Blaney Park

Blaney Park

A Novel

by
Rebecca Calanni
and
Matthew Diment

SANTA FE

Sunstone books may be purchased for educational, business, or sales promotional use.
For information please write: Special Markets Department, Sunstone Press,
P.O. Box 2321, Santa Fe, New Mexico 87504-2321.

Library of Congress Cataloging-in-Publication Data:

Calanni, Rebecca, 1961-
  Blaney Park : a novel / by Rebecca Calanni and Matthew Diment.
    p. cm.
  ISBN 978-0-86534-579-9 (pbk. : alk. paper)
  1. Self-realization--Fiction. I. Diment, Matthew, 1958- II. Title.
  PS3603.A424B57 2008
  813'.6--dc22
                        2007024546

Published in

WWW.SUNSTONEPRESS.COM
SUNSTONE PRESS / POST OFFICE BOX 2321 / SANTA FE, NM 87504-2321 /USA
(505) 988-4418 / ORDERS ONLY (800) 243-5644 / FAX (505) 988-1025

Dedications

I wish to thank my family for their love, patience and continuing support and belief in my abilities as a writer and artist. A special thank you goes to my parents for their support of all my artistic talents and for the typewriter they made available to me at age five, despite the fact that I had yet to learn to read and write. Lastly, thank you to my husband, Jim, for his unmatchable gift of music, for his love and friendship, and his unending support and belief in this project.

–Rebecca Calanni

I dedicate this book in loving memory to my father and best friend, Robert E. Diment. Special thanks to my mother, Constance, two sisters, Pam and Tracey, and my brother Rob for their love and support over the years. Thanks to my son, Morley, who is today my reason for living and my best friend. I am blessed to have him for a son. Also, thank you to Chelsea Rose for believing in my abilities and who encouraged me to write this book.

–Matthew Diment

Foreword

Emily Stewart, a free-lance artist and author of the study of upper Michigan wolves, is compelled to abandon the life and family she has been a part of since college and return to the soulful wilderness of Michigan's untamed Upper Peninsula. She discovers more than just a familiar love of the environment with the help of Elsie Brooks, a retired native of Blaney Park. With Elsie's wisdom as her guide, Emily faces both the ghosts of her past and the calling of her soul to become the free spirit she has longed for since childhood. She meets her first adversary in Conner Morley, a businessman whose only agenda is to profit from the destruction of both the land she loves and the pack of creatures who adopt Emily as one of their own. As they struggle to understand one another, they discover not only a love that may never be realized, but strength within themselves to face unimaginable challenges and true tests of character. Together they must choose between what civilization has defined and nature demands. While seemingly sacrificing all that is important to them, they are on a path to finding gratification within themselves beyond all expectations, as well as a bond to each other only understood by an alpha and its mate.

1
Blaney Park

October, 1974.

"Hey, gimme a hit!" Roger reached for the joint Derek was holding delicately with his teeth.

"Watch it," giggled his girlfriend, Judy, as she squirmed in fake protest of being sandwiched between them in the Nova's back seat. "You drop any ashes on me and . . ."

"...and what," Derek interrupted. "You'll ride in the trunk?"

Laughter filled the car. Judy twisted her face and stuck out her tongue at Derek. She then smiled and blinked flirtatiously at Roger, tipping her pint of Southern Comfort upward with her lips fully covering the mouth of the bottle.

"Okay, okay!" Greg, the only sober one in the bunch, glanced nervously in his car's rear-view mirror. "I'm not driving all the way to the bridge with you clowns in this condition. We're stopping for the night. You guys are nothin' but trouble."

"Are you crazy?" said Roger. "There's no decent motel between here and St. Ignace! I'm not sleepin' in this piece of shit, if that's what you have in mind."

They had just reached the eastern end of the Sceney Strip. To a Northern Michigan University student lucky enough to find a ride home for the weekend, it was the longest and most boring stretch of flat pavement in the entire Upper Peninsula.

"Not hardly. Just bear with me a little longer. You'll see." The ride was always a bigger party than actually going home. Greg was smart enough to recognize that trying to go much farther would only end up badly for everyone. He knew of a place, a perfect place, where they could continue their fun all night and no one would care.

Jackie snuggled close to Greg's shoulder, wrapping her arms around his. She smiled at him, knowing exactly what he had in mind. They had been here a couple weeks earlier and never made it downstate. He was scheming to spend the night with her again, before dropping her at her parents' house in Indian River the next morning.

Emily, sitting next to Jackie, stared out the front passenger window into the darkening night sky. She wanted to go home, not spend twelve more hours with this bunch. They were good friends and she was enjoying her sophomore year sharing a dorm room with Judy. However, being paired up on this trip with Roger's roommate, Derek Stroebel, wasn't her first choice. Derek's dad had inherited farmland in the northwest part of Oakland County and made a fortune on property development. Derek was the youngest child, and a spoiled one, at that. He was known for his Detroit connections and always had enough marijuana to go around. His dad had laughed off his bad behavior as typical for a smart boy who wasn't being stimulated by his teachers. The naïve freshman girls fought for Derek's attention, and he knew it. Emily thought he was a jerk.

"You sure, Greg?" she asked. "I can drive, if you're tired."

"Jesus, take a break, Em," Greg laughed. "Have a hit or two. You might even enjoy it." The rest of the group laughed at her expense.

Emily ignored them. She never enjoyed marijuana. A barely-sipped half pint of blackberry brandy remained between her knees. At parties, she always felt like she was standing outside the circle, just an observer. Tonight was going to be no exception.

Just as the moon slipped out from behind a cloud to light up the pine forest, their car reached the bottom of a hill and they crossed a bridge above a wide river, it's current barely rippling beneath the moonlight.

"Awesome, man!" Derek laughed. "Virgin territory!"

"Ya, you wish," Roger teased. "Fresh cut lumber from around here is as virgin as you'll ever get."

"Fuck you," Derek responded.

"Look, you guys. There it is!" Greg was pointing to the opposite side of the river at what appeared to be an old, deserted town of small, white buildings. Most of the windows were boarded up.

"We're staying here?" Emily was horrified.

"Just wait," Jackie whispered closely to Emily's ear. "It gets better."

Greg turned the car into a narrow gravel drive leading to what appeared to be a large, Victorian-style home. A sign, which read *Harrison* hung over its porch. A dim glow could be seen inside.

"There's life here! Let's go!" Derek threw open his door as Greg stopped the car. Jackie smiled as she got out with the others and then leaned back against the car, watching Greg walk confidently toward the main entrance.

"May I help you?" Elsie Brooks stepped into the small foyer and smiled with familiarity at Greg.

"You bet, ma'am," he replied, bowing dramatically to her.

"A few more this time," her eyes looked past him as she smiled at the laughter on her front lawn.

"Ya, well," Greg glanced over his shoulder. "A full car helps pay for the gas, y'know?"

"You're a smart boy, Gregory." Elsie handed him three keys. "You get the same room, plus the two down the hall. Have a good time, but respect the environment of Blaney Park. Leave it as you found it."

"No problem, Miss Elsie," he winked. "You have a nice evening."

Elsie, the Harrison's proprietor, laughed lightly to herself as she watched Greg turn to go back outside. He leapt from the top step onto the walk and danced towards his friends.

"Miss Elsie is being more than generous tonight, guys. Who wants a key?" Greg extended his hand upward, dangling the keys above his head. He pocketed one and threw one to Roger.

"Where are you sleeping tonight, Princess?" He winked at Emily as he tossed Derek the remaining key.

"Greg, don't be an asshole," she snapped. "Roger, you and Derek better plan on sharing a room."

"Forget it!" snapped Judy. "I'm spending the next two days with my two little brothers. Tonight, I'm having fun. Find your own roommate."

"Never happen," Emily glared at Derek, who was dangling the third key from his tongue. Walking away from the car into the darkness that surrounded the old bed and breakfast, she could hear the group laughing behind her.

"You'll be back," Derek called after her. "Begging for me!"

Next to an old propane heater in the Harrison's parlor, Elsie sat in her rocker and smiled at the laughter of her guests while her mind drifted back to when she was their age. Greg understood the history of this beautiful place, and Elsie was confident he would keep his friends in line, while allowing them to have a good time. Her only payment for their stay was the company they provided her and the life they breathed back into the Harrison's old walls. She was grateful for their presence.

Behind the house, Emily found the backyard gazebo and remained there for over an hour. She listened to the group's laughter on the front porch and was disgusted by their intoxicated behavior. She stood up and stared out into the grounds surrounding the gazebo. It was a beautiful, clear night. Perfect for a walk in the woods, like she had done so many times as a child. She knew the sooner she began exploring this tranquil place, the better her chances were of not being followed and becoming the subject of Derek's drunkenness.

Emily stepped into the darkness in the direction of the woods, knowing the river lay not far beyond. Having grown up near the Hartwick Pines National Forest, she was not intimidated by the black night of northern Michigan, but rather felt called by it over the noises inside the Harrison as they dimmed behind her.

She walked into the woods and felt the pine trees closing in. The moon, once again escaping the cloak of a cloud, lit her path as she stepped into a clearing. Emily caught her breath at the beauty before her. Standing at the edge of a small clearing that blanketed the gentle river's southern bank she smiled, remembering her childhood play along the Au Sable River.

Okay, she told herself. This was definitely worth it.

She grinned and her pace quickened toward the rippling water. Almost immediately, she was stopped dead in her tracks by the sound of slight rustling in the thicker grasses along the embankment. Upon hearing a weak growl, fear knotted in Emily's stomach.

Shit, she thought. This is not Grayling, it's the U.P. I'm in deep trouble.

A faint whimpering told her it was an animal in danger, and the nurturing side of her immediately replaced her fear. Moving forward, she pushed back the grass with her shoe, revealing a young female wolf which, she guessed, was six to nine months in age, with its leg hopelessly caught in a poacher's trap.

"Jesus!" Emily said aloud, taking a few steps backward. The wolf growled and jerked its body, as if to scare her away. Blood was caked around the trap, evidence that it had been there for some time. The wolf was weak. Its breathing was heavy and it squirmed nervously at Emily's presence.

"I'm here to help you," Emily's voice was soft and she crouched low to the ground, putting herself on equal terms with the wolf. "But I... I'm not sure how. Just please don't bite me." She took a deep breath and slowly extended her hand towards the grip of the trap. At the sound of Emily's soothing tone, the wolf gradually ceased its whimpering, as if it trusted her. After all, Emily was the first living creature to come across the young wolf since it was gripped by the slamming of sharp metal into its leg.

"It's okay. You'll be okay, you'll be fine," Emily whispered. Her hands moved slowly, reaching the back paw of the animal and sliding over the trap. The wolf dropped its head down into the grass and instinctively gave in to Emily's presence as its only hope for survival.

The trap was strong. Emily's heart was beating wildly with adrenaline. She hated poachers. She had come across many such traps as a child, usually too late, only to find a half-eaten, dead animal left without concern by the trap's owner for what may have been captured. Such animals were frequently left to die or to be consumed by either their enemies or the large scavenger crows and seagulls that hung around Michigan farms.

Her steady hands pulled with equal strength against the trap's tension. With one quick movement, Emily separated its sharp jaws, releasing the mangled leg of the wolf. It yelped slightly when the trap was removed from its flesh, and Emily quickly slid the trap out from underneath its bloody leg.

"I'm sorry," Emily whispered, as she carefully closed the trap. The wolf lay back in the grass, panting heavily. Emily rose and moved a few steps backward, waiting to see if it would attempt to run off. She concluded that the wolf was too weak and too wounded to even rise.

Wondering what to do next, she heard a noise in the woods behind her. She whirled around, still clutching the trap, and saw the silhouette of a man standing a few yards from her. He held a short-barreled shotgun in one hand with the barrel resting in the palm of his other. A cigarette dangled loosely from his lips, and the shadow of a long knife blade extended from his belt.

Emily was frightened. Her upbringing told her not to show it. She squared her shoulders and stood still.

"That's my trap, young lady," the old man growled.

At his words, Emily realized he was the one responsible for the pain this animal had been enduring. Her temper flared, as she knew he was only there to claim his property and the prize that was caught in its grips that night. His only concern for the wolf that lay in the grass behind her was its black pelt.

"Oh, really?" she asked sarcastically, and lifted the trap into the air. "You mean this trap?"

"Yeah. That trap."

Emily's eyes narrowed in the darkness as she felt her blood surge.

"Then swim for it!" she hissed at him, flinging the trap over her shoulder. It splashed into the river behind her. The stranger's only response was another long drag from the cigarette still held between his lips.

Emily was shaking as she turned back to the wolf, now lying unconscious in the grass. Wondering if it was still alive, she knelt down and placed her hand on its chest cavity to feel for its breathing. Ignoring the fact that this shadowy figure still lingered so close to them, Emily continued to whisper gently and slid her hands under the wolf's body. As she embraced the limp creature against her, Emily rose back to her feet and turned to face the silhouette in the moonlight.

"You know what you're doin?"

"Absolutely," she snapped as she walked around him. "So, get out of my way."

Archie Phillips didn't follow her. He just stood there, staring toward the river and smiled to himself. He liked her. Emily was the first person who had stood up him in a very long time. He dismissed the trap lost in the river's current, and turned to watch her struggle as she carried the wounded creature back up the dark path toward the house. Emily possessed a feistiness he hadn't witnessed in many years, rarely in a woman, and it pleased him.

"What the hell are you doing?" Jackie squealed from the large front-porch swing. The others turned to see Emily standing on the front lawn with the wolf in her arms.

"Jesus, Emily!" said Roger. "What the hell is that?" He stood up, shocked at the site of Emily, her arms barely supporting the body of this wild creature. Judy and Jackie screamed and ran inside the Harrison House, alarming Elsie.

Emily said nothing and sank onto the lawn. She was just about to give up saving the animal, when Elsie emerged from the house, wearing an old, tattered wool jacket and carrying a small black leather bag. Ignoring the outbursts from the rest of the group, she walked quickly down the front steps and across the grass to where Emily crouched over the young wolf.

"Stand up," Elsie commanded. "You brought it here, so it is your responsibility." Elsie turned her back to Emily and began walking away from the house, into the darkness. "Come on."

Emily sensed something in Elsie's voice that caused her to feel at peace with her decision to help the wolf. Still cradling the animal in her arms, she rose once again and followed Elsie into the darkness.

Once they were out of range from the lights of the Harrison, Elsie slowed her pace, allowing Emily to catch up with her, and turned on a flashlight to guide them through the darkness.

"That's a poor creature you have there," she commented, as she heard Emily shuffling up behind her.

"Y...ya," Emily panted, fatigued from carrying the wolf.

"Think she'll make it?"

"I don't know.... I... I hope so. What do you think?" Emily looked at Elsie, her eyes begging for help. Elsie did not raise her eyes to meet Emily's, but continued to look onto the path in front of them, following the beam of the flashlight.

"I think she has a good start. The right one found her." Elsie's words encouraged Emily. "Which one are you?"

"I'm Emily, Emily Stewart," she replied, her arms weakening against the weight of the wolf. "Where are we going?"

"Right here," Elsie stopped beside a large barn. She unlatched the door, and slid it back on its large track.

"Just inside," she directed Emily. "To the right just a bit... there's a spot that's all hay. Lay her down on it."

Emily walked into the blackness of the barn, slowly moving forward and felt the floor thicken with hay. She stopped to squat down and lowered the young wolf into the dry, soft bed. Elsie knelt beside her, opening the small medical case.

"She's hurt pretty bad," Elsie commented. "She had to have lost a lot of blood to conk out like that. Wolves are pretty tough. That leg's got a deep wound, maybe even cracked the bone some, but she won't lose it."

"Thank you," Emily managed to say, still panting from carrying the heavy animal so far. "Thank you for helping me, for helping her."

"Ha!" laughed Elsie. "These wolves owe me enough already. They're used to me. You see, when I was much younger than you are, they took me into their pack, in a sense. I was one of them. They were the only playmates I had as a child. It's one of the reasons why I don't leave, just stay here. People think I'm lonely. I'm not. I just have a different family than most. Don't mean I'm more alone, just means I'm different. Most people, though, don't like different."

"What's that for?" Emily asked, watching with fascination as Elsie removed a syringe from the bag and carefully filled it with a clear liquid.

"It's for making sure I don't get bit," Elsie smiled. "And, it also lets this poor creature relax a bit. She's been through enough tonight already, and will be very anxious as I tend that wound. A little relaxation will do her good and allow her to sleep tonight. She needs to regain her strength so that she can return to the woods in the morning." Elsie looked at Emily's strained face and smiled at her level of concern. "Don't worry. It's only a mild muscle relaxant and will wear off well before dawn. She'll be fine."

"Wow. I'm so glad you've done this stuff before. And, I'm so glad I found her. She might have died out there."

"Most certainly she would have. If not by her wounds, by her enemies."

"Enemies? What could possibly take on a wolf around here? Do you have bears around here?"

"Not bears," Elsie shook her head. "This one is part of the good pack. Those who just run the grounds, eat off field mice and small animals. We have other wolves around here, Emily, and they are not as kind. Not all wolf packs are non-aggressive. There is a small pack of scavenger wolves that, for whatever reason, seem to hang around in these woods. I'm not sure what keeps them here. They never come near the house. They frighten me, much more than the bears occasionally wandering through the Park. Just be careful when you visit, okay?"

"Okay," whispered Emily. She watched Elsie clean and bandage the wolf's wound with ease.

"I know this one," Elsie tilted her head and examined the wolf. "She's young, but strong. She has more spunk than her brothers. Definitely an alpha. She'll head a pack one day."

"A pack? What's an alpha?"

"There." Elsie stood up, brushing the hay from her knees. She rested her hands on her hips, satisfied with her work. The wolf's eyes were closed, weak from the experience and from the drug. "Let's leave her alone now."

"But, what if she...?"

"Listen to me," Elsie turned her head and gently placed her hand on Emily's shoulder. "This is a wild creature. We can only assist when it is a matter of life-and-death. And, even then, we must limit our involvement. This is all we can do. Now, we must walk away and let her own care for her." Elsie reached down, took Emily by the arm, and pulled her to her feet. The wolf opened its eyes, and its ears moved back, but it did not raise its head from the bed of hay.

"Let's go now," Elsie whispered, as she firmly pulled Emily back into the moonlight slipping through the entrance of the large door. They stepped out, and Elsie closed the door all but for about a foot. Emily looked at her curiously, and then knew the smile on Elsie's face meant this would give the wolf its freedom, if it chose to take it.

"It's past my bedtime," Elsie smiled. They walked back toward the Harrison. The moon was out fully now and there was no need for a flashlight. "You're not like the others. You enjoy them?"

"Not really. Well, Judy's my roommate, and...."

"Roommates don't always make an impact on your soul, Emily. You have more depth at your young age than they do. That young wolf could feel it. If she didn't, you would not have been allowed to help her. It took courage to do what you did." Elsie turned from the path toward the back door of the house. "Good night," she called, waving her hand above her head.

As Elsie walked away, Emily stopped on the dark path, staring after her. She closed her eyes, trying to burn into her memory every word Elsie had said that evening, everything she did. She then opened her eyes and looked up at the house in front of her, thinking about her sleeping options. She opted for the gazebo, and pulled her jacket tightly around her, knowing it would be a cold night.

2
Emily's Choice

More than an hour passed, as Emily sat in the gazebo listening to the laughter and music cascading down from the open windows of the Harrison. As the voices began to diminish, she could not bring herself to return to the house and chose to stay outside in the cold where she could feel the night air and monitor the barn door. It was well past midnight when she rose from the bench and heard the music's volume lowering in unison with the lights at the top of the house. She stood and watched as the last light on the third floor finally went dark.

The last thing Emily wanted was an encounter with Derek. She feared he would pursue her now that the others had paired off into the other two bedrooms. She truly despised him and his arrogant behavior. Derek was attractive, and wasn't lacking in the area of self-confidence. He had convinced himself that having a good time meant flashing himself and his lifestyle all over the city of Marquette. He arrived to every party on campus with a date. The fact that his dad was a successful Detroit land developer helped Derek's image at Northern considerably. Daddy could buy everything, and Derek wasn't the least bit hesitant about taking advantage of that situation.

Emily rose and stepped out onto the back lawn. The frigid darkness spooked her, as she replayed Elsie's comments about bad wolves roaming the area, and she decided to go back to the house and sleep on the couch in Elsie's parlor. She began to move slowly forward and stopped at the edge of the shadows just before entering the front lawn, unable to keep her thoughts from the young wolf that lay in the dark barn behind her.

The front door to the Harrison began to open slowly and creaked against its old, iron hinges. Startled by it, Emily moved quickly to hide herself in the shadows and decided to bolt for the barn. She ran lightly, trying not to risk being heard by whoever was now outside. She ran straight to the barn, slipping inside the door Elsie had left partially open. Once inside, Emily ducked behind a row of large, metal milk cans and crouched low to the ground beneath a window. After several moments, she began to relax and her breathing slowed.

Someone or something was definitely approaching the barn. Emily maintained her crouched position behind the milk cans and waited for the intruder to be exposed by the moonlight shining through the barn door. The movement outside the barn grew closer, stopped, and then it seemed to be moving away. Her mind was racing. Was it Elsie? Had she returned to the barn to check on the wolf? Emily was already planning future stops at Blaney Park to spend more time with Elsie in order to learn about this place and the creatures that lived within its grounds. Being caught back in the barn might mean losing Elsie's respect, as she had clearly instructed Emily to leave the wolf alone for the night.

The movements drew closer. Emily's heart was racing. What if it was the poacher from the clearing? Perhaps he was angered by the wolf being released from his trap and somehow knew it was here. Had he had come to claim his prize, after all? Emily was now fearful for herself and the wolf. How could she protect them both?

The moon was extremely bright on this night, and the lack of cloud cover allowed its illumination of the lawns around the Harrison and surrounding buildings. Its glow entered the barn door and reached the edges of the hay bed where the wolf lay. Emily considered pushing the door shut, just a little, in hopes of blocking the moonlight from revealing the sleeping creature. She decided against it, knowing the noise of the large wooden door straining against its pulley would most certainly draw the attention of whoever may be looming nearby. A large shadow in the moonlight entered through the doorway, and was soon followed by the presence of its owner.

"Well, this is where they brought the little river rat, huh?" Derek's voice echoed in the large barn. "Because of you, I lost my date for the night."

It's only Derek. Of all the fears she had for who or what it could have been, she expected him to have fallen asleep with the others in the Harrison. Her heart's rapid beating slowed at the sound of his voice and Emily felt both relieved and irritated at the fact that he was even out there. She heard him shuffling towards the place in the hay where she and Elsie had left the wolf. His movements were erratic and, from his heavy breathing and soft laughter, Emily knew that he had been drinking, and drinking a lot.

"God, Derek," she said aloud, stepping out from behind the milk cans. "It's only you. You scared me."

"Emily," Derek was surprised to see her. "So, where have you been all night? I'm not used to having my dates stray from me. If I didn't like you so much, I would be offended by such behavior. Are you going to come back with me to the house so we can make up for lost time tonight? I really don't mind if you take care of some mangy animal, as long as you also take care of my needs, too."

Derek turned away from the wolf and surveyed the barn. He went to the wall and extracted a pitchfork that was hanging against a large support beam. He then walked around all four sides of the barn, removing different items from the walls. Emily did not know what to say nor understood what he was doing. She looked at the wolf whose eyes were open and blinking slowly, as it fought the affects of the relaxant. The look in the wolf's eyes no longer reflected approachability. She could only assume that the wolf was troubled by Derek's intrusion.

"Derek, I'm staying out here tonight. Thanks for coming out to look for me, but why don't you go back to the Harrison? We can have fun tomorrow during the drive downstate."

Derek did not respond. Intermittent stumbles and fumbling with the items he was carrying confirmed to Emily that he was either high or drunk, but definitely under the influence of one or more of the many substances that were available to the group that evening. While she was not pleased with his presence, he was the better of all the possibilities that were on her mind while she sat behind the milk cans.

"Were you hiding from me, Emily?" Derek asked with a slight smile on his face, as he continued his walk around the barn walls.

"Hiding? Why would I be hiding from you?"

"That's what I kept asking myself this evening. Why would a woman like you not want to be with a great guy like me? Let's hold that thought for a while."

"Derek, what are you doing? You come into the barn, say nasty things about the wolf, and then walk around taking things down from the walls. What exactly are you up to?"

"Oh, so now you are interested in me?" Derek closed the door, and slid the large plank board into the door's side brackets, locking it into position.

"Derek, please don't do that. Elsie asked me to keep the door open."

"Elsie? Elsie?" Derek leaned forward and shook his head at Emily. "First the wolf and now some old hag who doesn't even know what day it is.

Come here, Emily. I want to explain something to you."

"Derek, you're drunk. I think you are a nice person, but you are beginning to make me uncomfortable. You are not acting right."

Derek began laughing. He placed the items he had removed from the walls neatly on the barn floor, as if he were taking inventory of them.

"I am not acting right?" he repeated. "So, you tell me, Emily. What's right and what's wrong? Better yet, who cares about right and wrong? I don't, do you?"

"Yes, I do, Derek. My parents raised me to know that doing what is right is important."

Derek began to chuckle with an evil presentation. "Parents, parents, parents... so, now you think you have better parents than me? First, you are too good for me. Now, you are trying to say you have better parents than me. Who do you think you're talking to?" His tone and words turned sarcastic and this alarmed her, accelerating her heart beat. She realized that she was locked in the barn with Derek and couldn't allow him to see how afraid she was. She looked to the wolf. It was now looking directly at her, as if warning that danger was present. Emily's mind began considering her options.

"Derek," she sighed. "I'm sorry. That's not what I meant. I don't think I am better than you. I'm just not the right type of girl for you. I'm doing you a favor by telling you, you can do better."

"Exactly," Derek responded. "I agree. I am better than you, Emily. There is no doubt in my mind that my family is far superior to the country hicks you have for parents. But, you are all I have for this weekend. I think you could do a better job at showing me the respect I deserve from white trash like you. You should be feeling fortunate to be in this barn with me. And, while you don't dress like a woman, I am pretty good at undressing with my eyes and imagination. I would bet you are all woman underneath those farm boy clothes of yours."

"Go to hell, Derek!" Emily was now feeling her back to the barn's wall and her pleasant approach was not working. It was time for a new strategy. She thought back to her mom's lectures of never allowing herself to become vulnerable to men. Her mom was concerned about Emily's journey into adulthood and had explained that you never really know a person until you get to know them well. She had cautioned about placing being in any vulnerable situation with a man. Emily didn't really know Derek, and was now in a very uncomfortable predicament with him.

"Exactly," Derek smiled. "Now that we agree on what's happening tonight, we can get started." He unbuckled his belt.

"Derek, don't be an asshole! Why are you doing this? I have no interest in you. I am saying no. Do you hear the word no, Derek? I do not want to have sex with you or spend any time whatsoever with you for the rest of this trip. Now, open the door because I am walking out of this barn - alone."

Derek slid his belt from his pants and went over to the wolf. To Emily's horror, he lifted his arm and struck down, whipping the animal once. It yelped softly, unable to call out for help in its sedated state. The look in the wolf's eyes was of great pain and fear at the situation.

"You bastard!" Emily screamed, as she lunged forward and pushed him back. She then knelt next to the wolf and began whispering softly, trying to calm the trembling animal. Risking an attack on her, Emily reached out and gently petted the wolf, knowing full well that this was very dangerous. She turned with clenched teeth toward Derek.

"Get out of here, Derek. So help me, if you hurt this wolf again, I will kill you! Or, I will call somebody and you will be in more trouble than your daddy can fix!"

"I thought you knew who I am, Emily," Derek laughed. "Who gives a damn about this wolf except that senile old lady and you? No one else does. So, do you honesty think my dad would allow some country bitch like you to accuse me of anything? You're nothing. This wolf is nothing. Besides, who says you didn't kill it to put it out of its misery, maybe with this pitchfork." He picked it up and placed the blades lightly upon the neck and shoulder of the wolf. Emily didn't move. Her hand was still comforting the animal and only inches from the pointed fork. As her anger and fear collided, she began to cry softly.

"That's it, Emily. Show me how much you care about this insignificant little river rat. I love it when people are about something. It makes them stupid. I, personally, don't understand why anyone would waste their energy on anything besides money, sexual satisfaction and the thrill of the power that comes with being me." He laughed in Emily's direction. She would not look up at him and was doing her best not to provide him the satisfaction of placing her in a submissive position. She was confused, as she realized Derek had her. She slowly moved her hand and grasped a blade of the pitchfork, lifting it from the wolf.

"I am so sorry," she whispered, thinking that if she had left the animal in the woods at the mercy of the trap, its pain would be over by now. She had wanted to save its life, and now felt she had only prolonged the agony.

"I will give you a few moments to be with your dog," Derek stepped back holding the pitchfork. "But don't take too long, sweetheart. I want you to be a good dog and obey me."

Emily stared at the wolf as tears clouded her vision. She no longer felt afraid of the creature. They were on the same side now, both at the mercy of the pitchfork. She leaned down and buried her head behind the wolf's shoulder, wishing the wolf would turn its head and bite her neck. This would be appropriate compensation to Emily for placing the wolf in this predicament, and might cause Derek to run for help. She could smell the bitter odor of the wild in the wolf's fur. It was not a pleasant smell, but Emily hoped her apology would be felt and she could make sense of the decision she was facing.

She hadn't dated much during high school, or in college. She had, however, cared very deeply for a couple of young men. As much as they urged her, she never felt the need to give up her virginity. She was the only one in her circle of friends who had not experienced a sexual relationship and had always felt good about her decision.

Now, Emily had to choose between the safety of the wolf and a threat to her sexuality. Her tears soaked into the wolf's fur, moistening its skin and releasing more of its wild odor. The decision was too difficult. She knew if she denied Derek's wishes, the wolf would be killed right in front of her. If she consented, part of her soul might die.

Clearing her mind, she wiped away her tears and lifted her head, turning to see Derek tossing the knotted end of a heavy rope up over a beam. It had a slipknot and swung down beside her, hanging a few feet off the ground.

"What's that for?" Emily asked.

"You didn't really think I'd put a pitch fork through that animal, did you? Hell, no! I think hanging it by its fucking neck would be much more entertaining. I used to do this to dogs and cats in my neighborhood when I was a kid. It was a treat to see the legs kick while the animal would struggle to survive, only to make the rope tighter. It was truly a lesson of survival for me."

Emily was now trembling with anger instead of fear.

"Or. Now, Emily, this is a big or, okay?" Derek walked a few feet to her, and unzipped his jeans. "Or, you can crawl over here and suck on this for a while, to take my mind off it. Oh, and don't forget to take your clothes off, too, so I can enjoy the beauty and softness of your body."

"Derek, you are sick! You disgust me. Do you really think you are going to get away with this?"

"Ah, but I do. It's not like I haven't gotten away with it before. This shit excites me, baby. Especially when I have a high going like I do tonight."

With that, Derek vaulted the pitchfork into the hay pile, just past the wolf's body. Emily looked at the rope dangling from the beam. If she fled from the barn, she would undoubtedly come back in the morning only to find the wolf dangling lifelessly from the rope. She had no choice. Derek had won. She looked, once again, into the eyes of the wolf. The creature tried to lift its head towards her and Emily smiled, sensing that the wolf was asking to die. She gently caressed its paw, a gesture of one last connection between them, and then stood up slowly to face Derek.

Laughter from the hallway brought Emily to consciousness, and she opened her eyes to the morning sunlight streaming in through the bedroom window. Derek was lying next to her, still asleep. Her mind quickly awakened with the nightmare she had lived through and tears fell from her eyes. Every crevice in her body ached, every muscle cried with her as she looked to the ceiling for answers around what had occurred the night before. Trying to calm her mind, Emily slowed her breathing. She needed resolution to her experience before the long drive downstate with the others.

Emily's eyes focused above her. The ceiling was beautiful, a true work of art. Its architect had not just slapped up some mud and paints, but had put much love and time into it, creating something special within this house. It had contours and lines that were uncommon to just any ceiling. It was one that was crafted with care and concern. As she scanned the vaulted ceiling, her eyes tracing the lines, she noticed a crack in one corner that had become stained yellow with age and water damage. It was unsightly and took away from the overall beauty of the ceiling. Her thoughts turned back to the artist who came to this room perhaps some forty years earlier. How that creator would be disappointed to know that the roof had been neglected and allowed to leak, blemishing his beautiful work, leaving it scarred by the outside elements of nature.

She looked back at Derek, spread out next to her, naked and sleeping peacefully as if nothing wrong had occurred the night before. She blinked hard as the tears slowly trickled down from her eyes into the sheets. There was only one pillow and Derek had it under his head. She looked back to the ceiling and tried to settle her emotions. Her life was now going to be like that ceiling. Her architect had been an artist, too. He had created her lines in such a way she felt beauty within herself. Her parents had protected her, taught her to protect herself, and all were determined to keep the outside elements from staining her image.

Her wrists were tingling, and she lifted her arms above her face. They were red and swollen from the rope burns she received as she hung from the wooden beam while Derek had his way with her. All of her wounds began to awaken, as she felt the delicate muscles and flesh of her vagina throbbing to her heartbeat from his abusive treatment the night before. She had not fallen asleep, but had fainted into unconsciousness from exhaustion, and was now taking inventory of her being and knew she was deeply damaged by her experience. Emily was like the corner of the ceiling, except the plaster and paint could be repaired. Her wrists would heal, but for the remainder of her life, she would see the scars around them and be reminded of that horrible evening. Her mind was racing and she knew what she wanted. She must tell someone. He must be arrested. Derek must be punished. Emily suddenly wanted to call her mom and dad. She wanted to speak with them and ask that they come to her, bringing whatever was necessary to fix what had been broken in her.

Derek, had rolled from his stomach to his side, and was now facing away from her. She so wanted a knife to stab him in the back and find satisfaction in the revenge of killing him. Just the fact that he had the nerve to lay there next to her after what he had done made Emily realize that he would have no regrets, or sorrow.

She rolled away and slowly lifted her body from the edge of the bed, suppressing her whimpers from the stiffness and aching she felt. She did not want to awaken Derek. She looked to the floor to find her clothes, not remembering how she came to the bedroom or became undressed. Emily had not wanted to give Derek the satisfaction of seeing her body during his assault and had struggled to keep her clothes around her body for protection. She knew he would not rip them and provide proof that she was not participating in his advances on her.

She looked around at her feet and bent over, carefully and quietly collecting the wrinkled items from the floor. Almost underneath the edge of the bed lay her light blue camisole. Emily stared at it. She looked at the delicate lace edging, the satin straps and again fought back tears as she remembered shopping with her mom for new clothes to take to college that fall. It was a time when womanhood was settling in and, for the first time in her life, she had decided to purchase a few things that would enhance her femininity. A lump rose in her throat, as her eyes focused on the delicate silk fabric now stained with semen. One of the straps had been torn away from the lace bodice. Emily did not touch the camisole, but instead took her foot and slowly shoved it beneath the bed. She never wanted to see it again.

She dressed, and slipped from the room, pausing on the landing at the top of the stairs. She had held her breath while she was dressing, afraid Derek would hear her, and now was breathing deeply as she tried to capture all the oxygen available for her lungs. Emily sat down on the top step and turned to look out through the window behind her. It was a beautiful morning in Blaney Park, as the sun shown warmly on the river. Canadian geese had settled there for the night, and were diving for food as they swam across the smooth water. Once again, she looked at her wrists and decided she would do whatever she had to do in order to heal them. After all, she did have a choice as to how it was going to impact her life. It would take time, and it would take courage. Emily promised herself that one day she would bring justice against Derek and he would pay for this.

She would despise men like him from this day forward. She would hope that the emotional scar inside of her, along with the physical scars that she had been given, would soon heal without notice. She pulled down her sweatshirt, thankful that it was oversized and she would not need to worry about hiding the marks on her body.

Emily began to slowly descend the staircase and paused at the bottom. The smell of the morning's breakfast told her food was waiting, yet she could not bear to eat along with the others. Instead, she slipped out the front door and decided to check on the wolf. As she rounded the back of the Harrison, she broke into a run and stopped at the barn's entrance. Her heart sank at the sight of the empty hay.

"She's gone," Emily heard Elsie's voice and turned to see her standing by the milk cans. She was wadding up the remnants of the gauze bandage she had used on the wolf the night before. "Her bed was cold, so she probably left before dawn."

Emily stared at the hay. For some strange reason, she felt emotional and tears welled in her eyes.

"Her pack will care for her," Elsie said gently. She walked over and patted Emily on the arm. "They always do."

Emily blinked, and wiped the tears from her eyes. She squared her shoulders, as the car horn blared from the front of the house. She then looked to her left, at the rope still dangling from the beam. She slowly turned toward Elsie, who was also looking at the rope. Elsie's expression had gone more serious and she looked back, staring intently into Emily's eyes.

Emily said nothing for a moment, as she returned the woman's gaze. She sensed Elsie's confusion about the rope. It was not there the night before when they had left the wolf and returned to the House.

"I'll be back," she whispered, dropping her eyes as she turned toward the door.

"Emily," Elsie reached out and clutched Emily's wrist, causing her to wince with pain. Emily did not turn back to face her. Elsie gasped at the sight of the burns on Emily's arm. "What happened here last night?"

"I..." Emily's voice began to crack, as she struggled to respond. "Nothing."

"Look at me," Elsie said, sternly, and she turned Emily toward her. She put her finger gently under Emily's chin and lifted her face. Emily's eyes were filled with pain, as the tears began to fall again, and she looked up to Elsie. "My God, child." Elsie embraced her, and the car horn blared again.

"I can't go with them," Emily cried.

"Stay here, do you here me?" Elsie directed. "Do not leave this barn until I come back for you." She stepped out of the barn, pulling the large doors securely shut behind her.

Emily began sobbing uncontrollably, as she lowered herself into the hay. She curled into a ball, holding her knees tightly against her chest, and waited for the doors to reopen, for the sunlight to return.

3

The News

Spring, 1994.

"What? You have to be shitting me. No way. Oh my God, Sharon. What do we know?"

"It looks like the cancer is in the lymph nodes," Sharon said to her brother. "I can hardly breathe, Conner. I can't believe it. It's breaking my heart. I just can't believe it."

"When did this all come about?"

"Well, you know he hasn't been sleeping well. He would wake up with the sweats. The doctors, at first, thought he had the flu. When he stopped eating and he was losing weight, the doctor sent the cultures off to the lab. They came back positive."

The phone line became silent for some time, as Conner was in shock.

"Are you okay, Conner?"

"No," Conner Morley was sitting alone in his living room. "No, I guess right now I am not okay." The lights of the room suddenly didn't provide sight. They provided irritation. He went to the fireplace and started the gas logs that he had purchased to provide instant fire and ambiance. He then went to the light switch and turned off the lights that were beaming down from their canisters high in the vaulted ceiling. The cordless phone was the best money could buy, but it was not providing the clarity he needed from his sister's statements of what all this meant.

"Sharon. Is he going to die?"

"Well, Conner, if it is lymphoma and it's not in the bone marrow, he has a decent chance."

"Christ. I mean I know he's no young pup, but this is a shock to me. I never worried about him. I guess I thought he'd live forever."

"I know, Conner. I felt the same way."

"Hey, thanks for calling. How are Linda and Ken holding up?"

"I guess they are doing okay. We just have to wait for the tests to come back. We can only hope and pray for the best."

"Have you spoken to Mom?"

"Yeah, she's pretty shaken. She isn't, and hasn't, been well for a long time now. She just never thought much about Dad being vulnerable to any illness. He was always so strong and healthy. It's put her in shock, too, I think. We all took for granted he'd be around for a very long time."

"What can I do?"

"Nothing now except to pray. He's going to be going through some very challenging weeks to come. He will be on chemo, I would think, no matter what we find out. And Mom will not be much help, considering her own health issues."

"God, Sharon. Dad has always been such a rock. It's just hard to believe."

"I know."

"Are you okay?" Conner asked.

"No, I'm not. I don't want to lose him, Conner. He's too important to me. I want my kids to know him better and they are still too young to appreciate him. I want Lee to have a chance to learn sports from him. There is just too much living to be done before any death occurs in our family." Sharon began crying very hard.

"I know, sweetheart, I know." Conner repeated the phrase over and over, having no good answers for what was happening to the man both called dad. And the world they knew was changing. He was shaken by the news and felt very alone. He hadn't seen his wife in two weeks and he felt very detached from her. He wanted to call her, but didn't see the point until he received definite information about what his dad's condition was. It was still in the discovery stage and he knew his wife was going to Europe soon. He didn't want her to have to feel anxious about choosing between work and family. He may also not like her choice.

"I will call you later, Sharon. I need time to think about this. I will be calling soon. Thanks for letting me know. Call me if you need me."

"I will, Conner. Hang in there."

"You, too. Give a kiss to the kids for me and tell that husband of yours I said hello."

"Okay. I have to call some others who I think will want to know, so I need to get going, too."

"Okay, Sis. I love you. Thanks for calling."

As they hung up, Conner could feel the emotions swell in his body. The news was a shock to his system.

4
Search for Solitude

Rrring! Rrring! Emily flinched at the sound of her office phone.

"Damn it!" She closed her eyes and slumped back in her chair.

Shit. There's another great thought blown right out of my mind. I can't write here. Why can't I concentrate anymore?

"Hey, you." Austin was standing quietly in the doorway of her office. He was a tall, handsome man with prematurely gray hair. Most would guess he had done some modeling, as he possessed those GQ magazine looks that men didn't really like, but all women appreciated.

Austin had grown up in the plains of the Midwest. Attending college during the late 60's was a financially difficult thing for most and, with two brothers and a sister competing for the family college funds, Austin had turned to the military for his college education. He discovered during his enlistment that he had a great interest in planes, and spent his four pay back years at the U.S. Air Force base in Omaha, Nebraska, while taking private flying lessons. When his commitment was finished, he eagerly accepted a teaching position at the University of Michigan's business school. He was anxious to see a different part of the country and Michigan's Great Lakes area offered a welcome change to the heartland plains and tornado alley.

Teaching was a fun challenge for Austin, but it didn't hold his interest for very long. During his fourth year on the education payroll, he wandered into a courtyard one September afternoon and found himself completely distracted by a young art teacher diligently working on the preliminary sketch of a wolf. It was Emily. She was very striking in appearance, with long, brown hair and green eyes. Seeing her dressed simply in blue jeans, a cream-colored cotton sweater and leather moccasins, Austin couldn't take his eyes off of her. Three months later, they moved into an apartment together and married the following spring.

Emily had graduated from Northern Michigan University with a dual English/art degree and, after taking a few months off to work on her first book, she accepted a part-time teaching position in Michigan's fine arts department. Soon after they were married, Austin was offered a position with the General Motors Business School in Detroit, and Emily was eager for a change. Oakland County was growing, and they decided it would be an ideal place to start their family.

While pursuing her writing and artistic talents as a stay-at-home mom, Emily raised their two daughters, Tammy and Megan. Austin, meanwhile, taught during the week and built a small, successful charter flight company on the weekends, flying primarily Detroit's business leaders to the resort getaways of upper Michigan for retreats, team-building sessions and occasional escapes with one-time companions who Austin never dared question. He was paid well, enjoyed his job, and never judged the indiscretions of his clients. He would, however, often joke with Emily that if she ever ran out of topics for her fiction writing, she should just tag along on a few weekend charters with him. The activities and conversations that took place in his small aircraft were sometimes better than a soap opera. And, the customers always treated Austin as if he were invisible, focusing their conversations on the latest business merger or even each other, if the group contained those who were more than just business associates.

As much as Austin enjoyed listening to their lives, he was glad to be in the cockpit, rather than in one of their suits. Their world was one empty of soul and feeling, and only about value-added effort and productivity. He sensed from some of his more frequent guests that their rendezvous of pleasure were also lacking of emotional and soulful depth. Even the cases of corporate infidelity seemed less about romantic, emotional connection and more about business and compensation.

That was then, this was now. Austin loved his wife, but the years were pulling at his shirt tails. He wanted to be as free as the birds which flew around his plane. Yet, he had kids to think about and he wasn't absolutely sure Emily was ready to call it quits with him, despite her success as a free-lance artist and writer. God knows, he'd given her enough reasons. After Emily and he married, Emily's dad fronted Austin with enough money to pay off the balance on his flight business, as her dad had money to burn after his retirement from a corporate management career that exceeded over forty years of service.

After two kids and all the excitement of traveling, Austin often thought about how different his life would be without the responsibility of family and marriage. He loved Emily, but she was always in another room writing books he didn't understand nor cared to read. He felt trapped again, just like while he was in the military. It felt like a tour of duty.

Tammy would be graduating in a few years, and would be joined soon after by Megan. With the girls gone off to college, they would become empty-nesters. Both Emily and Austin held their own silent concerns about there being enough reasons for them to continue sharing a life together, as their interests and hobbies had taken such different directions over the years.

Emily opened her eyes.

"What's wrong?" Austin was puzzled by the look on her face.

Emily stared at him, hesitating to admit how she felt about their home at that moment, a place that should have provided her comfort and where she should be most content. They had lived there for so long. Lately, it seemed a place filled with distraction and unrest. Emily had been increasingly confused over the past few weeks, unable to understand why she felt so uncomfortable in her own home. For the past two months, she had this growing sense that her soul was called to be somewhere else. Some days, as she drove toward Ann Arbor to substitute teach at Michigan, she felt an overwhelming urge to turn north onto the US-23 highway and follow it northward to the Mackinaw Bridge and the tranquility that lay beyond. The feeling had intensified recently, and the harder she tried to ignore it, the stronger it became until she was almost unable to concentrate on anything except the urge to run away.

"Austin, I just can't work here anymore," Emily looked down at her desk, trying to compose herself. "I know that sounds terrible. This is a great house, a great office. You and the girls have always been so good about giving me the time and space I needed in here. The problem isn't... it's not our home, it's me. I... I'm just not here."

"So, what do you suggest?"

She thought for a moment before responding. "I haven't got a clue. This has been eating at me for weeks. I just figured it was just all the stuff around the girls and school that was distracting me. But this year's pretty much done now. I've been trying, but it seems like right about the time I get back into it and everything starts to flow, something happens. Like someone at the door, or the phone ringing. There are too many interruptions for me to work here."

"Ya, sorry," he smiled, apologetically. "That call was for me, by the way. I'm flying north tomorrow. Some corporate team-building bullshit again.

These guys have the greatest excuses for hanging out in resorts for a few days. But, what the hell, it's an easy flight and, at these rates, that new plane will be here real soon."

Emily smiled and stared at Austin as he leaned against the door, his arms folded loosely in front of him. His world was so simple. He taught, flew, hung out with the girls and had few concerns beyond how to purchase the latest toy for his business. She thought about how attractive he was and how well he had maintained his sex appeal over the years. His appearance was one of his characteristics that had so strongly attracted Emily to him. But she was feeling more each day that it was his independence which would cause him to leave her after the girls both went off to school. It was a thought she continued to fight and put out of her mind. As much as she craved her solitude, having them all gone seemed almost frightening to her.

"Maybe I'm the one who needs a vacation," she joked. "Maybe I should take a month off and go on a retreat or something this spring."

"I know a pilot who can give you a decent deal on a ticket," Austin winked. He straightened up from the doorframe and turned to walk away. Emily watched him, and he suddenly stopped.

"Em! I got it!" He whirled around and walked back into her office, leaning over her desk in front of her. "Why don't you go up to Blaney for a while? You know, that old town in the U.P., the one you said you used to always drive through when you were in college. I fly there all the time now, you know that."

"Blaney Park?"

"Why not? Some new owner took it over a few years ago and... well, that's another story. Anyway, they made it a resort or something, and the airstrip's great. That's where I have to go Saturday. Why don't you and the girls come along? I'll have only three paying passengers, so we'd have plenty of room. We can drop you there, if you think it looks okay to stay, and I'll spend Saturday on the Island with the girls. I can pick you up next weekend. Okay?"

"Austin, are you crazy?" Emily blinked at him. "That place is probably falling down by now. It's in the middle of the woods. The only place to stay other than the Harrison, I think, is in one of those little ratty cabins. Jesus, I'd have to drive to Marquette just to shop." Emily stopped suddenly and looked up at Austin, who was grinning from ear to ear.

"Perfect," he straightened up and crossed his arms with satisfaction.

"Austin," Emily smiled at him with excitement. "You are so smart. Perfect, nothing - it's great! That is, if it's not a hole by now." She leaned back in her chair again.

"I have it on personal knowledge that it is far from being run down. Besides, it can't be too shabby, considering the clientele it's getting these days. Make some calls. Find out what's up with the little cabins, if you can rent one for a week or so, and let me know." He leaned again over her desk and kissed her lightly on the forehead.

"Then go pack," he smiled.

"Thanks, sweetie," Emily whispered.

Blaney Park. She closed her eyes and tried to imagine the rolling landscape, covered with pines and hardwoods, the large river that ran not far from the grounds of the Harrison House. It had been over twenty years since she had last driven through it. It must be terribly run down by now, unless the new owner had really turned the place around. It could be crowded and full of tourists or, worse yet, a bunch of those annoying Detroit suits trying to prove their manhood by roughing it in Northern Michigan. Her mind drifted to the one time during college she had spent the night there and felt a lump begin to form in her throat.

"Quit it," she said, shaking her head. She knew Blaney was the answer, regardless of her ghosts. It was, indeed, perfect. Any doubts that were entering her mind were being quickly erased by her soul telling her she had to go there, she needed to go there. She sat up, took a deep breath and reached for the phone.

* * * *

Once they crossed over the span of water that flowed beneath the Mackinaw Bridge, Emily's heart began to pound. She began pointing to the different buildings beneath them. The girls were smiling at her, as Emily talked about her college years. She laughed at her own accounting of the crazy trips she and her friends braved in the middle of the wicked Michigan winters just to go home for a 24-hour period to party with their friends who had stayed downstate to attend college. They followed the US-2 highway along the southern coastline of the Upper Peninsula, and Emily provided a documentary-style tour of the landscape.

Emily and the girls were ignorant of the boredom displayed on the faces of Austin's three paying passengers, who were obviously saturated with her history lesson. She had sensed, when they boarded the plane, that these three were not happy about sharing their privately chartered flight with her and the girls, but she had overheard Austin politely telling the female passenger, who appeared to be the senior of the group, to 'get over it.' From the glare she received, Emily concluded this was someone who was not accustomed to being overruled, especially by another female.

She was glad to know that, once the plane landed, she would soon be in the solitude of her cabin and she planned to isolate herself as quickly as possible from the Harrison's paying guests. There was only one person Emily planned to interact with, and she looked forward to seeing her friend, Elsie Brooks, after so many years.

When they reached the intersection of US-2 and M-77, Emily could see the clearing that led to Blaney Park. It was the clearing that had once been used as an airstrip during prohibition days by private airplanes that brought Detroit businessmen and their companions to the northern woods for an escape into the passionate world of free spirits.

The sun broke through the sky's light cloud covering just as they began their approach to the airstrip. Emily's heart was beating wildly. Her sense of unrest had been replaced by a sense of homecoming, but it was mixed with an underlying fear that she dismissed as simply being uncomfortable with going back to a place that held so many memories for her, and they were not all pleasant ones.

The plane landed.

As they neared the hangar, an old man stepped out of the doorway and approached the plane. He dropped the tire blocks around the base of the plane and waved up at Austin. As they stepped out on the ladder, Archie Phillips extended his hand to them.

Emily did not recognize him. He had aged poorly, and his mannerisms had grown softer. She didn't know this man, the same man who confronted her the night she had angrily hurled his trap into the river. Archie had been silhouetted in the darkness of the trees that night, with his back to what little glow of light came from the moon. Archie looked under the brim of his hat at Emily and provided her a slight smile, which she did not see, so he transferred it to her girls. He knew she hadn't recognized him and this pleased him. He liked Emily then, and now would be more at ease knowing she did not remember him. Somehow, Archie always knew the circumstances around those who visited by the time their planes had completed their taxi to the hangar where he stood waiting.

"Welcome to Blaney Park," he nodded, but did not smile.

"Thank you," said Austin. "Good to see you again, Archie."

"You, too. Let me help with those bags, and I'll walk you over to your wife's cabin."

"What about us?"

"I will be back to get yours," Archie replied over his shoulder to the obviously more irritated of the two corporate gentlemen, while the woman stood with her arms folded, rolling her eyes. He pointed to a wooden picnic table next to the hangar door. "You can wait on that bench."

"I'll stand, thank you," the woman sneered.

Emily was standing a few yards from them, staring toward the buildings. It looked the same to her, just fresher, cleaner. The paint on the buildings was still white but brighter than she remembered, and the grounds were neatly groomed. There were no long grasses or weeds, only the dried stems of last year's wildflowers. Daffodils, crocuses and tulips were beginning to break through the surface of the dirt in the flowerbeds. The grounds nearest the hangar had been freshly paved for the airstrip, and were bordered by an open field dotted with grazing cows and horses.

"Hope they don't ever walk in front of a plane," she joked.

"Oh, they do, sometimes," Archie replied, "but they get out of the way soon enough. Don't like the noise of the props much." Emily laughed at seeing Austin stare at Archie in disbelief, certain he was imagining his plane landing on a cow.

As they passed the general store, the girls begged to go inside.

"No way," said Austin. "You're not spending my money just yet. We've got plans later. Let's just get your mom settled, and we'll be on our way."

Archie led them past several small, white stick-built cottages, and stopped in front of the first one built of full log design.

"Number six," he announced, turning the doorknob.

"My lucky number," Emily smiled, remembering she her last visit. "This is where I stayed the first time I came here." Emily looked away as Austin winked at Archie. Austin liked taking any and all credit, even when it wasn't quite deserved. He knew, however, this time it was his.

Archie turned and handed her the key. "Won't have much need for this, but here you go. No locks here, ma'am. Your only intruder is the moon."

"I'll take it, anyway, thank you." Emily took the key, as Archie took her bag inside the dark cabin.

"Anything you need," he continued, as he stepped back outside. "I live in the bunk, in the back of the hangar building. My number's on the wall by your phone, in case you need something, any time, 'round the clock. The wolves howl most every night, so if you hear them, remember they ain't as close as they sound. Please don't be calling me about wolf noise. I can't do anything about that. It's their home, we're just visiting. Enjoy your stay." He turned to walk back toward the hangar and waved his hand above his head.

Emily smiled, as Archie was talking her language. Wolves would not spook her. She knew much about wolves. She planned to study and write about them while she was here. This was something she had wanted to do since she first visited the Harrison so long ago. She looked down at the key that lay in the palm of her hand. It was the human race that she planned to lock out.

Emily stepped inside the cabin, and began shaking. She felt a sudden urge not stay and turned quickly to Austin, who was reading her body language.

"You'll be fine," he smiled reassuringly and wrapped his arms around her.

The girls were inspecting the cabin and their city upbringing echoed in protests throughout the open room.

"Mom, you're not really planning to stay here alone for a whole week, are you? It smells funny."

"There isn't even a hair dryer on the wall!"

"Yes, she is," Austin scowled. "Now, say good-bye, girls. We're having dinner on the Island, remember?" He turned to Emily and wrapped his arms around her again, whispering, "You brought your phone charger, didn't you? And you have my knife? Are you sure you brought everything?"

"Yes, yes, yes. We packed three times, Austin. I'll be fine. I'll call you later on your cell, when I'm settled." Emily tilted her head back, and smiled up at him. "Now get these girls out of here, would you? I have work to do. Don't worry about me."

"I always worry about you," Austin smiled and turned toward the door, clapping his hands together. "Okay girls, we've been officially kicked out. Give your mom a kiss and let's go."

"Be sure to get some fudge while you're there," she whispered, hugging both the girls together. "And hide it from your dad so there's some left for me."

The girls giggled and nodded at her. They each kissed good-byes on her cheek and ran outside to catch up with their dad.

Emily stood leaning against the doorway, waving to them as they walked with Austin, one girl on either side of him with arms wrapped around his waist. The girls were chatting wildly, and Austin tipped his head back with laughter at whatever they were telling him. Emily watched them, affectionately. Lately, she had enjoyed his relationship with the girls more than her relationship with him. The girls adored him and he knew it.

Her family had left her and she suddenly felt the loneliness that followed their departure. She began to open her computer bag, when she heard the engines on the plane fire up. Emily slowly sat down on the edge of the bed and continued to listen until the noise from the props grew further away, drifting quietly to the east toward St. Ignace. When she could no longer hear the plane, she lay on her bed and allowed herself one good cry.

"Is this what I want to do?" she said aloud. "Is it worth it?"

Feeling the tension release from her neck as fatigue overtook her, Emily gave in to her need for sleep. She turned her head to look at the fireplace and was relieved to see it well stocked with wood for the evening, undoubtedly by Archie. She wiped away the tears, smiled and then fell asleep without bothering to unpack or even undress.

5
Legacy of an Old Friend

"Shut up!" Emily pulled the pillow over her head, trying to block the loud calls of a blue jay that sat perched on the windowsill outside the cabin's kitchen sink. The bird continued, and Emily was soon wide awake.

"You are the most obnoxious alarm clock ever!" she yelled, as she sat up and threw the pillow at the window. The bird flew away and Emily flopped back down onto the old mattress.

Wow, I'm really here. She blinked her eyes and pulled a large, green comforter over her as she looked around the room. The fire was hissing softly and Emily knew that she would have to bring in more wood soon if she were going to have any prayer of keeping it going. Starting a fire from scratch was never anything she was good at, despite her efforts to learn while camping with her parents.

She swung her legs off the bed, and her bare feet came to rest on the cold, wooden floor. Emily smiled, as the bright morning sunlight streamed in through the windows, and she reached to the floor beside the bed for her socks and hiking boots. It may be cold inside now, but she knew the day was going to warm up quickly outside and she planned to enjoy every bit of it. She was anxious to visit Elsie. They had exchanged letters over the years, as well as an occasional phone call. Elsie was overjoyed when Emily had phoned to say she would be returning to Blaney Park for an extended stay. The Park hadn't been a stopover for the students at Northern for many years. The most recent owner was very strict about trespassing, and when the Harrison finally completed its renovations and opened its doors for business again, the young visitors stopped coming altogether. Elsie missed them and their laughter. They kept her young.

Still wearing her jeans and cotton shirt from the day before, Emily lifted her bag from the floor onto the mattress. She opened it and pulled out only a thick sweater and a pair of gloves. Certainly, as she hiked around the grounds in the warmth of the sun, she would have enough adrenaline to keep her warm, and would not require a coat.

After she had finished her breakfast of coffee and toast, and completed her journal entry for the morning, she packed a small bag with sketching materials, a writing pad, a camera and a bottle of water. Smiling to herself with excitement, she turned the old metal knob on the front door and stepped outside.

The path leading to the woods behind the cabins was rough, as it had been rarely traveled on over the past twenty years. The cabins of Blaney had received few visitors Most either spent their time in the Harrison and hanging around the more touristy areas, or they came to hunt and went straight out of town early in the morning with a tracker or hunting guide. There wasn't much at the end of the path except the river. And, the river was exactly where Emily planned to spend most of her time.

She was breathing heavily when she reached the clearing, obviously out of shape from her years of city life. She laughed out loud at herself as she bent over to rest her hands against her knees, trying to catch her breath. When she stood back up, Emily was overwhelmed at the landscape in front of her. It was late April, the peak of springtime, and there were still thin ice sheets jetting out from underneath the riverbanks, protected by the frozen ground. The current was moving swiftly at its center and sounded like a heavy rainstorm. Near the banks, the melting ice dripped into the pools around the rocks and fallen tree branches that had washed along the sandy bottom and embedded themselves beneath the mossy overhangs along its sides.

Emily was taking it all in and not focusing on any one thing. Her eyes ran along the opposite bank and she gasped as her vision was drawn to movement at the edge of the trees. A mother wolf and four half-grown pups ran out from the shelter of the thick pines and they moved playfully toward the river.

She remembered watching deer on her family's farm and dropped quickly to her knees, crouching low to the ground so the wolves would not see her and run away. The mother cautiously looked around and approached the river, lowering her upper body and stretching her head down to lap at the cool water. She then crawled backward upon the safety of the grass and stood still in order to allow her thirsty pups to lick the cool moisture from around her mouth.

Emily watched as one pup suddenly became curious and ran away from the rest. It tumbled toward the river and leaned dangerously over the edge while the mother was busy managing the rest of the pack, not noticing that one had strayed off. Emily heard the pup yelp as it toppled over onto a sheet of ice. The mother wolf dashed to the edge, but it was too late and the ice broke free, plunging the pup into the icy river which immediately began to carry it downstream.

Without thinking, Emily jumped into the knee-deep river and fought the current as she tried to run through the icy water across to the pup. She caught up with him and plucked him from the river's swiftness. He cried out and Emily soothed him, holding him gently against her sweater for a moment.

As she smiled at the beauty of this creature, Elsie's words from so many years ago flooded her mind: we can only assist when it is a matter of life-and-death and, even then, we must limit our involvement.

Emily was suddenly gripped with anxiety. She looked up and realized she was standing just a few feet from a very nervous alpha female, bearing its teeth in a low growl. Her hands trembled with fear and excitement at finding herself this close to a wolf family and she knew that the calmer she remained the better for all of them. Emily leaned forward to gently place the young wolf safely on the edge of the bank. She was numb to the cold water flowing rapidly around her legs, but managed to straighten up and slowly move backward to position herself more in the middle of the river, never losing eye contact with the older wolf. The pup ran to the safety and warmth of his mother's fur and nuzzled her closely.

Emily and the mother wolf held their eyes locked on one another, and the wolf ceased its growling. It seemed there was a moment of maternal understanding. She no longer felt afraid, and the mother wolf's disposition had softened slightly. With the others running playfully around them, the mother wolf nudged her wet pup ahead of her and turned to guide her brood back to the safety of the forest. As they turned away from her, Emily looked more closely to see a small gathering of wolves beneath the shadows of the pine trees, just at the edge of the sunny clearing. Her trembling resumed at the site of more adults. The pups had played openly in the clearing and Emily had not noticed the rest of the adult pack that still lounged in the shade.

Some of them rose and joined the alpha female and the pups as they retreated back into the forest. One particular adult, however, seemed to linger behind the rest. It finally rose awkwardly and, as Emily watched, she noticed the animal was limping slightly. She looked more closely at the back legs of the wolf and realized one leg was thinner than the other, slightly deformed above the paw. She then took notice of the wolf's dark charcoal fur, almost black coloring.

Emily gasped when the creature turned and looked directly at her. There were less than 30 yards between them and their eyes locked.

"It's you," Emily said aloud, as her heart was pounding wildly. "My God, it's really you. You did survive!" The excitement she felt at seeing what she thought was the female wolf she had rescued from Archie's trap so many years ago provided a rush that left her dizzy. She laughed and stepped further backward into the water, now ignorant of its icy temperature.

Emily watched as the wolf limped into the woods with the others. As strange as it seemed, she felt young, as if it was 1974 all over again and she stood in Blaney Park for the very first time. Seeing the black wolf brought back so many memories and, at least for this moment, the good ones shielded her from the painful twinges that were also creeping back into her mind. Emily refused to think about them, for now.

When the wolves had all disappeared into the trees, the cold water around Emily's body saturated her. She turned to fight through the current and walk back across the river, knowing she would have to quickly get back to her cabin and dry off.

"Well! You certainly haven't changed any."

Startled by a familiar voice, Emily looked up to see Elsie Brooks standing on the riverbank next to her backpack, with a large wool blanket draped over her arms.

"Is that for me?" Emily smiled.

"Who else? You'd think by now you would know better. All these years, and I'm still helping you out of a mess." They laughed as Emily reached the bank and climbed up onto the dry ground to kiss her friend warmly on the cheek.

"Here, wrap up in this and I'll pour you some coffee. I'd give you a hug, but you're soaked!" Elsie handed her the blanket and turned to pick up a thermos from the ground behind her.

"Thanks. It's so good to see you. You look great. How did you know I'd be here this morning?"

"Now, where else do you think I'd find you?" Elsie teased and shook her head, handing Emily the cup of steaming coffee. "I know you think a lot of me, but I also know I'm second place next to those guys." She nodded toward the other side of the river.

"Elsie, she survived! Did you see her?"

"Emily," Elsie laughed. "That old wolf died years ago. This one's a daughter from her first litter and auntie to that little guy you just rescued."

"But she's limping."

"Another victim of Archie's hobby. Surviving his traps must run in that pack. Never known him to catch a black."

"Oh," Emily looked back across the river with disappointment.

"That was not the smartest thing you could have done, y'know."

"I know, I know. But, the pup..."

"Honey, have you ever seen a dead wolf pup at the edge of a river?"

"Well, no."

"Ever see a wolf swim?"

"Y, ya."

"Someday you'll figure out that they can take care of themselves." Elsie smiled broadly, and then frowned when she noticed Emily shiver. "Come on. Let's get you back."

The two old friends walked back along the path to Emily's cabin. By the time Emily had changed into warm, dry clothes, Elsie had a roaring fire built and the cabin was glowing inside. Emily stood staring into the flames, thinking about the morning and how glad she was to see the wolves.

"She came looking for you a few times," Elsie offered, rocking slowly in the old wooden chair by the fireplace.

"Who?"

"The one you brought to the barn. Every now and then, I'd be in the yard, maybe out by the barn, and I'd see her, limping along the edge of the grounds, never getting' too close. The dogs usually chased her off. But, I knew why she came."

"Oh?" Emily still didn't look up from the flames.

"You saved her that night, but she couldn't save you."

"What happened to her?" Emily asked, ignoring Elsie's last comment.

"Old age, most likely. One day she just stopped coming. I was glad to know she was gone. Too much pain in the soul of that one. She carried the memory of that night in her heart, too, you know."

"You knew, didn't you?" Emily asked softly, as her eyes billowed with tears. Her knees weakened and she sank onto the floor beside Elsie's chair.

"Of course I did. Why do you think I let you stay the weekend, instead of going on downstate with those so-called friends of yours? Why do you think

I told them you were sick, and wouldn't let them see you? Putting you on a bus back to Marquette was the best thing for you."

"Why didn't you call my parents, or the school? Report it all to somebody."

Elsie sighed deeply before answering.

"I thought about it. I decided it was your choice, your decision. I had to let you do what you needed." She chuckled a little. "That boy was sure upset with me."

"Derek?"

"Was that his name? The cocky one. He threatened me, y'know."

"He what?" Emily looked up at Elsie, irritated at this news.

"The others were in the car, I think he told them he'd forgotten something and came back in. The little bastard got in my face and told me if I ever accused him, or caused trouble for him, he'd have the Harrison burnt to the ground with me in it." She laughed and shook her head. "I've been up against a whole lot worse than the likes of him, Emily."

"Elsie, I'm sorry. I had no idea. I really didn't know what to do. I just knew I couldn't leave with them, with him. I didn't mean to cause problems for you."

"I know you didn't. And, you haven't. I never heard from him again, and I didn't expect to. He was just another one of those bullet-proof city kids. He didn't bother me."

Emily looked back to the fire. They sat in silence for several moments, and then Elsie rose from the chair.

"I've saved it, you know," she said. Emily looked up at her and wiped a tear from her cheek. "All these years. I knew you'd come back."

She walked to the wall opposite the couch and started pulling tacks out from the sides of a large, hand-woven throw that hung on the wall. "Come on, give me a hand."

Emily rose slowly as the tears began falling down her face. She knew what was behind that throw. They removed the tacks and Elsie let it fall to the floor.

"Oh, my God, Elsie," Emily took a step backward and lifted her hand to her mouth, her other arm circled her waistline. "I'd forgotten . . ." her voice faded and she began to weep. Elsie put her arms around Emily and held her, just as she had done then, the day she found Emily sitting on the floor of the cabin on top of a bed of wood shavings, tears streaking down her face and holding a paring knife in her bloodied hands.

Carved in the wood of the cabin's wall, was a large, ominous wolf's head, its eyes were cold and dark, full of pain. The eyes had an eerie look to them, too large and not quite like the natural eyes of a wolf should be.

"It got you through it back then," Elsie said, soothingly. "It was your pain. You left it in this wall, didn't you?"

"Y....yes," Emily whispered, resting her face against Elsie's shoulder.

"If the pain stayed here, in this wall, then I knew it would leave you alone." She pulled back, placed her hands on Emily's shoulders. "Look at me."

Emily lifted her head up.

"Your eyes are in there, aren't they?" She nodded her head back at the wolf's face.

"Yes."

Elsie smiled. "Everyone who's ever seen it always asked why the eyes looked so strange. Why so large, so dark and angry." Elsie bent down and picked up the throw to fold it. She then walked over to the door, opened it and turned back to Emily.

"I want you to do something for me in return for this."

"What?" Emily asked, looking up again. "Anything. Anything at all."

"I heard you sketch now as well as you write. Is that true?"

"I don't know, I suppose so. I've had some luck at a few art fairs and a couple galleries down state."

"Good enough for me," Elsie nodded. She pointed to the wall. "I want you to sketch her, on canvas, as close to the size of this one as you can."

"I don't understand. Why would you want a sketch of that?"

"I want it for the lodge, the main room. It belongs in there, too."

"God, Elsie, not the lodge."

"Emily. You made a choice back then. This wall has protected these cabins over the years and I want her to protect the lodge, too. The original model's been dead a long time, but you've got her family to work from, if you need. Black's run strong in that pack, more than the greys. You do that for me, okay? And we're even." Elsie turned and walked out of the cabin. "Supper's at six," she called as she walked away.

Emily watched her for a moment, and then turned to look back at the carving. She sank back down onto the floor and lifted her hands. Turning them upward, she traced the faint scars on each wrist with her fingertips.

Protect the lodge, huh? So, who will protect you? Emily began thinking about the wolves, how beautiful they were and how fascinated she had always been with them. She looked back up at the carving and breathed deeply.

"Okay, my friend. A portrait you'll get."

The quiet of the cabin was interrupted as her cell phone rang. Emily looked toward it for a second, contemplating whether or not to answer. She rose, walked over to the desk and picked it up.

"Hello?"

"Emmy!" Austin's voice was breaking slightly as the phone fought with the cell service in the area. "How'd you sleep? How's your first day going?"

"Hey, Austin," she paused, thinking about the morning's excitement in the river. She decided not to tell him, afraid that he would try to convince her not to stay. "It's pretty quiet here, just like I'd hoped. I slept like a baby last night."

"That's great, Babe. We're heading back down now. The girls fractured my visa card this morning on the Island. I'm not buying them anything 'til Christmas!" Emily smiled as she heard giggles coming from behind him in the plane. "Listen, we'll be back up on Friday, okay? You think you'll have had enough by then?"

"Actually, Austin, I'm going to stay a while longer, maybe a couple weeks." Emily was almost shocked to hear herself say these words.

"Really? Wow."

"Can you have the girls put some more clothes together for me? Jeans, hiking stuff, okay? I'm going to be outside a lot."

"Sure thing. I'll give you a call Thursday night from the house. I've got a couple fares scheduled to come up on Friday morning, some guy's wife and her assistant, I think. So, I'll bring you some stuff then, okay?"

"That's great, Austin. Thanks. I really needed this. Give the girls a kiss for me, and tell them to keep that kitchen clean. And remind them to bring my fudge."

"Okay," he laughed. "Try to be careful up there, hear me?"

"Austin, I'm losing you. I'll talk to you Thursday. Bye." Emily ended the call, abruptly, for fear he would sense something in her voice and become concerned. She had told him when they were dating about the events of that weekend at the Harrison, but assured him it had all been put behind her. No ghosts. When, actually, she had always remembered just sketchy details of that night in the barn. Her mind had blacked out a big chunk of the evening, perhaps as much as two hours. From the pain she had felt the next morning, Emily never allowed herself to remember. She didn't want to know.

She set the cell phone back down on the desk and decided to walk the grounds. Picking her backpack up once again, she walked outside and headed towards the general store.

I hope they sell scotch, she thought to herself.

6
The Phone Call

Conner's phone rang, cutting the quiet of his office. It awakened him from his mental looping about his life and the situation he had found himself to be in.

Detroit, Michigan. He was wealthy beyond anything he would have ever expected and he lived in Michigan. Why? Family. More than any other reason, it was because his family was there. Conner grew up in southern Michigan, and his parents had lived there for over 35 years before retiring and moving almost three hours north to Crawford County.

While he loved golf and warm weather, he hated bugs. When he traveled as a youngster with different sports teams, he was exposed to the south and all the bugs that were found there. Michigan's cooler climate provided some escape from them. Environmental cautions found in Michigan during the spring months didn't extend much beyond an occasional flood or small tornado. Nobody worried about earthquakes or hurricanes. Mother Nature was kind to this state.

Spring had been upon them for a short time now and the golf season was coming into full swing. The neatly manicured greens, fragrant with fresh-cut grass, were calling him and Conner was mentally laying his path to sneak out of his office at the Hartman Farm's exclusive professional suites. The sun was bright, and Conner knew Whispering Willows Golf Club would be a welcome escape from all the burdens of business and life.

Shit, he thought. What if it's Sharon? He thought of his dad, and slowly picked up the receiver.

"Conner Morley speaking," he said.

"Hey, man! It's Rick."

"Richard!" Conner growled, smiling at the sound of his old golf buddy. His mind flooded with the numerous rounds of golf they had played during the past eight years or so.

Rick worked for the same corporation as Conner's wife. Samantha had introduced them at an employee appreciation picnic while doing her internship. It only took one word - golf. The two became instant friends.

"How are you, you son of a bitch?" Conner laughed. "You've been avoiding me ever since I whipped your ass at Maple Valley last July. One hot day that was, huh? I played out of my ass... too bad we weren't playin' for money."

"Yea, Con Man," Rick laughed. "But, you know I don't bet. I don't make the big bucks like you, and I got three kids to get through college. I can't afford just giving my money over to the likes of you. You need to give me more strokes if you want to bet me, but I don't bet so don't waste your time."

"How are those kids of mine?"

"Tim is doing great in college. Listen, I need to get you to work with Lee this year. It's his junior year, you know. This is a big year for him. He really wants to do well, but he says he's just not that interested in working with you."

Conner's mind painted an image of Rick's younger son, and his heart sank slightly. Lee wasn't his kid, but Conner had felt a bond with both of Rick's boys, as well as with his daughter. He had coached them all, mentored them, one by one. He felt great disappointment at Rick's words.

"How come he doesn't want me to work with him?"

"I don't know, Conner. Tim has always said what you did for him was more than any coach he ever had. Hell, even me. Not that I was ever much of a coach, especially up against you. I think Lee was always a little envious during the time you spent with Tim. I think he felt like you weren't interested in working with him, and now thinks you'd do it just 'cause he's next."

"Hey, Ricky, you want me to call him? Maybe I can stop by the house one day. Talk to him. I mean, I have worked with every one of your kids. Debbie's the most fun, I must admit. I told her she's gonna be your best athlete and run circles around those brothers of hers."

"Con Man, would you do that for me? Call him, I mean? Or stop by, that would be good. You know kids, and I can't explain it. Lee's grades are good, real good. But lately, he's been talkin' about not playing basketball or even baseball this year."

"Not play? What the hell is that?"

"I don't know. Tammy's been telling him if he doesn't want to play, he shouldn't play. I asked her what the hell she was doing. If Lee doesn't play sports, then he's at high risk of falling in with the wrong crowd. She knows that, being that she teaches and has first hand knowledge of the high school kids who don't have any focus in their lives. Hell, Con Man, you know I have never worried about my kids 'cause they've always cared so much about playing sports."

"I know, man. You need to talk to Lee. He's a good little athlete, but we both knew he wasn't as interested in it, mostly because of his brother. He's just not that competitive." Conner had settled back into his chair, leaning back with his feet up on the credenza behind his desk. He was staring out the window at the hazy sky above Motown. His mind, however, was on the court, watching the kids, critiquing their moves. Then, without warning, Rick's focus brought him back.

"Well, enough about the family, Con Man. I called for other reasons."

"Yeah? So, what's up? I thought you sounded concerned and that's not like you. You're the most laid back guy I have ever met," Conner laughed uneasily. He was trying to be receptive to his friend, but Rick's sudden change of tone and focus made Conner nervous. "I envy you so much for your faith and family. Jesus, Rick, you have it made. I just can't wait for Samantha and me to start popping out athletes like you and Tammy."

"Quit it, Con Man," Rick's voice was developing tones of anger. "Don't do this."

"Don't do what?"

"Make me out to be some perfect person with the perfect life. I'm not and I don't. I am judgmental and leave work early to be with my kids while acting like I'm going to a meeting. You know that, so quit it. I hate it when you make me out to be a saint."

"Shit, Rick, what kind of crime is it to leave work early to go watch your kids, take them to practice or whatever? I can think of a lot worse things people do. Just the fact you find that bad tells me what a great guy you are. I love you, man!" Conner growled his last statement in imitation of a beer commercial. He was trying to pull Rick back to a level he was comfortable communicating with him on. Something was wrong, very wrong. He could feel it, and knew he may not want Rick to continue.

"Conner, stop it. I have been struggling with this for a while. But I can't turn away from it anymore. It's none of my business. I need to talk to you about something and I feel terrible about it."

"What is it, Rick? Jesus, with all the things we've talked about over the years, how can you be having so much trouble talking to me?" Conner was feeling angry now. He stood up and turned to look out his office window.

Putting Rick on speaker, he then walked closer to the glass, twining his arms around each other in front of his chest. He was trying to get away from the phone, from the message that was about to be delivered to him.

"Conner, are you alone? Can you talk freely?"

"Rick, I have an office the size of Texas and I run my own business. You know I clear out everybody and everything any time you call. What is your deal, man? It's as if you are telling me..." Conner's arms dropped to his sides and he spun around to face the desk. His heart was pounding. "Oh shit, Rick, you aren't sick are you? Jesus, I just found out my dad's sick. You better not be sick, man."

"Your dad?" Rick doubted his call, now. This may not have been the best time to have this discussion, or was it. "Conner, what is wrong with the rock? When I saw him in July I couldn't believe he was 68 years old. I thought he was just in his mid 50's he looked so good. No joke, my friend."

"Yeah," Conner leaned back against the window, feeling the sun's heat on the glass. "You know something, Rick? My dad always told me that I am successful because I hang around people like you. Good people who care about other people. Dad told me to know a man, just see what friends he hangs out with. I use to resent that saying until I got into my own business and realized it is true. The slime hang with the slime and the good always seem to keep no time with such slime."

Conner laughed at his own wit. He often found a way to rhyme his talk and it amused him. He also knew that slime was some of his best friends who would do anything for him, as he would for them. He laughed as much for the hypocrisy as the humor. No laughter joined him from the speaker.

"What's up with your dad, Conner?"

"It's the c-word."

"Oh shit, Conner. I am so sorry," Rick's voice stopped short, and the Conner's office remained silent for a few moments." You know I will pray for you. I'll put him on the intentions list at church. When I tell Debbie, I know she'll want to light a candle for him, too. We all will."

"Thanks, Rick. I know I can always count on you and the family for support and understanding. This is a fresh wound for you. How long has your dad been gone now, ten months? Jesus, it hasn't been a year yet, has it?"

"No, it's been ten. But, I didn't have the same close relationship you had with your dad. My dad was a drunk and could never keep the family together, you know that. You saw it. Hell, I learned more about how to be a man by watching my old man being less of one."

"Yeah, I remember. I wish it had been different for you. But hey, you made amends before he passed and that is most important. I don't need to make amends with my dad. We know each other as if we are the same person. I couldn't have asked for a more blessed relationship with a dad. I will never live up to him as a father." Conner's voice cracked and he paused to turn back to view of the city.

"Hell, Rick, at this rate, with as much time as Samantha's putting in at work, I will never have kids. You have to have sex to have kids, right?" Conner laughed at his own comment, although his envy for Rick's family was very real. "Well, you know, you have three of them. They are your kids, aren't they?"

"Shit, Conner." Rick laughed at Conner's trash-talking style.

"Rick, you've cussed twice, now. I don't hear you cuss that much in a quarter. What's up? Your heart sounds heavy."

"I can't tell you now, Conner. Not with the news of your dad. It just wouldn't be right. Another time, we'll talk."

"Rick, you know me. I don't retreat or hide from anything. You know I like it right between the eyes. I love you, man, you know that. There's nothing you can tell me that I will be mad at you for. We have too much history together. What is it?"

"Tammy and I have been seeing Samantha with Jim Gordy."

Conner stood quietly for a moment, waiting for more. Rick was silent.

"Shit, Rick, is that all you got?"

"No, Conner, I mean, we have seen them together a lot, y'know? Together."

"I know this, Rick. They've been working long hours together for about four months now on a project for some tool and die company on the east side. Samantha has apologized over and over for the time she's away. She's been working such long hours I purchased a condo close to her work so she wouldn't have to drive so far to the 'burbs each day. You know the traffic's is hell around here. It makes no difference if it's 275, 96, 10... all slow moving. I just couldn't see her wasting two hours a day in traffic, and you know my schedule. I have kept busy so I wouldn't miss her so much. When I call her, she's never available, always in those stupid corporate meetings that take up the workday. Now she gets time at night to do whatever real work she needs to do for herself. It's a vicious cycle and you know her work ethic. She wants to be Heritage Technologies' first female CEO. I am so proud of her, Rick. You know how tough a woman has it in corporate America, these days. Hell, you should know all this, anyway. You work for the same company!" Conner was becoming defensive, protective. He didn't like the direction Rick was taking.

"No, Conner. Just listen to me, please. The other night, we went to Cios, in Birch Lake, for dinner. You know, that new restaurant? High-priced place, but great food and all of H.T.'s big wigs go there to get away from the business deal restaurants downtown."

"Yeah, I know the place," Conner replied. "It's near you guys."

"Right. Well, when Tammy and I were walking into the restaurant, the host seated us in one of those cozy rooms in the back. It was our anniversary, y'know? When we walked past the booth next to ours, I looked in. Samantha and Jim were there, Con." Rick stopped, and swallowed hard. He was uncomfortable with what he was doing to his friend, but knew it had to be done.

"Go on, Rick."

"Conner, we could hear them talking. Hell, Tammy and I went there to celebrate, be alone. I had saved for months to take her there, and what did we do? We stayed quiet and listened the whole time to what they were saying."

Conner sank into his chair. He loved Samantha deeply. He had believed her, supported her efforts at work. He had given her blind trust, unconditional love. As he listened to Rick's words, he closed his eyes and thought of his dad. He suddenly felt numb, old.

"Okay. You have my attention."

"You mad at me?"

"Not at all. I told you, I wouldn't be mad at anything you tell me. You always tell me the truth and I know that. But I suspect I am not going to like what I am about to hear, am I?"

"No, Conner, you're not."

Conner's fists clenched, tightened, and he pursed his lips as he fought the lump in his throat. "Keep going."

"They were talking about how great they have it. Jim was bragging about having a wife who takes care of the kids and the house, Samantha has you to support her spending, and they have each other to have fun with. I am paraphrasing, of course. Never been a very good eves' dropper. They didn't have a clue anyone was around to hear them. Tammy and I were just amazed at how open and blunt they were about their whole relationship. They were in complete disregard for their spouses and family. Shit, Conner, Jim has kids. It disgusted us. Tammy kept thinking about his kids. How a man could do that to his family? How Samantha could do this to you?"

"Go on, Rick, and tell me everything now, please, so I don't have to guess what else there is. I have to know everything." Conner leaned forward in the chair, supporting himself with his arms on his legs. He felt weak, almost as if he would be sick. He was dizzy and his heart was pounding out of his chest.

"Conner, I had heard some rumors. But hell, Samantha has moved up in the organization so quickly and she's still so young. You know the rumors. Women always face this kind of talk from envious and jealous men, and women, that aren't advancing. People can be cruel. So, I tried not to believe it. I know how much you love her and you tell me how hard it is to be away from her so much. Hell, Conner, everyone at work is surprised you put up with it. Most men would never allow it. I always respected you for trying so hard to support her. I know those times when you'd call and tell me you were weak and you needed to know from me that all was okay, that she wasn't screwing around on you. I truly believed she was not. She being a pretty woman, Conner, I never wanted to make more of any one situation than can be expected. Hell, you even told me you expected some flirting to go on and that you knew she had to be open to some of it so she wouldn't be looked at with that bitch image you told me she was so against having. But what we heard and saw crosses the line, Conner." Rick paused. "Are you sure you want me to tell you?"

"Yes," Conner stood up abruptly, and kicked the chair back behind him. "And quit stalling, damn it! While I don't want to hear it, I need to hear it now or I won't believe it. I guess I'm lucky it's coming from you, because there is no one I trust more then you. So give it to me, the whole story. Before I come over there and kick your ass!"

"I'm sorry, man. Okay. Well, to my surprise, Tammy was as much a bird dog as I was. We told the waiter that we were waiting for someone so we didn't order. Samantha and Jim obviously were finishing up and they were drinking wine, a lot of wine. Tammy went to the bathroom and walked right by their booth. They didn't recognize her at all. I don't think Jim's ever met her, and Samantha was too focused on him to care. The wine was working on them, too, I imagine. Only two plates on the table, Conner, so we were sure they were alone. I can't believe that neither of them looked up when

Tammy walked so closely to them. I almost said something to her when we first passed them, y'know? But something prevented me. I am so glad that I didn't. Samantha would have heard my voice and then they wouldn't have displayed themselves like they did. It was Tammy's idea not to order a full dinner and just listen in on their conversation. It was horrible, Conner, to hear one of my best friends' wife flirting and advancing on that slime ball. I've never liked the jerk, anyway.

"I have to tell you now, Conner. Samantha is not the first one. This guy is slime, and everyone knows it. I know of two professional assistants who have been with him, for sure. One was going to file a sexual harassment suit against him. I would guess he dumped her for Samantha because it was after that when I didn't hear much about the guy. Then he switched departments."

"Well, Rick," Conner smiled and slouched back in the chair. "Knowing my wife isn't the first doesn't give me any feelings of comfort, understand? I'm dying here, buddy, but you have to tell me everything. You can't hold back anything because I need to know for many reasons, okay?"

Conner's voice had taken on a new tone, and Rick recognized it. He was more serious. It was like he was negotiating a business deal or preparing for a street fight. That's why he was the CEO. He was a rock, like his dad. No one could touch him in a boardroom. Rick heard something else in his tone. A vein of focus that he had only heard rumors about, something that went way back to Conner's childhood. It made Rick nervous. While he knew the professional side of Conner, people had told him how Conner's dark side from being city-raised was nothing to stir up in him. Even Conner's own dad, during the golf retreats that Rick attended, would make reference to loyalty and love for team mentality. Rick knew this was about family and Conner always said, 'don't mess with someone's family.'

"Tammy and I were up all night on our anniversary, Conner, and didn't even celebrate, if you know what I mean. We just lay there all night looking at the ceiling, praying to God to give us the strength to do what was right. Jesus, Conner, all you have done for us and our family, and I have to be the one to tell you this."

"Rick, don't worry about it, okay? I'm not sure I would have believed anyone else but you. It had to be you. It was meant to be you. I will be okay. Go on."

"By the time Tammy came back from the restroom, they were laughing and giggling. They were obviously kissing, with all the smacking going on, and nobody brought them anything more to eat. My stomach just fell to my knees. I didn't know what to do. If we walked out, we'd just give her another chance to see us, and she would surely recognize me. We felt almost dirty just sitting there and listening like we were. To my surprise, it was Tammy who insisted we stay put. She said Samantha wasn't going to talk her way out of this one and she wanted to stay long enough to validate that this was no misunderstanding.

"They were toasting each other and talking about their upcoming trip to Europe. I know that's the day after tomorrow, Conner. Tammy insisted you know before they leave. Anyway, Jim asked Samantha if she thought you had any inclination what was going on. Samantha laughed and said no. She told him you're dumb in love with her, and all she has to tell you is you're not supporting her enough and that puts you right back in line. 'He really wants to support me,' Samantha said, laughing. 'So, I let him pay my bills.' Then they both laughed even harder. Conner? Man, you okay?"

"Yeah. You just keep going."

"By now, Tammy was squeezing my hand. I think she wanted to go over there and beat Samantha up or something. Then, we could hear them getting up to leave and Samantha paid the check. She said, 'It's a business meeting. We talked some business, so I'll expense this puppy.' I know this sounds stupid, Conner, but I got really pissed when I thought about my shit bonus last year and now this was happening."

"Rick, I can see your point. I ain't too happy about it either. I have to ask Samantha to pay for our dinner once in a while. She expects me to pay each and every time. Shit, she makes damn good money. I guess this Jim must be some guy, huh?"

"Jesus, Conner, you know him. You've seen him. He's got a potbelly and wears a hairpiece or something. Shit, he has too much hair for the size of his head. It makes me sick just thinking about it."

"Okay, man, so now I'm ready to vomit. Is that it?"

"I wish it was, Conner. They made some more wise cracks and got up. Tammy got up first, after they turned away from us. I tried to get her to sit down, but she wouldn't. She said they'd obviously had too much to drink to notice us, and she was going to follow them to get as much info as possible. Shit, if Tammy would have had a camera, I know she would have taken pictures. You know, she has never said much about you, Conner. Sure, she was pleased with you helping the kids. But she never talked straight about you. Honestly, I was afraid to ask her because I know you come down on the kids hard when they complain, make excuses or aren't working enough. I always wondered if she resented you for that. But, I tell you what. She was like your eye spy that night. She was all over Samantha's situation, wanting to catch her at everything.

"So, when they got up to leave, Tammy grabbed her coat and purse and said, 'come on.' You know how that restaurant is configured, with the parking lot across the street out front, and that walk out area? With the breezeway canopy, we didn't even have to leave the building, at first. We just watched as Jim walked Samantha to her car.

"By the way, Conner, Samantha's skirts don't hide much these days, and this one was no exception. She was publicizing her legs, if you know what I mean. She always does that. Everyone at work knows you'd kick their ass if you found out anyone was messing with that. No one wants to cause any problems here, least of all, Tammy and me. I always thought everyone was looking out for you. Obviously, this deal with Jim has been going on for some time."

"Keep going, Rick," Conner said with a soft voice.

"Well, they were holding hands walking across the street and when a car came by, they let go of each other. When they got to the car, Samantha went to open the door and she pushed her butt out when Jim walked up behind her. He reached under her skirt to get a feel, and she turned around to face him. That's when they kissed, well, you know, Conner. One of those kisses. I am so damn sorry."

"Is that it?"

Rick sighed heavily. "Not quite. Samantha did a u-turn when she left, obviously to go back to town. She drove off the road, waiting for Jim to catch up to her in his car. That gave Tammy and me a chance to get around back to ours. Tammy told me to get in, she was driving. Because Samantha waited for Jim, we had no trouble getting up behind them. We held back and just followed. They went to the condo complex near the corporate office. I knew it was Samantha's condo you purchased, Conner. Samantha parked and they went to the side door, kissed and he opened the door. Guess he's got a key. They both went in."

Rick waited, but Conner didn't comment.

"That's all we saw, man. Tammy wanted to stay and I told her no. It was our anniversary and I wasn't going to sit there all night. Besides, you know me. I get into work real early, in case I leave for one of the kids' activities. I drove by the apartment building the next morning, and Jim's car was there. It was covered with frost, obviously from being there all night. I wanted to park and wait for him, y'know? But, I think it's obvious.

"I am so sorry I had to tell you, my friend. You don't deserve this, Conner. We know you are a kind man. Hell, no man should have to deal with such a woman. I don't know what to say."

"Rick, I love ya, man. You did the right thing. I'd have done the same for you, although I know Tammy isn't that way. I am sorry my life ruined your anniversary. Tell Tammy I will make it up to her. What my family does, I do. So, I fucked your anniversary. I promise I will make it up to you guys."

"Don't be stupid, Conner. I know you must be beside yourself. I don't know what I would do or feel if I had this happen to me. Please tell me we're okay, you and me. I need to know that."

"Rick, don't think about it again, you hear me? You did right. We are both in difficult positions and I am feeling every emotion created by God right now. I need some time." He paused and strengthened his tone. "Listen. I will call you next week, okay? We are not keeping in touch enough. Let's not let it go so long again before we talk."

"Sure, Conner, Maybe one early round of golf before the season officially opens and we have to compete for tee times with all the hackers, okay? Take care and I will talk to you next week. If you don't call me, I will call you."

"Thanks, partner; for everything. Give my love to the family."

Conner gently placed the receiver in its cradle. He stared at the phone, his hand still upon it. He leaned back in his chair, and the heat of the pain driving through his chest was almost unbearable.

NO, NO, NO, his mind was screaming. Please God, NO. I love her. Don't do this to me, please. He ran his hands upward along his face and through his hair. Tears began to swell up in his eyes, as the phone rang again. Conner jumped and jerked the receiver to his ear.

"What!"

"Conner? Jesus, man, what's your deal? Your phone's been tied up for over an hour!"

"Land man," Conner recognized the voice of his legal counsel and tried to compose himself, pressing the speaker phone button and slowly setting down the receiver. "What's the word?"

"Dump it! That's the word."

"Dump it. Dump what? No guessing games today, man. I'm late for my golf game and not in the mood."

"Okay, here's the deal. You know that piece of dirt in the U.P., the one I mentioned was in your possession and no one knows where it came from? When I came on board after Joey's retirement, I found it in the books."

"Yeah, I remember, the one that's losing money and we don't even know who or why it was purchased. The mystery land."

"Exactly. It's a bloodsucker. It's gotta go, Conner. And go now. I've got a developer who's interested. Wants to sell the lumber, put in vacation condos and is offering big bucks. There's good timber there, and he'll make a fortune clearing the land. I won't take no for an answer on this one. I know you love your raw land and we pay dearly in taxes for it all. But you didn't even know you had this property and we can make millions. Remember this is why you hired me. We can pay taxes for years on the other properties from the margin we will make if I close this deal."

Conner weakened and his arm dropped to his lap. He sighed and lifted the receiver back up from the cradle.

"Just arrange whatever you think needs to happen. Send me the paperwork." Conner slowly lowered the receiver back down. So much, he realized, was going on around him that he was blind to. First, his wife, and now some piece of land he didn't even know about. What kind of businessman, husband, even person, was he? The accumulative amount of adversity was overwhelming him, shaking his very core. He needed space, time and strength to think of solutions. If he owned land, he wanted to see it before he sold it.

Conner ran his fingers across the telephone, replaying the tapes of his conversation with Rick. His heart was breaking, yet he was too shocked to accept Rick's words. His heart told him it was true, that Rick was only validating what Conner had felt for months. The walls of his large office suddenly felt very close, too close for Conner and his heart began pumping faster.

I've gotta get the fuck out of here, he thought. Tonight.

Conner pulled his cell phone from the clip on his belt and dialed Todd's pager.

Todd Sullivan was flirting with the building receptionist when his pager vibrated. 4-4-4 was displayed. He knew what that meant. Fire 'em up, we're flyin' tonight. Todd took a quick look outside seeing the lightning and rain that was falling. He could only shake his head and tell the receptionist what an important man he was. The CEO wanted to see him. She blew him a kiss as he walked to the elevator. Todd wasn't smiling, he knew what 4-4-4 meant, and it never meant anything fun.

7

The Hood

"Con Man!" Todd walked into Conner's office with that cocky, crooked smile of his. "How's it going? So, you want to fly and die today. Weather isn't supposed to be that good, y'know. So, ah, maybe you should just look out that big window of yours. A storm front is about to move in and you still want to make a trip. Why, Con? Still tryin' to show me you is a real man, huh, Con Man? Well, I don't mind you putting your life at risk, but it bothers me when you place me at death's door. No one would miss you, but me? Many a people would be devastated if I wasn't on this paradise called earth!" Todd laughed at his own words. Conner was in no mood to put up with Todd's trash talk, as he did every day.

"Todd, fuck you!" Conner reached for his briefcase & jacket, as he scowled at his friend. "Today is not a good day to be fucking with me, okay? I don't have the patience. Just do your job today and get me where I want to go. That's what I pay you for and I do pay you handsomely, if you remember."

Conner's harsh words stung, but Todd had seen him this way before. He knew not to just come out and ask. Conner hated explaining business to him, and they both knew Todd didn't care about the business or its troubles. The fewer conflicts, the better for him.

Todd had a simpler life. He envied Conner's power and money, but wanted nothing of what came with those elements. He knew he was overpaid by this wealthy boyhood friend who was taking care of him. He also knew that Conner's life would have been over a couple of times if it wasn't for him. Todd watched Conner's back and that was worth a lot to Conner. Seldom did Conner mention compensation in their conversations. It was unspoken and unimportant, for the most part. Todd went to the bank and there was always money in his account. He didn't pay for his house, car, utilities or any other fixed costs. Spending money was always generous and after the month was over, the outstanding balance was placed in investments, and spending money was again provided. Conner never talked down to Todd and he appreciated that. He told Todd his job was to watch his back and prepare for retirement. Only a few times when Todd's accounts were exhausted and no investments were made did Conner call him in about it, and they talked about financial planning. He used words like protecting the dollars he worked so hard for, rather than throw them away.

Conner came from a solid family and Todd's was broken before he could drive. While Conner went to college, Todd barely made it through high school. There was a bond between them from a very young age and they both talked about how they were going to take care of each other. Conner lived up to that promise. Todd came to Conner out of the military, broke and nowhere to go. Every need of his was taken care of with only a few stipulations and Conner always made sure Todd had his dignity.

"Oh, you pissed at the wife again, huh?" Todd smiled, trying to cut the tension in the room. "I can always tell when you haven't seen her in a while and you are feeling ignored by the bitch. Why are you with that shit of a woman, Conner? She doesn't give you the time of day. She is no wife, man, she is a business partner. Let me tell you, there are a bunch of women who would love to have a dog like you, Con Man. Shit, Holly has some friends that would crawl on their hands and knees and wouldn't even ask you for a ride home when you've had your fun with them. Hell, I am going to have to keep an eye on Holly if you become available and she found out. If it weren't for my great looks, your money would be a worry." Todd often cut the anger out of Conner with humor, saying just the things that kept Conner feeling loved.

"Shut up, asshole," Conner snapped. "I don't do my best friend's wife. I want my wife, not yours, nor some bimbo you know that is just coming over as an imposter. I see those types of women all the time, everywhere I go. Women all fancied up as if they had somewhere important to go, as if they were something special to take home to momma. Then, sugar daddy walks up and you know what they are. A mistress gets all the fucking attention from this slime, while the wife is home keeping the family together. It makes me sick." Conner's face showed the pain of his own concern that his wife was the other woman of some big wig in the path of her career goals.

"Yeah, things aren't like when we were kids. If I told you once, I have told you many times, you have to check up on a woman like Samantha. Give her the space and she will dog you. I have to go file my flight plan if you are bent on being in the clouds today. I will be back and when I do, I want you to chill out and quit thinking about whether your wife is fucking around on you.

I want to see that attitude back to being the Con Man. So, what's the itin?"

"North," Conner walked to the office window. A storm had developed not only outside his office, but also inside his heart. He reflected on the time in life when he and Todd met. Life seemed simpler back then. It was a good time to be a kid.

Todd and Conner were not blood, but they were brothers. They had grown up together in Flint's inner city and had watched each other's back since the seventh grade when Todd's family moved into the city. It didn't hit Conner until they were both in high school that coming to the city wasn't exactly a direction of improved status. Most families in the late 60's were moving out to the suburbs because of the crime and perceived dangers, and frequently as a show that they were succeeding. It was a status thing to tell people your family was moving to the 'burbs. Todd's parents were having marital troubles and his dad's construction business was going bad even with a booming economy in place. Todd's family consisted of three boys, his mom and his dad. He was the youngest.

Todd and Conner met one September day in 1966. The neighborhood kids were playing a game of whiffle baseball in the school yard. The game was played with plastic baseballs with holes in them. The lightweight bats were plastic, as well. This equipment was necessary due to the much smaller field and the limited space available to kids living in a populated city neighborhood. The bases were shorter, and the base paths were worn down from extensive play the field endured during the previously hot summer days.

The school yard was bordered with four small houses the school board had converted into school buildings. The city schools were overcrowded with kids. Many people lived in Flint where they could get the good wages of a union shop job and a very affordable standard of living in the city. Those who worked their way to white collar positions, or who had businesses that took advantage of the growth and success of the booming automotive industry, would move to the suburbs. With the safety consideration of small kids crossing a busy city street during shop shift changes, the school board voted to remodel the four smaller homes into a school, allowing kids from kindergarten through third grade to be safely schooled in their own neighborhood.

Conner was sitting on top of the redwood fence that surrounded the school yard, when an unfamiliar figure approaching from the south caught his attention. He liked jumping up onto the fence because it gave him the feeling of being a wolf, watching over his pack from a high rock. City kids learned early to watch for danger and he was very good at it. He also liked jumping up on the fence because it provided him a workout and made him feel strong. He was always trying to get stronger at that age. He wanted to be as big as the high school kids.

Perched on the fence, Conner continued to spy the strange kid walking up to where they were playing. This was definitely a kid no one had ever seen before. He was chucking and jiving with everyone around him. Conner didn't say a word. He sat on the fence and acted like he was just watching the game, as his team was at bat, while keeping a sly eye on this cocky stranger.

The kid picked up one of the two plastic bats left for the summer play. Conner could feel the heat begin to draw moisture on his brow. He never enjoyed confrontation, but knew it was a necessity when the time came to maintain respect. If one acted weak, or proved to be such, he was eaten alive in this city. It was much easier getting a couple of stitches after the battle, rather than dealing with all the hassles that would come from showing weakness in the face of confrontation, especially in front of a crowd of kids who pounced on the weak. It was better to take one's bumps and bruises when they were offered and Conner's street sense told him he was dealing with a loose cannon in need of a good attitude adjustment.

It became Conner's turn to bat. Normally, he would use the other bat that was available. But, because he didn't want to waste any time setting this stranger straight to the ways of the hood, Conner politely asked him for the bat he had picked up. The kid looked Conner up and down. City kids always did that. They measured each other up before they made the move. There wasn't much dancing that went on. If you were looking for trouble, it usually came very quickly. Conner could see the stranger was unsure about him.

They were now eyeball-to-eyeball. Conner never brought any weapons with him to the hood field. Few hoodlums were ever seen there or around Conner's house, because of the location of the neighborhood. Every so often, though, it happened and the kids looked to Conner to keep them safe and protect their turf. He didn't know how he was designated the heavy, it just somehow always happened. He thought of his friends as cowards, but they were his friends and if he wanted to keep them, he had to overlook their pension for avoiding getting beat up at his expense. They were not all cowards, but he knew that he was fortunate not to live in the roughest area of Flint. Conner had been exposed to enough in his short life to know all the dangers.

His dad was one of the district's high school coaches and was very good at most any athletic endeavor. Because of his confidence and attitude, Conner stared directly into the stranger's eyes and politely repeated his request.

"Please give me the bat."

The kid reached out and handed Conner the bat. Conner then walked over to the other bat and picked it up, handing the bat he just took from the stranger to Kevin, a boy who was standing close to home plate and looking very scared, as usual. Conner placed his arm around Kevin and moved him further away so Conner could take his place at the plate. He whispered into Kevin's ear that if he decided to fight this guy he wanted Kevin to jump the back fence and run for help.

Conner was experienced in these types of things. Only an absolute idiot would walk into someone's hood all by himself and act the fool the way this kid was. Conner was certain there were others watching from the peripheral, somewhere waiting for the first blood to occur so they could expose themselves. It's an old city baiting trick used in hoods to entice a group of kids to challenge one person outside their territory and then when the cops came, it looks like the outside group was just protecting their boy from the other group. When Conner looked into the stranger's eyes, he sensed he was not on any drugs, flipping or anything like that. So, he had to be earning some respect, maybe an initiation from another hood. Conner stepped closer to the plate, fully realizing trouble was lurking around the corner.

"Hey!" said the stranger. "I thought you were going to use that other bat."

"I changed my mind."

With that, the pitch was tossed and Conner smashed it over the school that represented any fence in major league baseball. Conner gave his coolest home run trot. He went to first, second and then on his way to third he looked to home base to see the stranger wrestling with the next batter for the bat. Conner never made it to third base. Like a batter who had been hit by a pitch, he took a V-line directly to home plate. He changed sports in an instant, and was running full force when he barreled into the stranger who was wrestling with Nick. Nick was a small guy who Conner looked after not because he much liked him, but because Nick's mom was a friend of the family and had asked Conner to watch out for him.

The stranger lifted his elbow just before Conner reached him and it connected to Conner's lip, splitting it open as they both crumbled to the ground. The stranger was shaken from the blow and Conner fell on top of him. Even though Conner was stunned by the elbow and was seeing stars inside his head, he instinctively began punching, striking as many times as possible.

"Watch my back, watch my back!" Conner kept yelling to his friends, the others in the area. Any time now, Conner was preparing to have to deal with more intruders to their hood baseball field. But to his surprise, no one showed up.

Funny thing about fights. On television there is always a winner. This was not a reality when it came to hood fights. Two dudes would go at it and there may be a lot of fists thrown, but to throw a punch takes a lot of energy and cannot be sustained. No fight lasted more than a minute or two. The adrenaline of the fight provided extra incentive to keep fighting, but the stranger began covering up and Conner decided he was too tired to continue. With his friends watching his back and no other opposing players from other hoods present, he stopped fighting.

Conner stood up while maintaining a fighting pose, just in case his opponent was playing possum. The stranger got up and ran off around one of the nearby school units. As he ran, he yelled, through the normal street superlatives that occur when a confrontation has presided, that he would be back with his older brothers and Conner was going to die for this.

Conner was a tough, street-smart kid, and he did well when the occasional scuffle would occur. He used the cut on his lip as reason to leave the yard, knowing that to stay would be very ignorant. Time heals wounds and settles tempers. He knew this kid hadn't just engaged in his first brawl. Both were only twelve years old, but had experienced their share of skirmishes and Conner knew the stranger's threats should be taken seriously. Still woozy from the elbow blow he had received, he told those left watching to go home. Some of them did what most kids do when a fight breaks out, and had ran home as soon as the first blow was provided.

The game was over.

Conner went straight home from the park, enjoying the taste of his own blood as it dripped into his mouth along the way. He learned early in life that he had a high threshold of pain and actually enjoyed what pain came from competing, especially competition that included moments of injury which caused Conner to bleed. It was those times when an indescribable rush of adrenaline would occur and Conner felt his strongest. While some would crumble from the sight of their blood, it only excited and motivated him.

Conner reached his house. Knowing his mom would be upset from the sight of blood, he picked up a basketball from the yard and began to shoot baskets. The blood continued to drip into his mouth and he spat it out like a baseball player would tobacco. He wasn't the best spatter. He spat often, yet wasn't sure why. He saw athletes do it all the time, but to spit blood was different. Blood was stringy, thicker than saliva and, while he did his best, he was not keeping it off his shirt. He couldn't go into the house until his lip stopped bleeding and now he would have to hide his shirt.

As Conner was relaxing, trying to visualize the brawl and make himself a more dominant participant, he saw an El Camino car moving slowly up the street toward his house and his heart began pumping rapidly. Would they stop? Would they shoot him, or talk trash and move on? They didn't do anything. They just drove by the house. Inside the cab sat the driver, and the stranger from the baseball diamond sat next to the window. Another kid was in the bed of the car and raised his arm parallel to the ground, made a fist, pointed his thumb upward and outstretched his index finger, making the image of a gun with his hand. He then extended his arm and imitated multiple gunshots while pointing directly at Conner.

The next morning, Conner ate toast and cereal for breakfast. It was the first day of school after a nice long summer. It was a sunny morning, and Conner was still feeling the sting of both the fight he had the day before and his mom's disappointment upon seeing his bloody shirt. It didn't matter though, as he was going into the seventh grade and this year he'd be able to play on the school basketball team. He couldn't wait for football season to come and go, so basketball season would begin.

He stood at the kitchen counter, sipped the last drop of milk from his bowl and then dropped it into the sink. He kissed his mom good-bye and started out of the house. The small ranch-style home wasn't much, but it was enough. Conner's mom and dad both were teachers and, while everyone else in the family seemed to be rich, it never bothered Conner that his parents didn't have money. He loved sports and with his dad being a coach, he had grown up being either in the gym or out on the ball field. While he knew money attracted the girls as an adult, in school all the beauties liked the athletes. He was damn sure going to have a pretty skirt on his arm this year simply because he'd be a player.

Conner walked to school with his normally fast gate. It was a necessity all those years keeping up with his dad's stride. He was aware he walked faster than most people, but still had to have style and made sure he looked good while he walked. He was breathing in the fresh, cool morning air of his middle class subdivision. The entry road to his house came in and looped back out and thus his street only had one entry and exit route. This helped keep the gang bangers from coming around because the configuration of the neighborhood was pro neighborhood watch. Any trouble and they'd have to bust it. Gang bangers were like water, they take the path of least resistance.

The corner house was the smallest in the neighborhood and had been up for sale for a while. He had been in it once, because two kids he knew had lived there with their mom. He remembered going into the house and smelling the fowl odor of sewage. The house was a pit, and Conner had to leave soon after he entered. He could not believe anyone lived in those conditions. As he approached, he recognized the El Camino from the day before sitting in the driveway, with the school yard stranger sitting in its bed, along with his brother who had pointed the finger gun.

Conner's heart began to increase its pace.

Shit, he thought, what should I do? This was why he hated the streets and loved athletics. In the streets, nothing was ever over. Conner and this shit-head had their fight and it should be over with, but it never worked that way. Now, he had to fight again and again until he eventually lost. Then, it would be his choice to end it, if his life hadn't. Sports provided boundaries and when the game ended, everyone took their outcome and dealt with it.

He decided to keep walking. He wasn't going to cower now. The corner house was next to a very busy street. It wasn't that Conner expected anyone to stop their cars in order to assist him against his foes, but if he were left injured on the pavement, someone would surely call for help. His biggest fear was not to die, but to die a slow death. He'd rather get blown away in a drive-by shooting, than to be cut a bunch of times and suffer during his final moments.

Always aware of his environment, Conner was pretty good at adding up situations and he knew he was in trouble. If he had been paying more attention, like he should have been instead of feeling safe because he was still in his hood, he could have cut behind some houses and taken a different route. They had spied him and now they wouldn't let him go. He knew he had to face the challenge now or get hurt later. Might as well be now, he thought.

He wasn't much for hiding. He hated it. He wanted his medicine and the option to get it over with.

He continued toward the house and moved to the middle of the street. If they were going to throw down, they may have to stop traffic to do it and that would give Conner a better chance to survive. Winning isn't anything more than surviving that moment to get to the next day. This was going to be one of those situations. He could feel it.

As he approached the street, he continued to keep eye contact with the older kid. He didn't want any trouble, but he also didn't want to look meek to the animals that were preying on him. His mind was racing and realized they must have moved into his neighborhood. He could use that to his advantage.

"You live there?" asked Conner.

"Hell, yes," the older brother replied. "What you got to say about that?"

"Had I known you were hoods, maybe yesterday wouldn't have happened."

Conner was now feeling more confident that his language and position was superior. He was an articulate person for his age and smart beyond his years. The longer Conner could keep them talking, the better.

"You live around here?" The kid's eye was puffy and black from the fight.

"Yeah, I do."

"Where?"

"Where do you think? Your brother took a shot at me yesterday in front of my house."

"Very funny. You are a smart guy, aren't you, asshole?"

"Smart enough to know that I have to walk past this house every day and twice on Sunday. I want to deal with whatever is bothering you dudes now and be done with it. This is our hood and I don't need no shit here."

"No shit? Hell, you beat the shit out of my brother, you fucker. What kind of hood is this?" the brother jumped out of the car bed and fronted Conner.

"He was looking for trouble. He got it. Now are you looking for trouble?" Conner looked directly in his eyes.

The brother wasn't sure what to do now. Conner wasn't much shorter than this kid who was obviously of high school age and who, he now realized, he had miscalculated to be afraid of him.

A smile came to Conner's mouth. He knew the routine and, looking into the eyes of the older brother, he could see that while he may not win the fight, he would survive because this guy didn't have what it took. Now the question was, does Conner pull first? He knew that fights don't last long and who gets off first usually won. Conner could tell the guy wanted out and was going to give it to him.

"Okay, are we ready?"

Conner smiled and continued to look into the eyes of his opponent, while keeping his peripheral vision on the elbows. The elbows were the keys, they move first. If they did, Conner was going to take his forehead and bust this kid right on his nose. He knew when the kid fronted him he was not experienced at it. Never get so close that your opponent can grab your balls or bust your nose. You make them reach so you know their strategy. Conner was in a tactical superior position and was ready to do both to this guy and he knew it would be over quick. He probably wouldn't even want any of the medicine Conner was prescribing.

"After this guy, who I assume is your brother, and I get done kicking the shit out of each other, you and I will walk to school, my friend," Conner said, without looking at the kid now standing near the car.

"You are going to walk to school with him?"

"Yeah, he's in the hood. We have to watch each other's back. Now that I know he lives here, he's cool."

Shit, I lost my advantage, Conner thought, as the brother backed away a couple of steps. If they were to fight now, Conner would not feel so confident of victory. His opponent was both cocky and strong. That was a dangerous combination. Depending on the will and the heart of this guy, Conner was at risk of getting hurt now.

"You ain't out to get my brother?"

"Hell, no. Your brother is an asshole. He comes into my hood and acts like he's tough shit. You don't do that around here or you are going to get hurt. My name is Conner. Are we done dancing? Cause if we are done dancing, I want to get to school, where I can meet the new skirts."

"If you ain't out for my brother, we're cool."

"What the fuck is your name?" Conner started laughing.

Everyone began to laugh and Conner walked up and shook his hand.

"My name is Greg. I want you to meet my youngest brother, Todd."

"Hey, Todd," Conner said. "What the hell were you doing yesterday, anyway?"

"I was trying to make a name for myself in the neighborhood. My brothers told me I was going to get my ass kicked if I didn't step up right away. I wanted to make sure I wasn't going to be a whipping boy around here."

"Jesus, man. You're going about it all wrong. Come on, I'll walk with you and give you some city teachings so you don't get yourself killed. My lip looks like hell because of you. The skirts better think I am sexy or we are going to throw down again after school."

Todd and Conner started laughing again and shook hands.

"Oh shit," Conner said. "I even have to show you how to shake. Man, you can't be that stiff. Let your wrist flow and your arm swing. You shake hands like that at school and you may not survive the day. You do like girls, don't you?"

Todd laughed and jumped on Conner's back in a mock way, starting a lifetime friendship that would be filled with much success and many adversities.

8
Father and Son

The plane ride to Tri-City was a solemn one for Conner. Childhood memories dominated his thoughts. He stared blankly out the plane window as tears filled his eyes. The education received in school was minimal compared to the instructions and lessons learned by a son from his father.

Ewald Kenneth Morley had made his mistakes. He never tried to hide his weaknesses from his son, nor did he want them to show. Conner had the innate ability to see those weaknesses without any type of communication taking place between them. Conner loved his dad.

They were flying just above the clouds. Conner was amazed at how they pillowed the floor beneath the backdrop of a deep, blue sky. The diminishing distant lightning seemed symbolic of how Conner and his dad felt about one another. He respected strong figures and was introduced to many men in his life who were great leaders. None were any more impressive than Ewald. Yet, with cancer now beating on his dad's body, Conner felt somewhat betrayed at his dad's strength.

Never had Conner witnessed a tear fall from his dad's eyes. Not even when Conner's grandmother had passed away twelve years earlier did Ewald cry. This had disappointed Conner, because he was very close to her and had looked to his dad for guidance. Her death was devastating to him, and he had cried many tears. Conner felt he had disappointed his dad due to his weakness of openly expressing his grief. He had cried equally hard when his mom's father had passed away. Conner's grandpa often drove him to sports practices during the year. Football, basketball and baseball were all sports Coach Morley directed. Never did a day complete when Conner wasn't involved in the practices in some way. Just like the wolf packs that take care of their own, the Morley family did well to keep everyone involved.

Many times after practice, Ewald would take Conner to the coaches meetings. They were usually held in the school's film room, but there were times when the success of the team warranted a trip to the local watering hole for a more appropriate setting. A Friday win made a Sunday coaches meetings civil. This was where Conner got his best education and where he enjoyed listening, the most. Listening was the only thing Conner did during those meetings. Never was he allowed to speak unless spoken to, and never, absolutely never, was he to discuss the meeting with the woman of the house. Subjects on drinking, women, politics and sports were all discussed. Some of the language Conner heard was as fowl as an outhouse in July. Yet, Conner knew his place and made sure that he kept his distance. He would eat his meal, drink his soda and be rewarded with a candy bar for his good behavior.

Coaches were very proud people and they all had their opinions about each aforementioned subject. As the alcohol flowed more freely, so did the opinions of each man at the table, which held the many pitchers of their favorite beer. Always beer. Never hard liquor because liquor stayed in the pores longer and was more easily detected by the woman of the house when they returned home after the meeting had concluded.

Conner loved those meetings for many reasons. He felt like one of them, one of the coaches. Ideas and emotions ran free. He was able to see those tough men now smiling, allowing themselves some freedom in their behavior. Normally, they were all very serious and focused on their work. Victory had a way of making tough men kind.

The drive home after these meetings was also something Conner looked forward to. He enjoyed talking openly with his dad on a daily basis. What he most desired to know was the soul of this man he called Dad. It seemed during those special rides home, Conner could ask just about any question from his young mind and his dad would answer. Conner appreciated it when his dad treated him as a peer, rather than a boy. He learned more from his dad during that drive home than he did in an entire month of being with him for the routines of life.

Life. It seemed so easy back then to understand life. Sports put boundaries around life. There were rules and regulations, and to violate them had specific penalties and consequences. Conner knew that he was out of control and had little choice of influence on the two life-altering situations he put himself in: his wife's affair and his dad's cancer. There are no rules for such things and it seemed that the person who deserved to live the most was going to suffer the worst consequence. Conner was a religious man and believed in God. Yet, what game official would allow the cheater to endure the lesser of the consequences?

Todd landed at the airport. Conner stepped out of the plane to find his dad waiting to greet him. He knew immediately that the cancer was already playing havoc on his dad's body. The once burly and youthful 68-year old now looked sullen, every bit of his current age. The shallow look in his dad's face and slight yellow tinge to his skin took the breath from Conner. He had never imagined his dad to look so vulnerable. Never had his dad been anything but The Rock.

Todd tied down the plane as Conner and his dad walked through the small terminal to the parking lot. While it didn't seem to be chilly, Conner was shivering from the realization that his dad was truly ill. Losing was never an option for Ewald. This was the man who seemed to win at everything.

"Mr. Morley, how are you doing, sir?" Todd caught up with them at the car.

"Good, Todd. Damn, I haven't seen you in ages! You sure are doing well for yourself. You fly that contraption of a plane, huh?"

"Yes, sir. Your son buys me the fuel and I take it for a heavenly ride every chance I get. Would you like to go up?"

"No, Todd, I think I am going to try and keep my feet on top of the ground for as long as I can. I don't particularly have any desire to be above or below. On top will suit me fine, for the next ten years, or so. But, I have quite a challenge on my hands here. I tell you what, Todd."

"What's that, sir?"

"If I end up not kicking the shit out of this cancer, and if I pass...."

"Dad, don't say that," Conner interjected.

"Oh, be quiet, Conner. Remember, you are supposed to listen, not talk, when you are with your old man." Ewald smiled, but Conner didn't see the humor in his comment. "As I was saying, Todd, if I end up going in the direction of hell, I'll give you the signal. You dig up this old fucker, put me in that plane and take me to heaven, okay?"

"Damn right, I will do that. But, I am sure there is no place for you but right here on earth. Shit, you are the toughest man I have ever met. I can't see this disease doing anything but motivating you to fight!"

"Thanks, Todd," Ewald smiled broadly at the compliment. "Have I ever told you how glad I am that you came into our lives? You are more like family than you are a friend." He reached out and placed his hand on Todd's shoulder.

"Thank you, sir. I sure think a great deal of you and the Mrs. Actually,

I think of you guys as family more than I do my own." Todd was clearly uncomfortable with the conversation and made his excuse to exit. He had to sign the flight log and make sure the plane was fueled properly. It was the routine of the pilot to handle all of the checks to be done before leaving the airport. This was due to pilots either forgetting whether they did or did not prep, and there were too many instances where, typically because of weather, they were forced to fly out early. Nothing would be worse than having to complete all the pre-flight preparations when a pilot was in a hurry.

Conner and Ewald waited at the car for Todd to return so that they could drive him to his hotel for the night. Conner's mom had invited Todd to the house, but he declined, knowing that the family would be in a sensitive mood. Todd didn't like sickness or death. He didn't go to funerals, as he just didn't see the point in seeing someone dead when he had memories of them when they were alive and healthy. Todd already told Conner that he would not go to Ewald's funeral when that time came. So, Conner knew that if his dad passed, Todd would not be there to support him.

Ewald handed Conner the keys to his Ford Mercury Marquis and told him to drive. This concerned Conner. His dad never let him do anything. Conner couldn't even use a power tool by the time he was an adult even though his dad was once an industrial arts teacher. Conner was always expected to hold the wood, not cut it. Or, clean up the mess, not make it.

Many times without realizing it, Ewald challenged Conner's self esteem by never allowing him to control the job. Conner remembered his dad often saying, 'If you want the job done right, you do it yourself.' Conner never got to do anything beyond being the gopher. He would be so frustrated and would often try to get out of the work by saying he had a game to play or just sneak inside to watch sports on television. Ewald would scold his son harshly and often call him lazy. Conner made a few attempts to explain how boring it was just to clean up after his dad's work. Ewald would accept no excuses. You did what you were told. If Conner made excuses, his dad would simply turn away...again.

The car engine was running when Todd approached. Ewald was telling his son about all who had phoned him with their prayers. Conner knew those who reached out had touched his dad. At his age, Ewald had seen a few of his better friends pass away, and his mortality was confronting him. Conner sensed uneasiness in his dad, but was uncomfortable asking too many questions just yet. He would be visiting with his parents for a couple of days and did not want to start off poorly by asking a stupid question.

During the drive into town, Conner looked into the rearview mirror and caught Todd's eyes. They said it all. He, too, was concerned about the man who treated him like a son. He never had to do too much to be part of the family. All he had to be was Todd and, somehow, that was just okay with the coach. At times, this caused Conner more frustration, as Todd's imperfections were looked at as just being a free spirit. Yet, Conner was never given that same freedom.

'If you embarrass me, I will embarrass you,' Ewald had told him. That was the deal. Conner knew perfection was not always attainable, nor perpetual. He wanted the same deal that Todd received, but realized that being blood carried a price that Todd did not have to pay.

The drive to the hotel was an easy one. Todd would soon leave them, but not before making some wisecracks to Ewald about Conner's life situations along the way.

Leave it to Todd, Conner thought, to get the topic of he and Samantha off the ground before he even got out of the car. Conner gave Todd that 'asshole' look in the mirror, as Todd described her in such terms as slut, cheating bitch and the infamous whore. Conner knew his dad would not be offended by such references and may even be thinking highly of Todd's support for his son, but Conner did not like it when subjects were broached about his life when he did not initiate them.

Conner was relieved when Todd stepped out and removed his bag from the trunk of the car. Todd said his good-byes, and Conner began the drive to his parents' home while his dad slept. He was, again, deprived the chance for some soulful father-to-son dialog that he wanted so badly to engage in. It hurt Conner's feelings that his dad wasn't able, or capable, of talking with him about all that was occurring in his life.

Expectations can be so worthless and often only lead to disappointment. All the events and travels had taken their toll on Conner. His life, which seemed so solid and successful just a few weeks prior, was now 180 degrees to the negative. Downward trends were to be expected in his business, but he thought family and personal relationships were supposed to balance him and keep his life steady. Many had asked why he was married. One very good reason, he thought, was to have kids. Samantha never seemed very interested in kids, only in her career. He had concluded that marriage was ignorant without kids. His enjoyed great material wealth, but his soul was empty without family, a pack of his own.

He was dozing and had difficulty keeping the car between the lines. For years, he hadn't driven if he was tired. His successes afforded him options regarding the luxuries of life, and what he would have given at that moment to have Todd driving while he slept right beside the coach. What was first an irritant, his dad's somber state now became something he envied. Keeping his eyes open became easier when two white-tailed deer suddenly dashed across the highway in front of his car. With his heart now racing, his mind focused on the task of driving.

His parents lived on a channel of Shamrock Lake. Conner continued along the winding highway watching for the first turn toward his parent's house. He couldn't help thinking that maybe it would have been best for one of the deer to have not been so quick and instead taken out the vehicle, along with both Conner and his dad. His life was so upside down and he was so distraught with his dad's condition, he was afraid he would not have the courage to witness his dad's diminishing health and the impact it would have on them both. It was, to Conner, much like seeing a world class athlete getting beat in a major event. Everyone knew it would eventually happen, but when it did, the sport would never again be the same once the winning streak was broken. American's love winners and only tolerate losing under the most extreme circumstances. Conner did not want to see his hero dismantled without dignity.

Please, God, he thought, allow him his dignity during his fight.

He turned into their driveway and his whole attitude change in a split second. Conner always appreciated being at the lake. The setting within which they lived was settling to him each time he pulled into their driveway, both because of the surroundings and because his parents were so supportive of him. In many ways, it was a dysfunctional situation for him. On the one hand was the coach, unyielding in his opinions and expectations, never giving an inch even when he really might wrong. And, then there was his mom. The woman who Conner knew would love him no matter who he was or what he did. He used to joke that he could commit murder and his mom would somehow try to get him to feel good about his situation. Ann was an amazing woman and mother, yet, Conner was sensitive to her enabling ways and balanced his need for support with the level of support he received from her.

As Conner got out of the car, he thought about how awesome the human brain was and what it was capable of. With all that was happening, he was reflecting, debating and attempting resolution to three major issues in his life, all within the same hour. He thought he was either a very intelligent man, or a very sick one.

His mom greeted him with her normal warm welcome. The high school homecoming queen who was once so physically beautiful was still gorgeous, but more of the heart and soul than of her physical self. Never once in his life did Conner doubt her value to him and the lives of those she interacted with. 'Never take for granted what impact you have on people's lives on a daily basis,' she would always tell him. He'd have been in bad shape if not for that woman. She always took the time to sit and speak with her son, when her husband would turn and walk away. Although she was the person Conner turned to during crisis, he knew she could not handle his current vulnerability in his marriage with her husband in a life-threatening situation.

"Talk to your dad, Conner. He will listen to you. He's telling me he won't take the chemo-therapy."

"Not take the therapy? What the hell is that?" Such nonsense shocked and angered Conner. "That's the first I heard of that."

"Go to the porch. What do you want.... coffee okay? I'm making a fresh pot."

"Sure, Mom. That would be great. Are you sure you don't want me to get it?"

"Absolutely! When a mother can't get a cup of coffee for her son, that is the day her son better find another coffeehouse!"

Conner smiled and went to the porch to see his dad sitting in his chair, drinking a glass of water. Except for the occasional coaches meeting in the bar, Ewald never drank much. He stayed very sober at home and he always contributed his healthy life up to this illness to his lack of cigarettes and alcohol consumption.

"So, you've decided not to take chemo-therapy, huh, Dad?"

"Who told you that? Did your mother tell you that? Ann!"

"No, no, Dad... don't call Mom in here. I am talking to you, man-to-man."

"Don't tell me what to do. If I want to call your mother, I will call her."

"Jesus, Dad, relax. I didn't come all the way here to get into a pissing match with you. But I don't understand why you aren't going to take your chemo treatments. Please don't tell me after all these years of you telling me, 'don't give up, never give up,' here you are telling me you are not going to take chemo. What's that shit?"

A defining moment for Conner occurred sometime in his junior year of high school. He was athletically and academically excelling at one of the four Flint Class A schools, Flint Southwestern. Sometime mid-year, he realized when he spoke to his dad, the conversation and posture of those conversations changed. He had, after all those years of being the omega, become the beta. His dad spoke to him as a peer. This included all the cussing and the freedom that went with it. No curfews and trust at the highest level. Conner had finally gained the respect and admiration of his dad. The coach was proud of him. Conner was now able to broach subjects with his dad when others would cower in front of him.

This conversation was going to be another defining moment. The cancer was non-Hotchkins Lymphoma and had not infected the bone marrow. Based on what doctors told Sharon, if Ewald could handle the chemo, he had an 85% chance of surviving. This was excellent. Without it, he would certainly die.

"So answer my question, Dad, I didn't drive all the way up here to dance around words and attitudes. Are you going to take the chemo, or not?"

"No, so there is your answer and now leave me alone."

"No, I won't leave you alone. I didn't live my whole life up to now respecting you for your toughness and resilience only to now hear that when the greatest of all challenges confronts you, you quit. Fuck that, Dad, and fuck you if you have been an imposter all these years."

"I am an old and happy man, son. I don't see the value to extend my life when God is calling me. I am 68. How much time can I possibly have after such a fight?"

"How do you know its God calling you and not the devil? With all the devilish things happening to me right now, I'd not put it by the devil to have a hand in your illness, Dad."

"Yeah, that's a fucking shame about Samantha, son. I am not surprised, though. When a wife isn't home more time then she is, she is fucking around on you. I never felt comfortable about that whole situation after the marriage, but your mother made me keep my thoughts to myself."

"Oh, yeah, right, Dad. Like Mom has any control of what you say or don't say. That is bull shit, too, Dad. If it were any other woman on this earth than Mom, you'd be divorced. Talk about loneliness. You know how much time Mom spent alone while you were coaching and traveling? You weren't home either. It's all about one's character and value system, Dad. Being away from me isn't what caused Samantha to stray, it was her character. And if you don't take the chemo treatments, I will never forgive you for not trying. I will never forgive you for your lack of character, integrity and, most of all, your lack of concern for your family who is not ready for you to die."

Conner stood and walked outside, down the hill to the dock and onto the pontoon boat that sat in the channel. To hear that his dad was an imposter from his dad's own mouth was like a knife in his chest. He was stepping very close to being out of bounds and Ewald was in no shape for a knock down, drag out fight with his oldest son.

He had to balance his anger for his personal situation with his dad's. Double standards were never acceptable to Ewald, so Conner wasn't going to allow it now. He stepped away and replayed the events. So many things he could have, or should have, said. This was common for Conner. The strength of his dad was evident in all their discussions, even at age 39. He knew he'd had his moment and he let his emotions get the best of him. Ewald would not be there for him to return and dialog with. There would be no more conversation on this day. He'd have to wait until tomorrow.

That evening, they sat in the living room drinking coffee and talking about the sports news of the day. ESPN was on the television, as it always was. His mom would have the time for her favorite programs, and the rest was dedicated to his dad. More times than not, the event blared from the set. Conner recognized a few years back that both of his parents must have been losing their hearing. At times, the television volume was so loud that it annoyed Conner, but he always kept quiet and respected that in their house, things were done their way.

His mom announced that she was going to bed early. Conner did his normal son to mother kiss-and-hug routine, looked at his mom and her eyes were watering. His mom was such a compassionate woman, she cried about everything. He knew that she was afraid of being without her rock. He winked at her and she smiled as her tears began to fall.

"Its okay, Mom," Conner whispered, as he hugged her. "He may have quit, but I will not. I will keep working on him to take the chemo."

As his mom left the room, she looked at Conner, stopped and put her index finger first to her eye, then to her heart and then pointed at him, a sign of her silent love for her son. She did that most often with her grandchildren. Conner realized with his pending decision to divorce Samantha for her indiscretions that he would never have children who would know them.

The game was not over and Conner looked to his dad. Ewald's eyes were closed and he was asleep. Conner knew his dad must be drained to have let this particular game complete without his full attention and criticism as to how the coaching and officiating was being performed. He took the remote and clicked the television off. The game no longer mattered to Conner, either. He sat on the couch and watched his dad's breathing. What a miracle the human body is and how fragile its ability to function can be at an advanced age. Conner noticed again, just how much older his dad looked to him. It seemed just a couple of months ago he was amazed at how young and active his dad was. After all, his dad was still a 6 handicap at the local golf club where Conner provided a membership to his dad each Christmas day. Conner had days when his dad gave him as stiff a competition as anyone could who didn't have his tour card.

Ewald's cheeks were expanding and restricting, as his breathing was laboring. His cheeks looked like those of a trumpet player, as his slumber became more deep and rhythmic. While Conner wondered how the game would end, he decided to go to bed, leaving the room silent and his dad in a peaceful sleep. He removed an afghan from the couch and covered his father, looked at him for a few seconds, and then kissed him on the lips. His emotions were again getting the best of him.

When he was a youngster, Conner always kissed both his parents good night. While in the 9th grade, he walked into their bedroom one night, kissed his mom and then went to his dad and put out his hand to shake. His dad looked surprised.

"Dad, I am kind of getting older now, maybe it would be better if we shook hands. What do you think, Dad?"

"Son," Ewald motioned for Conner to sit down next to him, "I was eight years old when my dad died of cancer. I kissed him every night before I went to bed... every night. After he died, it took me a long time to get over the fact that I would never kiss my dad goodnight again, let alone experience another day with him. So if you don't want to kiss me goodnight, that's fine with me, but it's your choice."

Those words had touched Conner. For the first time in his life, his dad had reached out and told him about his childhood and about the grandfather he never met. From that day on, Conner always kissed his dad goodnight.

The next morning, the aroma of fresh coffee awakened Conner. The cottage life was always good for him. He loved the water and he loved the fact that family always seemed so connected at the cottage his parents called home. His parents had purchased the cottage before they retired, so they had two homes during one stretch of their life. Even though it was truly a three-bedroom home with a detached two-car garage, it remained the cottage.

On a normal Saturday morning, unless Conner was going to go water-skiing out on the main lake, he would just shut his eyes and go back to sleep. On this morning, he didn't want to waste a single second with his dad, nor his mom for that matter.

When Conner walked into the kitchen, there sat his dad, drinking a cup of coffee. Ewald rose to get Conner a cup of java. Conner started to interrupt his kindness and tell his dad to sit and relax while he made his own cup. Then he thought it better to let it go, because his dad would see that as Conner telling him he was incapable of getting it.

Conner's dad always asked what he took in his coffee. After some 25 years of coffee drinking together, his dad always asked this when making Conner's cup. His mom just knew and always placed a cup in front of him, just the way he liked it, but his dad always asked. This was amusing to Conner. Hell, he knew what his dad liked in his coffee and he hardly ever made him a cup.

"How do you feel?" Conner asked, as Ewald sat down next to him.

"Like hell."

"Did you sleep well?"

"Hell, no. My son just left me in a chair to sleep. I usually sleep in a bed."

"Okay, Dad. I just didn't want to wake you up. You seemed to be sleeping soundly."

"That's okay, son. I actually slept well. I just wanted to give you some shit."

"Wow, that is a surprise."

Both of them laughed and then the kitchen table conversation went silent. It was 5:30 in the morning. Any other Saturday, everyone would be sleeping and resting for the days festivities of watching sports on television.

"Son, how are you doing?"

"Well, Dad, it was once said that a son pays for his father's sins during his own lifetime. I sure wish you could have been a bit more godly during your years." More laughter came out of the kitchen.

"Yeah, well, son, I guess you may be right. My dad must have been an angel. I have had a good life. Yes, I have seen and done many things I wish I could take back. But I look to the future. I don't look back. As you know, I don't dwell on my failures, I build on my successes."

"You have had a lot of success, Dad. You have touched a lot of people in your life. You have always put your kids first when you coached and you have been a great father. That's why I don't understand this decision not to take chemo."

"Chemo won't help me, son. It's terminal."

Conner heard the words, but he didn't want to believe it. "Terminal, Dad, no one told me it was terminal. Terminal as . . .?" Conner's voice faded, as he asked his dad to say what he already had said. He hoped for a different answer if he asked again.

"I didn't want to upset your mother. The doctors told me to kill the cancer I'd have to find alternative medicines or go on some aggressive procedures that would basically take the few months I have left and put me in a near death condition. I don't want to waste my time, son. I want to live these next months and when I go, I go."

Conner couldn't hold his emotions in any longer. He knew his dad would want him to be strong, so he crossed his arms on the table and began crying even harder than he had the night before in order to put himself to sleep. Expecting his dad to walk away from the table in disgust, Conner instead felt a touch on the back of his neck. Reaching out to him for the second time in Conner's life, Ewald rubbed his son's neck and allowed him to cry. Conner was not the type of person to shed tears in front of other men. He wished he could be more compassionate and supportive, but Conner always knew his dad was there for him and he felt better about being a man knowing his dad had been a man's man. And now, he was going to be a fallen hero. Conner almost felt guilty that he had believed his dad was quitting on him and the family.

"Conner," Ewald said. "I don't have much time. I need to make sure your mother is taken care of and that my estate is protected from the goddamn government. They've had their share of me. I want your mom and you kids to get what I have."

"I don't want anything . . ."

"Conner, you always say the right thing, son. This is no time to speak, you need to listen." The words Conner had heard so often and resented, he now was more than willing to listen to and wanted to be there for his dad, to listen to his words. He knew that soon he'd only have memories of this man who raised him to be a man.

"Son, look at me. Look at me in my eyes."

Conner's red and swollen eyes were losing the battle to purge the tears spilling from a broken heart. He looked into his dad's eyes with disbelief, as the rock who never shed a tear was about to drop several.

"I am so proud of you, son. I want to tell you that you are the greatest pride in my life. You are the man I wanted to be. I know you have gone through some tough times recently and I am going to add to that load. I don't want to leave this earth without you knowing that I am proud of who you are, not what you have accomplished. I love you, son," Ewald rose from his chair, as did Conner, and they embraced. "I will miss you so much. I wanted to love you forever, but I guess my forever has come."

Conner could not speak, as a range of emotions overwhelmed him. He held on tightly and, while a hug from his dad was foreign, Conner tried to express all those years in one hug, knowing it would be the only heartfelt hug he would get for the rest of his life. He wanted to exhaust his feelings so his dad would know the respect was mutual.

Several minutes passed. Ewald finally released his hold, and walked to a cabinet door. He opened it, and pulled out a photo album. He placed the album on the kitchen table and opened it.

Conner walked over to the sink, removed a couple sheets of paper towels from the roll, and used one to wipe his tears and blow his nose. He handed the other to his dad. Ewald wiped his own tears and acted as if the embrace had never occurred, as if he was embarrassed at the scene that took place. Conner's mind raced as to what he could say to put his dad's mind at ease, to tell him how long he had waited for such an encounter. But he passed at all thoughts, deciding it was best to say nothing, as if it did not happen.

Ewald sipped his coffee. Turning the pages of the picture album, he began to educate Conner about his own youth. He explained old newspaper articles about his dad during his athletic Hay Day, and told stories about how Conner's grandfather had worked as a railroad conductor and would sneak Ewald onto the trains for a trip, which was against regulations. How, when the train would hit a truck or car at the crossing, Ewald would have to exit the train and stand as if he was just a neighborhood kid watching all the commotion. How his older brother, Archibald, worked on the train, too. About how his brother would bring in a pie that their mother had baked, pull out his penis and wipe the pie with it.

"Jesus, why would he do that, Dad?"

His dad started laughing and asked, "Would you take a piece of that pie knowing someone had just wiped his dong on it?"

Both of them laughed and Conner conceded his point, feeling embarrassed for having asked the question.

"Dad, wait a minute. You have a brother?"

"Not really, I just called him that. Like you think of Todd." Ewald turned the page and moved on with the pictures. Conner sensed Ewald did want to expound.

It was a great morning filled with the passing on of tradition and family history. It was a father and son passing the torch of life from one to the other, the torch that would now be carried by a new generation.

Conner concluded that perfection was not perpetual, but it does happen.

9

Big Band

Archie Phillips walked into the office that doubled as the entrance to his apartment. He enjoyed living in the hangar next to the Blaney Park airstrip. It was located a fair distance from the main guest cabins which provided him some solitude, yet it was close enough to the main center of activities that he could keep a close eye on who came in and out of the area.

The days were filled with tourists, as well as a handful of local residents, who continually wanted his attention, causing Archie to look forward to his evenings of peace and quiet. He was not a people person and found it difficult to be around others for sometimes hours at a time during the day. Not enjoying the company of others had cost him dearly over the course of his lifetime. He couldn't understand why, but most everyone he met irritated him soon after he spent any length of time with them. However, he endured people because he must. It was vital to maintaining his good standing at the Harrison and avoiding any suspicions about who he was and where he came from.

Archie walked directly to the gray file cabinet behind his desk, and reached into the gap behind it and the wall. He retrieved its key from a nail just low enough in the wall to be out of sight. He unlocked and opened the top drawer, and pulled out a pint of Jack Daniel's whiskey with one hand, a pint of Chevas Regal scotch with the other. This was what he had been looking forward to since the previous night, when he had gone through the exact same process. He placed both bottles carefully upon the desk, closed and locked the drawer, and replaced the key on its nail.

He then walked to the office door leading to the main hangar and checked that it was secured. He reached up and pulled down the shade to cover the window, and again checked the door's lock. Turning back to the desk, Archie hesitated as he reached for the bottles. Instead, he returned to the door and flipped the lock open, then closed, even though he knew he had already locked it. He repeated this exercise three more times before satisfying himself that it was done correctly. Archie knew it was his own paranoia that caused him to behave this way, but he could not resist it. No mistakes. He must never make a mistake.

After the final check, he removed a small bell from his shirt pocket and placed it by its rope over the door handle. Archie felt relieved from concern for the door, as the bell on the door would ring if anyone turned the handle. This trick had always worked during his previous life. If it hadn't, he would not be alive at that moment, thinking of his paranoia. The bell also provided some peace against the haunting fears he kept buried within that his past would someday come back to pay him a visit.

Archie then walked to the two windows of his corner office and checked the locks on each of them, as well. He removed two more bells from his pocket, placed one on each of the window latches, secured the locks again and pulled down the shades.

Reaching down behind the water cooler that stood to the right of the windows, Archie retrieved a carefully hidden rope. The rope had a large loop tied at one end, which Archie tossed over the cooler. He then draped the other end in front of the windows and tied it to the heavy table on the other side of the room. Anyone who entered unnoticed or tried to crash the door with a running bulldoze technique would trip the rope and tip over the water bottle, making an alarm from it. Archie was smart to it all. He had used every technique known to people like him. He knew that the chances he would ever be bothered by his past were slim, as he had always made sure he left quietly and without trace.

It had been many years now, and most of the thugs he dealt with were now either dead or in prison. Each year he survived was like five years free from worry. He was never that important in the whole scheme of things. Archie was a worker. They called him a do'er. He was the man with the black hood, the person who set the table, but was never able to eat from it. His time at Blaney Park was both required in order for him to stay alive, and considered a cool down from being too hot with the police and the thugs. He also needed to be there for his soul, as it was losing the battle against the guilt he felt for all he had done in his life.

Archie was not comforted by the fact that he actually felt good about some of the horrible acts he had committed long ago, especially during his quiet times. He liked taking out the slime of the world, those people who would hurt their own mother if it meant they would make a few more bucks or get over on someone. Archie was comfortable with such vigilante work. He actually felt proud to rid society of certain bad elements that walked down the streets in his hood. It was when he had to take out someone who he knew was good people, but just down on their luck that bothered him. Certain thugs, given the right type of opportunity, would have been good citizens had they not been caught up in the hype and romance of the gangster life.

Archie was 79, yet he was still a bull. His face was worn and full of lines, making him look 100. Chain smoking and the hard liquor he had consumed over the years had caused those deep wrinkles, which were complimented by the scars, left from scuffles, which protruded from his face. Archie could still walk for miles and lug 200 pounds of wild game out of the woods when he had to do it. He would wheeze and cough the whole time, but he would get the job done. He had been at Blaney Park for almost 43 years. Most who visited or lived there couldn't remember when Archie wasn't at the Harrison. Blaney was an unknown place during its earlier years, used only by Detroit VIPs during prohibition for their chance to drink and live the free life with plenty of booze and companionship.

Nobody ever really knew who owned the Harrison. Anyone who became curious would soon receive a phone call from a stranger asking why he or she was investigating the ownership and what their intentions were. In a small town like Blaney Park, no one felt it was worth the insistence to know.

Archie arrived just before Elsie had returned from earning her doctorate in veterinarian school, something rare for a woman of her era. She was now much older than most of the staff at the Harrison. She had played around its grounds as a child and assumed she would eventually take her role with the rest of the employees when she had reached the appropriate age. She was a local girl who had never left town, except when she decided to go to college when she realized all of her friends were gone. The girls she had grown up with either went off to college immediately after high school or married their free ride out of the Park, and Elsie had stayed. She had many opportunities to leave when she was younger, but chose not to. She loved the land, the Northern Michigan seasons and, most of all, the wolves of Blaney. They were her true family.

Over the years following her return, she naturally assumed a more senior role and it eventually became a misunderstood fact that Elsie actually owned the Harrison and she loved that. She liked the idea that people viewed her as the owner, never being too quick to correct them. This provided status for her in this small town.

Archie tried many times to date Elsie during those earlier years when they were both young and tempted by those types of things. Elsie always said no to him. It was for the best, Archie realized later and especially now. For the longest time, the town residents harassed Archie, asking why he kept to himself and didn't find female companionship. Some felt bold enough to even encourage Archie to approach Elsie. One evening, she sat him down on the porch of the Harrison and told him, straight out, that she was more afraid of him than attracted to him. Archie was accustomed to this type of reaction from a woman. She told him that she really liked him and wanted to be very good friends, perhaps even like family, but never lovers. She had touched Archie that evening. He needed family. He wanted family. So, from that night on, he looked at Elsie like a sister and vowed to protect her like one of his own pack.

Over the years, as they both continued to work in the Park and no engagement announcement was made, the locals ceased their efforts to set up the two Harrison singles, as they were referred to. Besides, most were afraid of Archie. He carried that look, the look of a man that was not to be irritated. He never talked much, even after the night on the porch with Elsie. They were like family with one another throughout all the years that followed, and did so without much interaction. They just knew when one needed the other.

It was late. Archie had already covered and stored all the equipment used for that day's entertainment by the tourists. He put away all the fishing rods, refrigerated the bait that was left and covered the boats. There were many other things left to do, but Archie enjoyed the fishing tasks, most of all. The remaining ones would wait.

He moved to the very back section of the hangar, which was his living space. He closed and locked his door, placing a bell on the handle as he did with the front door to the office. Both bottles were with him, along with a shot glass and a pack of Marlboro cigarettes he would smoke before bedding down for the evening.

He went over to the phonograph. It wasn't the electronic, contemporary kind that most people have in their homes. It was the one like kids had when they went to school in the 60's and 70's. The top came up on a hinge, and it plugged into the wall. The record, a 33rpm, would be placed over the spindle and the needle set on the first track. The music of such greats as Count Basie, Greg Miller and Duke Ellington would now begin filling the room. Archie loved the big band music and he liked to play it loud. His distance from the cabins and the main living area allowed him to take liberty with his volume. He was quite the dancer, in his time. The swing style that went with the music demanded quick feet and good hands. Dancing was one way Archie could get female interaction without working at it. And, with his looks, he discovered early in life that he would need to have reasons for a woman to want to share time with him. Archie was a sharp dresser, always looking the best in the house, and made up in style what he lacked in looks. Once he stepped out on the dance floor and showed his stuff, women would come to him the rest of the night looking for a dance or two. When he was lucky, a woman would dance with him in a more private place and he would experience what love could feel like.

Archie grew up in Saginaw, Michigan. He enjoyed his work on the rails there, was a hard worker and never missed a day. Archie's only problem was his temper and it hindered his ability to get along with others. He was a quiet guy who knew how things should be done on the job. He continued to apply for management positions or advance to conductor on the train line, but he was turned down each time. Others would frequently tell him he had to chill out and not get so angry when management would do things he didn't agree with. Archie would argue with management when they placed people and cargo in danger. He was quick to speak out for himself and others when things were wrong, but didn't have much to say when things were going well. He often said, 'why talk about doing right, when you are paid to do it that way?' He was his own worst enemy.

His much younger brother, Ewald, came to work for the Bay Area Railway Company. He played on the company's baseball team in the summer and basketball team in the winter. If a game conflicted with the work schedule, the foreman on duty would always gladly redo it to accommodate the players, especially Ewald. Ewald got along with both peers and management. They liked him. This made Archie irate. While Archie was also a good player with his name on the roster, he'd always do his rail job first and wouldn't take the special liberties offered to him. He told his brother, in no uncertain terms, that if he was going to get ahead in life, he had to put away the games and keep focused on the job at hand. After only two and a half years of working on the rails, Ewald was promoted above Archie, and made conductor. It was a bittersweet party when Ewald had his promotion celebration. Archie was happy for his brother, but hated the company for bypassing him for so long and then promoting his brother above him in such a short time. He had mentored Ewald and always watched his back. Ewald knew that he never would have advanced so quickly, perhaps not ever, without Archie's help. At the party, Ewald proposed a toast to Archie, thanking his older brother for being the best rail man ever, the best big brother a brother could have, and for being the biggest asshole in the world so the company could promote him, instead.

Ewald sensed Archie's anger and knew he would never allow himself the freedom to express his disappointment. He would just let it fester inside and grow more wrinkles on his face. Everyone laughed at Ewald's toast and so did Archie, on the outside. But inside, he felt betrayed by his company. He was able to justify most of the times he didn't get promoted, but this one was a sour pill to swallow for him. Yet, Ewald was family and Archie was going to do him right and make no problems for his younger brother.

'Don't fuck with family' was what Archie told everyone, and he wasn't about to do anything to hurt his own brother and fellow union man. Instead, Archie chose to use an open mind and develop a strategy for utilizing the company rail system to make him some serious dough. He wanted out of that shit job. The rails had burned him and now the rails were going to help him help himself.

Archie was known around the pool halls and the bars of Saginaw. He liked knowing the who's who of town and feeling close to the action. He was a bar brawler and never afraid to pull the trigger if trouble came looking. It was the one place in his life where he was at ease and felt like he belonged. He had respect in that domain. Archie was a mean man when he drank. Hell, he was a mean man when he didn't drink. He found pleasure in not just winning fights, but dominating them. He wanted to create a situation where his opponent would think of him when looking into the mirror every morning from that day forward. Whether it was with a weapon, or his teeth, or his nails, Archie knew how to maim and he did it well.

He became even more that way one night after a fight in his favorite lounge in Saginaw when he let a smaller, outmatched man off from a good beating. That same person came back later with a 9-millimeter pistol to wait for him. When Archie came outside, he took one in the arm. He was fortunate that the gun jammed on repeated attempts to fire again and that the assailant decided to drive away. Learning from the experience, Archie swore from that day forward no man would be capable of revenge on the same night of any action with him. If they thought about revenge, they'd have to know Archie was not going to deal with them again.

He began taking his knife out after a brawl was completed and would cut off the lobe from his opponent's left ear, never before the fight was over, but after he had won. There was honor and protocol in those days. No weapons were used, it was hand to hand fighting until one or the other granted submission. It was the way. And it was also the way for all opponents to remember Archie after being defeated. It would thrill and satisfy Archie to see someone in a public place less one ear lobe.

During those prohibition days, Archie began smuggling both drugs and alcohol on the trains. He'd only do it when his brother wasn't the conductor. At first, the company was always putting Archie and Ewald together. Archie began complaining. He wanted the freedom to make his deals without putting his brother in danger. No one would have ever believed that Ewald was not involved in the illegal activity and Archie knew it. He had to go to his brother and tell him he didn't want to run with him, ever again. It hurt Ewald so badly, he decided to leave the train and return to school to play sports and become an educator. Ewald had set up the schedule and the situation to be just that way, to try to keep family together. He wanted to make things better with Archie. Ewald knew he was hurt over not being promoted.

Archie had another agenda and wanted nothing to do with his brother. He loved Ewald, but too much had been lost between them. Archie thought Ewald used his good looks, personality and athletic abilities to get him ahead, instead of doing his job. Archie just didn't get it and neither did Ewald. Even after complaining to both the company and to Ewald, Archie found he was once again scheduled with his brother on the last run before Ewald left for school. They had strong words, almost came to blows, and never talked again. Ewald told Archie to never come near him or his family. Fifteen years later, Ewald had a son named Conner, a nephew Archie never got to meet.

The music was finished and half of both bottles were, too. Archie was halfway through his pack of cigarettes, sitting on his worn out couch and staring at the wall.

This happened to him often. He'd listen to the stack of albums just once and the next day he'd wake up at 4:30am, still on the couch, with his cigarette on the floor and the last album just rotating over and over again. He'd always hold the cigarette over the tile floor when he smoked, because he knew he'd fall asleep with it lit, and wouldn't risk burning down the hangar. He never remembered putting out his last cigarette, and always found it on the floor with a trail of ashes leading to the bud.

After all these years, he no longer worried about it. He would drink himself to sleep every night, first listening to music while thinking about the old days, then sitting in his favorite chair while staring at the wall thinking about what if... what if he had a family, or if he'd gotten the promotion. He would dream about running his own business and be able to walk down the city streets in the best clothes, having people love and admire him. For all he did to be disliked or feared, his reality was he only wanted to be loved and cared for by someone. He just didn't know how to express it, nor to feel it.

The phone rang in his room. Archie slowly looked at his watch and then at the half-empty bottles. He contemplated letting it ring, but was concerned it was Elsie. Sometimes, a fishing group got a little too rowdy and stopped respecting the environment like Lady Elsie thought it should be. When this happened, she always called Archie to rescue her. All it took was for Archie to walk up to the group with his sawed off shot-gun, machete at his hip and the look of a man that would easily use both with pleasure, and things got quiet very quickly.

"Hello," Archie answered, trying not to sound too drunk, even though Elsie would know better. She always did.

"Well, I'll be damned!" he exclaimed at the sound of a familiar voice. "Tell me it's not you? You son of a bitch! Do you know I was just sitting here thinking about you and your boy? I have been seeing shit I ain't wantin' to be seeing up here, and I was just wondering when the time would be coming that I'd get this phone call from you, man.

"Oh shit, you ain't telling me the truth? Is he losing it? No, I mean is he fucking losing it? Is he going to kill her? You know, he should kill the bitch, if you ask me. Hell, I'd do it for fucking free. I won't even take any part of her parts." Archie started to laugh both from his humor and the loosening affect of the alcohol he had consumed.

He loved it when he'd get one of these calls. He was back in his domain, talking to his type of people, not those wishy-washy, golly-gee-whiz types he took fishing. He wanted to puke when he was with them and use whatever was usable as fish bait.

"You've got to be fucking me? He knows about Blaney? How in the hell did he find out about Blaney? No shit! I am going to find that fucking

Joey, idiot lawyer, and cut his ears off! I told him not to place it back on the books right away. I told him to retire and that I'd get him access later to place the property. I am going to find out where that bastard's grandchild is going to college and make him some fucking trouble. Damn it. I told him, don't fuck with family! Don't people listen anymore? Joey should know better. That asshole figures I must be dead by now. He's in for some big fucking surprise. I am still wheezing, but I am breathing." Archie laughed, using this opportunity to feel happy for a short time.

"Okay. Damage control, TS. You sure he has no clue, no knowledge. It's very important you know this for sure? Good. I hear his dad has one leg in the grave. So, he's hurting big time, with that all going on. Life is that way, I tell you. When it rains, it fucking pours. No one is immune, even Jesus had a bad day. And if fucking Jesus had a bad day, you know, you and I are in for some really bad shit." Archie laughed again with the person on the other end.

"Alright," he continued. "Here is what you do. Stay with him. He's going to want to kill either of them or fucking both. He's like me, I've seen his competitiveness before. He's going to want somebody's ass over this. If it were my world, I'd hand them both over for the fucking punishment. But I don't want him to be like me. It's worth it when it happens, but it deadens the soul later. He's like that, but he ain't like that, y'know? He's too much like his fucking dad and not enough like me. I should have been there, for Christ sake! He's like a son to me. Don't fuck with family. How many times do I have to repeat this to these people in the world? In my world, it was understood. These people are fucking stupid." Archie stopped for a drag on his cigarette.

"Alright," he continued. "We need to be careful. The first three weeks are most risky for him and us. You are a good man, TS, I know and trust you. You are like family. Hang in there with him, and watch his fucking back. He's vulnerable right now."

Archie hung the phone up. He took a swig out of both bottles of liquor again, set them down and looked at the shot glass that he always had placed in front of him on the table, but never used. He wobbled to his feet, trying to regain the balance stolen from him by the alcohol in his blood. He picked up the glass and threw it against the cinder block wall. "Don't fuck with family!"

After staring at the phone for a few more moments, he walked back over to the couch. He sat down carefully, making sure he was slumped far enough down for his hand that now held a cigarette to extend a safe distance from the couch. Archie got too comfortable, and soon passed out.

10

Dump It!

The visit with his dad came to an end at four o'clock that same afternoon. Ann woke just before nine to find the father and son already watching ESPN Sports Center on television. She offered them breakfast, and they both accepted. It was a usual cottage morning meal of scrambled eggs, sausage, toast, orange juice and coffee, and she placed a steaming cup on the table in front of Conner.

"Mom never asks me how I want my coffee."

"She doesn't care whether you appreciate her. I want you to know I am making it for you."

The two men smiled at each other. Ann sat down at the table with them. The two were jovial in their conversation. She sensed something had happened and tried to find an explanation in Conner's face. These two, who were fighting just yesterday, were now acting like they had just won a bet at the table. Conner smiled at her.

"I love you, Mom," he winked.

"Well, I love you, too," she replied.

"Please, not at the kitchen table while I am eating, for Christ's sake," said Ewald.

Everyone laughed and Conner accidentally spat out some eggs from his laughter. His dad's comment was so typical and actually sounded trite after all that had been said earlier in the morning. He was accepting the inevitable and he knew he would have to support his mom soon. But, not today. Today, he was going to complete his visit with his parents and then fly to Blaney Park.

He waved goodbye as he drove away from the cottage. His parents watched from the entryway window, as always, and waved back to him. He did his best to keep his smile and not allow his sadness to overtake him. He was heading back to pick up Todd so they could make the flight north.

Just as he got to the highway, his cell phone rang. Normally, there isn't much reception in that area due to a dam that controls the water levels of the nearby river and lake. It was Samantha calling him.

"Hey you," came from the other phone.

"Hey, sunshine, what's up?"

"Just wanted to call and tell you I will be working late and through the weekend. This job is going to kill me, Conner. I can't believe what they expect from me. I better get a damn good bonus this year."

"Yeah, you better."

"What's the matter?"

"Oh, just not feeling too well today."

"Well, I have to go. I just stepped out of a meeting to stay hi. Luv ya."

"Okay, Samantha. Thanks for calling me. Love you, too."

Conner ended the call and felt the pain that Samantha did not even ask about how dad was doing. Conner began beating himself up because Samantha always talked about expectations and how he always expected too much of her. Did he?

He turned into the hotel parking lot and realized his drive had been a blur, filled with deep thoughts of joy and sorrow for his parents. How fortunate he felt to have experienced that moment with his dad, yet, he wondered at what cost. To lose his father was going to be devastating. It would be his burden to stay strong for the rest of the family. After all, he was the oldest son. Ken and the girls would look to him for support and strength. Even though both sisters were older, he had always felt the responsibility to protect them.

Conner was irritated that Todd was not outside waiting, but at the counter of the hotel flirting with the receptionist. Todd did have the tendency around women to get off task. It was just to be expected. Conner would have been very upset if Todd was lazy or inconsiderate, but since there was a woman involved, he accepted Todd's actions.

"Hey, Con Man. How you doing?"

"Okay, Sully. You ready to go?"

"Yup, sure am, and the weather is looking good. Made the flight plan and called the terminal to let them know you are coming. Oh yeah, the rental car company will have someone there to take your dad's car back up to them. I gave them your parent's address, and they found a couple guys who live out there and carpool. Said they'd be glad to drop it off on their way home. They get off in 30 minutes, so that should work out just fine. Oh, and they are over-charging you, as usual, but I figured you wouldn't mind."

"Great, Todd. You did good, man."

"Are you sure you are doing okay, Conner?" Todd always used Conner's given name when he really was serious. Conner appreciated when Todd would take a moment to show he truly cared.

"I don't know if I am okay, Sully. But what choice do I have? I do know I have some difficult times coming my way before it gets any better."

"Hey, you know I am here for you, brother. I am watching your back. Always have, and I always will."

"I know, Todd. You have been a great friend over the years."

"But I ain't going to your dad's funeral."

Conner smiled, as the hotel's automatic doors opened and they walked to the car. They climbed in, with Conner driving and Todd got into the back seat.

"What the hell you getting into the back seat for?" Conner asked.

"Hey, I told the sweetie at the counter that my chauffeur was coming to get me. It wouldn't look good if I got into the front seat, now would it?" All that was going on and Conner still couldn't help but be entertained by this special dude he called his best friend. No way could he stay down and depressed when he was around Todd. Sully had the knack for getting a chuckle out of him. Even after the most difficult and most rewarding morning of his life, Conner was still moved by Todd's ability to ignore reality and always seeing the sun, never the clouds.

Todd called ahead to the terminal. It was a small airport and did not have larger planes fly into it very often. The Saab 340 was a site to be seen by those who worked there. A normal Saab 340 would seat about 30 people, but Conner's plane was customized, with extra bathroom accommodations, a business office, cushioned reclining seats and a full service bar. The plane could only seat six people comfortably. The door to the aircraft was open when they arrived. The rental person was there and Conner turned over his dad's car. After boarding the plane, he went straight to the bar and poured himself a stiff Jack Daniel's and diet Coke, then sat and waited for Todd.

Todd was outside the plane. His pre-flight routine included checking the twin props, the engines that powered them. He would check the wings for any cracks and looked to make sure the tires were inflated correctly. As humorous as Todd could be, he took being a pilot very seriously. Conner had much respect for Todd as a pilot. As a chauffeur, Todd was more neglectful. Getting the oil changed in the sedans was sometimes way overdue. Conner would scold him when the windshield fluid would be so diminished the panel light would illuminate. But the plane was a different story. He was proud of being a pilot and took even more pride in being a damn good one.

Todd boarded the plane, pulled up the door and locked it. He looked at Conner reclined with his drink in hand.

"You okay?"

"Yeah, I am going to come up there and sit in the co-pilot seat for the trip."

"Not with that drink in your hand, you're not. How many have you had in the fifteen minutes I was doing my pre-flight?"

"None, this is my first."

"Well, dump it and come sit with me. I'd love to have you. But you can't come to my cockpit drinking or drunk. It don't happen, Con Man. I don't care if you own it or not. When I fly, I am the boss."

"You de man," Conner grinned.

"Damn right, baby!" Todd smiled back.

Conner sat and watched Todd go through the mechanics of getting the plane ready for flight. Todd was talking to Minneapolis dispatch on the radio and Conner listened from the co-pilot headphones. Conner had already witnessed Todd fire the right engine. When he pressed the button to ignite, the lights in the cabin shut off and then came back on after the engines supported the voltage. The same thing happened when he started the left engine. All the switches and buttons Todd had to manipulate always impressed Conner, who always respected Todd just a little bit more after he'd fly with him. Todd would check and re-check his routine, never deviating from his checklist.

"Folks," Todd spoke into the microphone, as the plane began its taxi to the runway, "this is Captain Sullivan from the cockpit. We are number one on Runway 1-3. Suzie, please prepare for take-off."

"You don't have a stewardess," Conner rolled his eyes.

"Just practicing for my real job."

The flight to Blaney Park would be just 45 minutes. By the time they got to cruising altitude, they would have to descend and land. Conner loved the convenience of his plane, but its cost was another topic.

The take off went without a hitch. Conner waited for Todd to discontinue talking to the area traffic and Minneapolis air tower.

"Sorry for making you come with me, Todd. You can fly back in the morning and I will make it up to you."

"That's okay, Conner. Holly isn't pleased with me right now, anyway. No sense going home when all I will get is a good night's sleep."

"Oh, yeah? So, what's up?"

"She doesn't think I am spending enough time with the kids."

"Is she right?"

"Yeaaah... but, what does that have to do with anything?"

Both started laughing. Conner looked out the cockpit window as the plane ascended through the clouds. It was just turning dark. The days were getting longer with the beginning of the spring season. He enjoyed the scenery of trees beginning to bud and flower when the clouds were dispersed enough to see land. Otherwise, he'd just sit back and watch the sun settle to the west just above the pillow of clouds. It was a wonderful view and Conner's thoughts turned to his father who would soon be making his own way skyward.

Conner was just getting comfortable being in the air when Todd announced his intentions to land. Blaney Park had a nice lengthy airstrip. It was shaped like a large plus sign, which allowed for different landing patterns depending on the direction of the wind. Detroit VIPs used to fly in there during the 30's and 40's so they made sure the airstrip was long enough to accommodate bigger planes, and many of them. Todd requested clearance to drop into the airstrip from Minneapolis dispatch. As the plane made its final approach, Conner was able to see airport lights illuminating, as well as the glow from a couple of campfires. The site settled Conner as he thought of the fact that he owned this place. It gave him an unexpected sense of satisfaction, realizing that people were holding business retreats and taking vacations on his property.

The plane landed and taxied to the hangar. Conner waited on board the aircraft for Todd to shut down the engines and do his exit checklist. Todd left the plane first and when Conner exposed his head from the cabin, he looked out to see the beauty of Blaney Park. The moment he saw it, it reminded him of his parent's cottage. It made him relax and feel at ease. As he stepped down the stairs, an elderly gentleman greeted him. The man looked right into Conner's eyes and had a broad grin on his face.

"Well, what a nice welcome you have given us. My name is Conner Morley."

"Archie Phillips is the name. I am the gatekeeper here at Blaney Park."

Archie, Conner thought to himself, replaying the story his dad had told him of his brother, Archibald, from the rail days. Somehow, this man reminded Conner of his dad. "Well, Mr. Phillips, you have done a wonderful job to these trees, here. Wow, are they beautiful."

"Yup. Worked all day to get them like this before you got here."

"I called ahead, by the way. A woman named Elsie said you have one last cabin available for the night. Is that right?"

"Yup. Just one. You need to call in advance during this time of year. It's one of our busy times with the walleye running and all. The cabin you are stayin' in had bees in it earlier in the week, coming out of hibernation. We couldn't rent it out because of 'em."

"The bees are gone now, right?" Todd asked.

"Nope. You just don't want to leave no sugar out and you will be okay." He winked at Conner. "Sure, I got the bees out. Dropped the nest two days ago and killed the queen. All is well there, now," Archie said with a sly grin. He couldn't stop looking at Conner and it was making Conner nervous.

"Well, Todd, we had a long day. I guess we should be going to the cabin."

"Yeah, well, I have my cabin. Where you sleeping, Con Man? 'Cause I tell you, I heard there were wolves in these parts and I ain't gonna to be outside camping or nothing like that. I am getting a bed and a roof over my head tonight."

"Sully. We're going to bunk in the same cabin. What's wrong with that?"

"Nothin, as long as I get the bed."

"I will flip you for it."

"Nope, I am your employee. You need to take care of me. I will think you are taking me for granted if you don't let me sleep in a bed. As far as you are concerned, I am your bitch for tonight. Bringing me up to this wilderness in the middle of nowhere. No guessing what's on the floor or in the couch. Shit, just give me clean sheets and I know I will sleep like a baby. Sorry, Con Man, but tonight, you ain't nobody. You sleepin' on the couch for bringing me up here." All three men began to laugh.

"Archie," said Todd.

"Yeah?"

"Lead the way, my good man. I am looking forward to some good alcohol and lots of it. I want to pass out tonight so I don't have to think about how I may get eaten by bears or wolves. Damn, it does have running water here, right? I don't have to shit outside, do I? I hate spiders. There are no dangerous spiders here, are there?"

"Jesus, Todd," growled Conner. "Shut the fuck up, will ya? Archie is going to think we are a bunch of pussy city dudes if you keep talking!"

"Too late," Archie said, with a serious tone. His excitement at seeing Conner was beginning to subside as his natural personality returned.

"Sorry, Archie. My friend is used to having the best of everything. He's spoiled."

"Oh, I am spoiled, am I? That's the fucking pot calling the kettle black," Todd trashed Conner back.

Archie picked up the bags that were retrieved from the cargo area of the plane. Todd was only staying the night so he didn't even bring a toothbrush. He planned to simply awaken and leave in the morning, to be home before his wife and kids got up. All three followed the flashlight that Archie carried, as the daylight had left very quickly and in the Upper Peninsula, when it gets dark, it's as if there is no light to be had. Unless the moon is out, a person can't even see their hand in front of them without a flashlight.

"Uh..." Todd began nervously, "you have extra batteries for that flashlight. Right, Archie?"

"Nope."

Conner walked behind them and glanced around at the area. He couldn't see much, but what he could see made him feel exhilarated. He could see glimpses of activity. Some people were still outside, enjoying bon fires and laughing. Some cabins were dark. Those guests, Conner thought, must already be asleep for the night. A soft glow could be seen through the windows of others, coming from the fireplaces inside as the occupants attempted to stay warm on this cool spring night.

Archie went to Cabin number 4. Conner's favorite number.

"Look, Con Man, your lucky number! Shit, everything just works out for your ass, doesn't it?"

"It's a good sign to me, man."

Archie opened the door without a key.

"There is a key for this door, right?" Todd asked.

"Nope."

"Conner, man, I ain't stayin' in no place that ain't got no key. This is fucking bullshit, man."

"What, do you think a wolf is going to turn the knob and open the door and just waltz in and eat your ass?" Conner started laughing. "Hell, one smell of you and they'll think you are spoiled meat. You have nothin' to worry about, you chicken shit. I will be in there with you. I promise to protect you."

"Promise?" Todd said with a sheepish look, while giving Conner the finger at the same moment.

"Breakfast is from six to nine in the Harrison." Archie placed their bags at the foot of the bed. "The fire should keep it warm in here for the remainder of the night. Wood is just outside the door, if you need more. I'll tie down the plane, Todd."

"Sure, Arch, that's great. Thanks. Check the oil and fill 'er her up, too. Yeah?"

Conner was stunned. Todd was letting this stranger take care of the plane. That was odd. Conner made a mental note to ask Todd about that later.

Archie left without saying a word. Just before he closed the door, he took a second and looked at Conner again. Then, grinning, he shut the door behind him.

"Damn, that is one old ugly mother fucker!" Conner said to no one.

"He's cool, Con Man. I thought he was kick ass! Did you see his look? I'd hate to see him in a dark alley!"

"No shit," Conner responded.

Todd went looking for the alcohol and it didn't take him long to find it. A bottle of Jack Daniel's and two short glasses were waiting on the kitchen counter.

"Pour me a drink, too, eh, Todd?"

"What, do I look like your boy?"

"Come on, Todd, don't start this shit with me. I just asked a favor. Why you always dissin' me?"

"Because you let that bitch get over on you, man. I told you she was fucking around on you when she asked for that condo. You are a smart man, Con Man, but you can be very stupid sometimes, too. You know what? You are the only one in the family who didn't think she was fucking around on you. If she wasn't, she should have been, for all the time she spent away from you. And, you listened to all that shit about career and work ethic. Stupid, man."

"Let's not talk about it, Sully. We talked enough on the way here on the plane." Conner took his glass from Todd and walked back to the fireplace. "Damn, isn't this relaxing, man? Look at that fire. Wow, that shit is beautiful."

"Yeah, not bad. And since there isn't a couch, I guess you can enjoy that fire all night, sitting right there in front of the fire in that chair, there."

"Fuck you! I am sleeping with you in the bed."

"The hell you are, Con Man! You haven't had a bitch in months. You even told me. I don't want no woody woodpecker pounding at my cabin in the middle of the night. Besides, this ain't even a queen size bed, it's a little thing. There ain't no room in this bed for the two of us, and I ain't sleeping on no floor, in no chair or in no damn tent. I am sleeping in that bed right there." Todd pointed to the bed.

"You fucker," Conner mumbled.

"Call me what you want. I am solo in this bed tonight," Todd said, as he lay down, pulled a pillow from under the covers and closed his eyes in mock sleep.

Conner situated two large chairs facing each other. He sat on one and placed his feet on the other. He couldn't quite get comfortable. Todd opened one eye and enjoyed watching Conner fail at getting himself into position. He knew he'd let Conner bed down beside him if he had to do it. But he wasn't going to make it easy for him.

Before he knew it, Conner had the pillow behind his head and blanket over his body. Todd wanted to ask about how the visit was with his parents. He sat up, looking out the window at the moon exposing itself from behind the diminishing clouds. He didn't like being half way to nowhere at this place called Blaney Park. But, he had to admit, it was beautiful and he wanted to be with his best friend on this evening. He wouldn't allow Conner to feel sorry for himself. Todd was afraid all that had happened would drive him into self-pity. While he wanted to allow Conner to be weak, he knew it would do him no good, in the end. He and Conner were always straight with each other, always truthful with each other.

Todd leaned over, grabbed his glass and drank its contents down with one swallow. He shook his head in response to the hard liquor and harsh effect on his body. He then looked over at Conner who was now snoring quietly in what looked to be a very uncomfortable position. He felt some guilt that he did not offer Conner the bed. He thought they'd talk and have a chance to discuss the day and how all went with his life. Conner had fallen to sleep. Mentally and emotionally exhausted, it seemed no matter the accommodations. He was ready to sleep this day away, dreaming for a better tomorrow.

11
The Question

The next morning, Conner woke early. The fire had gone out during the night, leaving the cabin cold and damp. Stiff and uncomfortable from sleeping in the chair, he straightened up and glanced at Todd who was sleeping soundly in the bed.

Conner thought about his wife. The truth was never easy to deal with when it was bad. He decided to forget about it until he could do something at the appropriate time. He already knew the truth. He just didn't want to believe it.

"Hey! Thought you said you'd bring in some wood last night? And, I figured you would be gone by now."

"Ya, right," Todd mumbled, pulling a dark green army blanket over his head. "I'm off duty, remember? And this bed is too damn comfortable to leave so early. Besides, the wife ain't happy about this, so no need to hurry home to that."

Conner smiled, not really wanting to awaken his friend. Todd had few opportunities to be away from his day-to-day life, and Conner decided to allow him the indulgence of sleeping in. His muscles protested once again, and he thought of how he had left his dad to sleep in a chair, rather than help him to the comfort of his bed. Conner smiled at the ache in his muscles, the same ache, he was certain, his dad had felt from the night before. What goes around comes around, he thought. He rose stiffly, walked to the sink and splashed his face with the icy faucet water. Looking out the window, he felt as if he had been there before.

"Breakfast will be in the Harrison," Conner said loudly, hoping Todd was still awake. "I'm heading up that way now. I'll see you there, okay?"

"Yeah, now shut up and go," was the muffled response.

Maybe I'll walk around, Conner thought, trying to decide the best plan of attack for evaluating a property that was already as good as sold. He removed a jacket from his suitcase and stepped outside.

It was a beautiful day, clear blue skies and bright sunshine. There was still a cool sting to the morning air, typical of Michigan that time of year. It shook Conner awake, and he knew that if he didn't start moving he would certainly go back to the warmth of his cabin. He walked briskly toward the river. Halfway down the path, the smell of breakfast was calling him and he decided his rumbling stomach was more important. He turned and walked in the direction of the main buildings. The chill was too much for him to be comfortable and there would be plenty of time to walk the grounds after breakfast. It was early enough that most of the guests were not yet moving around outside their cabins. Perhaps they were still asleep or already fishing in the cool waters of the river. As he approached the large white, Victorian-styled building, he noticed an elderly woman pulling dead weeds from the flowerbeds around the front of the house.

"Good morning," he called out.

The woman sat up and smiled at him. "Morning. You here for breakfast?"

"Absolutely. I love breakfast."

"Good. The first batch is always the best. Let 'em know I'll be in directly. My name's Elsie, by the way." She stood, removed her gloves and extended her hand.

"Elsie, yes," he smiled, shaking her hand. "We spoke on the phone. Conner Morley. Very nice to meet you."

"Did you say Morley?"

"Yes, ma'am."

"It's a good name. Nice to meet you, too," Elsie smiled and placed her hands on her hips. She looked Conner over quickly, from head to foot. Conner smiled, and turned to walk up the front steps into the house. He liked her. She seemed like good people, and made a nice first impression upon him.

Shit, he thought, as he reached for the door. The last thing I need is to like it here.

Conner glanced around the Harrison's foyer, and was surprised at the eloquence and atmosphere of the place. It had been well preserved and the history of its character still radiated throughout. He sampled the strong odor of coffee, eggs, bacon and pancakes, and his stomach wanted it. Distant conversations could be heard, and he followed the sound of silverware and shuffling plates, undoubtedly the noise of other guests now seated in the sun porch and waiting to be served by Elsie's staff.

He stepped into the porch, and glanced around the long bench-style table set for breakfast. He nodded as a few guests mumbled a friendly 'morning' to him, and chose a spot at one end, facing the window so he could look out at the grounds. He turned over his coffee cup and a young, smiling waitress soon filled it with steaming java, while he looked down the table at the others who had assembled there with him. The group consisted of four men, all dressed in business casual attire and who were talking about that morning's Dow Jones figures. A middle-aged couple, obviously on vacation, sat across from them engrossed with their own sections of that morning's newspaper, and one other female guest was sitting at the opposite corner of the table from him.

It was Emily. Conner glanced at her, and then took a second look. She was plainly dressed in a sweater and jeans, and her long, dark hair was secured neatly behind her head with a red bandana. He stared at her for a moment, and then she looked up at him. Conner felt his face flush, and dropped his eyes to his plate.

"Hey, move over, I'm starving," Todd nudged Conner with his elbow. Conner looked up, and Todd smiled. "Didn't think I'd actually get up, did ya? I can smell that food from our cabin. They must fan that shit over there to make people show up."

"I never know about you."

"Coffee, sir?"

"Why, thank you, young lady," Todd smiled sweetly at the waitress and winked at Conner, who rolled his eyes and turned to look out past the guests, through the windows to the grounds. "It smells great. Did you make it?"

The waitress giggled and shook her head. She turned to walk back toward the kitchen and Todd's eyes surveyed the view of her backside.

"You're such a fucking pig," Conner spoke low enough so that only Todd could hear him. Todd laughed and nodded, as he picked up his coffee cup.

"Shit, I must be a horn dog. Even that looks good this morning."

Conner glanced around the room and looked back down the table at Emily. She was writing in a tablet, and seemed unaware of the others in the room with her.

Damn, talk about looking good, Conner thought to himself. I wonder who she is, what she's doing here. She sure doesn't look like the rest of the group.

"Con Man," said Todd. "Hey. Are you listening to me?"

"Huh?" Conner looked back at Todd, realizing he hadn't heard a word that was said. "I'm sorry, man. What'd you say?"

"Where were you, man?" Todd said, scowling at Conner with curiosity. He then turned to look in the direction that held Conner so deeply in thought, and there was the reason. Todd looked back at Conner, whose face had gone flush.

"What?" snapped Conner. "You gonna talk, or what?"

"Oh, no you don't," smiled Todd. He leaned over to speak more quietly. "You fucker. Don't talk about me. You ain't no better than me. You're here to condemn this place, remember? Don't go thinking with your penis now, man."

"Bacon or sausage?" the waitress stood next to them, holding a plate of food in each hand. Both Conner and Todd began to laugh at the coincidence of her question with the content of their conversation.

"I am sorry, we don't mean to be rude," Conner said to her, trying to explain that they were not laughing at her.

"Bacon or sausage?"

"Surprise me," winked Todd.

She giggled again and placed a plate in front of him, then the other in front of Conner. "Let me know if I can get you anything else."

"Yes, ma'am," Don replied. "I will let you know." She smiled and winked at him, before turning back toward the kitchen.

"Yup," Todd smiled. "I get the sausage and that bacon looks just like your dick. Gotta eat. I've got some exploring to do on my own." They both laughed.

"I'm going to walk around the grounds. If its lumber these guys are interested in, I want to see what they're buying." Conner stood up from his half-eaten breakfast. "I'll see you later, Sully. You leaving soon or sticking around?"

"What the hell do I have to do here? I am leaving as soon as I finish flirting with the waitress. Hell, if I have to keep coming back, which I hope I don't, at least I will have something to look forward to if she's as in love with me as I think she is."

Conner smiled and looked back toward the end of the table. Emily was not there.

"She snuck out the back," Todd chuckled. "Guess she didn't think we were that funny. Better get going if you want to catch up with her, boss."

Conner said nothing and turned to leave the room. He knew he wouldn't see Todd again until he returned to take Conner home, and that was fine with him. He had a lot of exploring to do, and wanted to do it alone.

Once outside, Conner headed down the small, paved street that led to Blaney Park's few private homes. He walked slowly, surveying each one, and soon passed the small country store. He smiled a good morning to three women standing in the doorway.

At the end of the street, he stopped and looked around. The pool and recreation areas weren't open yet, as it was still too cool for sunbathing and such activities. Conner wanted to be away from people, to see what else existed in this place, and headed toward the back of the hangar, into the woods. He felt there may be more here than he realized, and that selling it hastily might be a mistake. He had good feelings about this place.

Conner knew, at that moment, why he had come to Blaney Park. He wanted to see the property and do some soul searching. He wanted the land to talk to him so that he could decide if selling it was really what he was supposed to do.

He had been walking down a rough path, when it suddenly opened into a clearing. Conner stopped and could hear the soft babbling of the river.

"Good morning."

Conner jumped, not expecting to hear someone speak to him out here, and was even more surprised to turn and see Emily sitting on the other side of a large, pine tree.

"Hello," he said, finding his voice.

"Pretty, isn't it?" Emily nodded toward the river.

"Sure is."

"I saw you at breakfast. Is this your first visit?"

"Uh, yes it is." Conner was reluctant to strike up too much of a conversation with this woman, for fear of being asked what he was doing there. It was too late.

"Are you here on business?" Emily rose and walked over to him, extending her hand. "My name's Emily Stewart."

"Conner Morley," he smiled, shaking her hand. He then slid his hands into his trouser pockets and turned to look casually around the clearing. "Not really business. Just getting away for a few days."

"Well, you've come to the right place. Lots of good souls here, except for the business people, of course. I'm not sure why they come way up here."

"And which group do you fit into?" Conner nodded toward her assembly of camping chair, backpack, laptop computer and several drawing items.

"I'm a writer," Emily replied, "doing some research on the area. And, I sketch a little." She dropped her eyes and smiled.

"That sounds interesting."

"I was just about to walk the riverbank. Care to join me?"

"Um, sure," Conner swallowed. He had planned to spend the day walking around the Park, but never imagined he would be given a tour by someone who fascinated him as much as Emily did from the second he saw her.

They started west along the bank. Emily pointed out different trees and river bends, why the thick banks curved downward into the water from erosion, casually describing all that was around them. Conner was impressed with her knowledge and obvious affection for the area. They cut up into the woods, circled back to the clearing and Emily held up her hand, motioning for Conner to stop.

"Hang on a second," she whispered, as she pointed toward the opposite bank. "Look." Conner was shocked to see what he thought, at first, was a group of dogs.

"What are they?"

"Wolf pups."

"Seriously?"

"Of course, I'm serious," Emily laughed. "Haven't you ever seen a wolf before?" She backed up a few steps, and Conner followed her along the edge of the clearing back around to her spot by the big pine. They talked quietly, so not to interfere with the animals that seemed indifferent to their presence. It was obvious that this was not the first time they played with Emily nearby.

Emily watched Conner as they talked, enjoying his obvious fascination with the wolves. She was curious about him, and why he was there. He was an attractive man, with sandy blonde hair that appeared to have been combed that morning with his fingers, as it was still fairly tousled. He was tall, perhaps an inch or two over six feet, with an athletic build. His appearance confused her, as he was wearing expensive trousers and a leather jacket, not the look of a man who was out for a hike in the woods. Emily noticed through his open jacket that his shirt was wrinkled, as were his slacks, and she wondered if he had slept in his clothes. His shoes were spoiled with dust and mud around the soles from their walk along the river, yet they were expensive leather shoes, well polished and like new. She would normally be turned off by his city looks had she not seen him at breakfast and heard from Archie that a new guest had arrived the night before on his own private jet.

She looked up from his shoes and his gaze met hers. Emily saw his ocean blue eyes and the smile that existed below them and realized he had caught her checking him out. In her embarrassment, she focused on his jacket.

"What does the triangle-shaped insignia on your jacket mean?"

"Oh, this?" He placed two fingers on his jacket pocket. "This means everything to me. It represents my philosophy of life. I know if I live by it, I will be okay."

"Really?" Emily was intrigued.

"Yup. I call it the Triangle Of Life. At the top of the triangle is God, represented by this cross. To the right, family, represented by the heart." Conner pointed to each small symbol with his index finger as he explained them. "To the left is my self esteem, represented by the smiley face. If all intersections are connected, I am successful. God, family and then me. And, always in that order. It may sound silly, but it works for me." He smiled.

"Do you journal?" Emily asked casually, kicking at an imaginary grasshopper as she turned to watch the wolf pups playing on the opposite bank of the wide river. She looked up, and his eyes caught her again, as he seemed to look right through her.

What did I say? She thought. Emily knew nothing of this person. Nor did she have a clue why she asked such a question, let alone think it would touch him as it did. It just blurted out. No need or reason or logic involved.

"No one has ever asked me that," Conner replied. "Whatever made you ask me that question?"

"I really don't know... I'm sorry if I..."

"Yes, as a matter of fact, I do," Conner smiled. "Wow, you are good. I don't think I've ever admitted that to anyone."

"It's in your eyes, I think. You look at me and I feel like you are looking into my soul," she laughed lightly. "People like you always journal."

Conner looked at the large sketchpad leaning against the tree. There were large, outlining marks on the paper, and he could make out the faint shape of a wolf's head.

"What are you working on?" he asked.

"Just a project for the lodge," she leaned down to flip the pad shut, then turned back to him, smiling. "I don't let anyone see a project before completion. Here." Emily picked up an acorn. She brushed the winter's dirt from it before handing it to him.

"What's this?"

"An acorn," she laughed. "You've never seen one?"

"Yeah," he said. "What's it for?"

"Some say that we're like acorns. We grow on the tree and then fall to the earth. Only then, when our roots grow down into the earth, do we start to become what we were destined to be."

"Growing down, not up, huh," Conner rolled the acorn in his fingers and looked at her. His eyes stayed locked within hers for a moment, and they said nothing. Then he looked away, back across the moving waters. "Do they always act so indifferent to you?"

"Indifferent, no. Trusting, yes." She smiled, fixing her gaze once again on the opposite bank. "Sometimes, Wolfie swims across to me. Unless his mom catches him first."

"His mom?"

"The Alpha female. See? The bigger one." Emily lifted her arm, pointing towards the edge of the trees. "She's over there, just under that white pine."

"I don't see..." Conner's eyes quickly scanned the trees, unsure of what he was looking for. "What the hell is a white pine? They all look alike... they're green."

"There!" Emily laughed and grabbed his arm, turning his body.

Conner caught his breath as his eyes focused on a light gray form shuffling out of the shadows. The female wolf sped quickly in front of the pups as they tumbled and rolled over one another, edging ever so slightly closer to the riverbank.

"Shit," he mumbled. Emily smiled at his reaction, and pulled him down into a squatting position next to her in the grass.

"Watch," she whispered.

The alpha female circled her pups, growling and biting at their necks, as they whimpered and scurried into a tight pack, running clumsily back into the trees.

"Watch Wolfie. He's the darkest one."

The darker of the pups had circled back around behind his mother and was stopped in the long grass, as he stretched his head upward to see, his ears pointing up with curiosity. The female stopped and turned towards him.

"He's in deep shit," Conner chuckled.

"No, no...shhhh! Just watch him." Emily was still holding Conner's shirtsleeve and leaned her body against his shoulder and upper arm. Conner tried to concentrate on the wolf pup's play, rather than Emily's breathing as she watched with excitement.

"Emily," he whispered, and pointed toward the edge of the clearing where several other wolves were walking around, some lying in the grass. "Look over there. Is that a wolf? Man! It looks more like a bear. How come that one is so dark?"

Emily followed his hand, and recognized the rest of the pack.

"That's the rest of his family," she explained.

"This is amazing." Conner was almost speechless at what was taking place right in front of him. The darker adult moved awkwardly toward the river.

"It's limping," Conner noticed.

"Yes."

"Why? Is it hurt?"

Emily thought silently for a moment of the night she first encountered a Blaney wolf. "Trap injury. It happens around here, unfortunately." Conner shrugged it off, not caring enough about these animals to know what the story behind the limp was.

The wolf pup continued to look towards them and then slowly, cautiously, walked in a crouched position as he moved their direction, almost stalking them. The female did not move or attempt to shuffle him back to his pack. She just stared across the river, straight at Emily. Conner noticed that the female wolf was more interested in them than her disobedient pup.

"Emily," he whispered, "she's watching us."

"She's watching me," she smiled. "It's a game we play." Rising from her crouched position, Emily kept her eyes locked with the gaze of the alpha female. Wolfie stopped short, raising his head up sharply. Emily slowly backed up, still holding Conner by his shirtsleeve and he rose to move with her. He was fascinated by the communication between Emily, the wolf pup and his mother.

As they moved backward, Wolfie's ears lowered and he relaxed his posture. The alpha mother took a few quick steps forward, and he scurried back to her. Together, they loped back toward the rest of the pack and disappeared within the trees.

Emily stopped and smiled up at Conner, who was staring at her once again.

"That was amazing," he whispered. "They do that all the time?"

Emily laughed and shook her head. "Sometimes, if I don't back away, if I walk forward and crouch down in the grass, Wolfie will swim over to me. But that's usually only when I see them in the early morning."

Conner looked at her in disbelief. "Swim to you? Across the river?"

"You don't understand. We have this thing. It's really hard to explain, and I'm not sure you'd even believe me." Her eyes turned back toward the river.

"I'd like to see that sketch when it's done."

Emily didn't reply, as she bent down and began picking up her things, placing them into her backpack. "I need to go. Thanks for the walk. Maybe I'll see you around here again sometime." She smiled at Conner, hoisted her bag over her shoulder and walked away from him back in the direction of the cabins.

"Thanks for the tour," Conner called after her, as he watched her walk back down the deer path. It was the same path they both walked to get to the river, neither expecting to find another human being. He looked back toward the place where they had stood watching the wolves and felt blown away by what he just witnessed. He was consumed by the experience and knew his life would not be the same again. So much work, so much energy, so much pain had he experienced over the years. He was working so hard to make life livable, feel alive and successful. Nothing seemed to work, until now. One walk in the woods, one experience at the river's edge with a pack of wolves, one question asked and he felt alive again.

Someone must be praying for me, he thought.

Conner walked the woods for the rest of the day, playing back the tapes of the morning and soaking in the beauty of the area. Late in the day, he found himself back at the clearing. The sky was darkening and he realized he would have difficulty seeing his way back to the cabins if he didn't leave soon.

Movement in the moonlight interrupted his thoughts and he turned to see another wolf was at the river's edge. It was thinner, a more powerful looking wolf, and its fur more wild and shaggy. Conner didn't feel afraid because of what he had experienced with Emily. The wolf looked at him intently, without moving. A small group of wolves appeared at the tree line, like a pack calling to the one staring at Conner. There was now a competition going on. Conner realized he was not in his domain and it was no place for him to be. He broke the connection and began walking backwards towards the deer path. His heart was beating hard, as his content feeling was replaced by fear as he realized he was not Emily and the pack might attack. He walked backwards, keeping his cognitive mind on the wolf's movement behind him.

When the path curved around a thicket, he could no longer see the wolf and began to sprint back to the cabins. It was now very dark and he could hardly see the ground under his feet. If it wasn't for the brightness of the moon, he knew he would be lost. Finally, he got far enough down the deer path to see the cabins and found Number 4. He never stopped running and thrust open the front door, slamming it behind him. His heart was pounding, his chest expanding and sweat was running from his brow. All the business meetings and lunches had taken his conditioning away.

Now safe, he walked to the refrigerator for some ice. He dropped it into a glass and opened the JD bottle that still sat on the counter. This drink was different from the previous night. This drink was to celebrate a wonderful, exciting day. He hadn't felt this excited for many years. After filling the glass half empty, he looked at it and thought, half full tonight.

Conner still could not catch his breath from the awesome experience. He looked down at his clothes and saw that his six hundred dollar Italian shoes were scuffed, and his eight hundred dollar pair of wool pants were snagged and full of burs. These things on a normal day would have pissed him off big time. Tonight, he just smiled and, after finally catching his breath, took his first drink as the ice cubes cracked against each other in the quiet of the cabin. He looked toward the hissing of the fire, burning brightly in the fireplace. It had obviously been prepared by Archie, as there was no sign of Todd's return.

The quiet made his thoughts drift to Emily. He liked her. She dressed differently than the women he was attracted to from the city. She was a bit of a tomboy. She had asked him if he journalled. What had made her ask? How did she know so much of what a person has no business knowing. And, the wolves. How did she know they'd be there? That they wouldn't run off, or worse, attack them.

What a woman, he thought, gulping his drink.

As he poured another, he thought he heard a faint howl and looked out the kitchen window. To his amazement, he captured a silhouette of a wolf just at the edge of the path as it entered the woods leading to the river, with the moon as a backdrop.

"No way," Conner laughed. His heart leapt as he heard and watched the wolf make one more howl before turning back into the dark path.

With that, Conner flopped down on the bed. He watched the fire, thinking about Emily and what had occurred that day. The fire was crackling and its warmth, combined with the affects of the JD, made him tired.

Hell with it, he thought. They are ruined, but I am new! It don't matter anymore, anyway.

Just as Conner was falling asleep, he heard his cellular phone ring.

"Shit," he said. His thoughts and dreams of Emily, the way she leaned against him, the way she touched his arm, her scent, the warmth of her breath on his cheek, were interrupted.

It rang again. The fire had started to diminish, but there was just enough light to find the phone. Besides the battery, the phone had an LCD indicator. He really didn't want to answer, but he always would.

"Conner Morley speaking."

"Con Man."

He recognized the voice of his property manager. Phil Jackson had always been a loyal associate. Phil had made a ton of money on Conner and was brilliant at real estate negotiations. Phil did his usual, no niceties, right to business.

"Conner, I hope you are not getting too comfortable there in Upper Michigan. I just spoke with the developer who is interested in that worthless piece of property you call a park. Based on what I have seen, it's no park, it is overhead. Blaney Park should be called Bankrupt Park, Conner. It is costing you lots of money and doesn't bring in one penny for your bottom line! Hell, all it's good for is a write off and the way life is going for you, you don't need anymore write-off's. I've spoken with Joe and he's agreed to draft the paperwork as soon as you want to sign off."

"Phil, call me tomorrow." Conner hung up without allowing a reply. Phil's call bothered him. He put another log on the fire and, as he straightened up, noticed a flashlight on the mantle.

What the hell, Conner thought. Without bothering to take a coat, he turned on the flashlight and exited the cabin. He wanted to go back to the river and watch the moonlight. Just get away from that damned phone and recapture what he had felt earlier. Phil's call had such shitty timing. That had been the way of Conner's life over the last few months, hell, years. A failed marriage, a consuming work schedule, and a loss for the lust of life were erasing his passion for living. As he walked he became confused, wondering if he was still on the path or even going the right direction.

The flashlight batteries faltered and Conner questioned what he was doing out in the middle of the night with no protection. He was accustomed to being cared for. His money and position demanded it. At Blaney Park, he was just another animal. He shook the flashlight and it flickered in the darkness.

What a wolf I'd make, he smiled, almost tripping over a large tree root. I don't even have a pack. I am a lone wolf. Conner realized that his life had softened him. He was too pampered, a mommy's boy type. That was the ultimate needle in his side. He had sworn never to be a mommy's boy. Deciding to brave the path and continue his adventure, he could hear the flowing water of the river and soon found the bank. He walked along it carefully, until he found a large rock overlooking the water. It seemed like the perfect spot, with the river wide enough to allow the moonlight to shine brightly without interference from the trees.

Conner sat on the rock for only a few moments, when he heard movement in the water that was different from its flow. His eyes peered upstream into the darkness and he could see an image. Someone was in the river.

Who, in their right mind, would be out here in that cold water in the middle of the night? Straining his eyes in the moonlight, he saw the image rise from the water. He could see it was a woman by the beautifully shaped, protruding breasts, curving waistline and hips of the person. She shook her head backward and when he saw the full mane of long hair, he knew it was Emily. His heart was pounding wildly.

Can she see me? Oh shit, he thought. How would it look if she saw him watching her? Conner crouched down on the rock. She knelt and stretched out fully in the water, supporting her upper body by her arms. The thin layer of cloud cover was gone now, and the moonlight illuminated the river like a street lamp. Emily leaned forward, lowering her mouth into the stream and then raised upward, stretching her neck. Conner could see the water flowing out of her mouth, spilling down the sides of her face, along her neck to her breasts. She was caressing the stream and it fascinated him. Twice more she scooped the water into her mouth and let it trickle out down her chin and body.

He so wanted to join her, but how? This wasn't a city woman who would be impressed by his money and dress. This woman had substance. Was she even human, he wondered as his sensibility was clouded by the alcohol he consumed in his cabin. Maybe she was part wolf, after what happened earlier in the day. So many thoughts were going through his mind. The loneliness he felt was heavy on his heart right down to his feet. Then panic struck him. If he could see her, she could see him. He stood and tried jumping from the rock to a tree for more camouflage. He misjudged the strength of the tree and its limbs broke, plunging him into the water just off the bank. The icy water shocked him. He didn't go deep and, fortunately, was near the edge where Emily would not see him. What a sight that would have been for her.

Yes, I just thought I'd take a swim in my clothes at eleven o'clock at night. I am sure this impresses you. Conner lay there in the cold water trying to decide if he had broken anything. How embarrassing it would be if she saw him.

Conner, the Peeping Tom. What a field day the tabloids would have with that story. Emily could retire off the commissions if she could get pictures. Then it occurred to him, how in the hell was Emily swimming in this freezing water? It would do him no good to pursue her, there would be nothing left protruding to pursue with. This cold of water would only shrink his manly parts to a magnifying state. Finally, he got the courage to crawl out of the river. He tried to see if Emily was disturbed by the splash he had made, but he couldn't see her at that angle.

Good, he thought, figuring she couldn't see him either. But now what? He was cold and he was no penguin. He was wet and frustrated.

Can't leave a good thing alone. Man, talk about being in a slump. Meet a great woman and write her off because she wears hiking boots instead of pumps. Then, see her in the moonlight and I get so excited I can't keep myself vertical. Who could, with water this damned cold?

Conner shivered as he walked back to his cabin. He wondered what animals would be awake at such a late hour. They have to sleep at night, right? What about snakes? Bears hibernate, but that's in the winter. His mind was trying to decide what animal was going to chomp on him this night. The way his luck was going, it had to happen. He reached a crossroad in the trail and the wind began to gust.

Great. I'm already freezing and now the wind is coming up. Conner reached the cabin, and sighed with relief. The bells on the side of Emily's cabin were ringing softly. Their sweet sounds helped him find the cabins in the darkness. Clouds were moving in and blocked the moon. He stepped inside and grumbled about his wet condition. He ripped off the wet clothes and threw them into a heap on the floor in front of the fireplace, which had been stoked, once again. Archie had obviously been there again, as everything was made up.

What's with this guy, Conner thought of Archie. Is that all he does? It's after midnight. Oh shit, did he follow me? Did he see Emily? To hell with it, I am too cold, too wet and too tired to protect the world tonight. It's probably me being stupid again, overreacting. He pulled back the top blanket and curled into a ball in the bed, closing his eyes and welcoming his sleep.

"Shit, Sully was right," Conner mumbled aloud. "This is a comfortable bed."

12
Bad Cell

Conner was still lying in bed when he felt something vibrating against his hip. At first, he was startled. He didn't know where he was, or what it was that awoke him. He seldom laid his head anywhere but his own bed, and frequently woke disoriented at a sleep-over when he was a kid. Todd's concern of what could be in the cabin earlier had increased Conner's anxiety of what creature would come out after dark to touch him.

Oh yeah, I am at Blaney Park, he smiled. He felt the vibration again and remembered he had tossed his cell phone onto the bed earlier and must have slept on it. Who would be calling him at this late hour? He picked it up and answered it.

"Conner Morley, speaking," He paused, waiting for a reply, "Hello? Hello?" Instead of a response, he heard a conversation. Someone had indeed called, but did not know they had dialed his number.

"Jim, it's me. Listen, tonight's okay, really. Conner thinks I am working through the weekend. He has no idea what I am doing and why. I try not to be too specific so he doesn't ask too many questions. I told him a long time ago, my career is the most important thing to me and don't want him checking up on me all the time. God, he'd be so pissed if he knew I was having an affair. He can get very upset when people don't live up to his value system. I have no intentions of trying to live up to it. He even told me many times that he'd die for me. Who in the hell dies for anyone these days? What a thing to say!"

Conner heard Samantha's laughter. He sat up from the bed and concluded that Samantha had mistakenly hit the redial button on her cellular phone and called him, thinking she was leaving a message for someone else. His body was tingling with emotion and adrenaline. He tried to focus his mind on what he was hearing.

"For a guy who always says he's so street smart, he sure is stupid about us. I love being with you, Jim. You are so much fun. The way we can just take off and do our own thing, no responsibilities and all the fun. I love it. Conner is always talking about a budget and saving up to have kids. Who in the hell wants kids? I'd never tell him, but kids are born out of mistakes. No one in their right mind would ever have a kid on purpose. Kids ruin everything. I don't want kids. Shit, I am in my mid-30s. If I were going to have kids, I would have had them a long time ago. I'd be home all the time taking care of them and I'd have no freedom to do what I wanted to do. And they'd always be his kids, Jim. Conner would have them all loyal and committed to family, like being part of a team. He has this thing about team and how important it all is. He always talks about us as a team. We are no team, except when I ask him to come with me to buy clothes or furniture for me. He'd never have any money for me if we had kids. I have too many things I still want and kids would take my fair share.

"I love using that 'don't you trust me?' speech. It works every time with Conner. He so wants to please me and feel like he's being a good husband. I can just about take advantage of him any time I want. Like yesterday. His dad's dying and I didn't even ask him about it. He never asked me what I was doing or wondered why I didn't inquire. It was easy for me to just let it go and be with you, Jim."

Conner continued listening waiting for Samantha to realize what was happening and what number she had dialed. It never happened. He listened until there was no more to listen to on the other end. Conner finally decided he'd heard enough. He turned the phone to the fireplace so he could see to push the red END button on it. By now, he was seeing red. He looked around the room for no other reason but to try and remember where he was when he heard the news from his wife's own voice. She was truly cheating on him, just as Rick had said.

There were things that occurred in life when one knew where and what he or she was doing when it happened. Things like the landing on the moon of a NASA space ship, the Kennedy assassinations, as well as that of Martin Luther King. Conner remembered hearing people tell him where they were when they heard about the bombing of Pearl Harbor, and he remembered where he was and what he was doing. Now, he was looking inside his cabin taking in all the things that were there so he could remember the death of his marriage to Samantha.

He wanted Jim to die. He was feeling a hatred grow inside him that would have been comparable to the family members who died during all those tragic moments in life's past. Conner lay back down to try to go back to sleep. His head was on the pillow for several seconds when he stood up and returned the call to Samantha. Her phone rang three times when he heard the answer on the other line.

"Hey, you. How are you?"

"Well, I have been better. I just wanted to call and let you know that you had called me by mistake. You must have pushed your send button by accident. You really should lock your phone so that type of thing doesn't happen, you know. Especially when you are talking on subjects that you don't want the wrong person to hear. I was obviously your last call so the auto redial called me again. When I answered, I tried but couldn't get your attention. You were too busy leaving a message for Jim about marriage, family and your life together. So, I just wanted to call to let you know you had called me by mistake and to tell you mistakes do happen. I will be trying not to make many more going forward. Have a good day."

Conner didn't wait for a reply. He just hung up. He half hoped he'd get a call back and a tearful apology for what she had done and just said about him. He thought better of it. Conner was dealing with too much adversity in his life. He was feeling too hurt by it all.

Samantha was right. He did want to be a good husband. He did want to support her and not be overly jealous or question the relationships she was having with men she worked with. Many times he had questions. He did not ask, hoping that she was being faithful, wanting his worry only to be that of an insecure man missing his very secure wife. But lies and life were the same now. His life was a lie and she was not being the hard-working career woman she said she was.

He turned off his phone and placed it on the floor. He contemplated getting up from his bed and walking outside to throw up or, at the very least, into the kitchen where the Jack Daniel's was calling his name. Instead, he looked to the ceiling, searching for answers and decided better of it all. Better to sleep and find peace, than to drink and think of war.

13
The Fight

It was late June. Conner had spent six weeks meeting with his legal staff, setting course for his pending divorce from Samantha. He had kept himself busy between business meetings and spending time on the golf course with Rick and now the waiting game had started. It would be several weeks before the final court hearing and Conner knew he needed to get away in order to keep from going crazy. A trip to Blaney Park was the perfect solution.

Conner awoke with the sun shining through his cabin window. The beauty outside was like a picture hanging on the wall. The smell of breakfast came from the Harrison and he smiled. Intermittent aromas of fresh air and pine filtered through those of coffee, hash-browned potatoes and bacon.

Conner rolled over and looked to the ceiling. He grabbed the pillow from behind his head and hugged it to his chest. A lonely thought came to his mind. Samantha was cheating on him. The pain was tearing at his stomach. He wrapped his arms tightly around the pillow as if the hug from it was the only hug he'd ever get for the rest of his life. He loved hugging Samantha. He loved her. He would miss her and now all he could do was try to forget about it. His few attempts to call Samantha had been met by her answering services. She was not going to let Conner back into her life until she was ready to speak to him. Conner was crushed that she didn't feel the inclination to fight for him. She just gave him up.

Conner felt the tears swell up in his eyes. He had always said he'd only be married once in his lifetime, and never considered divorce. Now, he had no choice. Without trust and loyalty in his marriage, he could not be with her any longer. He had decided he wanted out and was calling his lawyers each day instead of his wife. There was much to do and much to protect from a woman who would betray family. No telling what she had already done to him, financially, if she was capable of cheating his heart. No doubt, his finances were at risk.

Conner stopped any more tears from coming to his eyes. He had a father with cancer and he needed to be strong. He looked to the window again. A soft, cool breeze was blowing in and a blue jay landed on the windowsill. There were some bread crumbs on the counter. Conner watched as the bird would hop down onto the counter and fly away with a crumb, only to return again a few seconds later. He lay there counting to himself the seconds it took for the bird to leave and return, and then wondered if there was more than one bird. There could be more than one bird. Hell, they all look alike.

How do I know? Conner thought. I don't know shit. I don't even know how to keep my family together. I am going to get that Jim Gordy. Sad thoughts were returning to him. He tired of waiting for the bird to return, thinking it had its fill.

What is Samantha going to do when Jim is done with her? Okay, that's enough! Quit beating yourself up, man. It's over! Move on. Don't let her keep breaking you down, asshole. Conner scolded himself as he did all of his life whenever he was allowing himself to be weak. He couldn't do anything, and knew he wasn't going to make solid business decisions if his mind was cluttered with thoughts of a cheating wife.

His thoughts turned to Emily. Do you journal? All Conner ever wanted from Samantha was for her to show some interest and affection towards him. Samantha was like Lake Michigan in the spring, appealing to the eye but cold to the touch. And, this woman asked such a deep question of him the first time they met. It blew him away and made him feel good inside, all at the same time.

Yes, he decided. That is what I am going to focus on today. Me, and how and what I do. Fuck her, she can't make a fool out of me! His attitude changed. He had to work through the heartache and issues that confronted him now. He did this often with his athletics. Adversity would hit him and he would overcome it, knowing all the issues and embarrassment was still in his life, but he wanted to win so he had to move on. He'd take blocks of time and work through the disappointment. First a minute, then an hour and finally, a day would go by when he'd be okay.

Conner thought again of Emily and the fact that she seemed to find him interesting. He thought of his friendship with Todd, the one person on earth who he could depend on and be straight with. There was much to be happy about if he thought of issues other than a cheating wife and an ill father.

Conner jumped out of bed and went to the bathroom. He showered and shaved, then brushed his teeth and decided to go get breakfast. On a small chair next to the dresser, lay a stylish pair of khaki shorts, white socks along with a pullover golf shirt. The shirt's logo read 'Blaney Park' with a wolf embroidered beneath it.

I don't think so, he thought, figuring Archie must have left them. Then, he reconsidered. What better way to thoroughly look over the business of the Park than by blending in with those who worked there?

Everything fit comfortably. As Conner reached for his dress shoes, thinking how silly he was going to look since they were all he had with him, he noticed a pair of hiking boots against the wall next to the chair. A perfect fit for him, size 10D. He was accustomed to being taken care of, but this was too much to ask for away from home. A pair of sunglasses and a hat lay on the table.

What the hell? Conner thought to himself, as he looked in the mirror on the wall. Ranger Rick, he laughed. If the boys back in the hood could only see this.

Conner exited the cabin and started up the path towards the Harrison for breakfast. He came upon a boy, probably no more than seven years old, throwing a football up in the air and catching it.

"Over here!" Conner reached out with his arms. The boy threw a perfect spiral to him. "Wow. Nice throw, son."

"Thanks, mister."

"Can you catch it back?"

"You throw it and I will catch it."

Conner tossed the football back to the kid.

"Great catch! Bet your dad is good at football, too!"

"I don't think so, sir," the boy shrugged, as he tossed the ball back to Conner. "My dad is in heaven."

Conner said nothing, and again tossed the ball back to the kid who caught the ball on the run. "Very good. You are good."

"Ah, this is nothing. I can catch the ball all different ways. I can catch it with my back to you, I can catch it left... I can ...right... I can..."

Conner stopped listening to the little guy. His smile stayed on his face and he kept eye contact with the child, but his mind turned to his self-pity. He was thinking how he'd never experience a son of his own and teach him to catch and throw. He felt bad for the boy who did not have his father, like Conner had his dad, while growing up.

"And," the boy continued, "when I grow up I am going to be another Terry Bradshaw."

"I'm sure you will, big guy. You keep practicing and, someday, I bet you will."

Conner left the kid still talking and tossing the ball up in the air, pretending to be someone he wasn't and hoping he would be somebody special himself, one day. Conner thought about how he was exactly like that little boy when he was a kid. His parents would take the family places and all he wanted was a ball in his hands. No need for a fishing rod, or a gun. Just a ball and his imagination were all he needed.

Conner was walking past the general store just as an elderly lady came out with a bag of groceries. He stopped and looked back. She was having trouble negotiating the cement block steps leading down from the store to the path.

"May I help you, ma'am?" Conner asked.

"Why sure, young man. Oh, you work here," her eyes scanned over his apparel. "That's fine. What a nice place this is, to have people to help me. Here, take my bag. I am in Cabin 8. Come along and I will show you."

Conner took the bag as, with sudden energy, she began walking to her cabin, expecting him to follow. Conner began to stop her and decided not to, since he really did not have any pressing tasks and the old lady obviously wanted some help. He followed her past the boy with the football, past his number 4 cabin and down the road to Cabin 8. The whole time, she was talking and Conner never heard a word.

"Okay, boy, here I am," she stopped in front of her door. "Thank you. Now, wait right there while I get you a tip." She reached into her small change purse as Conner placed her bag on the front step.

"Oh, that's okay, ma'am. I don't need a tip."

"Listen, you work here, I am sure Elsie ain't paying you much and you need money for a college education. If you want to be successful in life, you need college teaching. You hear, boy?"

"Yes, ma'am," he smiled. "I hear you."

"Didn't you listen to anything I said while we were walking to my cabin, boy? You can learn a thing or two from old folk if you'd just listen. That's the problem with you kids, nowadays. Too much talkin' and not enough listening."

"Yes, ma'am" Conner replied, trying to be respectful.

"Now here," she curled his hand around a bunch of coins. "Don't tell Miss Elsie how much I gave you, now. She'd not be too kind with me, knowing I was giving you more."

"Okay, ma'am. I won't. Thank you, ma'am."

"You are welcome, boy."

Boy, Conner smiled as he walked away. Don't call me 'boy', lady. He looked in his hand at the coins she had given him. 25 pennies. All of them wheat pennies dated before 1940. Conner walked up to the boy with the football, and told him to reach out his hand.

"Here's 25 pennies. Go buy yourself a victory candy bar when you win your game."

"Oh, thank you, sir!"

Conner started again towards the Harrison for breakfast. At that moment, he got the urge to speak with Archie. He wanted some history about the Park and what was going on here. After all, if he was going to make good decisions, he needed to ask good questions. He walked to the hangar.

"Morning," said a tall man working on a small aircraft.

"Good morning," Conner replied. He stopped to look at the plane.

"Austin Stewart," the man reached out for a handshake.

"Nice to meet you, Austin," Conner shook his hand. "Conner Morley."

"Yeah, I know who you are."

"You do?"

"Sure, any time a nice plane flies in here, I know about it. This one's mine," Austin nodded to the plane in front of them.

"She's a beaut."

"She does well. I am looking to buy another, here soon. I want a bigger one like you and Todd have."

Conner smiled at Austin's confidence, while wondering how he knew Todd. "Have you seen Archie around?"

"No, but he may be over at the pool. He vacuums it once a day and he hates doing it. He's always asking why, with all the water around Blaney Park, they ever needed a pool. I told him the pool's for all the city guests who don't really get wet, but want it for when they take their pictures of each other."

"Yeah, I think I know some of those types," Conner thought of Samantha. She'd be just the type to spend the whole day next to a pool and never get wet. "I am married to one, actually, at least for a few more months. She's one of those career women who want to look good, but not get sweaty.

I'm just waiting for my lawyers to pay her off."

"That's too bad," Austin shook his head. "Not my kind of woman. Mine likes to get down and get her nails dirty. Where does your wife work?"

"Heritage Technologies, Inc."

"Really. I fly a lot of H.T.'s management up here. One couple acts as if they own this place. They come here a lot."

"What are their names?" Conner's suspicions were rising. "I used to contract there and I knew a lot of their people."

"Well, it's against my policy to divulge my manifest. My passengers want to stay anonymous. But, I tell you what. Go sneak a peak at the Harrison's registrar and you might see some names that you know."

"Thanks. By the way, can I help you?"

"Sure."

Conner grabbed a bottle of cleaner and paper towels from the bench, and began wiping the soil off the wings of Austin's plane. He did that with Todd so they could leave their hangar quicker after a flight. If bug guts dried, they could be a bitch to get off. It also made for a more efficient flight if the wings were clean, and that kept fuel prices down. Every penny saved was a penny in the pilot's pocket. It was a pilot's chore to keep the plane clean of dirt and they took pride in it.

"You fly up here often?" Conner asked.

"Yeah. I started flying up here about two years ago when the couple I mentioned wanted to take some business associates north for the weekend. Next thing I knew, they started coming up here just about every week. Mostly during the week, which I found interesting. When do they work? They must have some cushy jobs."

"Maybe. They must be higher up in the company."

"Not sure. I almost want to tell you they are a married couple. They typically check in as Mr. and Mrs., yet there are times when they just use first names. But, like I said, I don't ask many questions. I just fly them here and collect my fare."

"They come here often, huh?"

"For two years now. Although, every time I fly them in, Archie gives the guy a hard time. I have asked him about it. After all, they are my customers. He told me to mind my own business. I'm sure there is something going on there underneath the covers. I think Archie would like to kick his ass, but I'll be damned if I know why."

Conner listened, but was finding it hard to keep working on the plane, now that he had a few tasks to accomplish. After cleaning the wings, Conner shook Austin's hand.

"You could be confused for someone who works here," Austin smiled sarcastically, pointing to Conner's shirt.

"Oh, you mean the clothes?" Conner laughed as he ran his hand across the logo on his shirt. "Pretty nice, and its embroidered, too. I wonder how they make any money around here giving away such expensive shirts. Actually, I already got put to work this morning by this old lady who made me carry her groceries to her cabin, and then gave me a full 25 cents." Conner grinned.

"Really, did she pay you in pennies?"

"Yeah, all 25. Why?"

"Well, if it's the lady I think it is, she tips all the college kids in collectable coins. Her husband was a big collector. Those pennies are probably worth some bucks on the market."

"Oh, shit! I gave them to a kid playing with a football. I told him to go buy some candy."

"Well, you probably just gave that kid a few hundred dollars worth of collectable coins, I figure."

"No shit! Well, I better get going."

"Thanks for the help, Conner," Austin smiled.

"No problem. Nice meeting you, Austin. Tell Archie I am looking for him if you see him."

"Sure. I don't go far from my plane and he eventually makes his way back here to the hangar. He may be out fishing with a guest, now that I think about it."

"Okay. Just tell him I am looking for him," Conner called back over his shoulder, as he walked quickly back towards the cabins. He ran up to the grocery store and looked inside to see the little kid standing at the candy counter section.

"Hey. . . kid," Conner was panting as he stepped inside the store.

"Yes, sir?"

"Did.... did you spend your pennies?"

"Nope. Got pennies right here in my pocket."

"Twenty-five?"

"Yup."

" I will give you a dollar for those twenty-five pennies."

"Nope. These are my pennies."

"Kid, I will give you one whole dollar for twenty-five pennies."

"Nope. These are my pennies. Not for a dollar will I give you my pennies."

"Kid, I will give you five whole dollars for twenty-five pennies."

"Nope. These are my pennies. Not for five dollars will I give you my pennies."

"Kid, I will give you ten whole dollars for twenty-five pennies."

"Nope. These are my pennies. Not for ten dollars will I give you my pennies. My asking price is twenty-five dollars for my twenty-five pennies."

"What? Are you kidding me? How can you ask twenty-five dollars for twenty-five pennies? You are ripping me off."

"Okay, then I will keep my twenty-five pennies and you keep your twenty-five dollars. Sir, you asked me for my pennies, and I am asking for twenty-five dollars to give you my pennies."

"Okay, okay. Twenty-five dollars for the twenty-five pennies."

"That's the deal, sir. Twenty-five dollars for my twenty-five pennies. Yup, that is the deal."

"Great." Conner said, relieved to be out of the negotiations with a seven-year old who, he was sure, didn't understand the value of a dollar. He reached into his pocket for his wallet and gave the cash to the kid. In return, the kid gave Conner the pennies.

Conner left the store feeling proud and relieved. He remembered seeing dates and wheat backs on the coins, yet it never occurred to him they might have been collectibles. He looked at the dates of some of the pennies in his hand and they were dated in the 80's and 90's. They looked recent and not old at all. He went back inside to the kid.

"Hey, kid! Are these the pennies I gave you earlier?"

"Oh, no, sir. Those were worth a lot more than twenty-five dollars. I saw you walking with Mrs. Evans before. I thought she might pay you in collectable coins. She does that sometimes, you know. Her pennies are worth a lot of money."

"So, why did you take twenty-five dollars from me for twenty-five pennies that weren't worth but twenty-five cents?"

"Sir, I think you got it all wrong. I only asked you for twenty-five dollars, after you offered me five, ten, and then accepted twenty-five dollars for them. My mom gave me new pennies to replace the ones you gave me.

You asked for this transaction, sir, not me."

Conner just smiled. He had been had by a seven-year old going on forty.

"Hey, kid."

"Yes, sir?"

"If you don't make it as a pro athlete. Look me up. I want to give you a job."

"Yes, sir. I think you need me, sir. You didn't make a good decision giving me twenty-five dollars for twenty-five cents worth of coins."

"Nope. You are right, kid. I didn't make a good decision. I have been doing that a lot lately. Enjoy the twenty-five dollars. Don't spend it all in one place."

"I won't, sir. I am going to put this twenty-five dollars in my bank account so it draws interest. Did you know interest is computed quarterly, and is compounded..."

"Yeah, yeah," Conner laughed. "I have to go, kid. I'll see you around. We can play more catch with the football and you can tell me all about it."

Conner left and headed back, again, toward the Harrison to get his breakfast. He walked up the steps and into the foyer. The front desk was unattended and Conner saw the guest registrar. He walked up and opened it. He didn't have to go far into it when he saw the names Mr. and Mrs. James Gordy. Conner's heart began to accelerate and he felt dizzy with emotion.

What do I do about all this? My world is crashing on me? Conner pulled out his cell phone and called Samantha. Her phone went directly to voicemail, so he left her a message.

"Samantha, I think we need to talk. Please call me as soon as you get this message. I know what's going on, Samantha. I'd like to talk to you about it. I think we owe it to each other to at least talk about it. Call me. Please."

Conner hung up. He hated himself for being so nice to her. He knew she was dogging him and that her affair had been going on for a long time. Now that she had Jim, why would she care about Conner or what he thought? He wanted the pain to go away. He wanted her to share in his pain. How could she not be hurting? He was losing all that he had hoped life would be for him and a life long partner to share it with. Now his partner was sharing her dreams with another man and his were left alone. The anger increased in his body. He needed to speak to her to get the answers.

"May I help you, sir?" Elsie Brooks had walked up beside him and reached out to close the registrar book. "Oh, Mr. Morley. I didn't recognize you with a hat and sunglasses on. You look quite handsome in our work attire. Do you want a job with us?"

"Good-morning, Miss Elsie," Conner managed a smile. "No, thank you, ma'am. I need to go. Sorry for interrupting your day." Conner turned and walked away out of the Harrison. He decided he'd go to the pool to see if Archie was there. On his way, he paged 4-4-4 from his cell phone. Halfway to the pool, his phone rang.

"Hey, Todd."

"What's up, Con Man? I just got home."

"Yeah, sorry. I need you to come back and get me."

"Already? What's up?"

"It's Samantha, man. She's here. She's been coming here for years with Gordy and I didn't even know it. I want to kill this fucker. I think he's here, too. I am losing it, man. I need you to get me out of here before I do something I will regret later."

"Okay, Con Man. Listen, I am coming. I may bring the wife with me, though. But I am coming."

"That's fine."

"Now listen. You listening to me?" Todd demanded.

"Yeah, I am listening."

"Whatever you do, don't hit Samantha. You hear me?"

"Yeah, Sully. I hear you."

"Fuck him up, if you have to. People will understand that. But, don't touch the wife, Con Man. Nobody will let that go down. Okay?"

"Okay. Just get here now. I think they are here right now and I don't know what I will do if I see them together."

"I am there in 75 minutes. Just go back to your cabin and wait for me. It's not worth it, Con Man. We can do this better for you than you can by yourself. Let me handle it. It's what you pay me to do, and you know I am good at it. I can't protect you, brother, if you do something stupid, and if you kick his ass, I can't do anything to him until it all cools down."

"I know, I know. But I ain't going back to my cabin. I can't. Get here, Sully, just get here. I am going ballistic. God, this can't be happening to me!" Conner cried out, as he ended the call. His mind was thinking at high speed. He was in conflict with himself. He wanted revenge now, but there was a part of him telling him he needed to go back to the cabin and let his emotions cool down.

Conner neared the pool and could see the building where the restrooms and dressing rooms were. He decided to walk up behind the structure so no one at the poolside would see him. He looked around the structure and there, off to the side of the pool, was his wife on a lounge chair lying face down with Jim Gordy putting suntan lotion on her back. Conner was now experiencing intense anger. He was finding it hard to walk away and let this moment pass for a better opportunity.

Conner didn't bother opening the gate, he jumped the fence. The noise caused Jim to look over at him while Samantha lay there, most likely sleeping. It was her way of sunning herself. Just to fall to sleep and let the sun bake her while she felt no responsibility to dialog with anyone. Conner had spent many a boring sunny days sitting next to her watching her sleep while her skin baked brown. While he didn't much like doing it, he sure as hell didn't like another man doing the same with her. Jim looked right at Conner. Conner used his index finger to call him over. Jim pointed at himself and Conner nodded. It was obvious, with the hat and sunglasses, that Gordy did not recognize Conner. They hadn't seen each other for at least a year. In fact, with the shirt and khakis on, he probably thought he was an employee of the Park. Gordy got up from his place next to Conner's wife and walked over to him.

"What do you want and why are you being so rude as to signal me over to you in such a manner. I am the customer and you..."

"Fuck you, asshole," Conner growled, as he grabbed Gordy by the balls and throat and pulled him into the men's locker room.

"Hey! What the hell are you doing? You're hurting me!" Gordy spoke with a gargled voice as Conner had his hands over his throat.

Conner slammed Jim against the lockers, released his grip and took off his sunglasses. Fear was pasted on Gordy's face, as the recognition of Conner was processed.

"Conner. Come on, man, let me go. You are hurting me. Let's talk about this man. It ain't my fault, man. Samantha asked me here."

"Ain't your fault? Ain't your fault? Aren't you a married man, Jim?"

"Conner, I..."

Conner reached down and again squeezed his hands over Gordy's balls, stopping him mid-sentence from finishing his rhetoric.

"Nothing but a yes or no answer is needed for my questions, asshole."

"Ain't you married?"

"Yes."

"Do you love your kids?"

"Yes."

"You wouldn't want anything to happen to them, now would you?"

"No."

Conner smiled at Gordy.

"I love this shit, man. You know how much I love this shit?"

"No."

"Well, you better find out, you fat fuck. Because, first, I am going to hurt your kids. Do you love your wife?"

Gordy did not reply, only glared at Conner with both fear and anger in his eyes.

"I said, do you love your wife?"

"I don't think I do."

"Oh, you are a fucker, Gordy. You let your wife bear your kids, but you don't stand by her. You need a good hurting put on your ass."

"Please, Conner. You are hurting me. Can we just calm down and talk? Please don't tell my wife about this. You wouldn't hurt my kids..."

"Me? Me? You have it all wrong you, asshole. It's you that have caused all this for your family. I tell you what. You will beg me to kill your ass when I am through with what I am going to do to your family. You fuck with my family, I fuck with yours. Eye for an eye. Tooth for a tooth, mother fucker. You will be beggin' me to kill you after you see how your kids treat you for what you did to them!"

Just then, a kid came into the locker room and saw what was going on. "Fight, fight!" he yelled, as he ran back out of the locker room.

When Conner glanced at the kid, Gordy pulled away from him and ran back out by the pool. Conner followed and lunged at him from the doorway, grabbing Jim's swimsuit and almost tearing it from his body. He began punching Jim hard to the body. First, in the head and then to the ribs. Gordy dropped to the ground into a fetal position, as he called out for Samantha to stop Conner.

"For Christ's sake, Conner!" Samantha screamed as she ran over, grabbing Conner by the arm. He pushed her aside, as if she was weightless. She fell to the cement scraping her knees and elbows. She looked up at him, shocked that he would ever do that to her. He had promised he'd never touch her. She began trembling as she realized the extent of his anger and backed away from them.

Conner continued his assault on Gordy, punching and kicking him, telling him to stay away from his wife. As a crowd gathered around them, Archie ran up behind Conner and grasped his arms at the elbows, putting a tight body grip on him. Conner was getting fatigued from all the punches he had thrown. He didn't have much energy to wrestle with Archie.

"Conner! Not now, man, not now! Chill out, son. Not now!" Archie was struggling to pull Conner back as he continued kicking at Gordy, who was on the ground in a ball trying to protect himself, yelling like a stuck pig. "Go to the hangar now, Morley! No one fights at my Park, no one! These are paying customers and you don't belong here if you are going to treat them like this!" He pushed Conner up against the side of the building, his hands on Conner's chest.

"Conner, you asshole!" Samantha sneered at him, crouched at Jim's side. "I hate you!"

"Samantha, how could you do this?" Conner said. "You are cheating on me?"

"Oh, grow up, Conner! So, I am cheating on you. What? Do you own me?"

"Own you? No, but I thought we had marriage vows..."

"Vows," she began to laugh. "Vows? That's too funny. Like wedding vows? Come on, Conner. Don't be so naïve. You've always known what I wanted and I will keep making more of myself and my own career. I am not going to be just Mrs. Conner Morley. You don't own me. You never expected me to just be with you, did you? "

"You bitch."

"Oh, so I am a bitch, huh?" She stood and walked over in front of him, thrusting her face up to his. "Come on, Conner, hit me. Hit me, Conner! You know you want to hit me. Do it, you coward!"

Conner turned to the door next to him and threw his fist toward it, knocking the door off its hinges and shattering a hole in the wood.

"Okay, that's enough!" Archie grabbed Conner again and pulled him away from the door. Samantha looked on in shock at the scattered pieces of the door on the ground around her feet. "You should return to your room, now, miss." He was growing concerned of the crowd behind them, and wanted this public display over with quickly.

"Go, Conner," Archie pushed Conner in front of him. "Go to the hangar, damn it!"

Conner turned to Samantha and held his bleeding hand up to her face so they both could look at it. Blood was running down his arm from the cuts he incurred from the broken and sharp wood edges.

"Why, Samantha?" he looked deeply in her eyes, knowing she could feel how he was hurting. "Why? I'd die for you. I wanted everything for you and this is what I get in return?"

"See, Conner? It's all about you. All about Conner." Samantha began to break down and cry.

"I don't know you. Who are you? What have you become, Samantha?"

"No, Conner, you don't know me. You never did. You were too stupid, too much in love with me to figure it out. I could never be who you wanted me to be. No one can."

Archie took hold of Conner's arm and moved him away from her. They stepped through the gate and Archie again told him to walk to the hangar. He then went back to Gordy, who was leaning against the building.

"Mr. Gordy, you are safe now. I am sorry about this, Mr. Gordy. I won't let this happen again."

"I think he broke a rib," Jim moaned. "I am having trouble breathing. I am going to sue this place if I am hurt, Archie. I am not going to stand by and be assaulted by anyone."

"Would you like to make a police report, sir? I'd be glad to call the cops. But I must tell you, we'd have to explain the why as well as the how. I am not sure you want the public notoriety, do you, sir?"

"No. No, Archie. You're right. It will be best not to make a big deal out of this incident. I will be okay, I think. No, no, don't call the authorities."

"Samantha," Gordy yelled, as he saw her walking away from the pool without him.

"Better give her some space, Mr. Gordy," Archie suggested. "The Mrs. seems a little upset."

"She isn't my wife, you ass. Jesus, Archie, haven't you figured out what just happened? That idiot is her husband and he wanted to kick my ass! Now, why would he want to do that? It ain't my fault his wife is fucking around on him, now is it?"

"Don't fuck with family," Archie said quietly, while lighting a cigarette and watching Samantha walk toward the Harrison.

"What did you say, Archie?"

"Oh, nothing, Mr. Gordy. Don't have anything to say, sir. I have other ways of communicating my feelings about all this. Nope, don't like this at all. It's a damn shame, I say, a damn shame."

14

The Imposter

Samantha was trembling as she walked toward the Harrison. Should she speak with Ms. Brooks and have Conner thrown out of the Park? Should she call the police herself? No, she could do nothing. Anything would open a can of worms about why she was there, and who she was with. She would not only be risking public humiliation by the revelation of her affair with Jim, but she would also be risking severe credibility damage to her career, if not to her job, itself.

"Damn it!" she said, out loud.

"Anything wrong?"

Samantha was startled by another voice, and looked up to see Elsie sitting on the front porch swing of the House.

"Oh," Samantha faked a smile. "I just caught my heel on a rock. These pumps are brand new. I'd hate to scuff them, you know?"

Elsie said nothing, just returned the smile and nodded her head as she rocked the swing gently in the breeze.

Not going in there, I guess. Samantha continued on the path around the front of the Harrison, not sure where she was going. She knew she wanted to be away from the pool, the hangar and the House, until she could figure out what to do about Conner.

She walked for several moments, crossed the highway and continued up the path toward the old lodge. Stopping in front of the steps, she looked up and noticed the door was open. Glad to have a diversion from the earlier events of the day, she climbed the stairs and stepped through the doorway. Samantha didn't expect to see someone inside and froze when she saw Emily, who had looked up at the sound of her footsteps.

Christ, isn't there anywhere a person can be alone around here?

"Oh, hi," Emily smiled. She recognized Samantha as one of the passengers on the plane when Austin had first flown her to Blaney.

"Hello," Samantha answered, glancing without interest at the canvas

Emily was sketching on. She walked around behind the easel and looked around the large mess hall styled room. "This is an interesting place."

"Yes, it is," Emily followed Samantha's gaze. "There's lots of history here. It used to be the main place for serving meals, years ago. They'd clear out the tables on Saturday nights, and use it as a dance hall. If these walls could only talk."

"You've obviously taken the history lesson," Samantha said, with faint sarcasm.

"Not really," Emily smiled, as she noticed Samantha was wearing pool attire. "I just know this place. Poolside meetings, today, I assume?"

"I took the day off, not that it's any of your business," Samantha retorted. "You're that pilot's wife, aren't you? Austin Stewart?"

"That's right. I'm Emily. And you are....?"

"Again, none of your business. No offense, but I come here for privacy, not to make friends."

"I see." Emily turned back to her sketching. "Then, if you'll excuse me...."

"A wolf?" Samantha interrupted, as she walked back toward Emily. She stood next to the easel for a moment, and then nodded. "Not bad. You're good. You do that sort of thing for a living?"

"No, not entirely. And, I don't suppose that's any of your business."

Samantha looked blankly at Emily, surprised to have her own style thrown back in her face with such ease. She realized Emily was not intimidated by her one bit and began to feel uncomfortable. Her paranoia about the events by the pool started to grow again and she decided that perhaps she could use a friend or two at Blaney.

"I'm sorry," she smiled, extending her hand to Emily. "My name's Samantha. I apologize for sounding rude. It's just been a horrid week, y'know? Too many meetings. I'm burnt out."

"I understand," Emily shook Samantha's hand briefly. "Sounds like you needed a day at the pool. Where's your husband?"

"My husband?" Samantha panicked, thinking of Conner. Then, she remembered Emily having seen her with Jim on the plane. "Oh, he's not... he's not much for the sun. Walking around the planes by the hangar, I think. What brings you up here?"

"My work," Emily smiled, clearly recognizing that her question had made Samantha uncomfortable. "I'm a writer, actually. I'm researching the wolves in the area." She looked back at her sketch pad. "Ms. Brooks has asked for a portrait to hang in here. It gives me a break from my computer and also from sitting out by the river all day long."

"A writer?" Samantha raised her eyebrows. How interesting, she thought, and how utterly boring. "I would think sitting out in the woods day after day in a place like this would drive you crazy. The research must pay well. What company do you work for?"

"I work for myself," Emily laughed. "And the research pays nothing. The end product will determine its value by its reception with the public."

"You do this for nothing?" Samantha was stunned that someone would actually put such time and energy into anything that didn't provide financial gain. "I didn't think pilots made that much."

"Excuse me?"

"Never mind," she shrugged. "I just can't see doing anything that doesn't have a bottom dollar. How do you rate your effectiveness? Your net worth?"

"I'm not sure we're speaking the same language, Samantha. You come from a very different world than mine. We evaluate our efforts much differently. I don't think I could ever work for a large company. Too much stress for me, thanks."

"That's only because you've never worked for one. It's pretty easy, actually. You get a degree, learn how to talk like a man, how to dress to distract them, and smile. Before you know it, they're buying you lunches and cutting you bonus checks." Samantha laughed and shook her head as she turned and walked down the length of a wooden table. "I've been bullshitting my way through the corporate world for years and getting promoted for nothing but a song. You should try it sometime. You're attractive, and seem intelligent enough. You'd be surprised how much time you'd have for sketching, and enough of a paycheck to go anywhere in the world to do it."

"Thanks for the compliment," Emily leaned back in her director's chair, resting her pencil on her leg. "But I'll stay with the writing." She watched Samantha walk around the room, wondering why this woman seemed so nervous. Who was she, really, and why did Emily sense so much plasticity within her? Samantha stopped in front of the doorway and turned back toward Emily.

"Well, thanks for the chat. Guess I'll head back to the House. It was a pleasure."

"Bye," Emily smiled, as Samantha walked outside. She listened to the clicking of shoes against the cement steps and then as they faded across the blacktop highway. Emily felt sorry for her. This woman seemed very unsettled with her life, a much different perspective than the first one of her Emily had formed during their plane ride together. Samantha seemed pleasant enough, but made Emily terribly uncomfortable. She seemed unreal, like an imposter. Her heavily tanned skin, styled hair and acrylic nails were accentuated by the obvious work of a great surgeon who was paid well to focus on the curves of her figure. Emily sensed an emptiness of character in this woman and wondered how she could be so successful. What were her true talents? Was it really all about how you smiled, as she said? Emily was smarter than that. She knew there were two kinds of women in the business world. Those that were there because they had earned it through hard work and dedication to their field, and those like Samantha.

Emily felt sorry for Samantha, and shook her head. How very sad to be so alone, and so misguided about what really mattered in life. She didn't realize that she had just conversed with Mrs. Conner Morley.

* * * *

Samantha's pace quickened as she walked back toward the Harrison. She was suddenly very concerned about Conner and what he was capable of. She never expected him to find her. What was he doing in Blaney Park? How could he have known about this place? Concern that he had been following her, or having her followed, flooded her mind. She knew he could be a very cold, calculating person and never dreamt she would be the recipient of such actions. She never expected her affair with Jim to be a big deal to Conner. He was so much in love with her, he was sure to forgive her, or so she thought. He would listen to her cry about how Jim had taken advantage of her, and she felt tricked by his affections and concerns for her continuing success at Heritage. She had made a mistake, a terrible mistake, and was certain Conner would forgive her, even though it would force him to go against his value system, against everything he believed in. Samantha was sure that her value to him was greater than his philosophy of life. Now, she realized she was wrong and this terrified her.

Shit, she thought, as she entered the House and hurried upstairs to her room. I need to get back, today. No telling what he's got planned, now.

Samantha called the hangar, and confirmed a seat out that afternoon with Austin. She then packed her things, and called for Archie to come after her bags.

"Leaving so soon?" he sneered at her, when he entered the foyer. Samantha rose from the chair where she sat waiting by her bag and walked past him towards the door.

"I'll meet you at the plane," she snapped.

"Afternoon, Miss Elsie," Archie nodded at Elsie, who had walked in from the kitchen.

"Was that Mrs. Gordy, Archie?" she asked, and then looked at her bags. "I thought she was staying until Friday?"

"Nope," he smiled. "Had a reaction to something earlier today at the pool. Sour bottle of sunscreen, I think. She decided to go back. Probably needs a couple of days at her spa, wouldn't you think?"

Elsie just laughed, and shook her head at Archie. He winked, and picked up Samantha's bags. As he left the Harrison, he felt good at seeing Elsie smile so. He knew he could always make her laugh and it pleased him. It was the one thing at Blaney Park he indulged in. Elsie's smiles kept him young.

When he reached the entry to the airstrip, Austin was waiting with the plane already prepped. Archie placed the bags into the cargo hold and secured the door. He waved to Austin, who stood talking with Samantha, signaling that all was ready for flight. Austin and Samantha boarded the plane.

Austin soon started the engines and pulled away from the hangar. After the plane had taxied out to the end of the runway, Conner stepped out of the hangar into sight. Archie didn't even need to turn around to know that he was there.

"It's a damn shame, son," Archie said loudly, as the plane took off above them. They both watched as Austin turned back toward the southeastern sky.

"I'm not far behind her," Conner said. "Todd should be here any minute."

"Yup," replied Archie. "You want me to go get your bags?"

"No need, Archie. I went after them while you were attending to Samantha. Thanks for all your help, sir." Conner extended his hand to Archie.

"My pleasure, son," Archie shook his hand. "Don't you worry about that Gordy fellow. I'll take good care of him for you."

"Thanks, Archie," Conner looked up as he heard Todd's plane approaching. "Guess that's my ride."

Todd pulled up by the hangar only long enough to allow Archie to assist with refueling and Conner to board. He wanted to get Conner out of Blaney Park as quickly as possible, before Conner reconsidered allowing Jim Gordy to live. Once they were airborne, Archie lit a cigarette and stared toward the woods.

Better check those traps tonight, he thought, inhaling the smoke deeply into his lungs. Haven't been out to the clearing in a few days. Gonna be a clear night, good night for a feeding.

Archie snuffed out his cigarette against the sole of his shoe and tossed the butt into an old coffee can beside the hangar door. He then started toward the cabins, on his final rounds for the evening to make sure that the guests of Blaney Park would have what they needed for the night.

15

Guess Who's Coming To Dinner

Archie knocked on the door of Jim Gordy's room. Jim opened it, and wasn't surprised to see Archie standing in the hallway.

"Come on in, Arch. That fucking husband of Sam's is crazy! Did you see that asshole go after me? Jesus! What the hell was that all about? I am going to get that guy when he least expects it, you can bet on that. Doesn't he know I have money?"

"He seemed to be a little pissed off," Archie nodded and entered the room. "Don't see many men get that pissed off anymore. Used to see it all the time back when men were allowed to throw a few punches, make their point with a few fisticuffs without being afraid of being killed or jailed."

"That was more than fisticuffs. I could see it in his eyes. Hell, he was actually smiling during some of it, like it was what he likes to do on a Sunday. He scared the hell out of me, Archie, when he started laughing about it. I was shitting my pants! I have never even been in a fight before, y'know."

Archie smiled at Jim's confession, as he removed a cigarette from the pack in his shirt pocket. He rolled it between his fingers for a moment, saying nothing, and then gently placed it in his mouth. After a few moments, he retrieved a matchbook, also from the shirt pocket, and lit the cigarette. He dropped the match on the floor. It was only then that he raised his eyes to Jim.

"Don't smoke in my room, Archie."

Archie inhaled from the cigarette slowly, and blew the smoke directly towards Jim. He had been catering to Jim and Samantha for two years, and he knew all about them. They had been coming to Blaney Park regularly during this time, acting as if it were their own private resort. Archie knew all about them. It was his job. It was his passion. It was his life.

Jim was never mean, but was a horrible tipper and whined about everything under the Upper Peninsula sun. To Archie, he would talk about his wife and two kids, and how he didn't much like being married. He liked to play around and find women who would have him because of his money and position, and then let them go when he was tired of them. Samantha was the longest affair he had ever had, and why not? She was moving up in the organization, and her knowledge and connections had business value to him. He had the best of both worlds with this one. Besides, how Samantha dressed would cause any man to stray if they had the inclination. She left only enough unseen to make all the men around the office take notice. Archie never said much to Jim, he would just listen. Never confirm or deny. Never give his opinion.

Now, as he listened, Archie thought back to when he had tossed Samantha's bags into the luggage compartment of Austin's plane while she stood nearby, pretending to adjust her hair in an imaginary reflection from the smooth side of the plane. He only asked her one question.

"Where is Mr. Gordy?" he had asked her.

"Sulking, I suppose," Samantha had shrugged and looked away. "Why should I care where he is? He can be such an ass. I told him to walk back to Detroit." She stopped suddenly, aware that she had spoken openly to Archie. "It is really none of your business, Mr. Phillips, why we fought, or where he is. He's staying back and will take another of Mr. Stewart's flights within the next couple of days. I have to get back to work and, quite frankly, I need to be alone. Feel free to take care of Mr. Gordy anyway you see fit."

Archie had smiled, pleased to learn that Jim would not be leaving just yet. He would be glad to take care of Mr. Gordy, in his own way. Austin had then emerged from the hangar, flight plan in hand, and walked up to Samantha.

"All set. Let's board. There's a storm blowing in later today and I want to get as far ahead of the front as possible. Are you sure your husband will not be joining us?"

"Yes, I am sure," Samantha had replied, not wanting to be referred to as Mrs. Gordy. It wasn't as convenient, now that Conner had found her and she didn't know who knew what about the situation. She just wanted to get on the plane and far away from Blaney Park.

Archie watched Austin's plane until it leveled out on its southern path for Detroit, and did the same when Conner left with Todd shortly afterwards. He had turned to the Harrison, with a clear agenda for the evening. He was going to provide Mr. Gordy his special service. A service reserved for only those unique issues such as this.

Now, Archie stood listening and exhaling deeply, blowing cigarette smoke across the room, as Jim looked at him inquisitively. There was something different about Archie tonight that made Jim uncomfortable.

"Come on, Jim," Archie finally said, as he blew out a slow drag of the cigarette. "I want to show you something." He opened the door and stepped into the hallway.

"Will you help me fuck up that Conner guy, Archie?" Jim followed him.

"Sure, I will help you, Mr. Gordy. I first need to show you how this is done, though. I need your permission, sir. I don't do anything in life without permission."

"Okay, okay. You have my permission. I'll go with you." Jim smiled, feeling that Archie was equally angry with Conner. He saw how Archie catered to Conner, and figured Archie was looking for some pay back because of the fight. "As long as you will help me kick the shit out of that Conner guy."

"Why would a man want to fight you, Mr. Gordy?"

Jim's mind began racing. Didn't I tell Archie I'm fucking Conner's wife? He wondered now if this information would help or hurt his chances to get Archie's assistance, something Jim desperately needed. He decided to lie.

"We were in a business relationship, me and Conner. Samantha had a part in it, too, and, after a while, Conner felt he was being mistreated in the negotiations."

"Uh huh," Archie blew out another puff of his cigarette. They had reached the path that led into the woods.

There was a slight cool breeze that evening. The moon was full and bright. The trees were full with leaves and swaying, casting shadows in the moonlight on the ground. While most of the trees were huge pine trees, there were intermittent oak and maple. All the different kinds of trees that fine quality furniture would someday be made from once the business deal with Derek Stroebel was made.

Archie walked slowly, side by side with Jim, who was beginning to get agitated. His movements were impatient and he continued to question Archie about why they were out walking through the woods in the first place.

"Where are we going, anyway?" he demanded. "Hey, can I have one of those?"

Archie was reaching into his pocket for another cigarette, and ignored Jim's request. He simply lit it, returned the matches to his pocket and kept walking. He always got a chuckle out of the fact that Jim would try to get free cigarettes from him, when he knew that Jim made over a quarter million dollars a year. Archie could always tell a cheater, as they would cheat everything and everyone all the time, no matter the situation. Jim most likely thought that Archie only made minimum wage and that a pack was something special, being what it cost nowadays. Yet, in all the years Jim and Samantha had been coming up to Blaney Park, Archie got a mere five percent tip for all he did for them and nothing more, not even a pack of cigs.

"We're almost there, Mr. Gordy," Archie raised his voice a little, as Jim had stopped walking, tired of being led into the woods. Archie continued ahead of him. "I will give you what you deserve once we get there. You do want what you deserve, don't you, Mr. Gordy?"

Mr. Gordy, Jim smiled at Archie's show of respect to him, and began walking again. Archie said Mr. Gordy on purpose to keep Jim's confidence and attention. Wanna-be men always reacted to Sir and Mr., and Archie knew this well.

They approached the opening of a small clearing, beautifully lit by the moon. From their view, the large white moon seemed to be directly in the middle of the clearing and one would have had to be dead not to appreciate the sight of such a God-given gift as the view that was in front of them. Archie did take that moment and cherished it. The tree tops shifted, as their branches and leaves swayed on the backdrop of the dark sky.

The breeze was stronger in the clearing, and it was a refreshing feeling to Archie. His cancer-filled lungs, weak from many years of smoking, inhaled deeply as he enjoyed every second of the experience. If God could heal man's diseases, Archie knew it would be done at a place such as Blaney Park. At that moment, he felt young again.

As they stood at the edge of the clearing, Archie thought briefly about the day he first arrived there, many years past. He just showed up one day, and asked for a job. Elsie Brooks liked him. He was not a good looking man, and carried the scars of a teenage complexion problem as well as many that he would never explain. However, he could be a charmer, in his own way, and was a great guide for the guests. He was an excellent fisherman and many a guest would tip him generously for all the fish they had caught and how much fun they had experienced. Many a parent brought a child suffering from a fatal disease to Blaney Park. It was known as a place where they could see what good God could do. With Archie teaching them how to catch, clean and eat fish, these kids would always leave with a smile, in contrast to their arrival when they carried the look of death.

Archie was reflecting in the moonlight about his life, and realized that he really didn't have a family, after all. At a very young age, he had made decisions that cost him the opportunity to become the alpha for a pack of his own. Oh, he was fertile, and capable of shooting quality bullets, but he would never place any woman and kids into the life for which he lived. There were reasons why men came to places like this and live out their survival. Archie was no different.

Elsie Brooks soon stopped fearing Archie, and began to love him like a brother. Archie was good to her, as well as all the guests. She often expressed that her best business decision was to hire him. He never said much, never asked for anything, but did his work and did his own thing.

Rumors around the area were that Archie poached animals - different animals. Like any relationship or situation, when someone likes you and hears rumors about you, most likely they will turn a deaf ear. Elsie Brooks spent years turning a deaf ear to the whispers of Archie's nighttime workings of the grounds. Each year, he would give generously to the schools in the area, and many wondered what he did to make his money. One year, the football program was at risk due to lack of funding. Archie walked right into the principal's office and told him to call the Board, the school had the money. So, while people thought he was doing illegal activity, they didn't work too hard to bust him since he did so much for his community.

Archie finished his cigarette and beneath the illumination of the moon ground its remains into the ground with the toe of his shoe. He was startled from his thoughts by the appearance of a man dressed in black with a dark hood covering his head. The man approached Jim from behind and grabbed his arms.

"Hey!" yelled Jim, as the man took him down hard, face first, to the ground. "What the hell is going on? You are hurting me, you mother fucker! Archie, Archie...help me! You son-of-a-bitch, just don't stand there like a coward!"

The man in black placed his knee in Jim's back and put handcuffs on his wrists. He placed a broom handle between Jim's elbows, in and out of his arms. This technique was used for much bigger people than Jim Gordy. The man in the black hood was a pro and knew what he was doing. The fear of death combined with pain and caused distortion in Jim's face. His mind had not yet registered that his life was about over.

"Arch, man, what's this about, man? I thought you and I were close. I thought you were going to help me?"

"Don't call me Arch," Archie reached into his pocket for another cancer stick. He raised it to his lips, and lit it. "Who in the hell ever gave you the permission to call me Arch? I always tell you one thing. Each and every time you arrive on Mr. Austin's plane, I tell you one thing. Do you remember what that one thing is, Mr. Gordy?"

Jim didn't even have to think about it. Every time for the two-and-a-half years, when he would approach Archie to give him his shitty tip, Archie would say, 'Don't fuck with my family.' The first time it happened, it bothered Jim. He asked a few people around Blaney Park about Archie, even the desk clerk, and all would just say Archie was a little different. Never mind Archie, they would say to Jim, he's had something happen to him in his life that don't make him right.

"Don't fuck with family. That is what you told me, Archie."

"So, why did you continue to fuck with my family?"

"Archie, you crazy son of a bitch! What are you talking about? I don't fuck with your family."

Archie looked down to where he had twisted his last cigarette into the dirt beneath his shoe. He then leaned down and dug his fingers into the ground, pulling up a clump of dirt and mossy grass. As he stood back up, he covered the cigarette with the dirt and then packed it down neatly with his shoe. Archie loved these woods and he made sure he was never the reason they died. He had seen too much death in his life. And some of it, he would admit to himself, he had actually enjoyed.

A smile came to his mouth, as he still had the next cigarette in it, and it was followed by a backhand across Jim's mouth. Jim collapsed, suspended by the huge man behind him and the broom handle between his arms. He was trying to get to the fetal position to protect himself, just like he did with Conner. Not this time. Archie's ways were more refined than Conner's. Archie and the man in the black hood knew what they were doing as if they had done it before, and Jim sensed it.

"That was for me," Archie said as blood began to trickle from Jim's lip. "Me and everyone whose had to hear your voice, your laugh and your demands, you asshole. I don't like leeches. I feed them to my fish. And, I don't like you. I am feeding you to my wolves." With that, Archie took a small rubber ball from his pocket. The man with the black hood grabbed a handful of Jim's hair and jerked his head backward, causing Jim's mouth to instinctively open from both the pain of his hair being pulled and the fear inside of his belly causing him to suck for more air. Archie's movement was swift as he thrust the ball into Jim's open mouth. Jim's response was a very short and weak moan, barely loud enough to be heard by the man behind him.

Archie always carried his blade. It was normal to see him with it. Jim never thought much of it, until now. Archie's hand slowly pulled it from its long, leather sleeve, gently placed the steel edge alongside Jim's cheek and drew blood from it.

Jim could do nothing. Tears were beginning to flow freely from his eyes as he choked and gurgled, attempting to scream for his life. But, the small rubber ball was now lodged securely within his mouth, preventing any discussion or catcall from him.

"Yes, I do poach animals, Jim," Archie lifted the blade in the moonlight and allowed the blood from Jim's cheek to run slowly along the shiny metal blade. "You asked me that question once, and I did not answer. You have asked me a lot of questions, Jim, and I never asked you one. In the two and a half years of speaking to you, have I ever asked you a question?"

Jim's tears were flowing harder now, and beads of perspiration were falling from his forehead down his temples to intermingle with the tears running down along his cheekbones to his neck. He slowly shook his head back and forth.

"That's right, Jim. I never asked you a question. I just made one simple statement each and every time you came here." Archie slowly lifted his blade to Jim's other cheek, and drew a fine line in the skin, allowing more blood to spill onto it. "Don't fuck with family. Isn't that what I told you? Hey, Jim, guess what? I am asking the questions now. How interesting it is you are not answering me. Oh yeah, you are shaking your head. But, hey, aren't you the guy who asked me a question and, when I answered with a simple nod of the head, it was you who said 'Don't you shake your head at me, I want a verbal answer any time I address you.' Wasn't that what you said to me, Jim? Like I was your boy, or something. Fuck you, man!" Archie laughed and leaned forward, placing his eyes directly in front of Jim's face.

"So, how did Sam lick you, Jim?" Archie leaned closer and licked Jim's cheek where the blood still trickled from the lance of the blade. "I eat blood from every one of my kill. It makes me one with them. It makes me understand their purpose in life. Everyone has to have a purpose in life, don't you agree, Jim?"

Jim made soft, gurgling noises as he nodded his head up and down in agreement. Archie's blade swung and buried deeply into Jim's left thigh, releasing a gush of blood. Jim could not move and he could not scream. All the pain remained inside of him and Archie knew exactly what he was doing. All the cuts, when and where they were delivered, were all for good reason.

Archie nodded his head to the man in the mask, who jerked Jim to attention. Archie reached out and unbuckled Jim's belt, unfastened and unzipped his pants. Jim's eyes were rolling backward, as his fear was approaching unconsciousness. He wanted to faint, wanted to die, yet he remained helpless. By now, Jim had to realize he was a dead person. The thoughts that were racing through his mind were not wasted on Archie, who was asking himself, what is this dead man thinking? God, I love this shit. If I could only get in this guy's mind to know what he was thinking during his journey to death.

Archie then bent down, pulling Jim's pants with him. He couldn't pull them down completely because the material of his pant leg had sunken into the muscle of his thigh with the thrust of the blade. Archie didn't care, as he had exposed all that he needed to expose.

"So, you like to fuck my nephew's wife, huh, Jim?" Archie always loved this part of the process. The truth was told and the victim realized why this was all happening Jim's eyes were as big as the shining moon above, now. Archie could see right in those eyes, and Jim now knew why.

"I tell you what, Jim. I will let you go," Archie paused to take a hit from his cigarette, "if you can get a hard-on." Archie's experience with life and death was deep. He, himself, had been left for dead many times, only to succeed in pulling through the grips of death and surviving. He knew he was bluffing by providing the one thing that Jim wanted right then. Hope.

Archie reached down and began to fondle Jim's genitalia.

"Come on, Jimmy boy. Think about Sam, you know those times I looked through a cabin window when you were getting a blowjob or you were behind her fucking for all you had. Yeah, Jim, you do remember." Archie knew it was instinctive. When a person was approaching death, they were also approaching ecstasy. The same brain chemicals that cause pleasure are also extracted by pain, and Archie knew this well. He just had to encourage Jim's brain to get into the correct state of thinking. With Jim's hard-on in hand, Archie drew nearer to his face.

"Fuck you," he whispered. "Fuck you for betraying your family, you asshole. Your wife, son and daughter will never see your cheating ass again. And, most of all, fuck you for fucking with my family!"

With that, the hooded man placed his knee squarely in Jim's back and jerked his shoulders back, causing Jim to arch backward, fully exposing his member. Archie swung the blade downward and sliced Jim's penis off near the testicles. The hooded man let Jim go, and he crumbled to the ground. The hooded man bent over Jim and removed the handcuffs. He then cut Jim's shirt off of him and removed all of his jewelry. Shoes and socks followed and lastly his pants and boxers. Archie knew Jim wasn't in any greater pain than he was with the chop to the thigh. What would be haunting Jim at that moment was the knowledge that his penis had just been completely severed and his dignity of his clothes lost. Not even death was more a priority to him in his mind than the fact that his manhood had just been taken from him.

The human body, with two main arteries cut, would die within minutes. Jim was a dead man breathing. Archie's only regret was that he could not be inside Jim's mind and know what his last thoughts were before going to hell.

Archie waited for the last breath of life to leave Jim's limp body. He knelt and said a prayer, not for Jim, but for his own soul and for Conner's.

Don't fuck with family. Archie completed his prayer, stood and slowly reached into his pocket for another cigarette. He found the last one and made sure it was distinguished. As he struck a match, the man with the black hood left without speaking a word. His duty was finished.

Archie sucked deeply from the cigarette and looked to the edge of the woods. The moon provided so much light Archie could easily see the wolves gathering at the edge of the trees. The cool breeze relaxed him. He knew that when he completed his cigarette and walked away, Jim would become wolf meal. For over 25 years, Archie carefully skinned the animals caught in his poaching traps, and brought the carcasses to this place. The wolves looked forward to moonlit deliveries of easy food.

With wolves, as with people, there are both good and bad packs. The bad were the ones Archie was in business with. They always wanted a free meal, and were willing to wait for it. Archie knew that when he walked away, Jim would be gone forever. There would be growling, and the sounds of ripping flesh, as the scavengers would shred Jim's body within minutes. What little remained would be spread across miles in every direction within the hour. Not even the bones would be spared. Wolves used bones to sharpen and clean their teeth after such a large feast. Jim was their bonus for many years of service.

Archie finished his cigarette and extinguished the lit bud down in Jim's ear and walked away with a smile.

"I told him," he laughed out loud. "I told him, don't fuck with family! Don't fuck with my family! Maybe he will listen now with a cigarette in his ear." Archie was speaking to no one and laughed aloud at his own words.

As Archie left the clearing, he heard the loping of the wolves as they raced to their feast. Soon the air was filled with snarling and sounds of tearing flesh and Archie knew the process had begun for an ending that he would never witness. He considered, for a brief moment, returning to the scene to be sure that all was gone, but thought otherwise. He had never done that before, and it would startle the wolves if he changed his routine, possibly causing them to turn on him. He continued his walk to the cabins and, upon reaching the door to the one Jim and Samantha used for privacy, he stopped and went in. He walked to the refrigerator and opened it to retrieve a Michelob Light. He then walked back out of the cabin and sat down in the log chair that was placed in front on the porch. He opened his beer and sipped it slowly. After about twenty minutes, much longer than Archie was expecting, the night air was pierced by the faint sounds of howling.

Archie closed his eyes and leaned back against the chair. It was done. The wolves had each taken their share and were praying for the Gods to bless their food. When the howling ceased, Archie stood up. He reached over and pulled the cabin door shut, and then turned to make his way back to his hangar, in anticipation of another day. He felt young again. He loved taking out the slime of the world, more than he liked to admit.

16

Blow Your House Down

Four hours earlier.

Conner didn't even remember getting into his Lexus and making the trip from the Oakland County Airport to his home in Birch Lake. His mind was filled with all that had occurred with his father, Rick's words, and then finding Jim and Samantha together at Blaney Park. It wasn't the right time for any of this. Conner never got the chance to tell Samantha how serious his dad's cancer was. To his knowledge, maybe she wouldn't even care anymore. Maybe she never did.

Conner needed her, he loved her and he had a deep passion for her. He met her at Heritage Technologies and had helped her be successful, for God's sake. She told him how valuable he was to her and her career. Many nights, she would come home sobbing about how she felt isolated in a corporate man's world. He would listen, and then put those bigots in their rightful place for her, while helping her build confidence and resolve to overcome them. He would defuse them, allowing a proper mind set for her in the work force. He inspired her to stand tall and to let her presence be the strength, rather than her gender the weakness.

He could hardly drive. His body was shaking, and his heart was racing. He wasn't sure he would make it home. She'd be at the house. She wouldn't go to the condo on this day, after everything that had happened. She would certainly want to speak with Conner. He felt all injustices to the core, yet believed all volatile situations could be resolved through open, honest dialog. He knew in the man's world, most men didn't know how to communicate. They would pull a pistol out and shoot themselves in the head, rather than sit down and try to tell someone their feelings. Conner's mom was a great communicator and taught him the value of conversation, even those that could occur with a raised voice and a few cursed words. That was what Conner was about to do. He called information for Jim's home address and number.

Hell, did I just run a red light? Conner glanced in his rear-view mirror.

His mind was focused on deciding his strategies rather than with his driving. Driving was just a necessary task to get him from the airport to his home. If Conner had his way, he would have simply instructed Todd to land on the front lawn and fuck what the neighbors would think about a Saab SF-340 twin-jet propelled plane suddenly turning their quiet street into a landing strip. He should have allowed Todd to drive him home and then he'd have had the time he needed. He had the resources to find the number all along, but there was no need to. He had previously discussed with Samantha her relationship with Jim. While Jim seemed too old, too fat and too self consumed to be any risk to Conner, she was easily influenced by any man who would seemingly help her career. Samantha would be blinded to all things important to her personal life if she thought being with Jim would assist her in advancing to the next corporate level.

Conner was concerned about her tendency to become infatuated with men of power and position, especially now that he had detached his career from hers. He no longer had a finger on the pulse of what she was doing. He had many issues and tasks for his own business, keeping them in the lifestyle they had become accustomed to, yet constantly worked to make sure they had quality time together. More often than not, it was Samantha who had a meeting or business trip and couldn't keep a dinner date or, even worse, manage to make it home to sleep in the same bed with her husband.

All possibilities now flooded Conner's mind. He embraced all the unconscious thinking that he had previously fought to the back of his mind so not to go crazy or mistrust Samantha so much that he would resent her for how she treated him.

The voice in the phone shocked him back to reality and allowed him to see the red traffic light in front of him. He stopped, just barely, before crossing the intersection. Good thing to, for as he was putting his mobile phone on speaker, he looked across the road and saw a Birch Lake police cruiser sitting at the corner, pointed directly at him. He'd have been pulled over, for sure, for this violation. And, Conner knew that he would have run from the cop until he had reached his driveway.

Shoot me dead or wrestle me to the ground and handcuff me, he thought, but I will be home with Samantha tonight, and be there soon.

"Mrs. Gordy, I presume?" Conner knew the routine.

"Yes, this is Mrs. Gordy," the woman's voice was pleasing. "May I help you?"

"You sure can, ma'am. I work with your husband at the Heritage Technologies and I understand he's away for a business meeting?"

"Yes, he is. He and an associate, Sam, I believe is his name, are traveling on business again."

As if he's working so hard for you and your two kids, Conner thought. Sam, huh?

Conner had the mindset to tell her right off, but knew his objectives needed to be met before he cleaned up on all the other peripheral players in this full blown act of betrayal.

"Well, we have an emergency situation with a very important customer and need Jim's counsel. This is a critical account for Jim and he needs to stay on top of it. However, we seem to have misplaced his cell phone and pager information. He'd be upset if he knew we were unable to contact him on this issue. So, if you could give his numbers to me, I think he'd be pleased that we contacted him, as it is also pertinent to that same meeting he is having with Sam. He will not be pleased to learn we called you for his number, however, interrupting your family's evening. I do apologize for that. I have a performance review coming up, and even though I don't work directly for Jim, I'd like to make sure he gets what he deserves. You understand, don't you, Mrs. Gordy?"

"I certainly do. I have had others calling me for Jim's number and some of them have seemed a little upset. I don't know how you people work under such pressure. Jim told me to never to give out his number, but you sound like a nice enough man, Mr...., what did you say your name was?"

"Morley... My name is Conner Morley, and you can let your husband know that I called when you tell him you have given me his number. I don't feel the least bit concerned about that, Mrs. Gordy."

"Well.... okay. His number is 555-8366."

"Thank you, Mrs. Gordy. You have a wonderful evening."

"You, too, Mr. Morley. Good-bye, now."

Conner ended the call. The light was turning green while he was turning red. He never liked men who cheated, but had never known a man who cheated with his own wife. Conner was not feeling too well and wanted to make sure Jim was not feeling any relief just because Conner was taken away from Blaney Park. No way would Samantha be so abusive to actually be with

Jim tonight. She would at least have the decency to be home, waiting to dialog with Conner about why she did this to him, and to their marriage. Conner dialed Jim's number. Never expecting an answer, he got one.

"Hello, Jim Gordy speaking."

"Mr. Gordy?" Conner spoke calmly, as if it were a business deal. "Mr. Morley here. James," he used the proper, given name, knowing it would confuse his combatant. Conner never liked the name Jim, anyway. He preferred James. This conversation would be Conner's way. "I just had a nice talk with your wife. Helen, right? She is a charming lady, Mr. Gordy."

"Please leave my wife out of this, Conner."

""Ha!" Conner laughed. "Please leave my wife out of this? James, James, James. What happened to the part of this scenario where you were supposed to leave my wife out of it? You fuck head." Conner cursed at Jim as if he just gave him a compliment. No change of tone, just smooth, confident and calm, even though his insides were frying and his heart was not just breaking, but falling apart.

"Conner, I didn't mean for this to happen. It just did. I had no intentions of ever being with Sam. We've been working together and all of a sudden we were sharing some personal information and we fell in love."

"Oh, so you love my wife, huh?"

"Well, no... yes... I don't know, Conner."

"Do you love your wife, James? Do you love your kids?"

"I don't know if I love my wife, but I do love my kids."

"Hear this, James. If you go near my wife again, you better make sure you take your time kissing your kids goodnight each evening, because something might just happen to them. Your life will never be routine again. It won't be so easy saying goodnight to your kids, if they aren't around. Do I make myself clear, Jim?"

"Clear."

"Do I make myself clear, Jim?"

"Crystal," Jim smiled, reminiscing about one of his own favorite movies. It was his only way to process what was happening as a fantasy, rather than the reality of his own ensuing death.

Conner's firm was one of Heritage Technologies' strategic partners. He knew many people there and many knew him. He was known for his competitive spirit, always participating in sports on the most competitive city leagues and that, combined with his upbringing and stories about a few violent confrontations he had as a teen, made him someone most dared not confront. For a corporate player, Conner did not grow up with a silver spoon in his mouth. He was a city kid to the core and even his mannerisms and dialect made it obvious to all that he was not country-club raised.

Several had approached Jim, warning him that he was messing with the wrong guy's wife. But love makes people do stupid things and Jim had been caught with his hand in the cookie jar.

Conner ended their call without another word, and Jim stared at his cell phone.

Where the hell is Archie? he thought to himself. I need that 'ol poacher. He will help me. He likes me, thinks I am a real player. I will pay him to take care of Conner, and he's just crazy enough to do it. Conner just threatened his kids and that scared the hell out of Jim.

As Conner continued to drive in the darkness, he realized he had just started something he may have to finish. To declare war and not proceed with the battle would not be smart. Conner hated this world. He never chose to be there, but he didn't know how to cope any other way. Eye for an eye. It was the way of the streets and it was survival of the fittest. Samantha had given him no other way out. She had placed the gun in his hand and now he was going to use it against everyone and everything that wronged him, including her, if necessary.

He began to cry. He could not hold it in. He would cry during private moments before an event to make sure the tears were purged so that no matter what pain or position he was put into, he would have his emotions in control. Crying was a conflict to Conner. His dad would never allow a tear, and would beat Conner if he shed even one. His dad raised a man, while his mom raised character. She would always sense when Conner was on the edge of breaking down, and give him a smile, before taking him to a private place where she would hold him close while allowing him to exude his true heart and soul. She let the hurt out, so it wouldn't harden Conner and make him impenetrable, like it did her husband. She wanted her son to have the sensitivity and heart of a man who could reach out to those he loved and express his desires. A man who could be a father and not just a provider of material need who would allow closeness and not feel weak in his child's presence.

Conner had become the man his mother wanted him to be, but he still had his dad's ways, too. They were conflicting values he struggled with often and he never enjoyed his dad's way. Those ways were what kept him alive and were how he gained respect from his homeys in the streets.

He kept driving. What good was life if your own family, your own wife, betrayed you? Conner had known loyalty and support from his own family. No matter the crisis, first there was dialog and then action that led to resolution. The force of the action depended on the effectiveness of the dialog. It was the same here. Without realizing it, he had reached out and given Jim a chance most of his peers would not. Where Conner came from, you don't cut the head off first, you cut off the appendages. First the fingers, then the arms. First the toes, then the foot. You cut off those things that bring the most pain to allow the brain, the heart and the soul to understand. It allows the central processing unit, the heart, and the disk memory, the brain, process all that was happening until the person wants to die, begs to be unplugged and taken out of misery.

Often, on television, people get whacked. The duck shows no pain. Not true in the streets. Death is a favor in Conner's world. Pain is what hurts. He would not whack Jim right off. He would go after the kids, then the wife. He'd have Jim begging for Conner to hurt him, not his family. It would get so bad that Helen might even put a bullet in Jim because of all the pain he brought to their family before Conner would ever need to touch him. And, if Conner did ever get to Jim, pain, lots of pain, would be inflicted before the unplug would occur.

Conner reached his own exclusive neighborhood and took the turn onto his street at 50 and accelerating from there. He couldn't wait to be with her, to dialog and get this all resolved. He didn't want a divorce and would try to be open minded to her story. Certainly, she must still love him. Hell, they had sex just the other week. Sure, it was the same old lay-there-and-take-it technique that Samantha preferred, but they did make love, so he thought.

He didn't even bother to open the garage door. He stopped short in the driveway and ran to the front door. Her Mercedes must be in the garage. She must be in the house. The front door and it was locked. Conner pulled out his key and opened it.

"Samantha?" He shouted her name. No reply. He ran to all the rooms in the house, thinking she was so ashamed that she must be grieving in one of the rooms. Downstairs, upstairs, outside on the porch.

"Samantha!"

She was not there.

Conner stood in the middle of their living room. He was devastated by her absence. He didn't understand and now judged her harshly.

"That bitch!"

The phone rang.

"What!" Conner answered.

"I am so sorry, Conner." A faint voice came through the receiver.

"Samantha, Samantha..." he breathed with relief, "where are you? Please come home. Will you just come home so we can talk? We need to talk, sunshine."

"No, Conner. I don't want to come home. I am at the condo. Conner, I am so sorry. I didn't mean for you to get hurt."

Conner was in disbelief at her words, yet tried to stay focused and calm.

"Samantha. Please come home. We can't fix this with you there and me here. We've been apart too long, we need to be together and talk, honey. Please, come home. I will send a car to pick you up, Hell, I will come get you myself. This whole episode is breaking my heart."

"I am home, Conner. This is my home."

"What do you mean, that is your home? This is our home. I purchased that place so you'd be rested for work, not to take the place of home! Not find space away from me, from us."

"Conner, I am confused and I don't know what I am doing. I am so sorry for hurting you. Are you okay? What were you doing at Blaney Park? I can't believe you and Jim got into a fight. Why do you fight everyone, Conner?"

"Me? Samantha, what are you saying? I was fighting for you. I was fighting for us! What did you want me to do? Just say, 'okay, Jim, you can have my wife. I am not going to say anything, so just let me know when I fit in, and give her back when you are done with her?' No fucking way. I will fight for us, Samantha. I will die for you!"

"Don't swear cuss at me, Conner. I don't like swearing, you know that."

"Oh, but adultery you like, huh? What are you doing, Samantha? Please come home, please."

"No. I am going to stay here tonight, Conner. I think we need space."

Conner paused before responding to her.

"What we need to do is talk. Who is Jim to you, Samantha?" Conner's heart was beating out of his chest as he waited for her response. He knew at some points in life there are defining moments, and this was one of them. Not just for Samantha, but for him, as well. He had his mindset. She betrayed him and he was working at overcoming it. But, if she betrayed him with this answer, he was lost to her. He knew he would have a difficult time with anything but a heartfelt apology and her assurance that Jim was just a toy who she used, once again, to advance her career.

"I have deep feelings for Jim, Conner. I don't know what I feel for him, exactly. We have gotten very close and I know I want to continue to see him."

"Do you love him?"

"I don't know if I know what love is, Conner."

"Do you love me?"

"I don't know."

"You fucking bitch! I can't believe you! You are fucking around on me, and now I want to talk to you about it and you give me this? What kind of shit is this?"

Conner tore the cord out of the wall, threw the phone on the ground and stomped on it. He looked at the counter. Several greeting cards he had purchased to give to Samantha lay neatly in a pile. He gave her cards often, to show her he was thinking of her. With his fist, he started to beat on top of those cards. The thickness of the pile kept him from breaking his hand as he viciously pounded the counter, until the marble top finally broke through. Conner knew how much that island was enjoyed by her. The kitchen was her source of pride even though she wasn't home much to enjoy it.

The phone rang again. Conner ran to the next available phone, the one in the office, and calmly picked up the receiver, saying nothing. He knew it was her.

"Are you done?"

"Am I done doing what?"

"Verbally abusing your wife?"

"Abusing you? Are you serious?"

"Yes. I could call the cops on you right now for what you just said to me."

"You are joking, right?" Conner was unsuccessful at holding back his laughter. "Tell me you are trying to make light of this situation in order to defuse us and not that you are so brain dead that you are actually accusing me of anything at this point! What did you do to me? You don't call that abuse? Fucking around on me, taking a rendezvous to Europe with this guy and calling it a business trip. Jesus, Sam! Are you feeling okay? Are you on drugs or something?"

"I am going to see Jim until I figure out who I love. I don't want to make a mistake here, Conner. I don't know what I want."

"So, you expect me to just sit here and wait until you fuck Jim's brains out and then decide 'okay, I have chosen who fucks the best? Bull shit! You can kiss my ass, bitch! Fuck you! Call the fucking cops, bitch. I am calling the insane asylum for you, as you have totally lost your mind!"

With that, Conner threw the cordless phone on the hardwood floor and it scattered into pieces. He then took the base and launched it on the floor with the receiver and it also shattered. Then, the phone rang again. Conner ran to the bedroom and picked up the receiver.

"Don't touch my stuff."

"What?"

"Don't touch my stuff."

"Take your stuff? What do you mean, your stuff?" Conner said, in a soft controlled voice, breathless from the rapid heartbeat from destroying the phones.

"Don't touch my stuff," she repeated.

"You mean our stuff."

"No, Conner. I am getting it all. I talked to the lawyers and they said I will have no problem getting what I want out of the house."

"Oh, is that right?"

"Yes, that is right and I want it as I left it, asshole!" Samantha hung up.

Conner kept the phone to his ear and heard the dial tone, followed by the beeping noise that Ma Bell shrieks when a phone is off the hook for too long. A smile came to his face, as his eyes turned cold and distant. He looked at the phone that was in his hand and then at the mirror that hung on the wall. Conner had bought it for her. He got a nice night in the sack for that purchase. One pitch and the glass shattered everywhere.

He then walked to her huge closet and began to pull every piece of clothing off the hangers while shuffling the neatly placed shoes to the sides of the closet. He made a total mess. In his destruction, he threw a shoe box that did not contain shoes. The lid came off, scattering cards and letters everywhere. They were love letters. Letters from Jim. Some asked Samantha what color panties she wore. Some asked what she wanted to do to him the next time they met. One described a negligee she had purchased for their trip to Europe. There were also cards for Jim, already signed and waiting for the proper moment to share. He choked, as he noticed that several she had received were dated three years back.

Conner began to cry uncontrollably now, as he realized that his marriage had been a lie all that time. Here he was fighting so hard to keep it together, keep passion and romance in their marriage, and felt like such a failure. He was fighting to keep Samantha's love for him strong when, in fact, she had already moved on. He was a wallet to support her shopping addiction. He was had, and he knew it. He sat in the pile of shoes, clothes and letters, with a runny nose and tears streaming out of his eyes. He needed to purge the pain quickly, because he was about to go Dad's way and be the only kind of man he knew how to be. A man who takes no shit when has been wronged and who believes betrayal was not acceptable.

Conner picked up another piece of special Samantha stuff, a hand-blown glass vase she had purchased at an art gallery. He looked for something else she found special, and you can be sure there was a lot of special stuff in the house. He destroyed both with one good athletic toss. Each time Conner saw an item break, he saw a piece of his heart go with it. His tirade would not go unnoticed. Some would understand his ordeal and others would think he should have just left. However, he wasn't the just-leave type of guy. He was a stay and fight man, and that's what he was doing. He was sending the message in the only way he knew how. Know what was important to your enemy and snuff the resource right out from under them. They would fall quickly and with less of a fight. In some ways, he wondered if this knowledge prevented him from ever wanting to be too close to something or someone. If he cared too much, it could be used against him. His knowledge was also his curse. It was a vicious cycle. He wanted love and he wanted money, but he wanted neither if they could be leveraged against him. Life was all about leverage and he didn't know how to think any other way.

Now, he was doing a bang-up job of banging up his house. While ripping up wedding pictures and throwing them everywhere, Conner knew he had made his stand and could not go back. It was over. Hell, it was over three years ago. He just now found out and was both pissed and feeling ignorant to the fact. Mirrors, clothes, tables, art pieces, furniture... he even picked up the corner of his huge bed, the bed he made love to her in, and shoved as much of it as he could through the large, bedroom window. Assuming Jim had been there at some point, he wanted it out of the house.

After he exerted all that effort to destroy everything he and Samantha worked so hard to accumulate, he sat on the bottom stair and looked at his destruction, as the realization hit. He had that defining moment and it was his way. Would he be proud of himself? Would he feel like he did the right thing? It didn't matter.

All the lights were on, and the cool outside air was entering through the broken windows. Conner heard sirens. Did a neighbor call the police? Probably.

His eyes then fell to the slate floor beneath the walnut and leather bench that sat in the foyer. Among the debris, sitting under the bench was an acorn. The acorn Emily had given Conner as they stood beneath the tree by the river at Blaney Park.

Conner got up and walked over to it. He slowly bent down and picked up the acorn. He put it in his pocket and looked around one last time. He walked to the one hutch he didn't break, and removed a picture of his mom and dad from its top shelf. Clutching both the portrait and the acorn, he contemplated leaving the house quickly to avoid the police. If he chose to leave now, returning would never be the same for him. Never again would it be home.

17

The Visitor

Conner looked at himself in the mirror that stood tall in the hallway which led from his bedroom to his bathroom. It was the same space he once shared with Samantha. He would lounge on their bed and watch her get dressed. He enjoyed watching her dress. She took such pains to look good, and she did look good. He felt a bit lonely there, staring at the same mirror he once shared with the woman he loved. It was one of the few items he did not break the night almost a month earlier when he let go of his dream, his marriage, and broke up the house he had shared with the woman who had betrayed him.

I look good, he thought. He was dressed in his black tuxedo, with a dark mock turtleneck underneath. He never liked bow ties, so he preferred the look of a silver tee or mock turtleneck-style shirt under his coat.

It was his birthday. Number 40, of all birthdays. Samantha was throwing him a party. It had been planned for months. The recent events and their fast-approaching divorce hearing should have cancelled such an affair. Yet, Conner still tried to keep his dignity and his commitment. After all, both their families would be there, too. He despised Samantha for what she did and was even more offended by her insistence that he attend when she called him to beg for his presence.

"People purchased gifts," she told him.

Like he cared about gifts at a time like this. He knew that his close friends and family would completely understand why he wanted nothing to do with such a party after they heard what had occurred.

"Business associates and very important people will be there," she told him.

Who gives a fuck about them, Conner thought to himself, as he stared at his reflection in the mirror. Why do I let her manipulate me like this? He put on the finishing touches of his clothes.

The doorbell rang. Conner knew it was Todd. He walked to the front door of the home he now despised even the mere existence of, to let Todd in.

As he walked through the house, he looked at the spots where nice, expensive furniture and art sculptures once sat. Only the indentations of the carpeting remained as proof that such items once stood there. The house seemed empty now. All he ever wanted was to have her there with him and instead, he had been living with her stuff. The three weeks since his temper tantrum gave the cleaning crew the time to repair most of the damage. Samantha had come back to the house and saw what he had done. She could have called the police, but she did not. She did take some of what was left that she valued, afraid that Conner would, once again, take his anger for her out on her stuff. Conner now despised her stuff. He realized that her stuff was what she cared more about than him.

When he got to the door, he was surprised not to see Todd, but instead an attractive woman wearing sunglasses. He opened the door.

"May I help you?"

"Yes, I don't know why I have come. This is the Morley residence, isn't it?"

"It is. I'm Conner Morley. Do I know you?"

"No, you don't know me. May I come in?"

"Please, come in," Conner stepped to the side. The woman seemed very distraught and this concerned him. She came into the house and stood there looking at the home, scanning it as if taking a picture of each wall with her mind, not wanting to forget what it looked like. He waited for her to speak and was curious why she continued to stand and look around the house.

"Sorry for the mess," Conner stated. "I kind of did some remodeling without getting professional assistance." He smiled, hoping to break the ice with this woman and also try to explain why some walls had holes in them as if someone punched them out, even though that is exactly what had happened. The woman never laughed or showed any emotion. She still had her sunglasses on.

"I am a teacher, you know."

Conner began to respond and then decided not to and allowed her to continue.

"I graduated and received my degree in just three years. My husband had just lost his dad. He committed suicide. He was hurting. He said he wanted a family, he wanted me. We went through a lot of tough times to get where we are today. I really didn't want to have another baby. He wanted a boy. So, now we have Larry. He's only four years old. I thought he'd be so proud of me that we had a boy. I thought he'd be dedicated to us. He cheated before, you know. I also have a 15-year old daughter. She's been through hell because of his cheating. She hates him now. But I wanted him to be happy. I thought I could make him happy. He's never really been a good husband, but I kept trying. I felt sorry for him. His dad committed suicide and he said it hurt. I tried to give him a family. Now, he's going to put his son through hell."

Helen Gordy. Conner realized, as the woman was speaking, that this was Mrs. Jim Gordy. The front door was open and Conner saw Todd walking along the sidewalk leading up to the front door. He placed his hand out like a traffic cop. Todd knew what it meant, and turned around to go back to the limo.

"Would you like to sit down?" Conner slowly closed the front door and extended his hand toward the carved wooden bench in his foyer. It was the kind of bench that allowed people to sit while removing or pulling on their boots during the winter. It was as large as most living room couches. Even with the destruction, Mrs. Gordy could see that this home had success in it, if success was measured by material value.

"My name is Helen Gordy," she began, as she sank to the bench. "You said you are Conner Morley, right?"

"Yes, ma'am, I did. Can I get you a drink of water or something?"

"No, thank you. You have a beautiful house, Mr. Morley."

"Thank you, and please call me Conner. It's not so beautiful, anymore. I don't even much like it now."

"Is this the first time you have been cheated on?"

"By my wife, yes. I have had many a person cheat me, Mrs. Gordy, but never my own family. First time for that."

"I suppose it was what drove you to do so much destruction to such a beautiful house."

"Yes, ma'am," Conner smiled at her awareness of what had really happened. "I'd like to tell you I did not do this. I'd like to tell you I had more class. But I guess when my wife cheated on me, she took most of my dreams away from me and I just didn't see the reasons not to break a few things of hers, take back a few of her dreams."

"Do you know why I am here, Conner?"

"No, I really can't say that I do."

Helen Gordy slowly removed her sunglasses. She was surprisingly attractive to Conner. He had pictured her as overweight, a maid-type wife to Jim and thus the reason for fucking his wife. But Helen had attractive features, although her face was swollen from the obvious signs of the deep emotional distress that she was feeling. She stood up and looked around a little bit before looking Conner in the eyes.

"My husband did a very wrong thing to a lot of people. This is not the first time. I was praying that you truly had a business issue when you asked for his number and I did what I always did. I convinced myself that everything was okay. My husband and I are building a house, or were building a house, much the same size as this. He was trying to make up for all the times he betrayed us, for all the times I received calls from men telling me that he was advancing on their wife. Each time, I tried to keep our family together and work with him. He is a lost soul, Conner. I was trying to save him."

"I appreciate your pain, Mrs. Gordy, but what does this all have to do with me?"

"Jim called me, that night after I spoke with you, from a 906 area code. I saw it on the caller ID and had the number traced. He called me to tell me that I needed to watch out for the kids, that some man was going to hurt them. He said that man was you."

"He did, huh?"

"I am not a stupid woman, Conner. When I heard my kids were in danger, I went to work to find some answers. I looked through his things and I found Samantha's work number, her condo number, and even her cell phone number. It didn't take me long to figure out that Sam, is Samantha."

"I am sorry to say she is."

"I haven't heard from Jim since he called that night. He told me you and he got into a fight. He was brief and not very concise about the situation. But he was very demonstrative that he feared for our children's lives. Now, Mr. Morley, I may be ignorant to let this man abuse me emotionally and ruin my life with his actions. But, as a mother, I will be damned if he's going to place my kids at risk. I want you to know this. If you are planning to hurt us to get back at Jim, take me now and don't hurt my kids." She began to cry.

That fucking coward. Conner was shocked, and even more upset with Jim. The guy calls his wife and tells her to protect his kids. He wanted to hurt Jim even more than he had before.

"Please, Mr. Morley," she continued. "Do what you want with me. You would actually be doing me a favor by taking me away from this hell I live in.

But, I beg of you, please, don't hurt my babies."

He reached his hand out to Helen. She took it in her own, moved to Conner and hugged him. They hugged, as she sobbed uncontrollably. Conner could feel her pain. He could feel the years of mistrust, anxiety and worry coming out of this woman. She was defeated and beaten down not by the man, but what he was doing to her kids. Conner held her close and tried to stay quiet. A tear started to swell up in his eye.

How could two people be so selfish? He had envisioned this woman not to be this kind and beautiful soul, but a woman who was domineering and ugly in all facets of her person. It was a humbling experience for Conner, and he whispered in her ear that all would be okay.

"Please look into my eyes, Helen." He pulled away from her.

She caught her breath and slowly pulled away from him.

"I promise you. I give you my word. You and your kids will not be hurt due to your husband being a cheating piece of slime. I am pleased that you came to me. It was a courageous thing to do. Be sure that I hear your request and I will adhere to it."

Helen nodded silently at his words. She was emotionally drained. She turned and, while still crying, walked slowly to the open door. Conner followed her outside and around the winding sidewalk to her car.

"Todd," he called, motioning toward the limo. "I need you to take this woman home. She is in no condition to drive."

"You don't..." she started.

"Nonsense," Conner interrupted her. "Please, let me start healing us both by allowing me to do this for you. It would make me feel better. There is a bar in the back seat. Pour yourself a stiff drink and gather yourself before you get home to your kids. Give me your keys and I will have someone take your car home for you. It will be there within an hour of your arrival." He opened the back door and Helen climbed into the roomy limo. Conner looked at Todd and shook his head. He wanted no conversation with Todd. He just wanted Helen to be gone from his home. It was unsettling to have met the woman whose kids would have been used as pawns in the game of love and war. It bothered Conner. He wanted her gone. He knew he'd stand by his word and not hurt the kids. But he was angry that his hand had been called and it was Jim's wife who was playing the game with him. It should have been Jim. He leaned down and looked inside the door before closing it.

"You are a brave woman. Your kids should be very proud of you. You saved them from some very difficult experiences, Helen. I would not have hurt them, physically. I would not do that to them. You saved their emotional health. I suggest you go save your own emotional being."

"Thank you, Conner, for listening."

Conner closed the door without saying another word. He couldn't see through the window of the limo, but he knew she was looking at him. He could feel her anxiety returning and her fear pulsating through the car window. She had no reason to trust Conner. Hell, her own husband betrayed her more times than any woman should have to put up with. He knew that as soon as Todd turned on to Cedar Lake Road, she would have already started thinking how she was going to protect her kids. She would have lost the trust and bonding that had occurred from the encounter in the house. That is what happens to people when they are betrayed as often as she was betrayed. They become senile. They no longer believe in anything or trust anyone. Conner was wondering if he'd become another Helen after his experience with Samantha.

As he turned to walk back to the front door, Conner pulled out his cell phone and called a crony to follow up and get Helen's car to her within the hour, as he had promised. He then hung up and called the limo.

"Todd?"

"Yeah?"

"How is she doing?"

"She's sobbing back there, boss. What the hell did you do to her?"

"Nothing. It's Helen Gordy. She came to ask for me to leave her kids alone."

Todd knew to close the window that separated him from the passenger seat in the back. Helen would not hear a word he was discussing with Conner. "You are fucking kidding me! He sent his wife to beg for him?"

"No, Todd. She came on her own. Gordy called her from the Park and told her to protect the kids, 'cause someone was out to harm them. She was smart enough to do the investigation and put the pieces together."

"Damn, Conner, what a way to live, huh? He needs to fucking get kicked in the head. What a piece of slime, he is."

"I agree, Todd. But listen, I am changing our strategy. Call Luna and tell him the play is off. NO PLAY. You got that?"

"No play. I got it, boss. Man, she is a courageous woman. Not bad looking either, huh, boss?"

"Shut the fuck up, Todd. Jesus, sometimes you just piss me off with your off-color comments. The woman needs a doctor. Are you nuts?"

Todd began to laugh. Everything ended in a joke with him. Conner hung up the phone and took a few seconds to think about how easy Todd had it. Good wife, good family, and so laid back he could find humor in even the most despair situations. He was going through hell and Todd was still oblivious to his hurt. It was as if Todd just didn't get what pain was about. His life was always just fun and humor.

The mobile phone rang again.

"This is Conner Morley."

"You are coming tonight, aren't you?" It was Samantha. "Conner, are you there?"

"Yeah, I am here. I will be there. I may be a little tardy."

"Conner, it's a surprise party. You can't be late."

"I can be anything I damn well please!" Conner wanted to call her a bitch, but did not. "I don't even want this party. I can't believe you were fucking around on me and at the same time you were planning this party for me. You are one sick puppy, you know that, Samantha?"

"Conner, can you not swear at me? Why are you swearing at me? You know how I feel about swearing."

Conner shook his head. She was acting as if the events that had occurred never happened. How could she even request that he be anything but pissed, after what she did to him? Just the mere fact that she was so nonchalant angered him.

"Conner, now don't you make a scene tonight. I know you are a little upset with me, but there are going to be a lot of people there who will not understand if you are in a bad mood. They will think I did something to you or that business is not well."

Jiminy Crickets, Conner thought. It was not like anything he'd normally think. But, when situations became so unbelievable, he would think of words or phrases that were just as outrageous. You did do something to me. How in the hell could she be so naive to how a person must feel after what she did to him? His wife had cheated on him, his dad had cancer, his mom was worried to death and his business was such that he didn't even know what to do with Blaney Park. Oh, yeah, he was in a great mood to go to a party.

"I will meet you at the Club. I am not picking you up."

"You have to pick me up! We can't go in separately!"

"The hell, we can! We will go in separately. You lie so well, Samantha. I am sure you can tell our guests something that is palatable. I don't want you near me all night, though, you hear me? And, you find your own ride. Oh, and by the way?"

"What?"

"If I see Jim there tonight, I am kicking his ass, no matter who is around. So you better make sure his cheating ass is nowhere near my party."

"He won't be there, I am sure. Would I do that?"

Conner hung up his phone without saying goodbye and thought of the irony. No, she wouldn't do that, but she'd sleep with him and cheat against her own family with him. Conner started counting the things she had done to him and concluded, yes, she would most certainly do that.

He walked into his home office, and sat down at his computer to check his e-mail. He was surprised to find one from Emily. 'Happy Birthday from the Wolves of Blaney Park' said the note. Conner smiled, wishing he were there, instead of here. He didn't even know she had e-mail access and it was a pleasant surprise. He sat there reflecting on life and waited for Todd to return so he could go to his birthday party. Conner was actually looking forward to seeing a lot of people he hadn't seen for a long time. Samantha had to tell him about the surprise party at Plum Hollow Country Club because Conner was going to avoid her. He wanted to punish her for what she did. Now, he would fulfill this event because he cared more about making his family and friends happy, then about hurting Samantha.

Todd had helped Conner come to the conclusion to attend, but Conner knew Todd had ulterior motives. He wanted to dance with his wife and with the receptionist of the building. Todd's wife was very attractive and laid back. She put up with Todd's flirting and would always say, 'Todd can have as much fun as he wants, but he's going home with me.' Conner always admired her for her unconditional trust. For all that Todd did, he never cheated on her. He was a faithful husband and a good father.

Todd walked up to the front door and went straight in, not bothering to knock. He knew Samantha was not home, so there was no reason to maintain such protocol. He would not have done that if the woman of the house were home. While Todd was like family to Conner, he never wanted to be at the house when Samantha was there alone. It was just their way. Conner would never stay and visit Holly if Todd wasn't home. Holly took offense, at times, when he would graciously decline to visit with her. It's not that the two boyhood friends didn't trust each other, they didn't trust their wives. The friendship meant too much to them to risk innuendo or a misunderstanding. The chance that a woman may try to use one friend against the other and try to come between them was too risky. It was more to save their marriages than their friendship. Because they knew if either wife were to accuse one of them, the friends would trust each other over their spouses. Both were flirts who knew what could be heard or perceived by the wife of the other from their friendliness. Neither money nor women would ever come between them and they both had the unspoken rules of engagement. Both would tease that the other's wife was thinking of them during their intimate activities. It was just too important to keep outside influences from destroying a close, family-like friendship.

"Conner! Where are you, YOU OLD MAN?" Todd yelled out as he entered the house. "Hahaha lulululu dododoododo!" Todd screamed at the top of his lungs. He did this because the vaulted ceiling in the foyer echoed when he did so. Todd always teased Conner that he lived in a museum, not a house.

"Jesus Christ, what did you do to this place?" Todd spoke to no one as he looked around at the broken mirrors, the holes in the walls and all the places where once there was something hanging on the wall and was no more. "Whew! You were one pissed off human being there, Conner! Damn, man. Why did you destroy this shit, man? You could have given it to me!" Todd laughed, and sat down on the foyer bench to wait for the guest of honor.

18

The Warm Up

Not much was said during the drive to the club. Southfield was closer to Conner's office than to his home. He didn't like going home much anymore and besides, his golf clubs were always with him. Without Samantha, it was just a house and she hadn't been around much for the last few years. It seemed every year she was home less and less. Now, he knew why. Seeing her later that night was not something he was looking forward to at all. The fire of anger was burning in his stomach and his heart was smashed from the knowledge that his wife was an imposter. Todd drove up to the Plum Hollow's guest drop off area, stopped the car and sat there waiting for Conner to get out.

"Ain't you going to get out and open my door?" Conner asked.

"Nope."

"Hey, man, we are at the club. You are supposed to come open my door. Besides, it's my birthday. You'd think for once, you'd come open my door."

"Are you asking me to open my door, walk around the back of this car, open your door and act like I am helping you out of this car?"

"Yes, that's exactly what I am asking of you."

"Nope, I ain't going to do it. Number one, I am pissed at you for breaking all that shit in your house. People are going to say you are crazy 'cause you broke that shit. Now, I will stick up for you, and I will tell them, under oath I tell you, that you are crazy because you didn't give that shit to me. Secondly, I did that whole chauffeur thing for that woman earlier today. I don't think my self-esteem could handle that routine two times in one day. Lastly, you are fucking old as dirt today. You are 40 years old. You need the exercise. Now get the fuck out of the car, so I can park this piece of shit. And, you can wait for me at the door and we can walk into the party together, or you can be a ass and go in without me, depriving me the opportunity to show all in attendance that you and I are close. But I am not catering to you just because it's your birthday. No way am I doing that."

Conner smiled and said nothing in reply. He opened his door and exited the vehicle unassisted. He waited for a moment until the car turned the corner to park in his reserved parking place. As soon as the car disappeared, he smiled and started his walk to the ballroom where his party would be. He knew that Todd would want him to wait, but no way was he going to do that now. It was a perpetually antagonistic relationship between these two best of friends, but they never took it personally. It was all in fun. Conner knew Todd would be cussing up a storm when he saw he had not waited for him. If Todd was sure Conner wasn't waiting for him, he could have entered from the back door, the service entrance. Conner knew Todd would be expecting Conner to wait for him.

The clubhouse and the restaurant were connected by a breezeway. Guests would normally enter through the front door, but not Conner. He always entered through the locker room. In the locker room was a gentleman's bar. It was where the golfers would go to drink and count up their strokes from that day's round of golf. While some used the room just to get away from their wives, others would use the room to play cards and gamble their time away. There was always money being bet somewhere, everywhere at the club. Some of the bets were substantial and ruined lives.

Conner was walking past the bar when he saw Carlos there. Carlos was a heavyset Latino man who had, most believed, not been dealt a full deck of cards. He was not the sharpest knife in the drawer, but God gave him the gift to serve. He was tremendous at running the bar. He remembered the name of every guest and what they drank. By the time they sat at a stool or a nearby table, he had the drink poured perfectly to that member's liking. He knew which members wanted to talk and who wanted no conversation with him. Most didn't speak to him because they saw themselves as better and Carlos as a nobody, insignificant to their world. Carlos never took any of it personally. He shined shoes for the members and treated them all the same, with great respect. No matter how rude they were to him, they'd find their shoes shined and placed neatly on top of their lockers. Conner respected Carlos for his patience of wealthy ignorance.

"Carlos, how's it going?" Conner asked.

"Mr. Morley, happy birthday, sir," Carlos had, of course, remembered Conner's birthday, since it fell on the same day as his own son's. "This drink is on me, sir."

"Don't call me Mr. Morley," Conner always told Carlos this. "Every time you call me Mr. Morley, I look around for my dad."

The first time they saw each other, Carlos had called Mr. Morley and they agreed that, from then on, he would call him Conner. Conner was one of the few members at the club who allowed Carlos to call him by his first name. It made both Carlos and his manager uncomfortable. But Conner insisted that Carlos not call him Mister anything. Conner felt it was degrading to Carlos to be forced to do that in an age when such protocol was not a normal act. He felt no more significant than Carlos.

"Carlos, thank you, my man," Conner reached out to shake Carlos' already extended hand. "Pour yourself a drink, my friend. You are my drinking partner. You and I are having one together, mono y mono."

Carlos went to the refrigerator and took out a pint of chocolate milk. He didn't even bother to get himself a glass. He had already poured Conner his JD and diet Coke and placed it in front of him on the bar. Conner raised his glass and toasted himself, then turned to Carlos.

"To you, Carlos. The man who treats me better than any person I have ever met. To you."

"No, no, no, Conner. You are going to get me in trouble again with the boss man if you be toasting the Carlos man. You the Con Man. You are the one who feeds my wife and my children. I appreciate you, Mr. Conner."

"Okay, Carlos... to the Con Man."

"To the Con Man," Carlos repeated, as Conner tapped his glass against Carlos' milk carton. Carlos downed the whole pint of milk in one slug.

"Carlos," Conner teased. "You have to quit drinking like that, man. You going to get drunk drinking that fast." Both men laughed. Carlos went to the end of the counter and brought over a bowl of peanuts.

"Mr. Conner," Carlos asked, still trying to play the protocol game, "Why you sitting in here with me, when you have a room filled with people waiting for you?"

"Carlos, I have no idea. But you know what, buddy? I'd rather sit here the rest of the night and drink with you then go into that room. Life ain't always what it seems, my friend."

"Carlos knows, Mr. Conner. Carlos knows. I shine shoes and I pour men drinks while they pour sour souls to me. But, I did not know you had a sour soul, Mr. Conner. You seemed like the gentle heart, the peaceful heart."

"Yeah, I thought I was too, Carlos. But I am an imposter, just like all the other fools who come to this club, spend their hard earned money on all this shit and think they are more important than they really are."

"Mr. Conner, you are very important to me. You are one of the nice guys around here. It make me sad to see you here when you have all those friends in there."

"Carlos, when do you get off tonight? You have to be close to shutting down here, right?"

"Oh, Mr. Conner, I know what you are thinking. Carlos can't be out there with all those people. They're not my kinda people, Mr. Conner."

"Carlos, you are better than ninety percent of those people. You are good people."

"Mr. Conner," Carlos swapped Conner's drink with a fresh one. "It don't matter like that. What matters is that I have a family at home, and I need to go home to them. Mama be having my dinner on the table and she ain't too happy with Carlos if he late. Mama keeps me on time." Carlos laughed, as if he told a joke.

"I went by your new house the other day. It's a very nice house, Carlos."

"Thank you, Mr. Conner. It has two bathrooms and three bedrooms. It has a basement and a porch. I smoke the cigars you buy me back there, as if I am here and Carlos is important."

"That's right, Carlos. You are important to your family. You go home to your family. That's where you belong, my friend."

"Okay, Mr. Conner. And, you go to your party. The boss man keeps asking me if you are here. If he comes in now and sees you, he will think I was not being honest with boss man. I have new house, Mr. Conner. Carlos has responsibilities. I don't want the boss man mad at me."

"Okay, Carlos. I won't get you in trouble with the boss man." Conner smiled and finished his drink.

"Happy birthday, Con Man," Carlos grinned broadly. He finally called Conner what had been asked of him from the start. Carlos handed Conner his drink ticket. At the club, no money ever exchanged hands. It was placed on a tab and every quarter the money was in a club account where the tab was reconciled.

Carlos took Conner's glass from him and began to clean up around the bar. Conner signed his ticket, and stood up.

"Later, Carlos. I love you, man." Conner said that often to Carlos after a good day on the course. Carlos appreciated hearing it shouted from Conner in front of all the regulars who treated him so poorly. Carlos was happy to hear it again, even when there was no one left at the bar.

"I love you, man," Carlos called back and smiled at their friendly interaction while he began to enter the transaction into the bar's computer. Carlos was going to void the tab and pay the bill himself. After all, it was Mr. Morley's birthday. As he was about to do it, he looked at the bill. $1,000 was placed in the tip section along with this note: Carlos, you take this or we are no longer friends. Oh, and happy birthday to Kenerto.

Carlos smiled and registered his tip. He shook his head and thought how Mama was going to be happy with him. He had planned to stop and get some flowers for his wife and an affordable bike for his son. Now, he would buy roses for Mama, too, and the more expensive mountain bike for his son. Kenerto so badly wanted the mountain bike, but Carlos knew he could not afford it. Carlos remembered, and so did Conner. It would be a good night to go home.

19
The Party Begins

Conner slipped into the hallway. He could hear the commotion coming from the ballroom, but did not want to enter. He wasn't sure he could hide his hurt and anger for Samantha and did not want to be near her. So many people, who Conner would have loved to see on a normal day, were there for him tonight.

How could she do this to me, Conner thought, and, then expect me to act as if nothing happened? He was struggling with his decision to attend, yet he knew he would be happier to see his family and friends more than hate to see her.

"There you are, Con Man!" Todd walked out of the ballroom. "Where did you go?"

"I had a drink at the gentleman's bar before coming out."

"People are waiting for you, man. You need to get in there. People are wondering if you are even showing up. Some of them are talking, Con Man."

"I don't give a shit about any of this, Sully. My world is crumbling and I am supposed to walk in there and endure this shit as if nothing has happened?"

"Yup," Todd simply responded. "I am just glad I found you first, out here lost like a God damned puppy dog. Now, I can walk in with you just the way I planned and this will make me look good. This may not be good for you, but it is excellent for me. I will get at least a handful of more dances with the skirts. Have you seen the skirts that are here tonight, my friend?" Todd smiled smugly at Conner, who smiled back.

The two friends entered the ballroom. A lookout posted at the door signaled the DJ that they were entering, and as Conner moved from the doorway, Hail to the Victors, the University of Michigan fight song, played in recognition of where Conner had received his degree. The lights dimmed and a spotlight shown on Conner and Todd as they walked into the center of the ballroom. Todd was hamming it up, as usual. Conner was eloquent in his approach, but was very reserved. He just didn't have it in him to play the game. Samantha ran up to him and gave him a hug.

"This isn't a funeral, this is your birthday," she whispered into his ear. "Can you at least smile?" She hugged Conner, irritated at him for not placing his arms around her. "Don't be a fool in front of all these people, Conner. Hug me. You are making an ass out of yourself."

Todd could see what was happening, so he grabbed Samantha's arm and moved her out of the way. He then wrapped his arms around Conner and they embraced each other in a bear hug.

"I always knew you liked me better than her," Todd laughed. "Happy birthday, man. Now, have some fun. Don't let the bitch ruin your night."

Samantha moved away, rolling her eyes and laughing like everything that happened had been staged for the guests' entertainment. But she knew differently, and could feel his anger, his disapproval. She took a risk approaching him, expecting him to give in to her like he always had before. Conner was not the same man. His love and trust for her was lost, and she could feel it. She was no longer family, no longer his sunshine, no longer important. It made him feel no better, how he felt about her now. It made him no more pleased, that he was now capable of turning her away. It made him feel worse.

After the hug from Todd and hearing his words, Conner came out of his funk, and the first people he saw were his sisters and his mom. Then, he saw his dad standing behind them. Family was what he needed tonight. He went to his family and they embraced in a group hug. Everyone except Ken, his brother, who was already talking to friends instead of standing with the family to greet Conner. That was not unusual for them. Ken felt Conner never gave him the time of day. They both agreed they didn't walk the same side of the road and it hurt Conner that they were never close.

Ken never cared to stay in touch with Conner unless he needed a favor and it usually had to do with money. That never went over well with Conner, who believed that if Ken had spent as much energy on finding his niche in life as he did trying to scam friends and relatives, he'd be very successful. Ken's love was conditional.

Conner was given a JD and diet Coke by Ruth, the hostess for the party and his favorite of all the staff members who worked in the main restaurant. He thanked her for his drink and gave her a light kiss on the cheek. Ruth was a true professional, and he was pleased it was she who brought him his drink and words of happy birthday.

Todd was still standing next to Conner as his family went to their assigned seats. Conner scanned the room, amazed at how many people were at his party, and at how many of the guests he did not know. Samantha had invited many of her work associates, no doubt posturing to gain esteem from them. This irritated Conner, especially after all that was happening. It was his 40th birthday. He should know everyone in the room. There were certainly several not invited who should have been, and who would be disappointed at being snubbed by his wife. Samantha didn't frequent the club much. She'd come on specific nights when the menu was to her liking or if she wanted to entertain an important client of her own. Sure enough, Steve, Jerry and their wives were nowhere to be seen. These men were his golf buddies and now would provide much trash talk to him for their snub from his birthday party. Their wives will be more upset, that was certain, but he would make it up to them. It would not go away easily. That was the way of the world at a golf club like Plum Hollow. People expected to be included in the influential events most talked about once they were completed. Conner's birthday party would be such an event. He was also looking hard to see if Jim was attending.

"Jim ain't here, so quit looking around for trouble, bro," Todd said.

"Thanks, man. I was looking for who I didn't want here, but I am also looking for who I needed to be here."

"I know. She called and asked me. Hell, I didn't know. I wanted to say, shit girl, if you don't know who he'd want at the party, how do you expect me to know? But, because she's your wife, I kept my mouth shut."

"Well, feel free to tell her anything you fucking want to say, now. I am so done with this shit, man."

"Relax, Con Man, you have a long night ahead of you. Don't drink too much because your tude is sharp and may make you want to act out on someone. Hell, I know there are many you don't know here, but they have been invited for some reason. No reason to give them a bad opinion of you."

"Thanks, Sully. Keep me off the juice, okay? Cause right now, all I want to do is drink and fight. God, I want to kick his ass."

"Seems to me, you already did, man. I have good word that he is lost. Poor bastard can't seem to find his way back home. Wife has issued a missing person report and it will be interesting if they come asking questions of you. I know they will be talking to that wife of yours. Now please, don't go try to be Robin Hood and save her. Let her get herself out of this one. She did it to herself. The bitch needs to fry."

"I won't be helping her. Really, Gordy is missing?"

"Yup. I spoke with Archie. They want to know the next time you are in town up there. The state boys are not on it yet, just the local guy. But, they do want to talk to you. Helen said you threatened the family."

"Fuck, Todd. I don't need this shit."

"Con Man, it's your birthday. I have been with you 24 by 7, man. I am your alibi. No one is going to get you for anything."

"Problem is, Sully... I wanted to kill the fucker."

"Yeah, but you didn't, man. I know that. If he's missing, it's not because of you. Now have fun."

Conner took a drink and his eyes glanced over near the entrance, just as Emily and Austin walked in. Conner lowered his glass, and his mouth fell open. He reached over and placed his hand on Todd's shoulder. Todd's eyes followed Conner's gaze.

"Holy shit, Con Man! Is that the wolf lady? Damn, she's more of a woman than I gave her credit for, Con Man. Sure beats the hell out of baggy shorts and sweatshirts."

Conner didn't say anything to Todd. He just let his friend carry on with his undressing of the beautiful woman at the door. He looked away and then back to her many times. The receptionist was giving them their nametags. Conner shook his head at the fact that Samantha had ordered nametags for his party. The thought of people needing them at a birthday party made no sense to him. Yet, he knew in some strange way, Samantha would rationalize that it was for him.

"Hey, Mr. Morley." Conner's thoughts were interrupted by the approach of a strange man. He quickly looked to the nametag that all of a sudden seemed like a brilliant idea. It read, 'Derek Stroebel.'

"Mr. Stroebel, how are you tonight?"

"I am wonderful. Happy birthday. This is quite a party you have here. You certainly know a lot of people."

"Well, I don't know about that. I think this is a combined birthday party for me and a business party, thanks to my wife." Conner smiled at the irony of standing there in front of a man he'd spoken to on the phone but never met in person. Derek was a potential business associate, so he couldn't very well place his displeasure with Samantha. At least she did get some of his players involved. Conner was uncomfortable speaking to Derek, knowing he was reconsidering the sale of Blaney Park.

"Well, I love a good party, no matter what the reason. May I call you Conner?"

"Sure, what the hell. You are at my birthday party, I suppose I wouldn't want to be rude to a guest."

"Great, Conner. I hope you keep that approach towards me, because I sure want to purchase Blaney Park. It has great value to me, both for business and personal reasons."

"Con Man, you son of a bitch!" They were interrupted by the approach of an old high school friend. "How are you doing?"

"Dennis, how are you?" Conner nodded at Derek. ""Excuse me, won't you?"

The dinner music began and the guests began finding their seats for dinner. Conner never took his place next to Samantha. He wasn't hungry and although it was rude to speak to guests while some were eating, he went to those he knew would be more pleased to speak with him than to eat. When he had exhausted all the tables, he used the fact that he had a business call as an excuse to leave the room.

Sully was sitting where Conner should have been, which irritated Samantha. She did not approach Conner again. After the hugging episode that began the evening, she was intelligent enough not to place herself in another uncomfortable position. Conner eventually just took an empty chair and placed it at his family's table and began to talk with them. He had no inclination to be with her, and was working hard to get the night over so he didn't have to feel so fake. The best part of the night was seeing his family, friends and, of course, Emily.

Wherever he sat, whenever he walked around the room, Conner always tried to be facing her direction. His heart was jumping and he couldn't understand why. He knew he didn't have a chance with her. Austin was damn good looking and she seemed to be very pleased with her life. It was Conner's luck. He loved for looks, not substance. She was beautiful on that night. Conner had thought she was cute at Blaney Park. He liked her soul and her style. Each time he saw her, she had on similar clothes and her hair always seemed to be up in a bun or under a baseball cap. Her dress, on this evening, was simple but elegant, made of smooth black silk, which seemed to glisten as she moved. Her hair was pulled back away from her face, with loose curls that were long and free flowing along her neck and shoulders. Her green eyes seemed to glow like emeralds in the ballroom lighting.

Todd had little luck keeping Conner from getting juiced. Conner had two very strong drinks with Carlos and had taken drinks off of friends at their tables, and was feeling quite well. Every now and then, he'd look to the back of the room where Emily was sitting, and think about her in the river. How attractive she seemed to be from 30 yards away in the dark. Now, he was wishing to ask Emily to excuse herself, jump on the plane and fly back to Blaney Park with him to take one of those walks they often took together. Conner always enjoyed the party side of business. Now, he was feeling less comfortable with all these imposters and was missing the solitude of Blaney Park.

Dessert was served and Conner could see Todd talking with Samantha. It was certainly unusual, as Todd never talked to Samantha much. He was somewhat intimidated by her. He was accustomed to speaking with women who acted more like women. Sam, as he liked to call her because of the masculine reference to her name, talked down to him because she felt he wasn't a man of power and wealth. Todd often would call on Conner's mobile phone just so he didn't have to hear Samantha answer their house line. Then, he could ask if the corporate bitch was there. He never came over when she was. She had now betrayed his best friend, and Todd didn't much care whether she was Sam or not, he'd stand up to her.

Samantha looked up and wiggled her finger to and fro at Conner. It used to be enjoyable when that occurred, because she would always joke, 'I just wanted to see if I could make you come with one finger.' The jokes had long left their marriage and their friendship. Now, it was nothing. Conner was numb to her soul and hated her heart. He approached Samantha.

"Todd wants to do the toast," she stated confidently. "I told him I was going to give a toast. Conner, I planned this party and I put it all together. Todd said he'd be making a toast either before or after, but he was making a toast. I don't want him near that microphone."

"Okay, let me take care of this."

Samantha looked at Todd with a mock smile, as if to say, 'see, it will be my way.'

Conner approached the podium and, as he walked by Todd, gave him a wink. The DJ handed the microphone to Conner.

"Good evening, everyone," Conner began. "I want to thank all of you for coming and I hope you enjoy the festivities throughout the night. As most of you know, there has been a mistake in my birth certificate. I am not a day over 35."

The crowd laughed.

"If I was 40 years old, which I am not, but if I was, I'd be so thrilled to have such a nice party at such a wonderful club. I want to thank Plum Hollow and their staff for being such gracious hosts. I have been a member here now some ten years, and I have loved each and every one of them. So often people speak of clubs as being click-ish and snobby and, of course, somewhat prejudice. My pride in this club comes largely from the fact that it is none of that. I'd also like to say that I was told Samantha was going to offer me a toast. Well, with her permission, I have changed the plan just a bit." Conner smiled and nodded towards her.

Samantha's first reaction was shock. Realizing people were watching, her grimace turned to a smile and she returned Conner's nod. He continued to smile. He enjoyed turning on her in this situation, for she had no choice but to play along. She had hurt Conner and it was brutal. Now, he was attempting to get some shots back without harming anyone or anything but their relationship. Samantha would never deviate from her need to keep the image of the perfect marriage, when it was she who had destroyed it.

"I have had a wonderful life," he continued, "and many good things have happened to me. I started out in information technology, learned my trade and worked hard. I then decided to go out on my own and try to make it in this world as an entrepreneur. I was so lucky to open my computer and communication business just at the right time. Those of you out there who supported me by giving my company business, I so much appreciate you all. You all know the story. After my first year showed a substantial profit from the contracts we signed, an anonymous investor provided me the money that meant my family would never need anything again. Because it was anonymous, I was never able to thank that person. I did not want to leave tonight without thanking all of you who have supported Conner Morley in his life and his dreams of doing good things in life. I have tried, and hopefully succeeded, at giving as much back as possible." People began to clap and Conner waited for them to finish.

"If the person who invested in my company, and in me, happens to be in this room, I thank you from the bottom of my heart. I can never begin to express the difference the financial backing has made. As all of you know, without dollars, there is no business. But more than just my business, it has given me tremendous joy to be able to donate substantial dollars to the charities I am passionate about. So, thank you, if you are in this room. Before

I pass on to heaven, I hope I find out who you are. I try to thank you, now, by how I do business and how I treat people. God, family and oneself are so important and I take pride in all of them." The crowd clapped again.

"After all these years, I finally get to control the microphone. It feels great to be alive and have friends like you people and I thank you for coming. Please, drink responsibly and, if you need a taxi, the Club has been informed to offer them at no cost to you. Getting you home is more important, so please don't drink and drive. But have fun tonight. It's the law." More laughter and applause echoed the room.

"Okay, I am done. Other than my immediate family, the person who has been selected to roast, I mean toast, me has been my very best friend in the whole world. I can say that, had it not been for this man, I would not be here talking to you today. I love this guy. I also know he's not going to say anything nice about me, so I don't know why I am giving him control of this voice device. But, he is the right man for the job. He is my right hand man and my brother. So, here to toast the 40-year-old Conner Morley, is 39-year-old Todd Sullivan." The crowd clapped as Todd took the podium and the microphone from Conner. The two shook hands and then embraced for a quick hug.

"Folks, I don't speak too much to audiences. I am not the suave and..., well, whatever that other word that goes with it is..." The crowd laughed and Todd relaxed. "I look at the Morley's as much my family as Conner's. They are people who took me in when I had no place to go. And, you know what is special about the man we're celebrating tonight? Well, I am going to tell you. I am not the only person he has brought into his life who don't have anywhere else to go. He's a man who cares and has compassion for his fellow man. Yeah, I have saved his ass when he could have lost it, but he has done that for me ten times over. I love the man, I love what he represents. He's God-fearing and a true gift from the Almighty. It wouldn't matter if he had millions or just ten bucks, he would still try to help people with whatever resources he had. We all know it, and most all of us in this room know what I say is true. And, those of you who were invited and never met the man, I suggest you take some time and introduce yourself to him. Because he's the man we are here to celebrate. And, I know he celebrates because God has given him the gift of caring.

"I want to propose a toast, to Conner." Todd turned to look towards his friend. "The last time I toasted you was at your wedding, and I am pleased to get the chance to do it again. Be pleased with your forty years, my friend. You have done well with them. Now, don't screw up the next forty by thinking you can get along without me!" The crowd laughed again.

"Really, man, you are my brother and that's all I need to say. Be happy and enjoy continued success! To Conner." Todd raised his glass and the guests raised theirs.

"Okay, folks, the dancing will begin and there is only one rule in Conner's house, you must have fun, 'cause it's the law!" Todd ended to a round of applause and gave the microphone back to the DJ. He then walked up to Conner, who shook his hand.

"Thanks, Sully. That was great."

"Great?" Todd replied. "Just great? Fuck you! That was outstanding and much better then you can ever do."

"I know, Todd, you are so much better than me. How do you live with such perfection?"

"I don't know. I do know it must be hard, because Holly tells me I am hard to live with all the time." The two friends laughed and walked off the stage. As Conner stepped down from the platform, he caught another look at Emily. Never, was she looking at him. He felt somewhat disappointed and also guilty. She was a married woman. Feeling the way he did was against everything Conner believed in.

The music started and Conner loved to dance. Samantha approached him.

"Are you going to at least dance with me? If you don't do that, it will be obvious to everyone that something is wrong. Can't you just keep it together for tonight?"

"Sam," Conner replied, purposely using Todd's expression of the masculine version of her name, knowing it would irritate her. "I have no intentions of dancing with you tonight, tomorrow or ever. I thank you and appreciate all that is good about tonight. But, you know what? I think you should just get in your fancy car and go back to James Gordy's arms. You deserve each other. I don't want you here. My family knows everything and I don't feel the need to put on a show for those who are here tonight. So feel free to go see your boyfriend and just leave me alone to enjoy my 40th birthday party. The best birthday present you could give me is to not be present."

Samantha's eyes began to tear up as he walked away from her. She had been caught first-handed and realized the consequences of such action. She so wanted to tell Conner she was sorry, that she really did love him and that she didn't know how it all happened the way it did. Samantha was a weak person. She needed, and valued, different types of things than Conner. He diminished her, and Samantha resented him for it, because she could not live up to his standards. He loved her so much, but his success and strong beliefs in right and wrong diminished Samantha's self-esteem and he didn't even know it. On top of it all, she was not capable of communicating her feelings to him. She knew in her heart that she was susceptible to straying from her marriage if she felt it would benefit her. He loved her for her physical beauty and who he thought she could be, given the opportunity, rather than who she was. Yet, she depended on her physical looks for success and subsequent advancement in the corporate world, never confident that her intelligence was enough. Conner was not naive that it could happen, but never would allow himself to see the obvious. He was married to a cheating woman who had no intentions of living up to his standards, when it came to matters of the heart and soul. She wore the same short skirts and revealing blouses back then, but they were for him to enjoy. So, he had no complaints. He trusted there were people watching his back, and she knew any inappropriate behavior would be exposed. Conner knew everyone. But when he left to run his own business, he lost what she was looking for - a man who could assist her career. Conner no longer had the time, or the knowledge to assist her, so she went looking for someone who could, and found him in James Gordy.

When Conner asked her to leave, Samantha realized she no longer had leverage with him. While they both felt her physical beauty was her key to him, it was her inner ugliness that cost her marriage and the advantages of being his wife. It all ended that evening in the ballroom. She knew Conner would still love and care about her, but never again give to her. It was over. Samantha turned and walked away. Conner watched, and so wanted to go after her. He couldn't shut off his feelings, his dreams with her. But he was destroyed by it all. Pride stood in Conner's way and he knew it. He couldn't let this go and try to work it out. Too much had been lost.

Just as he was talking himself into running after Samantha, Emily and Austin approached him. All night, he had wanted to approach Emily. Now, she was right there in front of him and their eyes met. Conner did not want to let her eyes go, but Austin reached out to shake his hand.

"Happy birthday," Austin smiled.

"Thank you," nodded Conner. "Thank you very much. I'm very pleased you both could make it tonight. Are you having a good time?" He turned and faced Emily, as quickly as he could without raising suspicions of his inner thoughts.

"Happy birthday, Conner," she moved toward him, giving him a hug and kiss on the cheek. While they were the same wishes as Austin's, the effect of each was completely different. Austin's was met with appreciation, but overall indifference. Emily's... Conner only wondered if she could feel the heart that was pounding just about out of his body in response to her greeting and well wishes.

"May I dance with your wife?" He looked back at Austin.

"Be my guest," Austin agreed, and laughed lightly. "Somebody should dance with her, as I don't dance!"

Conner led her to the dance floor. His heart was pounding and he was feeling like he was fifteen years old, taking his first dance with a woman. He was a good dancer and, in most cases, would be on the dance floor to show off and feel good about his ability to shake a leg. But, on this dance, all he wanted was a chance to get close to Emily and speak with her. He missed her. He cleared his mind of Samantha. While he was seeing himself as divorced, he knew Emily was not and he had to keep his composure and his manners. Conner pulled Emily close to him and they began to dance to the music.

"Are you having a good time, Emily?"

"A wonderful time, Conner. What a nice place to have a party. And so many people... you must be doing something well to have so many friends."

"Well, it's a long story and also a long life. The combination of those two elements brings all these people here together. What brings you and Austin? What a pleasant surprise to see you here."

""I guess your wife felt it appropriate to invite Austin, as he flies a lot of your associates, including her, up to Blaney Park."

"Oh, that's right," Conner smiled. "So, how is Blaney Park?"

"Wonderful, as always," Emily replied. "No offense, Conner, I am glad to be here to help you celebrate, but you seem to have plenty for that. Honestly, though, I'd rather be there."

"What? No way." Conner teased. "Blaney, instead of with me? I don't blame you, girl, I'd rather be at Blaney Park, too."

"Really?" Emily smiled with surprise. "You? Rather be at Blaney?"

"Sure! Why do you find that so surprising?"

"The way you dressed when you were there the first few times. It would be like me coming to this party in my shorts and sweatshirt. You just looked out of place."

"Me? Look out of place? Impossible!" Conner laughed and twirled her around the dance floor, as she followed his lead. "Hey, you are a good dancer there, wolf lady."

"Well, we wolves are known for our quick feet and ability to move when situations change suddenly." Both laughed again.

"I miss you, Emily." He pulled her in close to him, and their eyes locked.

"Now, Mr. Morley, you behave. We are both married. That is not an appropriate thing to say to me."

"No, Emily, I want to tell you," he said, hoarsely. "I miss you. I miss Blaney Park. I miss the wolves. God, I miss it all."

"Conner..." She stopped dancing and stood to look at him, still holding herself to him. "You are serious about how you feel, aren't you?"

"Yes, I am."

At that moment, Austin walked up and tapped Conner on the shoulder.

"May I cut in?" Conner looked up to see Austin and relinquished his position with Emily.

"Sure, Austin. Thank you for allowing me a dance with her."

"A dance? You two have danced five songs in a row. I came to rescue her from you, even with my awkward feet." Austin laughed, but Conner felt he was half-serious and perhaps irritated that they had danced for so many songs.

Conner bowed to them, and then returned to the lounge area where Todd was leaning against the bar.

"Great speech tonight, brother."

"Thanks, Con Man. What was up with that?"

"With what?"

"First, you send Samantha out the door, and then you dance with the wolf lady for five in a row! Not a smart move, dude."

"What?"

"What?" Todd said, in mock fun. "People are coming up to me asking me what's up with you and Samantha. Then, you go dance with the wolf lady and there is enough electricity to light Detroit."

"It looked that obvious?"

"Fuck, yes! It's one thing to dance, but when neither of your feet were touching the ground, it was obvious something was in the air. Good thing you have baggy pants on or your woody woodpecker would have been poking at her." Both began to laugh.

"Okay," smiled Conner. "I will set things straight." The music stopped. Austin and Emily approached Conner to say goodbye.

"Conner, happy birthday," Austin extended his hand. "Em and I are going to take off, now. I need my sleep. I am flying tomorrow. I do need to use the restroom before we leave, if you'll please excuse me?" Conner smiled and nodded as Austin left.

At that moment, Derek Stroebel came up behind Emily and winked at Conner. This guy was beginning to bother Conner and he didn't even know him.

"So, who is this beautiful woman, Conner?" Derek asked.

Emily felt the skin on the back of her neck prickle at the sound of a familiar voice from a very long time ago. She caught her breath but didn't move. The voice was too familiar and she told herself that it couldn't be. To her horror, she looked up and recognized him.

"Derek Stroebel," Conner bowed his head, slightly. "Emily Stewart."

Derek reached out his hand, and Emily slowly gave hers to him. He took her hand tightly and kissed the top if her wrist, directly along the faint scar line left from their last encounter. Emily jerked her hand away, and Conner looked at her with curiosity. It was so unlike Emily to be jumpy, so seemingly uncomfortable, and pull her hand away when a man was being cordial. Sure, Derek was an asshole, but Emily didn't know that. Did she read him the same way, perhaps?

"Nice to meet you, Mrs. Stewart. It is Mrs., right?"

"Yes, it is," Emily replied, coldly. Her eyes had gone dark, the same darkness that Conner had seen in the portrait hanging in the lodge at Blaney.

"Don't I know you from somewhere, Mrs. Stewart?"

Conner, sensing her uneasiness, jumped in. "No, Mr. Stroebel. I am sure you do not. Emily isn't from around here, and spends most of her time at Blaney Park. She is an exceptional writer and artist. Very talented."

"Yes, she is talented," Derek replied, with a crooked smile while looking directly in Emily's eyes. "Blaney Park, huh?"

Conner felt unusual vibes between them, as Emily dropped her gaze to the floor. At that moment, Austin came up behind Emily with her shawl and excused them both. Emily turned quickly and walked away without even acknowledging Conner to say goodbye. He was both confused and a bit hurt that she left in that manner, and was also irritated at being left to talk with Derek who he knew was there only for the property deal.

"Damn, she is still a fox," Derek smiled. "I saw you dancing with her, earlier. You poking that beauty, my friend?"

"Listen. Number one, I am not your friend. Secondly, she is married and I am not poking her, as you put it. Lastly, I don't appreciate your approach, here, Mr. Stroebel. We don't know each other well enough for you to be acting like this. I would appreciate you to be a little more polite and less aggressive to my guests."

"Chill out, Conner, "Derek smiled. "If I were you, I'd be taking that shit, if it came to me. I just thought you were exercising your right to a fuck on your birthday."

"Excuse me," Conner walked away. Derek got the message, smiled and left the ballroom. He did his job for the evening and, to his surprise, he even got a bonus. He saw Emily again. He had always hoped for another chance to encounter with her, having so enjoyed the first one, often fantasizing about what they had experienced together.

Conner was in conflict. He had earlier sent his wife off to be in the hands of another man and didn't feel the least bit uneasy about it. Now, Emily was going home with her husband and it bothered him. He cared about her so much. He wanted to ask her why she left so abruptly without saying a formal goodbye to him. What was wrong?

What is wrong? he asked himself. Everything.

Everything was wrong.

20

Emily's Defining Moment

Emily shivered. She was shaken to the core at not only seeing Derek after so many years, but more so by actually engaging in conversation with him. This was too much for her to handle, and getting out of there as quickly as possible was all she could think about.

"You okay?" Austin was looking at Emily with concern as he handed the coat room attendant the claim ticket for her silk wrap.

"Yes, I'm fine. Guess I just got a chill."

"In July?"

Austin nodded a thank you to the attendant and placed Emily's wrap around her shoulders. They said nothing to one another as they walked across the front entrance area of the Club and stepped outside. Austin handed the parking ticket to the valet, and they again stood in silence as they waited for their car to be brought around to the front entrance. The evening sky was clear, with the typical summer humidity of southeastern Michigan still lingering in the air. Austin glanced at her several times, but said nothing, and she knew his mind was racing with questions. She couldn't hide her reaction back in the ballroom and Austin, more than anyone, had picked up on her uneasiness. She wondered if he had also picked up on her reaction to Conner.

Once inside their car, she began trembling again. Austin hadn't even driven out of the parking lot before he spoke.

"Emily, the guy that Morley introduced us to, Derek Stroebel. That wasn't the same Derek, was it? The one from college?"

"Yes, it was."

"God, Babe, I'm sorry. I knew as soon as I saw your face... when Conner was telling him about you and your work up there." He reached over and placed his hand on hers, which were folded in her lap, trying to comfort her. "You okay?"

"I think so," Emily continued to stare out of the car window. Her tone was without emotion as she spoke. "I just wasn't prepared. I never dreamt I'd see him again, let alone at something like that party. It was just a surprise. Don't worry about it. I'll be fine."

They drove in silence until they had reached Maple Lake Road, and began their wind through the Lakes area of West Bloomfield to their home. Austin knew that the best thing he could do was to allow her some time to process what had happened, so that she understood how, if at all, she was impacted by seeing Derek again after all these years.

Emily's mind remained occupied by the events that had taken place at the party. Seeing Derek had upset her greatly, and she couldn't get his image out of his mind. He was from a time in her life that she kept little memories of, and definitely not the bad ones. How could this possibly be resurfacing now?

"Emily," Austin began again, this time with a different set of questions. "Conner's wife. She's one of my clients."

"Yes, I know."

"You do? How? You've seen her at Blaney?"

"Just a couple of times," Emily's mind thought of their brief conversation at the old lodge. "From a distance, mostly. She keeps a pretty low profile when she's there. Always stays in the House or out by the pool, and always has a private parlor where she takes her meals. She never eats in the dining room. Some guy is always with her."

"Ya, probably the same guy who flies with her, Jim Gordy. I didn't know that was Conner's wife, until tonight. I thought she was married to Gordy. God, it shocked me to see her and realize she's married to Morley. I'm surprised she even invited us, because she'd have to know I'd recognize her. But, then again, maybe she didn't care. Maybe she figured I wasn't paying any attention. I'm just the pilot, y'know." He laughed at his own expense.

"They've been having an affair for years, Austin," Emily sighed.

"So, you know?" Austin's tone told her he was clearly irritated at learning so much was happening around him, and he was oblivious to it all. Now, it was impacting his life much too intimately and he didn't like it one bit.

"Yes... no, I didn't know then. I didn't know she was Conner's wife until recently. I thought that Gordy guy was her husband. There was a problem at the Park recently. A fight. Elsie told me about it. And Conner."

"Emily, what the hell is going on?" Austin pulled abruptly into their driveway, turned off the car and looked at her. "You've spent so much time up there. It's like you have a different life when you're there, and now it's consuming you and your life here, as well. I feel like I've been gone for six months, and came home to somebody besides my wife. Jesus, I don't even know you right now."

Tears began to trickle down Emily's cheeks, and she was looking out the window toward the night sky. Her mind was in a different place, where the air was not so humid, and the stars shone a little brighter. She said nothing as she thought about what he had said and how right he was about it all. She did have a different life when she was at Blaney. It was a life that provided her more peace, more happiness, than she had felt for a very long time. She didn't want him to question her further, because she wasn't so sure she could explain it to him.

Austin was growing impatient at her silence, expecting an answer to his question. He said nothing, got out of the car and began walking toward the house without her.

After a few moments, Emily climbed out of their car and went into the house. She found Austin standing in their living room, staring out the window. She draped her wrap over the small bench in the entryway, and walked into the room behind him. The house was quiet, as it was still early enough that the girls hadn't come home from their own activities.

"I'm going back in the morning," she said, finally. "I'd like you to take me, but I'll rent a car if you'd rather not."

The room was quiet for several moments, before he responded.

"I'll take you." He paused before continuing, and then turned to face her. "I got a message earlier, anyway. Wasn't going to tell you about it, because I didn't expect you to be going back so soon and I didn't want to worry you. I really wasn't sure if you knew anything about it. The constable there wants to ask me some questions about Gordy. Apparently, his wife's filed a missing person's report. I wondered why he wasn't on the plane with Samantha."

"Missing person's report? No," she replied. "I didn't know anything about that. Why does he want to talk with you?"

"I'm not sure. Probably because I'm the one who flies the guy up there all the time. I would guess it's just routine. Nothing to worry about."

"Austin, I'm not worried about it. They don't have anything to do with me. You're right, it's just routine questioning." Emily squared her shoulders and looked directly at him. "I'm going anyway, you know."

"I know," he smiled at her courage, a remnant glimpse of the fearless farm girl resurfacing. "Gordy most likely just skipped town 'cause he got caught with his pants down while hanging out with someone like Conner Morley's wife. For Christ's sake, talk about finding a slightly risky target! If Jim knows anything about Morley, he'll wish he were on a different continent." Austin walked to the desk and picked up his flight planner. Their discussion had turned to business, as usual, and he was focused on procedures again. "When do you want your return scheduled?"

Emily stood motionless in the middle of the living room, and Austin looked up at her, waiting for her to give him a date to write in his planner.

"I'm not coming back, Austin," she said, quietly. She had realized during the party that her life was seemingly in suspended animation. She could not go back to her life with Austin and the girls or forward with hopes of a life with Conner. She was isolated from everything she came from, and denied everything she dreamed of. Emily felt defeated by the circumstances of both worlds, and didn't feel she had the strength to fight for either one. How could she? How could she fight for something that didn't exist, didn't welcome her, a world that had no place for her and one that she clearly didn't fit into? She was truly alone and suddenly realized she would be alone for the rest of her life. Emily had decided, almost in an instant, that she would go to Blaney and live there, purposefully isolating herself from a world that had betrayed her soul for the last time.

Austin stood silent for a moment. He then placed his planner carefully back down on the desk and leaned back against the wall, his eyes glassy from his own tears.

"At least we had one dance together," he said with great calmness in his voice. "Unlike the five dances in a row you shared with the guest of honor."

Emily dropped her head and began to cry softly, hurt by both his indifferent recognition that their marriage was over, and the ease with which he managed to throw one last wave of sarcasm at her.

"I'm not even sure you realized it was more than one. Remember me? The guy who pays attention? How well do you know him, anyway, Em?"

"Very well."

"Has he been there?"

"Yes."

"How often?"

"I don't know... maybe a half dozen times."

"With you?"

"Not in the way you mean, Austin. I'm not sure why he's there, actually. We just talk. About nothing, about everything. He comes by the river sometimes, when I'm working. I've shown him around the grounds, the woods. We've talked a lot."

"Obviously, since he introduced you as the gifted writer doing the research up there on the wolves of Blaney Park. You've never mentioned him to me. Not even when I told you about this party, did you suggest you knew him. Why?"

Emily stared at him, blankly. She hadn't even thought about it when Conner had introduced them to Derek. Austin never flinched. She realized now that he had to have wondered how Conner knew her at all, let alone what she was doing while at the Park.

"But you don't know why he's there?"

"No, Austin. I don't, really. It just... we've never discussed it, now that I think about it. Maybe he's been watching her. I don't know," she threw up her arms and turned towards the window. "What difference does it make?"

"I don't know that it makes any difference. I'm just trying to make sense out of all this. Jesus, Emily. Conner Morley?" He flopped down on the couch.

"I'm sorry, Austin."

"So am I." He was rubbing his face with his hands. "What should I tell the girls?"

"I'll talk to them," she sighed. "I want to leave early in the morning. I'll call them tomorrow night. This can't be a surprise to them, Austin. You and I both know they have sensed some distance between us for a long time, now. You know that."

"Yeah," he walked up behind her and draped his arms over her shoulders. "I just always thought we'd work through it. We've always worked through this kind of stuff, Em. Why is different, this time?"

"Because I'm different. Because I can't be who you think I am, who I was..." her voice trailed as she reached up and rested her hands on his arms. "Because I don't know who I am right now."

"But you can't figure that out here? You need more time alone? What, Em?"

"No, Austin. I can't. You and the girls will be fine. I'll be back, you know that. You'll still be flying people up there and everywhere else. I've still got my work here, the agency...it's not the house I'm leaving."

"I realize that. I'm just a little challenged by this, y'know? I feel like I just woke up from a very long dream."

She turned around to look at him and smiled. "Besides," she shrugged, "you're so busy, you won't even miss me."

Austin's jaw clenched as he looked at her and a tear fell down his cheek. "Ya," his voice was hoarse with emotion. "You're probably right."

"Then you'll take me?" She dropped her eyes, trying to control her emotions and not to react to the pain in Austin's voice.

"Of course, I will. Em. Look at me."

"What?" her eyes came back up to meet with his.

"Are you in love with him?"

Emily dropped her hands from Austin's arms, and turned around to face the window once again, her back to him.

"I'm in love with his soul."

Austin stood silent for a moment, and then turned her around to him again, and embraced her against his chest. Emily buried her face into him and cried softly. They stood together for several minutes, and Austin held back his own tears while Emily fought to regain her composure. Then, after a few deep sighs, she leaned back to look up at him.

"He's not why I'm going, Austin. He won't be there."

"I know," Austin smiled. "And, I know you need to go there. I guess I've known for a long time. Just never thought it was a big deal. You had your books, your wolves. I had my teaching and the plane. The girls are almost grown. I guess I just thought this is the way it would always be. I'm okay with it, really." He then looked down at her, having processed her last comment. "What do you mean, he won't be there?"

"He won't come back. He may never come back."

"Does he love you?"

"I don't know."

"Have you told him how you feel?"

"No," her voice was emphatic. "And, I have no intention of telling him."

"Emily..."

"Austin, please. Don't. Let's just let it go for tonight, please. I'm tired, and I want to pack before going to bed. I don't want to pack in the morning when the girls are here. We can talk on the way up, if you want." She pulled away from him and wiped her eyes.

"Don't imagine we have much to say, at this point. Do you?"

"Maybe not."

"I love you, Emily. I hope you know that. I always have and I always will."

"I know you do, Austin," her voice was shaking. "I love you, too. That's why this is all so hard, so very hard." She turned to walk down the hall towards their bedroom. Austin watched her, as the tears began streaming down his face. He had enjoyed his life, his family. He realized, at that moment, that his enjoyment had caused his indifference to what was going on around him over the years, including Emily's growth. She had grown up and developed her own life, a life that didn't include him. And, although he was aware of it, he really didn't see it or understand what the impact would be on their lives as a family. Oddly enough, he wasn't angry, even at her feelings for Conner. He just suddenly felt very empty, and very much alone.

He had been sitting in the dark living room, thinking about their conversation and what it would mean to them in the morning, when lights flooded the room as a car was turning into their driveway. Austin knew the girls were home. He was glad Emily had left the room before they arrived. The girls were very perceptive of their mother and very connected to her, emotionally. He didn't want them to see her so upset.

My girls, Austin smiled, wiping the last few tears from his eyes. They were his joy, the sunshine and the moon of his every day. He adored them completely and they felt the same for their dad. He was their world, their hero. They loved him and expected him to be with them forever. As long as Austin was in their lives, they feared nothing and felt the world was theirs for the taking. They would fly through both the sunshine and the storms of life, embracing it all, with their dad as the pilot.

He listened to them climb out of the car, yelling thank-you's and good-bye's to their friends, laughing and chatting with each other all the way to the front door. They were his real purpose, his life. They had been since they were born. They wouldn't understand why their mother would be gone from home so much, or why their parents' marriage was ending. Yet, he knew they would accept it, no matter how much pain they felt in the process. They knew everything would be okay, just because he was with them, and because he would tell them it would be.

21

Conner's Return

Three nights had passed since Emily had arrived back in Blaney Park. The sunlight glowing through her closed eyelids drew her from deep sleep to a conscious awareness that the morning had arrived. It was her first restful sleep since she had returned. The intense activities at Conner's party on Saturday night had exhausted her and seeing Derek had given her nightmares for two nights.

Her third night back, she ate dinner with Elsie. Elsie always helped Emily place things, including her fears, into the proper perspective. After a brandy and good conversation in front of Elsie's living room fireplace, she walked back to her cabin with peace in her soul again, and spent the remainder of the evening naked, wrapped in blankets and lying on the cabin floor in front of a slowly dying fire. Now, it was dawn and the fire had long been out. The cabin was cold and filled with the damp, Michigan morning air.

Emily shivered and curled deeper into the blankets, searching for a warm pocket in which to drift back into her dreams. The blankets refused, and her efforts to escape the morning chill only brought her further out of her slumber. Finally, she gave in, and her awakening was greeted by thoughts of Wolfie. She smiled, feeling renewed at his image in her mind and became anxious to start her day. The weather was perfect, and she was looking forward to the day's activities by the river. She rose from the pile of blankets and searched for her jeans and sweater. She pulled them on quickly, along with thick socks and her hiking shoes, and walked to the kitchen. Emily wasn't much of a coffee drinker. She rarely made it through an entire cup and only drank it first thing in the morning. She could have skipped it completely, but it seemed more a part of her morning routine than an actual need for a caffeine fix.

It was Wednesday morning. Conner wasn't due back up until Friday, at the earliest, if he returned at all. Emily thought about him as she walked along the path toward the river. She was thankful to know she had at least a couple of days alone before he could arrive back at the Park. She had felt very vulnerable towards him recently, especially at the party, and her thoughts were confusing her. They had so little in common. He was from the city, she from the farm. He was a corporate giant, she was a writer and a mom. Conner was a man who was surrounded by people who anticipated, and provided, everything he needed. She was a woman who hung out with a pack of wolves in the middle of nowhere.

Emily thought of Samantha. Conner's wife. How beautiful she had looked at the party. Her hair was dark, but had reddish-gold highlights, undoubtedly the magic of a beautician, which accentuated her strikingly large, brown eyes. Her fingers were dressed with an expensive manicure of long acrylics painted a deep brownish red and highlighted with gold flecks. Samantha's jewelry was large and expensive. The unique shapes of her rings, earrings and bracelets dripped with money, and Emily knew they were all one-of-a-kind creations, undoubtedly from one of the best jewelers in Detroit. Emily couldn't compete with Samantha's exquisite taste and style, nor did she have any desire to try. Samantha had no soul. All she had was what she created herself to be. Unfortunately, what Samantha had become was exactly what society applauded. Emily wanted no part of it. Seeing Conner standing next to her in a tuxedo, drink in one hand, shaking hands of guests with the other, Emily was trying to imagine where the man was that she knew from the Park, the one she met by the river. She searched his eyes for the one in expensive jeans, but who had great soul and who would stretch out in the grass next to her, regardless of the mud collecting on his $500 shoes.

"Just forget about it," she said aloud, as she reached the clearing. Emily looked up, breathed deeply and exhaled. She closed her eyes as her breath left her, allowing all the remaining discomfort of the party to float out of her body. She opened her eyes, saw the river gleaming in the morning sun, and smiled. This was all that mattered. Dancing along the riverbank with the inhabitants of this city was the only party Emily cared to attend.

It was early, only ten o'clock, yet Emily could already feel the humidity rising. It would be hotter than normal today. More than would be expected this far north, even for a day late in July, as this was typically a dry period. Emily was glad she had risen early with the sun to enjoy as much of the day as possible. When she had arrived at the clearing, the sun was barely high enough to burn off the dew of the night before. Emily loved this time of the morning. It was the time when the scents of the earth were most vibrant, most invigorating to her. She stretched out fully in the damp, cool grasses and balanced the cold chill of the earth, which soaked through her clothing to the skin of her back against the warmth of the sun as it baked her face, neck, and arms. She kept her eyes closed, and ran her hand upward beneath her sweater, lifting the bottom hem to expose her stomach in order to feel the heat of the sun on her skin.

An hour or so passed. Then, soft rustling noises from across the river drew a smile to her face, despite her closed eyelids. She recognized the sounds of Wolfie and his family, as they ventured out from the trees to play in the sun. Emily lifted her head, and propped herself up on her elbows.

She watched the younger ones play, in and out of the river, for a few moments and then she looked further back to locate the old female. She finally saw her, standing close to the edge of the trees. Emily knew, by the old wolf's actions, that she was getting beyond her active years, old enough that one day very soon she would cease as part of the pack.

Today, the old one was particularly less active, and it saddened Emily. Despite the warmth the sun brought to the earth and how it released the smell of honeysuckle and goldenrod into the air, Wolfie's elder walked slowly away from the rest of the pack, to the side of the clearing and nearer the river. She sat down in such a way that she was facing Emily. They simply stared at one another for several moments. Emily didn't even feel compelled to capture the image on paper, so her sketchpad lay untouched beside her in the grass. Emily knew this was an image she cared to only capture through her eyes and into her heart. She broke their gaze and pulled her eyes in the direction of the other pups.

Where was he? Her eyes soon found him, as usual, challenging the rest of the pack to follow him to the edge of the bank, daring them to the cold water of the river. Emily laughed aloud as she watched the little daredevil. He feared nothing, he knew nothing to fear. He had experienced the river once, and was not met with death. Emily had saved him. The river did not represent danger to him, but rather risk that would be buffered by his new friend, this strange being that did not resemble the rest of his pack, yet was very much a part of it and who was always there, on the opposite bank.

Emily noticed the pups, including Wolfie, look up suddenly towards her side of the river, and they retreated slightly back towards the edge of the trees. Simultaneously, she heard footsteps behind her and turned to see

Conner walking into the clearing from the footpath.

"Hey," he said with a large grin on his face. "What's up?"

"The sunshine," she smiled with pleasure at seeing him. "Now I know why." The Park had not been the same to her since he had left almost two weeks before his birthday. Emily had so enjoyed his company during the spring and early summer, yet didn't realize just how much until recently. They had walked together in the morning, shared picnic lunches that sometimes consisted of little more than crackers, whatever overly-ripened fruit they found in their cabins, and warm sodas and sometimes a few swallows of whiskey. It never mattered. Just grab whatever, Conner always said.

Emily so enjoyed his relaxed mood, his spontaneity, the way he found pleasure in just being there. Conner questioned everything. Why did the wolves come out to play so freely only in the early morning hours? Why didn't the bees and the black flies swarm until the humidity peaked during the afternoons? Why did she insist on not bathing until the evening in order to keep away the mosquitoes? Why did he have to crouch in the grass whenever the wolves were out, rather then stand on the riverbank in order to get a closer look? Emily had explained her world to him, while imagining what it was like to grow up in his. She knew she would feel as much out of her element in his childhood domain as he now did in hers. Conner was successful, strong willed, fearless and intuitive about life. Teaching him the way of nature, of the river and the wolves, gave Emily a sense of equal footing to him. She could share something with him that he had never experienced before. She could be the teacher, and he, the student.

Conner bent down slightly, remembering to lower his body language so not to scare the wolves off.

"Who's here today?" he asked.

"Everyone. Look," Emily pointed at the black wolf. "Welcome back, by the way."

"Thanks."

"How has your week been so far?"

"Fast. Slow. Difficult. I'm glad it's over."

"Me, too. I'm not even sure why."

Conner looked curiously at her watching the wolves, a smile of contentment and peace on her face. The pups tired, and began flopping down in the grass. It was approaching midday and they were becoming sleepy beneath the heat of the sun.

"Lunch time," Emily suddenly turned her head and looked at Conner. "I didn't bring anything today. Didn't expect to see you, y'know."

"That's okay."

"Are you hungry?"

Conner laughed. "I'm always hungry."

"Come on," Emily rose to her feet, extending her hand to him. "Let's go for a walk."

Conner's heart rate increased as he reached up and took her hand. Emily's demeanor surprised him, it was different than before. She seemed warmer and more relaxed. He didn't even ask where they were going, just held her hand. He looked back over his shoulder, across the river and saw Wolfie. Emily's constant companion was sitting with his head upright, ears forward, paying very close attention to what she was doing, where she was going.

"I think someone is upset with you," he teased, pulling gently on Emily's hand. She looked back at the pack.

"Oh, he'll be okay," she smiled. "He won't follow this time. He knows better."

They walked along the river until they reached a bend that was on lower ground. The land was softer, more moss grew around the tree stumps and Conner's new hiking boots soaked up a little moisture from the earth.

"Here we go," Emily stopped suddenly and bent down. "Lunch time."

Conner looked curiously as she reached beneath small, low plants that looked like the rest of the forest's weeds to him. These plants had very shiny, dark green leaves and she plucked red berries from beneath them. "Try one," she offered, holding out her hand. Conner held up his open palm and she dropped four small red berries into it. He looked at her, with hesitation, and she burst out laughing.

"Oh, I see. Big city kid, no fear of death, but afraid of a wintergreen berry or two! You are something, Conner Morley."

Feeling very much put in his place, he grinned, and lowered his mouth to his palm, gathering the berries up with his tongue but never losing eye contact with Emily. He was pleasantly surprised at the cool, mint flavor of the berries and their crispness when he bit into them.

"Wow," he said. "These are great, but I can't survive on this."

"I know, I know. That's just your appetizer. Come on." Emily took his hand again and they turned away from the river, walking uphill toward the trees where the sunshine was streaming through the branches. They reached the top of the ridge, above the river and walked another hundred feet into a clearing. They stood in knee-high bushes and Emily, once again, crouched low to the ground.

"This is much better," she pulled him down beside her. "Look."

Conner watched, as Emily used her forearm to bend back the tops of the bushes, and then flopped her leg upon them in order to free both her hands to collect what lay beneath. He was astonished at the site of large, blue clusters of berries, each one frosted slightly with a thin, white film.

"Blueberries!" he exclaimed. "Unbelievable. How did you know they would be here?"

Emily laughed. "This is my world, remember? I can take care of you, here."

Conner looked up at her, as he was plucking and tasting the rich, juicy berries. They were warmed from the sun and seemed fresher than any pie he had ever tasted.

Emily leaned back against her elbows again, leaving her leg upon the tops of the bushes to expose the berries that lay abundantly beneath. She watched him, his hands and his fingers, his mouth consuming the fruit. She watched the smile on his face, saw it in his eyes. She leaned forward and reached beneath a bush to strip a handful of berries into her palm. With her other hand, she took two berries between her fingers and slowly lifted them up to Conner, offering them to him. He hesitated, and looked at her for a moment, but said nothing. Then, keeping his eyes on hers, opened his lips just far enough for her to drop the berries into his mouth, one by one. They kept their eyes locked upon one another, as he slowly rolled the berries with his tongue and then pressed them against the roof of his mouth, allowing them to smell slowly, savoring them. Emily lowered her eyes to his mouth and she watched as he swallowed the berries. She watched his jaw, his throat and his neck as his muscles worked together to consume the fruit she had offered him. She lifted her eyes back up to his and Conner saw her passion for him in the shining pools of moisture surrounding her green eyes. Her lids were lazy above them, and he felt her looking deeply into him. She dropped her eyes once again and rose to her feet.

"Time to go back," she said, quietly. Conner stood up beside her.

"Emily...." his voice had softened.

She did not look at him, but rather just smiled and gazed toward the ridge. "We should get back before dark."

"Okay, whatever you say."

Emily reached down and took his hand, once again. She led him back towards the river, walking much slower than she had earlier. Conner was not just a follower, now. He was looking at the ground, the undergrowth and the trees. He was seeing so much more than he realized existed when they had first stepped into the woods. He was overwhelmed by the multitude of activities taking place around him. The calling blue jays, the distant drumming of the partridge, the wild sweet fern, lady slippers and Indian paint brush. A puff adder slithered by them while they rested by the edge of the stream, and Emily pointed it out to him. He realized that he was truly in a city - the city of nature. So much going on, so busy, so little time and yet, to someone who couldn't see, it all appeared to be so very boring. Not so, he realized. It was so much more alive than any city he'd ever been in.

When they returned to the clearing, it was approaching dusk. The wolves were gone and the sun had lowered just far enough to be slightly shaded by the tops of the trees. A small group of deer grazed along the far edge of the clearing and were barely visible in the evening shadows. The air was no longer warmed by the rays of the sun and the humidity was now creating a chill in the air. They continued along the path towards the cabins, saying nothing while listening to the sounds of the evening whippoorwills and other birds making their community calls. The deer moved across the clearing and along the edges of the thickets as if beginning an evening dance, their turn in the moonlight.

"Bonfire night," Emily announced, as they approached the back yard of his cabin. "Are you interested?"

"A bonfire, huh? Sure, I guess. Can I bring anything?"

Emily stopped, and turned to face him on the path.

"I've got lots of wood. You bring the J.D." She smiled and turned from Conner, leaving him speechless on the path next to his cabin. Watching her walk away, seeing her movements within her well-fitted jeans aroused him greatly. He watched until she disappeared around the next cabin, and then turned to grasp the doorknob, hoping he would have enough Jack Daniel's to last the evening.

Emily heard his footsteps draw closer to her in the darkness, and recognized Conner's gait. It was something she learned from the wolves, from their reactions as different things happened in the woods. They would respond uniquely to all noises. Emily enjoyed closing her eyes and seeing images with her hearing and mind, rather than by sight.

"Hey."

She smiled, not looking up from the fire, but continuing to poke at it with a large stick.

"Guess what I found in my cupboard?" Conner held up an unopened bottle of Jack Daniel's.

"Good ol' Archie."

"Ya, he's great. Doesn't say much, though."

"You just don't know how to listen." She lifted her eyes up sideways to meet his and nodded her head toward the trees. Conner looked up and saw Wolfie standing in the glow from the fire.

"Whoa," he whispered.

Emily held her hand out and Wolfie approached, cautiously. She didn't move until he reached her, sniffing her hand, then turning his head down in order to offer her an ear. Emily scratched him slowly and then he pulled away, backing up a few steps and lowering his body to lay a few feet from them.

Conner watched them closely and was deeply moved by the obvious bond between them. This was Wolfie's world, his domain. Emily was an outsider that had been accepted into the pack, into the hood. Conner thought of Todd and the friendship they had nurtured into a bond that equaled family. Todd had been the outsider, the intruder. He had won a place within Conner's heart and they had become family to one another. There was a similar bond between Emily and Wolfie that allowed them to communicate with one another so well.

"He's here almost every night now," she said. "I'm not sure if that's a good thing, or bad."

"I'd say it's pretty awesome," Conner watched Wolfie closely. "You're amazing, Emily. Thank you for sharing all of this with me."

"Thank you for coming here," she replied, looking up at Conner through the flames of the fire. The flames danced around her eyes and Conner was suddenly drawn to them. There was something familiar about her eyes, something he hadn't noticed before. They said nothing to each other for a long time. Emily stared at him, occasionally sipping her glass of whiskey and he was mesmerized by the dance of the fire around her eyes and on her face.

Emily was also caught in his gaze. Conner's face had softened that night and she sensed something very vulnerable inside of him, something she could not pinpoint just yet, as he had seemed so strong, so chiseled from the city. Hard, fast, successful. It just hadn't seemed to fit him, and tonight she could see it in his deep blue eyes, in his soul. It was a hunger, a craving, like the wolves for their pack. She still didn't fully know why he was here. He avoided the subject whenever she brought it up.

Her heart began pounding, as she sensed herself wanting to know him, understand what made him feel empty, what brought him joy, yet, at the same time, knowing she would either fear what she found or love it. If she dared to get close, she may not be able to pull back again, as her soul would mate with his and change her life forever.

"It's getting colder," Conner said, after a while. "Maybe we should call it a night."

"Out here, anyway. Why don't you come inside? I'd like you to read what I've been working on."

"I'd love that." Conner rose, and kicked at the fire's glowing logs.

"Don't worry about the fire," she said. "I'll check on it later. Come on."

Wolfie rose with them, and Emily turned to face him.

"Not tonight, guy," she smiled. "Better go back with your own, okay?" Wolfie looked at her for a moment and then turned to slowly disappear into the darkness.

"Awesome," Conner observed, shaking his head. He turned to follow Emily around to the front door of her cabin. There was little light inside, beyond the glow from the fireplace. Emily walked around to her desk, opened her laptop and turned it on.

"Have a seat," she said, pulling the desk chair back. "I'll pour while you read."

"Cool," he shrugged and sat down in front of her computer.

Emily walked into the kitchen, feeling slightly nervous about sharing her work in its rough format with someone like Conner. He was probably used to reading business proposals and monthly stock reports. Accounts of a bunch of wild animals may be terribly boring to him.

She poured their drinks slowly, glancing up frequently in hopes of catching a reaction in his face. She was disappointed, as he read without showing emotion. Emily picked up the glasses and walked up behind him.

She held her own glass in her left hand and leaned forward around Conner to place his glass next to his right hand which lay on the desk beside her computer. Her breasts brushed slightly against the back of his head and shoulder and he breathed in deeply at her touch.

"Do you mind if I read over your shoulder?" she asked.

"Not at all," he replied, lifting the glass to his lips. He sipped slowly and then replaced his glass on the coaster next to her laptop.

What is happening to me, she thought, as she reached around him once again, placing her glass down next to his. His hand still rested on the desk and Emily retracted her hand by pulling her fingertips lightly across the top of his hand, up his wrist and arm to his shoulder. She rested her hand on his shoulder, waiting for him to react. Conner continued to read and Emily drew her left hand up to his left shoulder, equal with her right. She began to caress his shoulders, massaging his muscles with her fingertips, as he read. He closed his eyes at her touch, rolling his head backward and then around to the sides above his shoulders. She drew her hands up closer to his neck, tracing the tendons up from his collarbone to his earlobes. She pressed her fingertips into his neck behind his ears and pushed her hands gently into his hair, up along the sides of his head and ran her fingers through his hair until they locked together at the top of his skull.

"What are you doing?" Conner moaned, softly.

Emily said nothing in response. Although she felt a tremendous desire to reach out to Conner, she fought the sensation that he was in more need of her friendship. He was most certainly in tremendous pain as he faced his divorce, the ending to a life he had believed in and worked for more than anything in his life. Emily closed her mind to her intense feelings for him and focused, instead, on the pain he was most certainly experiencing. She released her hands from one another and again ran her fingertips lightly down the sides of his head. She firmed her grip as she rubbed down his shoulders to his arms and lowered her head next to his. Emily's breathing was stronger as she opened her mouth and closed her lips around Conner's earlobe. He leaned his head backward against her shoulder and she kissed him lightly along his temple, down the side of his face and neck. She ran her hands beneath his arms, down his ribs and sides, bringing them together in front of his chest and locking them tightly around his waist.

'Stay with me tonight," she whispered.

"Emily..."

"No, Conner. It's not like that. Just please just stay with me, next to me, next to each other. Neither of us needs to be alone tonight. Please."

Conner rose from the chair and turned to face her. He looked deep into Emily's eyes and cupped her face with his hands.

"I'll stay. If you want me to, I'll stay."

Emily closed her eyes and reached up with her right hand to grasp his. She then opened her eyes and, taking his hand, stepped backward towards her bed. She led Conner to it and guided him to a sitting position on the edge of the mattress. She crouched at his feet and began untying the laces of his hiking boots. After pulling his off, she began removing her own, while he watched.

She stood back up and lifted her sweater above her head, exposing her tank top. Emily gently pushed Conner backward and he slid back on the bed to lie down on the pillow facing the fire. Emily crawled up next to him, with her back to him and snuggled backward against his chest.

"Just hold me tonight," she whispered, reaching for his hand as he lowered his arm around her waist. "Please, Conner. Just hold me."

Conner buried his face into her neck and closed his eyes. His passion for her was growing wildly, yet he knew he would never expose it to her. He kissed her neck lightly and then allowed his mind to be consumed by the effects of the whiskey.

Emily watched the dying flames of the fire, and listened to each rise and fall of Conner's breathing until she knew that he was beginning to drift asleep.

"Conner," she whispered.

"Mmmm," he moaned, and then began breathing heavily again.

"After your divorce, please come back to Blaney."

Conner didn't respond, only sighed and drew his arm more firmly around her waist.

And, I will be here, she thought to herself.

As the firelight died, so did Emily's consciousness, as she allowed herself to be consumed by sleep and drifted into a place she longed to be... a place that was hers and Conner's, if only for one night.

Archie stood silently outside Emily's cabin, watching all that took place within. He was not surprised by it, but rather at the amount of time it took the two of them to give in to the obvious passion between them. Archie envied Conner and felt great sadness for him, at the same time. He knew that

Conner was weakening to a passion for a woman that would never be his. Archie knew that this only meant Conner would live the rest of his life with an empty heart.

He watched them fall asleep together, fully clothed, and knew that this was more erotic and powerful than any bar pick-up Conner would ever experience in the city. Archie felt Conner's love for Emily and sighed heavily as he realized he was now responsible for her safety, as well. Emily was not family, yet Archie knew that Conner's weakness, his feelings for her, would create a situation where Archie must now treat her as such. He had always liked Emily, always felt she was special. Yet, realizing how she had now touched Conner caused him to look differently at her. She was married and so was Conner. Despite his fondness for her, to Archie she was now an imposter and a threat to Conner. He knew he would have to place her appropriately in his mind.

The fire died and Archie turned back to the darkness, thinking only of his traps, those that he must inspect and empty before dawn.

22

Truth Serum

September 8th. Conner's divorce hearing concluded at 12:03pm. Todd had him in the air by noon. They were heading north and said nothing to each other. He could see the hurt and anger in Conner's face and knew this was one of those times they would exchange no words with one another.

When they landed, Archie quietly took Conner's bags to his cabin and he, too, said nothing. Conner followed in silence, his mind was spinning with all that was happening. Loneliness was filling his existence. Life had never been too difficult for Conner, as he had always seen the positive in it. The positive wasn't obvious this time, however. Breaking up the house had sealed the end of his marriage to Samantha. Conner never wanted to admit it, but he knew she was capable. As he thought about their courting, Samantha had never been without a man. She jumped from one to the next, and Conner realized he had been nothing more than the means to her end. It was Conner who had worked at nurturing their relationship.

And, Emily. There still was Emily.

Conner watched as Archie dropped his bag in the middle of the room. Before he turned to leave, Conner saw him toss something on the coffee table. It was a half-full pack of Winston cigarettes. Conner didn't usually smoke and was now smiling with curiosity at Archie's perceptiveness.

He stood motionless as Archie pulled the door closed. He didn't even bother to turn on the floor lamp, as was his usual routine upon arrival. As always, Archie had the fire lit and the cabin was warm, glowing softly from the flames. Conner stared into the fire, then walked to the table and reached for the pack. He slowly pulled out a cigarette and tapped it against the side of his thumb. Not that he really knew why it was done, but everyone who smoked did it. He didn't even realize he was supposed to hold it filter down when he tapped.

Emily.

Conner rolled the cigarette between his lips, and his mind returned to her. He even liked the name. Emily. It rolled off his tongue and was fluid in his mind. She was not there. Archie had informed him that she had unexpectedly flown downstate two days prior for a meeting with her editor. Her book on the wolves around the Sceney Wildlife Refuge area had been well received, and Emily had been issued a grant by the State of Michigan to continue her research and studies of that area. Conner knew he would not see her until the weekend and he was pleased. He wasn't ready to see her, just yet.

Conner's arms suddenly felt tired and sagged at his sides. He went to the kitchen window and opened the cupboard containing his J.D. and enjoyed a whiff of the cool refreshing breeze blowing in through the window. He never closed it, even when the temperature dropped during the night. As long as the fire was stoked, the cabin remained like an oven and Conner could enjoy the cool air.

The J.D. and diet Coke, sometimes just the J.D., kept Conner warm until the time when he would pass out. He never respected people who drank themselves to oblivion. But it was his time now and he was doing just that. He never was one to revel in self pity, but the current wave of adversity was more then he wanted to handle while sober.

His business would be fine as long as he didn't leave it for too long. All his people were allocated and the pipeline for the next three quarters was set. He was losing motivation and inspiration for his business. What value was there to work so hard if there was no family to come home to who would appreciate his efforts? Hell, he thought, Samantha never appreciated what he did. Her career was most important and everything revolved around it. If someone spoke negatively about Conner, she would agree instead of supporting and defending her man, sometimes even when he was part of the conversation.

Conner had only consumed two drinks. He was still standing in the cool afternoon breeze as it rolled in through the kitchen window, and he was feeling more stupid than hurt. He closed his eyes and the room started slowly spinning. He placed the bottle next to the sink and walked back to flop down into the chair by the fire, allowing the alcohol and his sleep to overtake him.

The next day, Conner did not leave the cabin. He heard some movement outside around midday and knew Archie was nearby, most likely checking on him. Archie did not attempt to knock at the cabin door. He would clearly see the smoke billowing from the chimney and know that Conner was, at least, tending the fire. Conner needed to be alone, needed to grieve. Archie knew this and felt sad. This was his nephew, yet he couldn't reach out to him as such. He couldn't allow Conner to know that they were related. The cost was too great.

Saturday morning. Three days after he had arrived, the noise of Austin's plane could be heard as it touched down just before ten o'clock. Conner was still sitting in the chair, staring at the fire, when he heard Emily's light laughter pass by his doorway as she and Archie reacquainted with one another on the way to her cabin. Conner had barely eaten since his arrival on Wednesday. Two empty bottles of Jack Daniel's sat next to the kitchen sink and a third bottle stood open on the coffee table by his chair. He had not showered or shaved, and barely changed clothing.

Emily stopped by a few times during the two days that followed and each time knocked lightly on his cabin door. She always waited, knocked a second time, waited and then left. Conner knew it was difficult for her to leave him alone, knowing what he had been through and most assuredly worrying about him. He had sensed her affection for him growing during the months they had spent together and, although he longed to seek comfort in her, he could not find the strength to reach out.

Emily.

Who would have ever thought that Conner would be used and abused. He was spanked like a rented mule and he knew it. Good looks and the thought of being successful had lured him into marrying a shallow and self-centered woman. As he drank another shot, he thought of his mom. Samantha wasn't anything like her. His mom possessed qualities of class, integrity and loyalty. Samantha had none.

Another drink brought Emily back to his mind. Now, that was a kind and wonderful woman. Damn, she's married. Why did she have to be married?

The evening darkened with the setting mid-September sun and Conner threw more wood on the fire. Becoming more and more intoxicated, he now began talking out loud instead of thinking to himself.

"I am a good man," he said drunkenly, as he poured another shot. The diet Coke had been omitted from the equation for the last four drinks.

"Emily would be a fine woman to have as a wife. She likes Wooolfie and aaaaall the wooolves." Conner's speech was slurring as his mind was spinning.

"Eeeeeeeverrrybooody lllooovesss Emmmillly. I looove Ewillly, tooo! Hahahaha!" He laughed, dropping his glass to the floor just before passing out.

Emily had been sitting behind her cabin, watching the flames in her fire pit, when she had heard his voice coming from his window through the still night air. She rose and pulled her sweater around her shoulders. After hesitating for a second, she slowly began walking toward his cabin. She felt that he was perhaps finally open to a visit from her and she had missed him. As she walked closer, his voice stopped and Emily was confused by the silence. Rather than knocking, she walked around to the kitchen window, which still stood open, and peered inside to see him lying on the floor. Emily panicked. Was he asleep? Perhaps sick? Was he having a heart attack? She ran around to the front door and went in, just as Conner was attempting to rise up on his hands and knees.

"Oh, God, Conner, let me help you," she said, noticing the near-empty bottle on the table, and the glass lying on the floor at his feet. He smelled of sweat and stale whiskey. Emily threw her sweater over the back of his chair and struggled to help him toward his bed.

While Conner continued to mumble, pass out, mumble some more, pass out again, Emily cared for him, taking off his hiking boots, his belt, laying him out fully on his bed. She then stoked the fire and cleaned up the broken glass from the floor.

"Emillly... Emmmillly... you aaaaaaare in my cabin. I liiike yoooou in my cabin... aaaare we go, goin' to sllleeep togetttther?"

Emily smiled at his drunkenness, but did not respond. She continued to straighten up, while listening to Conner's rambling.

"Kiiiss me, you beeeeeautifull thing. I haaave beeen waaaiting fooor yooooou aaalll weeek."

"Shh," Emily whispered, holding her finger softly against his lips. She enjoyed listening to his uninhibited words.

"Haaave yooou everrr frrrench kisssssed a Woooolfffie? Hahahahaha! Did I telll yoooou that I ammm paaart wwwooolfffie? Hahahaha! You better ssstay the nnnight wiiith me... the booogy maaan might be out therrrrrrre. Hahahahaha!"

Emily unbuttoned his shirt and helped him lean forward. Her hands slid inside his shirt at his chest and slowly pushed the sleeves from his shoulders, down his arms. Her hands closed in around his, and her heart began to pound. The feel of his hands - they were strong hands, yet soft and warm.

"We'll fork with each other...hhhaaahahaha!" He slurred, breaking out in uncontrollable laughter. When he regained his composure, Conner corrected himself. "No, nonononono, not fork! Spooonnn each other. Hahahahahaha!"

Emily smiled and pulled the shirt away from his body.

"Hey, now! Are you making a move on the Con Man? Hahahahaha! You better be prepared to wear my shirt in the morning if you are going to be in it all night. Hahahahaha! I like underwear. Are you wearing underwear, Emily?" Conner leaned against her breasts as she pulled his undershirt from inside his belt. She repressed light laughter at his drunken state, and gently lowered him back onto the bed pillow.

"Whatever you say, Con Man. Yes, I am wearing underwear."

"I like the way underwear covers the aaasss and oh, isn't it beautiful!" Conner was leaning to the side, trying to look at Emily's ass. She smiled as she slid his belt from his jeans.

"No peaking," she teased. "Besides, you'll fall on the floor again."

"Hey, hey! If you can get into my shirt, can I get into your shorts?" Conner began laughing hard again at Emily's smile. "My turn!"

Conner reached for Emily's shirt and pulled it out of her shorts. He then reached for the top button, but Emily slapped his hand back.

"Hey, yooooooooou are not playing fair here! No fffffair! We need equality here! Wooooomen always want equality, and here it is, fffolks! Con man gets to take this foxy lady's shirt offf. Why? Because I can! Hahahahaha. Hey, Emmmily, let me help!" Conner unbuckled his jeans and pulled down the zipper. "Okay... your turn, Beeeeeauuutiful!"

Emily reached to the foot of his bed and picked up the cotton throw. She draped it across Conner's chest, both to warm him and to hide him from her gaze. His skin was smooth, his muscles well formed. Emily's body was reacting to how he looked to her, how he smelled, and her attraction to him was swelling.

Not tonight, she told herself. Don't go there, girl. You know better, this isn't right.

"Here, let me do that," she said, putting her hands over his. "You just lie back and let me do the work." Emily knew if she could just get him to lie back in the warmth of the blanket, the J.D. would take over from there.

Conner, in his drunken state, tried to look sexy at Emily, who knew what he was trying to do. She walked to the end of the bed and quickly grasped each of his pant legs, then pulled each leg of his pants off at the same time.

"Hey, hey now, no fair! That's cheating...!"

"Who ever said I play fair?" She smiled teasingly at him

"Do you knooow my daaad. Have you ever mmmet him? No, no. You haven't met my daaad. Oh, cooome on... everyone knows my dad. He's the greatest! But, dooo you know what God diiid to him?"

Emily pulled the afghan from the back of his easy chair and draped it over his legs, as she fought the urge to look at them, at his thighs, the bulging in his underwear.

"What, Conner," she said, softly.

"He gaaavvve him cancer." Conner's words drew her back a step and she looked down at him in horror.

"What did you say?" she knelt down on the floor beside him. "Conner, your dad has cancer?"

"Yup," Conner's voice softened and he composed himself slightly. "The greatest man on this earth, and God is trying to get him on His team. But, I got news for God. He can allowww my wife to cheat on mmme... did you know mmmy wife cheated on me? He can cause me to have businesss prrrroblems, but he can't have mmmy dad. Nope! I won't let him do that."

Oh, God, she thought, closing her eyes as they filled with tears. Not now.... why now?

"Conner, I'm so, so sorry."

Your wife was definitely cheating. That's why he divorced her. She slowly slid her hand up the side of the bed, over Conner's arm and clasped his hand gently in hers.

"Conner, go to sleep," she whispered, leaning her head against his upper arm. "I'm so sorry. I'll stay with you tonight, right here."

"Dooon't be sssorry. He ain't going to die. My wife cheated on me, but my dad ain't goin' to die." Conner eyes begin to swell with tears. "My daaad is a rock. I mean, a ssstone cold rock! Boulder rock. No way will a little bitsy... little bitsy...." Conner put his thumb and forefinger close together, "...cancer going to hurt my dad."

Emily turned to look at him and the tears were spilling quietly down her cheeks. She reached up with her other hand and gently caressed the hair from his brow with her fingers. "You'll be okay. I'm right here with you. I'm not going to leave you alone - not tonight, not ever. We'll get through this... all of it. You and me. Okay?"

"You gonna stay with me," Conner smiled. "Okey dokey... but don't take advantage of me in this condition, okay, Emily? 'Cause I'm a little under the weather. I think we are in a tornado because the ceiling is spinning. I am going to open my eyes. I want to see your eyes real quick before I go to sleep, okay?"

"Okay," she whispered, rising to her knees next to him.

Emily was slightly over him now. She looked down into his face and smiled through her tears. She knew she could do nothing for him but just be there, stay there and listen.

Conner opened his eyes. He had to wait for the tears to leave but when his eyes connected to Emily's, his heart began to race. He reached up and gently brushed a tear from her cheek.

"Emily, I love you. I know we haven't... known each other for very long... but you are... wonderful. My wife cheated on me, you know. You wouldn't cheat on anyone would you?" Conner, in his drunken state, gave no thought to the fact that Emily was married. He was single minded and focused on his love for a woman he couldn't have.

Emily couldn't breathe against the lump in her throat. She looked into his eyes, two great blue pools filled with pain, passion, love and loneliness.

"I love you, too, Conner," she whispered. She leaned over and kissed him lightly on the forehead.

"That's nice... you better take cover, Emily. The tornado is gettin' worse. Wow! How does the cabin stay together through all this spinning? Good cabins. Well made."

"Conner," Emily moved and positioned her face directly over his. "I would never cheat on you, Conner. Never betray you - your friendship, or your love."

"I bet the person who owns these cabins is a great guy. Huh, Emily? Did I tell you I own these cabins? I own all of this, Emily. I bet you are impressed, aren't you?"

"Go to sleep," she whispered, ignoring his admission and pulling the blankets around his shoulders. Emily sank back down onto her heels and leaned against the side of the bed, her arms stretched over him. She smiled at his words. What a kidder you are, she thought.

"Okay, Conner. You own everything."

Conner didn't say another word. Hard breathing replaced the talk and he fell to his drunken slumber.

Emily stayed with him until dawn, stoked his fire and quietly slipped out of his cabin. She felt it was better that he awaken alone, without her there, and wonder if he had dreamt their conversation and the events of the evening before. She did not want him to be concerned or embarrassed by anything he might remember having done or said and by leaving she knew he would most likely believe it to have all been a dream.

Shortly after she left, Archie knocked roughly on the door and walked in.

"You look like hell," he snarled at Conner.

"Ya, well, who gives a shit?" Conner mumbled as he pushed himself up off the bed with one hand, holding his forehead with the other.

"Why don't you clean up and come out of this place? You just might find an answer." Archie walked back out, not bothering to close the door this time.

"Hey!" Conner yelled after him. "Close the damn door!" Realizing that Archie wasn't turning around, Conner angrily rose and walked to the open doorway. It was a warm, September afternoon, and the sun was shining through the trees. A light breeze was carrying the brightly-painted leaves down from the oak and maple trees that were scattered among the pines. Autumn had arrived and left. Conner hadn't even noticed. A blue jay screeched at him, and Conner looked up into the trees. He took a deep breath of the clear air and knew Archie was right. It was time to come out.

He showered, shaved the week's growth from his face and dressed in clean, warm clothing. He ate lightly, not wanting to waste too much time in the cabin before it was too cold to venture the grounds. When he left, he headed in the direction opposite of the path to the riverbank. He was sure Emily would be there, and he wasn't ready to encounter her just yet. The cool air smelled clean and he felt refreshed for the first time in two weeks.

Conner walked slowly down the path toward the old village buildings, not heading in any particular direction. He looked up at the old lodge as he approached it and there she was. Emily was sitting on the front steps. Conner stopped on the path, but knew he could not turn around without being seen, as she was looking right at him.

"Hey," he smiled at her.

"Hey, yourself." She stood up and brushed imaginary dust from her jeans. "I thought maybe you were tired of my company."

"Ya," he laughed. "You can be a bit of a pest, y'know."

Emily smiled and walked slowly down the cement steps toward him, her hands stuck loosely in her pockets. They turned and started down the path together.

"What's new?" she joked.

"Oh, I don't think you really want to know the answer to that right now. It's much too beautiful a day."

"Calm before the storm, I'm afraid. Archie says the word is, a storm coming in around midnight."

"No campfire tonight, then, huh?"

"Maybe," Emily smiled. "I am going to do some sketching this week. The editor of my book wants some of my wolf drawings to be incorporated with my story. He says it will enhance their character."

"That's great, Emily. Austin must be very proud."

"I suppose he would be, if he knew," she said quietly.

"What do you mean?"

Emily stopped on the path and turned to face him.

"I've left him, Conner. I arrived Saturday and it was to stay this time. This is my home, now. I have lots of work to do in my life, for my life, and have to do it alone. We separated right after your birthday and I've decided to stay here. At least, for now."

"I'm so sorry, Emily," Conner was shocked. "First, my divorce and now this. Is there anything I can do?"

"Sure," she smiled after a moment. "Come with me tomorrow afternoon. Meet me by the tree at three o'clock. Okay?"

"I can't, Emily. I have to go back."

"Back? For how long?"

"I'm not sure. I've got a business deal that needs some attention. I've been putting it off all summer, but I can't any longer. I need to close it as soon as possible." He noticed that Emily's face had gone expressionless and she stared out into the grounds. "What's wrong?"

"Oh, nothing," she turned and smiled, yet her eyes were glassy. "I just hoped...."

"I'll be back in a few days," he interrupted, taking her hand in his. "Emily, look at me."

"Yes, Conner?" The warmth of his hand around hers made her heart race and she felt her stomach quiver. Conner placed his hands on her shoulders and smiled.

"I promise I'll be back. Then, perhaps you can teach me to sketch." He kissed her lightly on the forehead. "Will you wait for me, please?"

"I will wait," she smiled, stepping back from him. "Always and forever." Emily waved to Conner, as she walked away from him down the path toward the main buildings.

Conner watched her and felt sadness at her news. So much sadness. He knew her well enough to know that leaving her home was undoubtedly a very hard decision for her. And she came here. Here, to a place that he was about to sign the death certificate for. This was her home now, she had said it.

Nausea began rising in Conner's stomach again, as he opened his cell phone to page Todd, and this time it was not from the alcohol he had consumed the night before. Life had sickened him. Life and all its broken dreams.

23

No Deal

Conner sat at his desk, looking out at the deepening colors of the Detroit metro trees and thinking about how the colors at Blaney were most likely finished and shedding their leaves in preparation of winter. So much bad happened so quickly, and yet, why was Conner feeling so delighted to be alive? He couldn't get into his work. Several yellow message slips were sitting right in front of him. It was ten o'clock in the morning and all he had done since he arrived was sit in his chair looking outside, praying for his father and thinking about Emily and the place he could find her. He closed his eyes, breathed deeply into his lungs and could almost feel the cool, refreshing northern Michigan air.

A golf course, Conner thought. Blaney Park needed a golf course. With a little bit of investment, perhaps he could turn the area into a moneymaking opportunity rather than sell it. After all, he was a good businessman. Business was always an inspiring act, but emotion had to be out of the equation. His strength was his ability to stay unemotional about his business deals. What is the margin? Revenue is everything and he knew that he had to start thinking of ways to protect his money.

The intercom beeped.

"Yes, Patti?"

"Derek Stroebel is on line one, Conner."

"Thanks."

"Conner Morley."

"Conner. Derek Stroebel, here. How are you?"

"Good, thanks. Listen, Derek, I was just going to call you..."

"Great," Derek interrupted, his tone marked with concern. "I'm anxious about closing this deal, Conner. Your lawyer told me you went to Blancy Park. You seeing that beautiful place hasn't obstructed your business sense now, has it?"

"Funny you should say that, Derek," Conner was irritated at the thought that this land-hungry developer knew his activities so well. "How in the hell did you find out that I owned Blaney Park? Hell, I didn't even know I owned it!"

"Well, ah, let's just say I have some fond memories of Blaney Park. I've made it my business to know about it."

"Then, why are you going to cut it all down? That doesn't make any sense."

"Look, Morley. I didn't call to get into a philosophical discussion on why one businessman sells to another businessman an opportunity that will make both very wealthy. Fact is, you don't really own it anymore, anyway. I am holding a purchase agreement in my hand and I am just waiting to pick up the keys."

"So, who all are you talking to, Stroebel? You know you've been talking only with my lawyers and if you look at that agreement you will see that my signature is nowhere to be found. I don't quite see business the same way you do. I am not feeling very warm and fuzzy over your approach to my property. Let me tell you a thing or two about business. Possession is nine-tenths of the law, remember? That deed is still in my name and you haven't given me jack shit for dollars for the property. So the way I see it, you ain't got a pot to piss in. I will be communicating to my lawyer that I am putting this deal on the ice block." Conner hung up the phone.

"Conner, I am.... Hello? Hello... shit!" Derek yelled, as he slammed down the phone on his desk. He then swiped the phone off his desk in a rage.

Derek flipped on the intercom.

"Kim, get that asshole back on the phone now," Derek shouted. "Can you do that? Can you do something for me today?"

"Patti," Conner pushed his own intercom button. "No more calls today. Actually, take the rest of the day off. I want to be alone. Lock the door on your way out."

"Yes, Mr. Morley," Patti replied. "Thank you, sir."

"Patti, you have been with me for ten years. I keep telling you, don't call me sir."

"You just gave me the rest of the day off. I felt it was appropriate."

Conner smiled, knowing that Patti's son was playing in a school concert that evening and parents were invited. Patti never really asked, she just told Conner what was occurring in her life and Conner realized what she needed. He hired her after a friend of a friend mentioned she was in a dire situation.

Her husband died of a heart attack when her son was just under a year old, leaving her with a stack of bills and no life insurance policy. She was living with relatives when Conner met her and had cried during her interview with him. Normally, Conner would have asked her to leave and compose herself. First law of business is to take the emotion out of it. But this woman was different. When Conner looked into her tear-filled eyes, he knew she was good people. He told her to take a week before she started in order to find an apartment, arrange for childcare and forward the bill to his office, lease a car and, finally, make sure she arrived at work before him each day and didn't leave before him. Simple enough, it seemed.

Conner was correct in hiring Patti. She screened calls better than anyone he had ever employed. She could distinguish the valuable callers from the time wasters, and she had a knack for asking the right questions at the right time. Like the time Conner was going to take a $400 bottle of wine to the beer distributor. Patti suggested to Conner that cigars would go better with beer than wine. He found out later, after the deal was in the bag, that Conner's competition brought an expensive bottle of scotch.

"Fucking threw him out right on his ear," said the client. "How dumb to bring alcohol to an alcohol producer... that's like taking ice to an Eskimo!"

Conner gave Patti ten percent of the deal. She used the money to buy back the house she and her husband had lived in before he died.

"You talk to Morley?" Derek's dad walked into his office. "You got that deal closed on Blaney Park, right?"

"Not quite, Dad."

"What the hell do you mean, not quite?"

"Well, he's changing his mind, I think."

"You think? What the hell are you doing to me, Derek? You come up with this gold mine idea and you can't execute? Execute, execute... Damn you, I keep telling you that you don't ask. You take what you want."

'I know, Dad. You've been telling me for years. But, I tried telling him and he got all pissed off and decided I was not who he wanted to do business with."

"Well, we'll see about that. You are a Stroebel, aren't you?"

"Yes, Father, I am."

"Well, then act like it, son! Close this deal or I am going to execute you! Why can't you be more like me, huh?"

"I don't know, Dad, I guess you're gifted..."

"Well, if you would have went to a real business school instead you went to that God-forsaken school for forest rangers in Marquette. And, then came home every weekend to see your mommy. When are you going to grow up and learn what being a man is all about? You have to take the bull by the horns or you will be gored!"

Mr. Stroebel walked out of Derek's office. But, before closing the door, he turned around and looked Derek in the eyes. "I paid for your damages at the Hawk Club. Why you have to go to those types of bars in the first place is beyond me, but if you do, will you keep your hands off the girls? I could have bought the place for as much money as I put into fixing it up after you and your friends had your little brawl there."

Derek stared through squinted eyes, angry at his father's words. Mr. Stroebel ended with one last stab at Derek. "Well, I guess I should be happy you aren't gay, shouldn't I?" Derek's jaw clenched as his father closed the door.

Derek's head dropped. He was defeated again. His father had been defeating him since he was born. Derek never did the right thing, in his dad's eyes, especially since his college days. He still had nightmares over what had happened and had remained scared the truth would come out about him. He'd been sick for a long time, but because of his position, power and his clean reputation, he'd never been exposed. He'd never been made accountable. That had caused him as much discomfort as the wrong he'd committed over his life. It ate at Derek's insides while he was alone and reflected on who he was and the reality of his life's vicious cycle.

On the desk was a mirror. His dad put it there to remind him of who he was and what he had to live up to. His dad thought it would motivate and inspire Derek. It only served to defeat him more. He swiped the mirror off the table with the back of his hand and left his office.

Derek drove to a bar out of town. It was north of the downtown pulse of things and he sat in his car waiting for the Oakland University girls he desired to come out. Derek knew the college girls. He was almost forty, yet looked younger and liked younger women. His sense of attraction had not matured normally. He was still living out his college days. It was a time when all that was required of him was to get decent grades and withdraw his allowance. It was a time when he could take what he wanted, as his dad demanded. Then, he'd have all the beer and drugs he needed.

Today, he was no different. He opened the quart of beer he had purchased at a corner convenience store and reached into his Jaguar's console for a joint that was already rolled. He'd been to this bar before. Derek had met the girls that would soon be leaving for their afternoon classes. The upper class took the later class times so they could be ready to party when their classes were completed in the early evening and sleep in the next day. Derek was sitting in his car, preparing for the one pursuit that made him feel the most powerful.

The girls walked out together. Derek started the car and slowly pulled up to them. They recognized the car and Derek. When a decent looking man with money and a hot vehicle drove up, it was natural that there would be at least one woman in the group who wanted to feel the pleasure of being the chosen one. Derek knew this, he relied on it. She had to be in a group because she would give into peer pressure. If she was alone she could easily refuse, but in a group it was like the process was patented, a done deal.

Derek knew Becky's routine. He'd seen her often in the bar. He had flirted with her, told her all the great things about his life that were not true. He made her feel what most girls wanted at that age, security. How easy would life be to have a wealthy man and not have to worry if she made any money? All the perceptions Derek knew well and played on just as he attempted with her aunt, many years ago. He just had to keep his play spread around the geographical scene so his slick wasn't exposed.

Even in the bright daylight, Derek had no fear of his situation because he had done it so often before and it always worked out. Yeah, he would worry for a day or two. If the phone didn't ring in the first 24 hours, he knew he was safe. Hell, even if it did, he had the confidence that if his threats didn't scare off an accuser, his dad would sure fix things up for him. He always did. That was the good thing about being a rich fuck-up son. Dad would always make things right with a few bucks either on the sly or a contribution to the right political player that would make things more palatable to them. Derek knew Becky's routine and who she was. Becky knew nothing of Derek.

The girls walked close by his car. All of them were looking, as he slowly approached. He looked directly at her.

"Hey, Becky, how are you doing? Can we talk?"

Becky looked at her girlfriends. They all started to giggle and gave her a little push to the car. It was obvious that Becky didn't want to approach Derek. After all, they only slightly knew each other. Derek's process was working as usual. Becky slowly walked towards him, as she looked back at her friends.

"Go, girl," she heard from one of them, in encouragement of the encounter. After all, all things being equal, Derek would be a good catch for a college girl in suburban Michigan. Dad would be proud to have that car in the driveway when relatives visited.

Derek's smile was wide and his slick was in progress.

"How are you doing, Becky?"

"Fine..... Derek?"

"Yeah, my name is Derek. You remembered."

"Well, it's kind of hard to forget you, since you gave me your business card five times and called my apartment three times. How did you get my number anyway?"

"Well, I have a knack for doing things," Derek replied.

Becky looked back as her girlfriends left her. Her instincts told her to run after them. She didn't feel right about this situation, but she knew that if she didn't at least speak with Derek, her girlfriends would dog her. They all told her she was way too conservative as it was and overly nervous about men. She was still trying to fit in, even after two years of college. Becky had seen too many documentaries on the horrors around campus life.

"Can I take you to class?" he asked.

"Oh no, that's okay, Derek. I can walk."

"Walk? You don't walk on this campus. You will need to take the bus now. It seems to me that your girlfriends cannot be all wrong. They left you with me to take care of you. The least I can do is offer you a ride."

"Well, actually, I don't have class today. The professor is ill and they just canceled class. I can't believe they did that. They never cancel, but just get a TA or someone to teach. That's why I was in the bar. I usually wait until after class."

"Yeah, I noticed you seemed serious about your education when I talked to you. I really respect women who have an agenda in their life." Derek knew full well that it was the focused woman with an agenda who was most likely to keep quiet, realizing what intrusion such an accusation would be on her life's goals. Derek knew all this, because he was sick to the act.

Becky was dropping her guard to Derek's smile, his vehicle, the music playing, the fall sunny day and the beer she had consumed. The fact that her girlfriends thought nothing of leaving her with him helped to relax her. Deciding she would be just fine and would save the three bucks for the bus fare, she accepted his offer.

They started north on I75 towards M24 and Clarkston.

"Where are we going?" Becky asked. "My apartment's in the other direction."

"Hey, it's a wonderful day out and you said you didn't have class. I need to stop by my house to get something and I thought we'd have a quick beer there before I took you home. Come on, what's your hurry? Besides, I want you to see where I live."

"Well, I guess that would be okay," she shrugged. "It is a great day for a ride in a car as nice as this."

Derek pulled into an exclusive neighborhood. He drove to the end of a cul-de-sac and hit the garage door opener. The house was a beautiful, contemporary home with two floors and balconies everywhere looking out to a lake that existed behind it.

I can handle a beer here, Becky thought, beginning to relax. This is way too cool.

Derek had accomplished his goal and convinced Becky. It helped him that she had a few drinks in the bar before he approached her. She had been feeling lonely because she was not dating anyone, a choice she had made. It was not that she couldn't get dates, but Becky thought of college boys as stupid and self-consumed. She did like Derek's style, his money and his approach. He seemed very mature and successful. Everything she was looking for in a man, even if he was a bit older than she was.

Ironically, Derek knew if he worked on this relationship and if he took the time to treat her right, he could have everything he wanted from her. But his true feelings were that he could not handle a relationship. That would mean he'd have to live up to expectations and be sensitive to someone else's needs. For Derek, this was unacceptable. He already used most of his energy to live up to his dad and sensitive was what his mom always said he was. He revoked the word and somehow misconstrued that being sensitive to others and being a sensitive person was the same thing and he hated both. He had no use for a relationship as he could hardly live with himself, let alone someone else.

Derek exited the car, walked around to Becky's door and opened it.

"Allow me," he said with a smile as he opened her door. The short skirt that Becky wore was tight, so she found it difficult to get out of the sports car without exposing the white panties she had under her skirt. Derek knew this would happen, it was his process. He knew she would have to flash him to get out and he stayed just the correct distance away.

"Well, that's all you are going to get on our first date," she said, laughing uneasily as she tried to make light of the fact that she was struggling with her skirt.

"Oh, come on, I didn't look," Derek responded, knowing that he did. He opened the garage service door and they walked inside.

It was dark when the cab drove up to Derek's house. He threw two hundred-dollar bills at Becky, who was crying from the horror of just what had taken place earlier. She adjusted her skirt in an effort to put her dignity and pride back together.

"Your cab is here," Derek's tone was flip. "Thanks for the fun, kiddo. And if you have any ideas, remember you got into my car, you came to my house and you flashed those white panties at me. I think you get my point. And if that doesn't suit you, think about the reputation you will have at school. Oh yeah, and your aunt? Whatever she does for a living, it don't matter. Approach this the wrong way and she is nothing because of you. Look around, sweetheart. My family has money. Maybe your aunt will be unemployed if the wrong thing is said about her at that school, huh? A couple hundred bucks ought to get you home and allow plenty extra to help you forget. Now, get the fuck out and if you ever see me again, you don't know me." Derek began to laugh as he opened the front door, feeling the pride and exhilaration of power.

Becky gathered her belongings and left the house, hearing the door shut firmly behind her. She was emotionless, feeling no pain, just numb. Her head was spinning from the drinks, or drug, that was given to her by Derek which left her dazed and incapable of preventing the events that took place in that house from occurring.

Emily had warned her not to be naive about men. They do bad things and there were many a bad man out there, she had always told her niece. Her words now haunted Becky as she was reliving the day's events as if they were in a movie. The cab driver opened her door.

"Miss, you okay?"

"Just take me home," Becky whispered, in just enough volume for the cab driver to hear. He had seen this before. "Do you want me to call the police, ma'am?"

"No!" She said emphatically. "Just take me home. Here." She handed him the full two hundred dollars.

"Well, where is home? You haven't told me where you live."

"Please, just start driving. I will tell you as we go. Please, just leave this place."

As they moved back towards Oakland University, Becky dictated directions to the cab driver. The neon lights around them seemed to glow as if she were in a dream. She so badly wanted the day's events to be a dream. She kept pulling down on her skirt, trying to cover her exposed body, while asking herself, Did I invite this? Did I show him my panties so did I deserve this?

"Hell no," she whispered aloud in the back seat of the cab. Emily's advice kept coming back to her. She could see her aunt right in front of her face.

Sweetie, Emily had said. If anything bad ever happens to you, don't keep it to yourself, okay? I am here for you. I can't be with you every second of every day, you know that. But if anyone ever does anything bad to you, I will help you. We can do what is right and be proud of that. Okay?

Becky replayed those words over and over, as she took out her cellular phone and speed dialed their home number.

"Uncle Austin? It's me, Becky."

"Hi, kiddo! What's up?"

Becky began to cry. The cab driver looked to the back seat, then turned off his radio and shut down the meter. He knew what had happened. He had seen it before where he drove a shattered woman to her home after being at a man's place. His culture would never do such a thing to a woman. He was disgusted to learn it happened so frequently in the country he had been told was the best place in the world to live.

"Is Aunt Emily there?"

"No, kiddo, sorry. She's up north again. What's up?"

"I'm so sorry," Becky sobbed. "I really messed up... I am so sorry. Can I come see you? To the house?"

"Honey, of course you can come," Austin was alarmed by Becky's tone, and his instincts were arousing very familiar feelings from deep within him. "Where are you? Tell me where you are."

"I am almost in your neighborhood. I'm in a yellow cab. When I get there, can you be outside waiting for me? I don't want to get out of the cab by myself. I can't." Becky started sobbing. "Oh, Uncle Austin, I am so ashamed of myself!"

Oh, shit, Austin's heart was pounding wildly. "Sure, honey. Come on. I'll be outside waiting for you. Everything is going to be okay, you hear me?"

"Yeah."

"Whatever has happened, I am not upset with you, okay? I don't even know what it is, but I want you to know we love you and you will be okay. We'll make it okay."

"Thanks... I love you, too."

Austin slowly lowered the receiver, thinking of Emily's nightmare in college and feeling as if he were in a time zone.

Please, God... not this. Not Becky.

Derek sat in the dark living room of his parent's home. He slowly lifted his wine glass into the air.

"To Emily," he said.

24

The Letter

My Dear,

Conner sat at the desk in Cabin number 4 with pen and pencil in hand, and looked up at the wall clock. He had a little more than four hours before he was to meet her by the tree, at three o'clock. It had become their time, their routine. He knew she was aware of his arrival the night before, as Todd's plane had pierced the evening's silence over the Park. She would expect him. They would spend a couple of hours, as they had each afternoon he was there, walking together and laughing, sharing stories and pretending to be more interested in the wilderness than they were in each other.

Today, however, Conner wouldn't be there. He couldn't. He had to tell her, had to end this. She had to know, and know soon. This would never, could never, be her home. Conner would stay long enough to deal with her anger and he would leave this place. His leaving would begin the execution. Conner would never look back.

How does he start the letter? Should he even be putting any information down on paper, let alone on letterhead? Maybe telling her would be better.

No way, he thought. He could not look at those beautiful green eyes, as they would scream out in pain when he delivered his message.

Dear Emily,

"Shit." Conner crumpled the paper and threw it to the floor. No salutation seemed appropriate. Conner had been a loyal husband, but he still had his share of female friends and associates. He always had the gift of the written and oral word. Writing letters to beautiful women was never a difficult thing for him.

He leaned back in his chair and looked around the room. The cabin he had been staying in, on and off, for more than six months now was beginning to feel like home to him, making Emily's news even more painful. It was so rustic, a place Conner would not have been caught dead in a year earlier. Conner came to this God-given place only to sell it and make a huge profit from its sale and now he found himself feeling like this was home for him, too. He felt lonely anywhere else on earth except this place that was once just a mysterious property on the books.

He never wanted to disappoint anyone he cared about. The land lawyer had been on his ass to dump the property, and now how could he? Stroebel was pushing him to finalize the deal, and Conner was avoiding his calls. It was not the lawyer, nor the developer, he was most concerned with. On the floor beside his chair, lay many wadded up pieces of his letterhead. This was quality stuff, the expensive paper that was usually reserved for memos to vice presidents and CEO's. This letter was equally, if not more, important. This letter was to Emily. Yet, the attempt to write it was beginning to feel like an impossible task.

How could he explain to her that he was a caring and passionate man who deserved her kindness and her friendship? How would she ever believe him when she was told that he was actually the owner of Blaney Park and that he planned to sell it? How would she react when he told her that, not only was he going to sell it, but execute the sale by providing, to the developer who would buy it, the magnet of the premier lumber and the precious land it grew from?

The root of anything had always been a symbolic metaphor for Conner. One of his favorite authors wrote about how successful people don't grow up, they grow down like the roots of a tree. Conner believed in that philosophy and he saw the gorgeous trees at Blaney Park as symbolism to longevity and growth. No tree could grow tall and strong without having the roots to support it. He was beginning to realize that he never had grown good roots and he may now be toppling over from all the heavy limbs he struggled to support.

Emily had always spoken so possessively of Blaney Park, of her wolves, her favorite tree and of the river. Conner's business sense had made him a good listener. He knew what people wanted not by talking but rather by listening, and he had listened plenty to Emily. She had broadened his horizons and made him realize there was more to life than the material fun of day-to-day reckless recreation and the accumulation of stuff.

Life had always been a competition and a game to Conner. Everything was scored and evaluated for value. If it didn't add to the bottom line, it was not worth holding on to. He didn't like to disappoint people, but when it came to those items that made him feel important, that made him feel like a man, no person was exempt from being pushed aside even if it meant a loss on the P&L statement.

So now, he was facing the truth. The business wheels were in motion and for him to stop them now would be risking a lawsuit. And here was Emily, who thought of him as this special man who was simply coming to visit this place and enjoy the environment. A virgin to woods and an imposter of its value, Conner knew he couldn't just walk up to her and say, Emily, by the way, thanks for the tour of the land, but kiss it goodbye because I just made millions and all this might as well have been blown up by an atomic bomb by the time industry is done with it.

> Dear Emily,
>
> In the coming weeks I will be concluding a business deal that will sell Blaney Park and all the forest around it. First the lumber industry will strip all the trees, even your favorite tree and all the wolves will be pushed out of their living dens....

"Fuck," Conner threw down his pen. "I can't write this to Emily."

Oh, God, help me, he thought. What is happening to me? Give me the strength to do what is right. Why did my wife betray me? Why my dad? Why do I feel such a connection with Emily who I have absolutely no reason to be feeling these things for? I need your help.

Conner was so tired from the travel and the emotional stress of all that he had been through recently. The Jack-and-cokes had taken their toll, even while he was writing this essential letter. He didn't even get up from the table. He laid his head down like he did as a kid when he was scolded in school and made to put his head down. Ironically, he was now scolding himself and how his life had positioned him.

Conner's understanding of life was most money and most toys win. Just like any competition, he wanted the most points and winning would take care of his happiness. He attempted to blow the candle out just before his head reached the hard surface of the table. He looked to the dwindling fire and realized for the first time in many years, he was looking to God for assistance. He told himself to get up and go lay on his bed, but the alcohol and the self induced punishment that Conner was capable of made him simply sit there at his desk, continue writing, hoping to pass out. It was a hope day, he decided. He hoped tomorrow would bring solution and resolution.

4:35pm.

Emily kicked at the grasses, occasionally turning to look back up the path toward the cabins. Conner always met her at 3:00. She was glad he had finally returned from Detroit the night before. She thought of the last time she saw him and the short walk they enjoyed around the main lodge after he found her sitting on the steps. Hoping to bring him some peace and change of pace from his difficulty of working through his divorce, she had suggested they meet at the tree and he could watch Wolfie play while she sketched pictures that were to go in her book. How disappointed she was when he had told her he was returning to Detroit, instead. Yet, he asked her to wait and wait she had. For four long days.

Conner was always the perfect businessman, always on time. He had seemed glad to see her and didn't hesitate to say yes at her invitation. Now she was confused and concerned that they would not see one another again that evening. The sky was beginning to darken with an approaching late afternoon rain shower. Emily decided it was best to return to her cabin and avoid getting soaked. She would stop by Conner's cabin on the way.

As she started past the tree, the wind began to pick up and she noticed a letter, nailed to the side opposite of her sketching place, flopping in the wind. Emily walked closer and recognized her name written across the neatly folded page. She smiled, at first, thinking that Conner was playing with her and the letter would ask her to meet somewhere else, in lieu of the storm. She hesitated before opening it and Wolfie's uneasiness around her got her attention.

"What's the matter, boy?" she smiled, as she reached down to rub his head. Wolfie jerked away from her, and ran ahead of her along the path, stopping just at the edge of the clearing. Suddenly, everything felt very, very wrong. She looked up and the sky had changed - a strong storm was brewing. She looked across the river and realized that Wolfie's mother was gathering the pack toward the thicket.

"Wolfie! Go on!" Emily tried to dismiss Wolfie to the safety of his family, but he stayed with her. She then felt terribly scared and not just for herself. She looked down at the paper she held tightly in her hand against the wind, as big rain droplets began landing on it, soaking through to the ink. Confused by finding the letter, she tore it open. Standing in the cold rain slapping against her skin, she shivered more from fear than cold, and she began to read...

Dearest Emily.

The door to Conner's cottage was banging against the frame, arousing him from his drunken slumber. He looked up and, through the fog of his condition, realized that there was a storm upon him. He sat up from his bed, wondering if he had dreamt everything of the night before. The many wads of paper on the floor confirmed that he did not dream this - he wrote the letter. He tried to focus and remembered stumbling along the path through the woods, to the tree. He had nailed the letter to the tree. She would be there, expecting him to join her.

Conner rose and pulled the door securely shut. He walked heavily to the sink and poured a glass of water. As he gulped its coolness, he thought of how the river must be churning with the storm. The river, he thought. The wolves. The storm. Oh my God, Emily. Where was she? Conner became concerned for all. In his self-indulgence of grief, did he forget about those around him who had brought him so much pleasure lately? Suddenly, all the lessons of the city abandoned him and Conner ran from the cabin, thinking only of the wolves and her.

He knew she would be there. She would share his concern, putting aside her own needs to care for her pack. The rain was cold and stung his face and arms like knives, yet he kept running. The wind whipped the branches of the poplar and pine trees like leather tassels against his skin. The ground was now rain-soaked and the well-hardened path that his feet knew so well became foreign to him. It betrayed him and he was unsure of his footing, sliding and stumbling along its path. He reached the edge of the clearing and the rain was pounding like a torrent. The sky had darkened, and he stood alone in the clearing. He struggled to look towards the tree through the rain. The sky had become as dark as the night and he saw no one near the tree.

The explosions of lightning illuminated the river, as the water swirled and splashed up over its banks. All that surrounded him was screaming in protest to his decision that he had so carefully described in that letter. He looked to the tree where he was to meet Emily and she was still not there. Did he or did he not nail the note to the tree? Did he or did he not want to sell the Park? Did he or did he not want to express his feelings to Emily? Conner suddenly felt like the devil.

Oh my God, what have I done? His heart was screaming at him.

There were no wolves, no Emily. Nothing. Conner felt alone, vulnerable.

The note was gone from the tree. He frantically searched the clearing, looking, praying to find it before she did. Yet, as the storm closed in on him, he felt it represented her shock at his written words. She had found it.

He wanted to be with her to explain, make her understand his world, his motivations. After all, she would understand, wouldn't she? Unlike his dad whom he never saw spill a tear, Conner had the sensitivity of his mother. He cared.

As the storm howled around him he just didn't feel like fighting right now. He fell to his knees still spinning from the alcohol induced sleep several hours earlier. He just lay there in the cold long grass as the rain spanked his body. He didn't care at that moment what happened to him. He just wanted the pain to go away. Tears flowed in unison with the rain falling into tiny rivers around his face. He gasped for air as the rain drove him down.

I have to get up, he thought. To lie here is to die and I'm not ready. I've just begun to feel and to know what it is like to live. I'm not ready for you yet, God. Whether it means great joy or great pain, I want to live.

Conner decided at that moment he was the true imposter. Thinking he was a builder of a great business and now he realized his life was falling down around him just as the trees would soon be doing. How ironic that those trees were looking down and witnessing his moment of great weakness. He lifted his shoulders from the thick cold mud that held him, and looked up through his rain-soaked hair, not knowing what was flowing harder his tears or Blaney's.

Then, in the distance, faintly noticeable among the screaming of the rain and the shouting of the thunderous storm above him, he heard the bells. Even through the thunder and wind, their chiming could be heard gracing the edges of Emily's cabin. They called to him, beckoned to him. Conner pulled himself from the mud and screamed against the wind.

"Emily!" he screamed, with every breath in his body. The thunder beat his own voice back to him, preventing his calls from reaching out to anyone or anything.

He slipped in the muddy path as he ran against the icy needles of the rain and the wind forcing him from the path. As the rain turned to hail pellets he realized the true fury of the storm and ran faster.

He reached Emily's cabin and leaned forward against the back wall, trying to escape the pain of the hailstorm. With his eyes closed tightly, Conner felt his way along the knotty logs of the walls, around the side toward the front. The wind was howling with great depth. He could no longer tell which direction the wind and the rain were coming from and Conner felt fearful of the answer and was too afraid to open his eyes. He heard tree limbs and debris falling and tumbling around the cabin, around him.

He reached the front of the cabin and felt for the doorknob. Not bothering to knock, he thrust the door open and fell forward inside. Conner was breathing deeply as he lay face down on the cold floor. He heard no one inside the cabin, only the storm beating against it as if it were trying to come after him. He was afraid to look up and not find her, yet his heart told him what he feared. She was not there. He slowly pushed himself from the floor and rose to look around. The fireplace was smoldering from the night's ashes. Conner stared into the dark pit for a moment, and then, with a heavy heart turned to face the storm once again.

As he turned toward the door, his eyes fell on the wall of Emily's cabin. The large tapestry rug that had hung there four nights earlier was crumpled on the floor. Conner caught his breath and his heart seemed to stop cold in his chest. A wolf. The portrait Emily had sketched for the lodge. It was here, yet he looked closer and realized this was not a portrait. The image was not protected by a frame. It needed no protection, as it was carved into the wall of the cabin.

Conner did not notice that the hailstorm was passing and that the sky was beginning to lighten. The rain and wind continued to invade the cabin through the open doorway, yet Conner ignored its fury. He walked to the wall. His hand was shaking as he reached out to touch it. He ran his fingers up to the face and the eyes. He stared at the eyes of the wolf and they again mesmerized him, as they had the day he first saw the portrait in the lodge. Only this time, they were not strangers to him. He recognized this image. The portrait was the old female, the one with the mangled leg. The image was of the wolf, but the eyes were of Emily.

Conner gasped and stepped backward from the wall. The eyes were piercing right through him. The joy he saw so many times as they walked through the clearings and trees, along the riverbank, was gone. These eyes were black as stones in the bottom of the river, and full of hate. He saw her soul in those eyes. She was one of them, one of the wolves. Conner choked as fear began to form within him. This was how Emily would look at him now, through those cold and angry eyes. He didn't know whether to feel pain, knowing the cabin and her world would soon be torn apart, or fear that he had, indeed, lost her to the storm and to the wolves.

He turned and leaned back against the wolf carving, his eyes closed and his face hardened with concern. He felt very weak and lost. After a few moments, Conner opened his eyes and looked about the room. This was Emily's room. Dried wildflowers hung from nails in carefully knotted bundles along the walls. There were candles evenly placed around the room. He breathed deeply and smelled her. The room carried her scent and brought goose bumps to his skin. His gaze fell to her desk. Her computer was upon it, closed and powerless. Conner walked over and sat down at her desk. Without thinking, he pulled open the desk drawer. Inside, was a very old, torn journal.

He picked up the journal and held it for several moments in one hand, while caressing its cover lightly with the fingertips of his other. He was careful not to let his rain soaked through his hair drip onto it. He lifted it to his face and sniffed its staleness, a sign of its age. Slowly, he opened the book and flipped threw the pages, not reading the words, but just studying her handwriting. As he neared the center of the book, a page caught his attention and he stopped. It was a page filled with dark, erratic pen marks, almost like scratches and they left indentations in the paper through about four pages. Conner's eyes focused on the words of the page with curiosity and what he began to read shocked him.

Emily had written a very detailed accounting of a night filled with horror for her so many years ago in the barn and the old main lodge. Conner's heart was racing as he read the words through the darkened lines.

"....my hands clenched tightly into fists, fighting the strangling pressure around my wrists as he drove into me. My nails dug into the skin of my palms and sliced it open, causing the blood rise to the surface and ooze from between my fingertips. I kept my eyes tightly shut with hatred for him and what he was doing to me, as the sweat from his forehead dripped around my mouth. I focused on my anger, not looking at his face yet wanting to reach it. I wanted to claw him with nails bloodied from my own skin and make him feel the pain that I was feeling."

"Jesus Christ," Conner said aloud, as he tossed the journal back into the drawer. He tried to leave it, let it go. It was not his business. He could not. He went back to the desk, retrieved the journal again and continued to read.

"I focused on the pain in my hands and the burning of the torn flesh around my wrists where the ropes had eaten away at my skin, my legs that had been ripped by the brush while being dragged along the ditch toward the old lodge. I chose this, the pain from everything else, rather than the pain I felt from Derek's hands as they pinned my arms beside my head, as he drove into me harder and harder, until my spine felt it would crumble against the wooden tabletop and my muscles went numb."

Derek? Conner thought. Who the fuck was this slime? Was this another book? Another story? His heart was pounding. No. This was not Emily's writing, not like her style. She wrote of sunsets, flowers, the wilderness and her pack. What was this? It wasn't real, couldn't be real.

Derek. The name was spelled unusually. Conner's hands were shaking as he flipped forward in the journal, ahead of where he had just read, to pages that seemed more an accounting of facts than paragraphs of expression.

"He laughed at me. I was the whore, the perfect whore. I would do what he wanted and enjoy it. Open your mouth, he told me. I choked against him, I couldn't breathe. You know you love it, he told me."

He had kicked her, over and over.

"I wanted to kill him. I wanted to drive the pitchfork into him and leave him for her breakfast. He pulled me to my feet and laughed at me. I stood face to face with him, the thickness inside my mouth was burning and I spat in his face, spat himself back at him. I didn't feel his fist, only watched as it came at me and I surrendered to the darkness, not caring if I ever woke."

Conner skipped past the rest of the pages that were scarred by the pen marks. He stopped at what seemed a list of details and read the notes in the margin from a more recent time, evident by the different color of ink.

Detroit, MI. Land development. 555-7563.

Elsie hid the camisole in the back shed. Use for positive DNA when the time comes.

Derek Joseph Stroebel – the demon. The devil, himself.

Conner slammed the journal shut and his mind was racing wildly, putting together the pieces. Derek Stroebel, that son-of-a-bitch! This was why he wanted Blaney so badly. He wanted Emily. Again.

"I'll kill him myself," Conner stood up, shaking, not able to decide what to do next. Todd, he should call Todd, call the boys.

"You fucking bastard! Get your hands off my journal and get the hell out of my cabin!"

Conner jumped at the sound of Emily's voice, screaming at him. The journal fell from his hands and he turned to see her standing, rain-soaked, the doorway, clutching his crumpled letter in her hand.

"Emily." His voice choked.

"Get OUT, I said! Get the hell out of here! This is my place, you have no right to be here. You son-of-a-bitch! Call your little errand sky boy and tell him to get you out now!" She was screaming at him, as her eyes grew wider, filling with tears.

Conner moved toward her. "Emily, please let me explain."

"No." She covered her ears with her hands and leaned back against the door. She then squared her shoulders, slowly dropped her arms and looked at him. "I don't want to hear anything else from you. You've explained enough already in your letter. You're one of them, those who only destroy what is beautiful. You have ruined everything, Conner. You can't be trusted, can't be believed. Go back to your world that feels nothing, nothing but materialistic greed. You disgust me," She was glaring at him, her voice low and cold. "You used me. Used me to take way your pain, used my love to feed your pitiful ego. You have nothing, now. And certainly not me, not ever. Get out of my sight!"

She reached slowly for the door and opened it, still staring at him in silence, without emotion, with the same cold stare as the one etched in the wood behind her. Her green eyes had gone black and cut through him like a knife, deeply into his soul and he realized for the first time the intense strength she possessed. Strength beyond anything he had ever sensed in her, strength of survival. She was staring him down, as if to defeat his purpose and he felt her driving him from her heart. He felt outside of himself, unable to even recognize who he was, and anything that mattered now. How could he go back and change everything, as it was most certainly too late. He looked at her eyes and then over her shoulder at the eyes in the wall, realizing that he had raped her, too.

"I thought I knew you," she said slowly. "I thought you were different and you were here because it all meant something to you. I trusted you..."

"Emily, please..." he whispered, sensing the finality in her voice.

"Why, Conner? Why didn't you just tell me when we met? All these weeks we spent learning about each other, you were learning about everything. I thought you loved it. God, I even thought I loved you. I dreamt of you loving me some day, of us being together." Emily's eyes narrowed again and his gaze dropped to her hand as it tightened against his rain-soaked letter. "You're the same, no different. You used me, too, and now I hate you for it."

"Please, let me just explain..."

With that, she turned and bolted from the doorway back out into the rain.

"Emily!" Conner screamed after her. "Please don't go!" He scrambled to his feet and ran out of the cabin. He looked around, but she had disappeared into the woods. Conner spun around frantically, looking in every direction. She was gone as quickly as she had appeared. He had lost her.

"EMILY!"

He looked at the path in front of the cabin, and saw his letter. Conner knelt and as the tears streamed down his face, he slowly picked it up out of the mud.

"I do love it, Emily," he whispered. "And, I do love you."

"Archie!" Emily was banging on the hangar door. "Archie, please let me in! It's Emily!"

"Hey, hey!" Archie walked up behind her, and took hold of Emily's arm. "Easy on the door! What's got you all worked up?"

"Archie," she looked down at his hand firmly gripped around her wrist. "Please, don't ask me to explain."

"Emily," he lowered his voice. "Your business is your own, but I've known you a long time. I've never seen you this upset. That was a hell of a storm that just passed over. You okay? Your cabin? Something happen to that pack of yours?"

"No, no, nothing like that. Please, just take me to Manistique. Now. Drive me there. Please, Archie." She looked up at him, her eyes begging him to help her. Archie paused for a moment before answering. He was confused by her state and by her unusual request to leave. Archie knew how much Blaney had become her home, a part of her. He had watched her independence grow over the past several months and his own heart had taken her in as the closest thing to a daughter he would ever know. Why was she asking to leave?

"You want to talk to Miss Elsie first?" he offered, hiding his concern for her.

"No," Emily shook her head. "If you won't drive me, I'll find a car myself. And, at the very least, I will walk there."

"Okay, okay. Let me call up and tell Her Grace I'm leaving..."

"NO!" Emily jerked her arm away. "Not Elsie, no one, do you understand? I have to go. Now."

"Okay, okay," he shook his head and pulled his keys from his pocket. "I don't like it, but you've made up your mind, so I'll take you. It's your hunt."

"Thank you. Please hurry."

Once they had pulled out of the driveway, Emily unhooked her cell phone from the waistband of her jeans and dialed Austin's number. Archie said nothing, just drove.

"Austin? Damn voicemail," she glanced nervously at Archie. "Listen, it's me and it's about 7:15. I want to come home tonight. I'm driving to Manistique and I'll wait for you there. Please don't call the Park. No one knows I've left, and I want it kept that way. Call me back on my cell and I'll explain." She closed her phone and stared at it for several moments.

They drove in silence the rest of the way. When they reached Manistique, Archie pulled into the Coach House restaurant's parking lot. Before Emily got out of his car, she reached over and placed her hand on his forearm, managing a smile.

"Thank you, Archie."

"Here," he said, as he reached into his pocket and pulled out a roll of fifty dollar bills surrounded by a number of one dollar bills and held together by a rubber band. The Saginaw Wad, as he referred to it. He removed the rubber band and arbitrarily selected a fifty and handed it to her.

"Didn't see your purse. Go get yourself a cup of coffee."

"Thanks," she replied, realizing she had left without any money or even her identification. She thought of asking for a smaller denomination bill, but noticed only the fifties.

"You're welcome, young lady. You gonna be okay?"

"Yes. I'll be fine." She looked up at him one last time and swallowed hard. "I don't know when I'll be back, Archie. Take care of Elsie for me, will you? And Wolfie."

"Nonsense," Archie scowled at her and tried to hide his own emotions with his gruff voice. "You just go tend to whatever it is that's got you so worked up and then get back up there, you here? The Park needs you." He winked at her.

Emily smiled, and a tear rolled down her face. She leaned over and kissed him lightly on the cheek. Without another word, she stepped out of his car and walked toward the front of the restaurant. Archie waited until she had walked inside the building and then turned the car around to begin his drive back to the Park.

25

Soul Friends

Emily stepped inside the small restaurant. She brushed away the strands of hair that were soaked by the rain and clinging to her face. As she looked around the room, a few patrons glanced in her direction and then turned back to their conversations, newspapers or simply turned away to stare back out through the window at the passing storm. This was a place they had come to wait it out. So had Emily.

"Just one?" asked the hostess, as she removed the top menu from the stack that sat next to the cash register.

"Yes, please," responded Emily.

"Smoking or non?"

"Non. Could I have the corner booth, over there away from the window?"

"Sure. Right this way."

Emily followed the young woman, keeping her eyes on the floor in front of her so not to make eye contact with anyone in the restaurant. She didn't want to be seen as upset and end up with a concerned bystander asking a lot of questions in an attempt to reach out to her, as so many people did in these small town establishments. Any other time, Emily would have welcomed a kind heart extended her way. However, this time it was different. She didn't know how she felt, or even if she understood what it was that was happening to her. Her life had gone through such a tremendous upheaval over the past several months. It was as if her entire world had been turned inside out and, after reading Conner's letter, she wasn't sure of anything or anyone. Anyone except Elsie.

"Here you are," the hostess placed a menu on the table in front of her. "Someone will be right with you."

"Thank you." Emily sat down on the side of the booth facing the door. She slid the menu off to the side and pulled her cell phone from her pocket.

"Are you ready to order?" A waitress had walked up to the table.

"No, nothing to eat, thanks. Just coffee."

The waitress was quite young, perhaps 16. Her reaction to Emily's order for coffee indicated she was obviously pleased that her required attentiveness to this booth would be minimal. Those who came in just for coffee were usually not in a hurry, and only needed to be checked on a few times. They also helped fill up a section, which made work easier. The younger waitresses were less interested in tables filled with customers ordering full meals, which meant bigger tips. They would rather spend their time chatting behind the counter about the latest gossip at school or their plans for the weekend.

Emily was about to dial her cell phone, when it rang. She recognized Austin's number.

"Austin?"

"Emily. Yeah, it's me. I got your message. What's going on, babe?"

"God, Austin," she sighed. "I really don't want to go into this over the phone. What time can you be here?"

"Emily, listen. I can't get there tonight. I can't pick you up until morning."

"Why?" Emily felt a lump rising in her throat. "Is something wrong with the plane?"

"No, the plane is fine. You just had a major storm front go through up there."

"Yes, but it will be long gone by the time you get here." She smiled and nodded her head as the young waitress placed a cup of hot coffee on the table, along with a few packs of sugar and a small, silver pitcher of cream.

"That's not the point. That's a large system that stretches from the U.P. all the way down along Lake Michigan to Chicago. There's no way I can get clearance to fly until at least morning. I'm sorry, Em, but you'll just have to sit tight. What's so terribly wrong that you have to come home tonight, anyway?"

Emily's eyes were brimming as she listened to Austin's words and she slowly moved a spoon around in her coffee cup, twirling the cream and sugar into the steaming black liquid. She was stranded, unless she wanted to rent a car and drive downstate. This would mean returning to Blaney, because, as Archie had pointed out in the car, she had left without her purse.

"Emily, are you there?"

"Yes," she finally answered. "I didn't realize the storm was that wide spread. It's okay. Just call my cell in the morning, as soon as you know when you can be here."

"You still haven't told me what's wrong."

"I know. It can wait until I see you. How are the girls? Everything okay at home?"

"Yeah, the girls are fine. It's been a good week, actually. I think they like having me around the house again."

"I'm glad," she smiled at the thought of Austin and the girls being together. "How's Becky? Has she talked to anyone yet?"

"No, still the same. Dr. Sherman wants to give her a few more days to open up on her own. He did say that if she doesn't, he wants to admit her for a week or so."

"In the hospital? What good will that do? She needs to be with family. Keep her at the house with you and the girls, Austin."

"She's not talking to anyone, Emily. You can't possibly believe she's okay. She's been through something very traumatic. You, of all people, should understand that. Don't shut your eyes to what's happened to her and stuff this in the closet like you did your own experience all these years. She's not as strong as you are. You know you're the only person she'll open up to so we can find out who did this to her."

Emily trembled with her anger. A very sensitive nerve was reawakening, one that had been brought back to life at Conner's birthday party when she saw Derek Stroebel and then again when she found Conner with her journal, the one place she dared to express her feelings, both past and present. Once again, her emotional sanctuary was being violated and not just by someone who happened across it, but by someone who went looking for it. The one person she had recently put her trust in, someone she felt she could believe in more than anyone else in a very long time, had now betrayed her, just like everyone else before him. The impact on her was much greater than she could have anticipated or unlike any hurt she had felt before. She was devastated and, as a result, almost immediately her internal defensiveness took over and her heart had gone cold. Realizing that Conner was lying to her caused her to shut down.

"Tell her I'll be there tomorrow, Austin. There's no proof that this is the same as what I went through back then and you can't possibly understand."

"It isn't? What's so different, Emily? I think you're kidding yourself because you're afraid of the truth. You learned the hard way that you couldn't run away from a nightmare forever and look what it's doing to your life now. You're throwing away a life that you've spent over fifteen years building. Your own daughters barely know you any more and you've obviously forgotten who I am. You've pulled away from me, from all of us. And, now you're doing it to Becky. What are you afraid of? Why do you keep denying what happened to you, and now what has happened to her? You protected her for all these years, but it wasn't enough, was it? Don't blame yourself, though, because you couldn't have done anything. It just happened, just like it did with you and you know it."

"I made a choice," she snapped. "I made the decision that I felt I could deal with best, considering the situation. It was my choice, Austin."

"If that's what you've been telling yourself all these years, then you are right. That was your choice then and how you carry it through your life is also your choice. But, you know if you play back the tapes, if you allow yourself to revisit what happened that night, then maybe you had only two choices and they were both ugly. You didn't have any guarantee if you chose one, that the other wouldn't have happened anyway."

Emily said nothing. She closed her eyes, and tried to block the flashbacks that were streaming into her mind, twisting and swirling around images of Conner, the words in his letter, her journal in his hands and his voice screaming her name against the thunder as she ran from the cabin into the storm.

"Austin, I don't think I can talk about this right now."

"I understand. I'm sorry for bringing it up. You have to realize something, Emily. Becky needs you. You are all the family she has here. She needs your strength and she needs your support."

"I know. Tell her and the girls I'm coming home tomorrow, okay?"

"Okay. What are you going to do tonight? Are you going back to the Park?"

"I'm not sure. I'll let you know. Just be sure to call my cell. In case I'm not in my cabin, okay?"

"You bet. Get some rest. I'll talk to you in the morning."

"Good night, Austin." Emily closed her cell phone and placed it on the table. She swallowed hard, as she thought, again, of Conner. Who was he? What was he? When they were in the woods together, wandering around the Park, she had allowed herself to be completely relaxed with him. The more they shared together, the more he seemed like someone she had known all of her life. Emily had grown to not only enjoy their time together, but had she misunderstood her comfort level with him as love for him? Perhaps she did love him and didn't know how deeply until today when she felt so betrayed by the news in his letter that he intended to abandon the Park.

"I'm such a fool," she whispered to herself.

Her eyes opened at the sound of the bell, banging against the restaurant door as a new customer entered the room. Emily looked up, as did everyone whenever someone new came in, and she caught her breath. It was Derek Stroebel.

I have to be dreaming, she thought to herself, feeling her heart pounding wildly in her chest. Emily quickly picked up the menu from her table, grateful that the distracted young waitress had failed to remove it when taking her coffee order. She opened the menu and held it up in front of her face, so not to be recognized.

Derek glanced around the restaurant as he brushed the rainwater from the sleeves of his jacket. Not waiting for the hostess, he walked across the restaurant and entered the men's restroom, stopping only for a second to speak briefly with the waitress who had brought Emily her coffee.

Emily was nervous. The booth next to her was empty, as were the two tables beside her. What if he was seated near her? What if he recognized her and sat down in her booth? She was, once again, cornered.

Emily waited and Derek soon emerged from the rest room. He walked to the cash register where a coffee-to-go waited for him. He reached into his pocket and pulled out a handful of change, which he tossed on the counter. He then picked up the coffee and left the restaurant, without another single glance around inside.

This was unusual for Derek and even with Emily's faded memory of a few encounters with him at college she knew that he must have something significant on his mind to stay so focused. And, because he was here, it had to be Blaney. He had finally come for her, perhaps to make sure she would never file rape charges against him. And now, after Conner's party, Derek knew right where to find her. She trembled as she again opened her cell phone. This time, she dialed the Harrison. Elsie answered.

"Hello?"

"Elsie," Emily's voice was trembling as well as her hands, making it difficult for her to hold the small phone to her ear, much less talk into it. "It's me, Emily."

"Emily? You're not quite clear, dear. Where are you?"

"It's the storm, I guess." Emily realized her phone didn't have good reception. "Please, Elsie, just listen to me. I'm in Manistique, at the Coach House restaurant just inside the city limits on the east end of town. Do you know where that's at?"

"At the what?"

"The Coach House."

"Oh yes, I know it. Whatever are you doing there? We had such a storm go through. I can't believe you went out in this weather. Are you alright?"

"No, I'm not alright. I need some help. I left my purse in my cabin and I really need it. Tonight. Is there any chance you could bring it to me?"

"Well, I don't know if Archie has filled up the car this week."

"Elsie, you know I wouldn't ask unless it was very important. I know it's late. Please, I need to talk to you and I don't want to do it there. Will you come?"

"Of course," Elsie smiled, pleased at being needed so much by her friend. "Of course I'll be there. Shouldn't take me more than about 45 minutes. You just sit tight, okay?"

"Thank you, Elsie." Emily hesitated and thought of Derek who was quite possibly on his way to Blaney. "Elsie, listen. One more thing."

"What is it, dear?"

"I want you to promise me something. No matter what or who you see on the way over here, you have to promise that you will just keep coming, okay? Promise me."

"Emily, I don't understand."

"Elsie, please just promise me."

"You're confusing me, but.... okay. I promise. I'll see you in less than an hour."

Emily sat back in her chair. She let out a big sigh and turned to watch the young waitresses, as they chatted with one another behind the counter.

Derek, she thought. What could he be doing up here? God, I'm reliving a nightmare.

An hour had passed when Emily looked up from her third cup of coffee at the sound of the restaurant door. Elsie walked in, removed her rain hat and shook the water from it as she looked around the restaurant. One of the waitresses approached her and, upon seeing Emily in the corner booth, she smiled and pointed toward Emily.

"Thank you for coming," Emily managed, as Elsie sat down and placed her hand upon Emily's arm.

"My dear, what is wrong?" Elsie asked. Her expression was full of concern.

"I don't even know where to begin." Emily dropped her eyes to the coffee cup as the tears began to well up.

"Just take a deep breath and start from the beginning." Elsie looked up at the waitress who had walked over to them. "Black coffee, please. And a couple slices of that apple pie you've got up in the case. Put a scoop of vanilla ice cream on one of them." She turned back to Emily. "Now, what's on your mind, my friend?"

"Elsie," Emily brushed away the tears from her eyes and squared her shoulders. "You've known me for a long time. With the exception of my family, you've known me longer than anyone."

"Yes, I can believe that," Elsie smiled.

"You know my history."

"You're referring to college."

"Yes. When I came back here in the spring, I wasn't sure what I would find, but I knew I had to come. There were things I had to face in my past before I could move forward." She smiled at the waitress who was setting the plates of pie down on their table. "I guess I found more than I was expecting."

"You're talking about Conner Morley, aren't you?" Elsie slid the plate served ala mode in front of Emily.

Emily looked up at her with surprise.

"Sweetie, I've seen a lot of people come and go at that place. I've seen a lot of things happen there. And, I've seen what happened between you and that man from the first day he arrived. You're quite taken with him, aren't you?"

"I thought I was," Emily said quietly. "After today, though, I'm not even sure I know him."

"What do you mean?"

"Elsie, how much do you know about the owner of Blaney, of the Harrison?"

"Well," Elsie thought for a moment, "not a lot. There's never been much to know. Just that the owner has wanted to remain anonymous and has left me in charge of running the place, for the most part. Why, honey?"

"Conner is the owner."

"Are you sure?"

"Positive. I found out today, from Conner himself. Oh, Elsie, I'm so angry. He also told me that he is planning to sell everything to a developer. He's closing the Park, the Harrison, everything."

Elsie sat quietly, shocked at the news, and took a few bites of her pie. "When?"

"I don't know. We spoke in my cabin, during the storm. I ran out. God, I'm so furious at him. All this time together," she looked up and the lines in her face were drawn tight. "Elsie, all this time, all these weeks and months, I thought he was just there. Just another guest trying to escape from down state. I thought he was different."

"I'm listening," Elsie smiled.

"He lied to me, Elsie. He's no different." She looked up again. "Why couldn't he have just told me from the beginning? Before the walks, all the talking, before..."

"Before you fell in love with him?"

"Yes," she dropped her eyes.

"I'm so sorry, sweetie."

"I don't want to go back, Elsie. I can't go back. Austin has his life in Ann Arbor and our girls are very much a part of that, very bonded to him. My life is here, with you and the wolves. I think it has been since college that I just either couldn't see it or refused to. Now, it's caught up with me and I can't fight it any longer."

"Emily," Elsie spoke firmly. "You just need a little time. Are you sure about all this? I've not talked to him very much, to Conner. I can't believe there isn't a reasonable explanation for all of this. I think you should come back with me. Stay in the Harrison tonight and we'll sort through it together, okay?"

"Elsie, I can't do that. I can't go back there. I don't want to see him."

"You don't have to see him, but you know you can't stay here. He doesn't need to know your staying in the House."

"Elsie," Emily shook her head.

"Listen to me," Elsie leaned forward and grabbed both of Emily's hands. "You are right. I have known you for a long time, long enough that you are like a daughter to me. I care about you very much."

"Thank you."

"I'm not about to leave you here, in the middle of the night. Now, I'm going to pay the check and we're going back."

"There's more."

"Tell me," Elsie leaned back.

"It's Derek," she blinked her wide eyes at her friend, watching for a reaction. "He's back. Here, at Blaney."

"Stroebel? Are you sure?"

"Yes, I'm sure. He was at Conner's birthday party, Elsie. Oh, God, it was awful. Conner actually introduced us, not realizing we already knew each other."

"You poor thing. How uncomfortable you must have been! Is that why you came back so upset?"

Emily nodded and sipped her coffee. "Derek was so enjoying it and I felt like throwing up. The rest of the night was horrible. Austin and I went home early from the party. I couldn't stay there. He questioned me about everything, even Conner."

"What did you tell him?"

"That I was coming back to Blaney permanently."

"Oh, my God, Emily," Elsie closed her eyes for a moment. "I'm so sorry."

Emily dropped her eyes again and stared at her cup. Elsie watched as the tears fell, one by one, from Emily's cheeks to the table.

"Then today. When I learned about Conner? About his plans? I didn't expect to see him back so soon. I was so glad to see him. Just when I thought I could trust my feelings again, just when I thought I could start over, he ruined everything. I feel like I'm going crazy some days, y'know? Like I woke up one morning and I was a different person, with a different life completely. No one around me is who I thought they were. And, I'm alone, Elsie. I'm very much alone."

"More coffee?" the young waitress interrupted.

"Thanks," replied Elsie.

"I can't go back," Emily sipped her coffee once the waitress had walked away. "And, now, I can't go forward. At least, not in the way I thought I wanted to. I don't know what direction to go in. The only thing I am certain of is that I trust no one, anymore. God, Elsie, this hurts so much. I've been such an idiot."

"Stop it." Elsie said, sternly. "Look at me."

Emily took a deep breath and raised her eyes.

"Does he know how you really feel? Conner, I mean?"

"No. And I have no intention of telling him. The quicker he leaves Blaney, the better. I'm going to fight him on this, Elsie. He can't have the Park. I've decided I'm calling a lawyer and fighting him. Will you help me?"

"Let's just wait for a day or two and see what happens," Elsie smiled. "First things first. You are coming back with me tonight. Tomorrow, we'll pay Mr. Morley a visit."

"Elsie," Emily shook her head. "I can't go back there tonight. You don't understand. I know Derek will be there. He was here tonight, earlier, before I called you."

"Here? In this place?"

"Yes. He just came in for a coffee and left. I don't know why he's here, but it can only be Blaney. After seeing me at the party, he must be going there. When we were introduced, Conner told him I was writing about the wolves. Elsie, I'm terrified."

"Okay," Elsie's mind was quickly putting to work her years of wisdom and experience. "Here's what we're going to do. I'm going to call Archie and have him watch for Derek, tell him to keep the man distracted while we get you back. He won't look for you at the House, he'll go to your cabin. You get a good night's sleep, and tomorrow we'll take care of everything, together." She leaned forward and grasped Emily's hands. "I'm with you all the way on this one, kiddo. Okay?"

"I don't know...."

"Okay?" Elsie repeated, firmly.

"Okay. Let's go."

"Check!" Elsie called over her shoulder.

26

The Storm

Archie sat in his car listening to big band music while still thinking of Emily and if leaving her at the restaurant was a good idea. Who was he to tell a grown woman what she can and can not do? God knows, he would never let anyone tell him what to do. But, she was a woman and he was raised to believe that women were supposed to be treated as special. Maybe he should have insisted on staying with her. Maybe he shouldn't have allowed her to go at all.

He had parked his pristine, white '66 Buick Le Sabre near the hangar. The bench seat was made of black cloth with white stripes. The dashboard was simple, with a speedometer that would register speeds to 140 miles per hour. The ashtray overflowed with cigarette buds and ashes. Only the ashtray was neglected, as Archie was as meticulous with the rest of his car as he was with the storage shed that contained all the entertainment toys for the guests.

Archie turned off the ignition. He then leaned over and reached into the huge glove box for a small silver flask filled with whiskey. The compartment was large enough to hold two pints of Archie's liquor. Yet, he only kept it stocked with his flask. Drinking directly from the mouth of the flask, Archie emptied it with one gulp and sat back against the seat. As he watched the rain splash off the floodlight hanging from the corner of the building, as it swayed against the light gusts of wind that accompanied the rain, he waited for the high caused by the alcohol to kick into his head. He didn't like to be drunk all the time, but the everyday pain and loneliness was sometimes just too much for him. He needed his alcohol. It was his companion.

Archie's thoughts were still filled with Emily. He thought back many years to when he first met her and remembered how feisty she was, even then. While he was not happy he lost a trap that night, he found amusement at her courage. He liked her from the get-go. Now, she was back as if she had never left Blaney Park, so mature and beautiful. Her caring nature for the wild animals and environment had remained strong over the years. She had a passion for it he never could understand and, in some ways, envied. As the alcohol buzz began filling his head, Archie contemplated what it would be like to have a family and especially a daughter. If he had, he would have wanted her to be just like Emily, strong and independent.

"Archie! Open up! You okay?" Startled, he looked out through the rain-streaked window of his car door to see Conner standing outside, soaked to the bone. He rolled the window half way down and the rain began dripping in.

"Conner, what the hell are you doing out here in this storm?"

"I am looking for Emily. Have you seen Emily, Archie?"

"And, what if I had, Mr. Morley? Do you expect me to tell you where she is? I don't do that to guests. Their secrets are my secrets."

"Archie," Conner struggled to keep his impatience from surfacing. "Your discreetness is commendable, but I need to speak to her. She is very upset and I need to try to set things straight. If you know where she is, I really need to know."

Archie wanted to tell him in the worst way. He knew she was safe at the diner, yet could not betray her trust. His value system prevented him from doing so and even though Conner was special to him, more special than anyone would ever know, he still lived by a code and even Conner wasn't worth breaking it over.

"Haven't seen her, Conner. If I do, I will tell her you are looking for her."

"Shit!" Conner yelled and banged his fists on top of the Buick. He turned and ran back down the path leading to the cabins.

Archie reached over to the passenger side and locked the door. He then opened the door, closed it and locked it again. He did the same thing three times before he was convinced the door was shut and locked. He reached to the passenger floor and grabbed a large flashlight that he kept under that side of the seat, opened the driver's door and stepped out into the pouring rain. He was going to check on the boats and on the shed where all the equipment was stored. There would be another drink there waiting for him, as well as the solitude that he needed after so much activity. Archie locked the car door, pushing in the button on the outside handle and closing the door while keeping the button pressed in. The older cars required this and it wasn't one of the better features for him to have on a vehicle. He pushed in the button to check that the door would not open. He took a few steps away from the door, just to turn around and check it again. He did it one last time before moving on with his task of going to the storage shed. He had thoughts of looking for Conner, but decided against it, having had enough of socializing for the night.

Conner hurried back through the rain to Emily's cabin, only to find her still absent. He knocked anyway, hoping against hope that she was in there. For the first time since he had been to Blaney Park, Emily's door was locked. She always joked that only the moon would intrude without permission and, even then, it would be pleasant.

Conner was feeling bad. He had been through so much over the last few months. Emily was the one sunshine in all the clouds of his life. He actually believed he could be in love with her, had she not been married, and was sure she was falling in love with him, too. It was a problem Conner normally would stray away from, but with their souls so intertwined, he just couldn't help but feel good about it all. Now, he had invaded her space. Not only had he been caught reading her journal, she now knew that he was selling the Park. He didn't even know why he told her such a thing. He really hadn't sold it yet. The conflict between personal gratification and business profits was always easy for Conner. Business always took precedence because relationships were never trustworthy. A dollar today would be a dollar tomorrow, he used to always think to himself. People and love came and went like the Michigan weather. How ironic the storm was occurring on the night Emily found out he may sell Blaney. Now she could be in danger and he hadn't a clue where to find her.

Conner went from the cabins to the barn. No Emily. As he stepped out of the barn, he saw Elsie getting into her car. He took off running, with no chance of catching her. He could only see her brake lights flash as she turned onto the road to wherever she was going. Thinking it was odd that she was leaving during such stormy weather conditions, Conner asked himself what was happening this night. It was all falling apart around him, and he decided to go back to his cabin and hope Emily would return.

Archie got to the storage shed and pulled the keys from a U-hook device that fastened to his leather belt. He had keys to everything at Blaney Park, as well as to some locks that didn't exist anymore. He would never throw away a key, just in case it matched something, and he always knew the correct key for a particular lock. He would amaze his guests by getting the right key on the first pull from so many. Now, his alcohol buzz was wearing off and a dull ache would soon fill his head. With the rain falling so hard on this evening, this was even more an irritant to him.

The building looked more like a garage than a shed. Archie removed the pad lock, walked in and reached to the wall on his right for the light switch. Fluorescent lights blinked on all around the room. It smelled of gas and fish bait. This was where Archie stored all the entertainment equipment for the guests at the Park, each item neatly positioned in its proper place. A hard worker, he would clean and re-clean this shed while storing the equipment until, after about the third cleaning, he would call it quits for the day. The last thing he'd do before leaving the shed was making sure his stash of whiskey or scotch was properly stocked.

Archie walked over to the medicine cabinet. He opened it and pulled out a false shelf, which contained Band-Aids and gauze, both of no use if anyone had the need, because they were glued to the shelf. It was his way of protecting his stash from intruders, especially kids who he often would find snooping around the shed looking for interesting things to play with.

Archie reached into the wall and pulled out his stash with a slight smile. He would always look around to see if anyone was watching, remove a paper cup from its dispenser and then pour a full glass of either whiskey or scotch into it. He was then careful to return the bottle to the wall and replace the shelf as if nothing had been disturbed. In the shed, he always used a paper cup so guests wouldn't see what he was drinking. He would wear strong cologne and chew tobacco to keep the smell of alcohol off his breath. But everyone knew because the smell was too much for anything to cover up. Most people accepted it of Archie and those who did comment, exposing his use, would have a tough day on the river and area lakes. He would take them where no fish would be found, just to spite them.

He walked over to the work bench and decided to work on a reel that had been tangled with fish line by an eight-year-old earlier that day. This was like a puzzle to Archie who, rather than being frustrated, would play a game with himself to try and see how long it would take him to untangle it. He would set the egg timer to whatever length of time he thought it would take, and then go at it. If he couldn't untangle it within the time set, he'd take the knife to it, cut it out and re-wind it with new line. He took pride in how few times he had to cut out the line on a reel.

Archie was feeling good again. His buzz was back, he was having some competition and no one was there to bother him.

Back in his cabin, Conner poured a drink and sat down. His fire was going out, which meant Archie hadn't been out to stoke it for the night, as he had always done.

Jesus, even Archie doesn't like me now, Conner thought. I am a mess.

He stepped out onto the front porch to get the fire another log. As he stood and turned to go back inside, he looked up toward the main drive to see car lights pulling into the Harrison. He figured it was Miss Elsie, returning from her evening drive or perhaps even Emily who sometimes borrowed the utility van to run errands.

"That's it," he said aloud, while putting the log on the fire. "She took the van. No wonder I couldn't find her."

That was it and now she was returning. He wasn't going to go running after her. He'd sit in front of the fire and wait for her to come looking for him to talk. They always talked. She came to her senses and now wanted to talk him, so he thought. However, they never had an issue with each other before. Emily had certainly been hurt by his admission of not only being the owner of her Park, but also being in the process of selling it. Maybe she wouldn't come.

Archie was not doing too well with the reel. The egg timer's bell sounded and his feeling of defeat was intensified by the affects of the alcohol. He reached back as if to throw the reel, but thought better of it. Over the years, he had damaged more than he wanted to admit due to his temper. He hated spackling walls and replacing windows was expensive. He had finally realized that acting out his anger caused him more frustration in the end than the frustration felt at the time.

"The little shit really tangled you, bitch," he said to the reel.

The heavy rain pounding on the roof caused concern in him that the river might rise over its banks if much more came down. He hated floods, more from the inconvenience than anything else they caused. The docks are of no use to him submerged under water and the currents prevented the river from being accessed. If the guests weren't fishing, they would be talking to him and he hated that.

Archie removed his pocket knife, sliced out the section of line that was so badly tangled, and replaced it. He was thinking he needed a buzz refill, but didn't feel like going to the medicine cabinet again. Instead, ready to listen to some good music and have a few drinks in his own quarters, he decided to lock up the shed and call it a night. The one place Archie never smoked was in the shed, as there were too many flammables. His need for a smoke was now as strong as his need for a drink and, with the rain coming down so hard, his only smoking spot was the hangar.

Stepping out into the rain, Archie noticed a light inside the hangar. It was a motion detection light. An old trick. He never worried about leaving a light on, because he knew when he walked into the room it would come on automatically. The light was on and that was a bad sign.

Not even bothering to lock up the shed, he made his move to the hangar, shuffling his feet as quickly as possible, as his hand instinctively went to his left hip. His knife was not at his side! He had left so quickly to drive Emily to Manistique that he did not take the time to place it in his holster. Now Archie was angry with himself. Dismissing his concerns, he decided that he must have left the door unlocked and someone just walked in.

As Archie approached the door, he saw that its window had been broken. He thought of returning to the shed for a weapon, but decided he didn't want to allow the person to get away. He didn't need to worry. As he entered the room, the person was still there, standing at the file cabinet with his back towards the door and looking through all of Archie's files.

"What the fuck do you think you are doing, asshole?" Archie snarled, as he entered the hangar office.

The man whirled around in shock, as he didn't expect anyone to be returning to the office until morning. He didn't realize this was where Archie lived.

"I am the new owner of Blaney Park," he stated. "I forgot the key that was given to me for this building. Since I came all this way, I decided to break the window and let myself in. It's important that I find some paperwork, that I know is somewhere in these files, to close a deal I am working on. Do you work here?"

"Hell, yes, I work here and I live in that back room," Archie pointed to the door beside the file cabinet.

"Well, that's good, old man. I am not going to take your room from you. You work for me now, and I want you to help me find what I am looking for."

"Like hell, I work for you! And I want your arrogant, smart-talking mouth and piss -poor attitude ass out of here now, before I throw you out! But, before I do, just who in the hell are you?"

"My name is Conner Morley. Like I said, I own this place."

"Like hell, you do. I know Conner Morley and you ain't him."

"I was afraid you were going to say that, my friend." Derek Stroebel reached into his jacket pocket and pulled out a revolver.

Archie was now angry at both the situation and at himself. He knew his knife was just around the corner and was feeling naked without it. Even against a revolver, Archie was a marksman with his knife and still very fast with it. He would not hesitate to make the throw to the chest that would instantly kill this person, even if he had a gun. Archie was weaponless, and now felt both irritated and scared. After all these years, now some young punk, preppy type who probably never shot a gun before had one aimed directly at him. He was at risk of getting killed not by some street tough hoodlum, but by a choirboy looking for a piece of paper.

"You really gonna shoot me with that? Do you know what the fuck you are doing, son? Maybe you should put the gun down and just walk out of here. I won't even try to follow you. You just go, and we will both say this never happened. Okay?"

"Fuck you, old man," Derek laughed. "I don't know what you do here. Take out the garbage or cut the lawn, maybe? You are way over your head, old man. You don't know who you are dealing with. I will fucking blow your head off, if I have to. So, what am I going to do with you while I look for what I need?"

"And what are you looking for?"

"The deed, asshole. Fucking Morley backed out on our deal. No one backs out on a deal with me. No one. I know it's in here, and I am going to make him sign it. With a little persuasion, if you know what I mean."

"You think Conner will give in to you?"

"Maybe. If I get that little sweet bitch in my grasps he will, or maybe that Elsie lady. I was there, watching Emily and Conner dance. Conner is a sucker for that kind of stupid shit. That wishy-washy feelings bullshit that doesn't add any value to one's bottom line."

"Conner ain't going to sign anything for you, asshole."

"Well then, maybe I'll just kill his ass. Some dude is already missing, last seen right here at Blaney Park. Conner comes up missing, this resort goes down the toilet, 'cause no one will come here for fear of their life. I'll buy this place for even less than I was offering now for it." Derek started laughing with the thought of getting a better deal by killing Conner. "Personally, I don't like the fuck anyway. He's all Mr. Everything. Conner this, Conner that... Fuck Conner. He ain't shit to me."

Archie looked directly into Derek's eyes. They weren't right. He was tripping on something and this concerned Archie, as he had gotten into drugs years earlier and knew bad things could happen without reason or logic. He had to keep talking to the man in front of him holding a revolver until he could decide what he was going to do. The kid didn't look like he was the type who had ever killed a person before, but Archie knew not to judge the book by its cover. He had treated everyone as capable during his life and some were taken down who would have never done such a thing. He wasn't going to make a mistake, although he already had. He allowed Emily to take him out of his routine and on this night of all nights. It may cost him his life.

Buzzing high from the liquor he had consumed while in the shed, Archie was feeling brave. As he was looking at this kid in front of him, he decided to make a run for his knife, thinking he would have a chance if he raced to a place close by. Going outside was not a smart thing because the kid was younger and could certainly out run him. Besides, with a revolver, Archie would only be target practice and knew he didn't have the agility to avoid the bullets that were sure to be aimed at him.

Derek kept the gun pointing at Archie as he continued to shuffle through files that he had pulled from the cabinet. The cabinet had been pried open with a crowbar, and papers were strewn everywhere. Derek's mind was altered by the drug he had taken earlier to give him the courage to make such a bold move as to attempt to rob Blaney Park of its deed in order to gain ownership of a place he wanted worst than life itself.

"My dad will not take no for an answer, man. If this deal falls through I am fucked and I am not going to allow that to happen. You see, I have worked too hard and been humiliated for too long to allow that to happen to me now."

"Sounds like you and your dad need to sit down and work this shit out, son."

"Shut up, old man! Don't tell me what I need. You don't have any idea of what it's like to be an outcast and not liked just because of what? Fuck, I don't know why my dad don't like me. He just don't. I'd kill him right now, if he were here, that fat fuck."

"Well then, let me see if I can help you find those papers." Archie faked like he was looking at papers on the floor while moving closer to the bedroom door where the blade was hanging just to the right of it. If he could only crash through and get access to his knife, one quick flip of the wrist and he'd have done mortal damage to this kid with a gun. Archie expected to get shot in the act, but he knew unless the bullet found a vital organ, he'd live to tell yet another story to the pictures on the walls.

"Yeah, you do that, old man. You help me find what I am looking for. You work for me now, you know. This is my place, my building, my papers... all this is mine and daddy will be pleased with me."

Feeling he had a good line to the door, Archie took a deep breath, knowing his advanced age wasn't going to give him too good of odds to succeed without injury.

"Wait! Where you going, old man? I see you moving towards that door. Don't even think about it. Do you think I was born yesterday, asshole? Now, you be a good man and just sit in that chair over there." Derek waved his gun toward the office chair that was near the door. Archie knew it was now or never. He made his move.

As he lunged at the door, the younger and stronger Derek met him just as he reached it. Derek never bothered to point his revolver. He held it by the barrel and clubbed Archie over the head with its heavy handle. The bedroom door gave in against their weight and they crashed through it to the floor inside.

I won't even be awake to see myself be killed, Archie told himself, as he slipped into unconsciousness. I wonder which way my soul will be going.

Derek raised himself off the floor. He had taken a hard hit and was a little unsettled. The drugs, along with the blow to the body had made him wonder if he had broken something. The door was in pieces next to Archie on the floor and Derek smiled in victory. He took the revolver that was still in his hand and placed the barrel of the gun to Archie's temple. He pulled back the hammer and did nothing. He held the gun there, wondering what would happen if he pulled the trigger and blew this man's head off. Did he have a wife? Kids? Maybe. Derek took the revolver away and disarmed the hammer. He had no beef with this old man. None. So, he was going to let him live.

Derek looked around the room and saw traps hanging on the walls. Bored and frustrated with looking for the deed, he was ready for a different approach. He went to the wall and removed a trap. He stepped over Archie and exited the hangar.

Emily should have come over by now, Conner thought, as he drank the last of his third JD and diet coke. What's keeping her? He was growing more impatient that she had not come to his door to discuss their issue. He wanted to explain to her that he still had ways of getting out of the deal, but in case he couldn't, he wanted to prepare her for the worst case scenario. After all, Conner didn't know about this heaven on earth called Blaney Park. He had no idea that it meant so much for so many. Nor did he truly realize how many people came here to relax and just be away from the hassles of civilization and enjoy the peace and serenity of such untouched country. Peace was so important to one's soul and Conner had learned that from Emily and the Park.

His patience was exhausted. He could not wait another minute. Even though he had just finally felt dry again, he decided to expose himself to the elements once more and go looking for Emily.

Conner first went to her cabin. To his disappointment, she was still not there. He made his way back to the Harrison only to find that neither Elsie nor Emily was there. He looked to the parking lot where the van was sitting, as always, in its spot. Confused again, he thought he'd go back to the hangar to question Archie one more time. As Conner approached the hangar, he noticed the door standing wide open and the broken glass. Inside, papers were blowing around the room from the strong winds of the storm.

Conner entered with caution, realizing that something was very wrong. He stepped lightly as he walked toward the back and carefully looked inside Archie's room. Upon seeing Archie lying on the floor face down, Conner felt his blood racing to his head as his adrenaline was fueled by his anger. Not yet sure that the perpetrator was gone from the hangar, Conner entered slowly and cautiously. When no one was to be found, he went to Archie and rolled him over. The bump on Archie's head was bleeding and Archie was mumbling as he faded in and out of his unconsciousness.

"Archie! Archie, are you okay? Come on, man. Talk to me!" Conner stood up, walked to the bottled water machine and filled two cups. The first one, he poured over Archie's head. He then carefully tried to sit Archie up, offering the second one by tipping the cup against Archie's mouth to allow the water to trickle into his lips. Archie spat out the water and jerked his head to the side.

"On top of the file cabinet," he gasped. "That's what I need."

Conner went to the front room and sure enough, on top of the cabinet, sat a bottle of JD. He unscrewed the top from the bottle, took it back over to Archie and offered him a slug. After Archie drank, Conner took a swallow. He helped Archie sit up and stood to replace the bottle on top of the cabinet.

"Archie, what happened? Who did this to you? Why did they do this to you?"

"Some young fuck," Archie replied, rubbing the back of his neck.

"Here," Conner pulled a handkerchief from his back pocket and handed it to Archie.

"You know some guy named Stroebel?" Archie asked, holding the handkerchief against the blood on his head.

"Stroebel? Derek Stroebel?" Conner was alarmed. "He was here? He did this?"

"I got a guy at the car rental desk at the Delta County airport in Escanaba. He called me and said Stroebel was in town. He'd arrived three days ago. But, when he didn't show the first two days, I figured he wasn't coming. Had his name on the list for a long time and never expected him to show. But it was him that did this to me. Fuck, I should have been more careful. Fucker thinks he's the owner of this place. He was lookin' for the deed when I walked in on him. I was planning to knife his ass, but he got to me first."

"Jesus Christ," Conner looked at Archie in disbelief. "Where is he now, Arch?"

"Don't know," Archie groaned, as he stood up. "We have to find him fast, my boy. He said something about making you sign the deed when he found it. And, he mentioned Emily and Miss Elsie. He's done his homework. They are in danger."

"Emily," Conner swallowed against a lump that had risen in his throat. His mind was racing to replay the words he had read in her journal. "Fuck, Archie! Come on!" He grabbed Archie's arm to steady him and they started out through the office.

"Wait!" Archie pulled away. He stepped back through his doorway and reached up to remove his knife from its place on the wall inside. He strapped it to his belt, as the corner of his upper lip curled into a smile that sent a chill through Conner. "Now, let's find that bastard."

27

Goodbye, Derek

"Archie, you have been hurt. That shot to your head looks bad. Maybe you should stay here and let me go."

"Fuck that, Conner! I ain't staying back and missing all the fun. That son of a bitch took a piece of me. Now, he's going to get back what he deserves." Archie pushed past Conner and started out the hangar door. Conner followed directly behind him.

"Where do you think he went?" Conner yelled to Archie as the winds of the second wave of the storm were building and the rain felt like small needles against his skin. While Conner was trying to shield his face, Archie stood stoic as if there was no hard rain hitting him on his bare skin like that which was hurting Conner.

"I don't know. Haven't figured it out yet. One thing's for sure, Conner. He wants your ass. Why don't you stay back and let me find him. I will take care of him for us both. I don't want you getting into any trouble from this situation. I can take care of the daddy's boy who came here to fuck with my family. It could get ugly. I am not sure what he took from the hangar, but I faintly remember him taking something."

"Look!" Conner yelled through the rain and wind, pointing past Archie.

"Shit!" Archie yelled, as both men looked to the barn. It had been set on fire.

"There he is!" Conner yelled and started running after Derek, who was leaving the burning barn, holding a trap and a flashlight in his hands.

"He's going towards the clearing!" Archie called back.

Conner continued to run another hundred feet when he looked back toward the hangar. There, he saw Archie on his hands and knees in the wet grass. Conner stopped running and returned to him.

"Archie! Archie, you okay? What is wrong?"

"Conner, I don't think I can go with you, son. I am out of breath and my chest hurts. Ugh, ugh..." Archie grabbed his chest and rolled over onto his back. He unbuckled his belt and pulled it out of the first two loops on his pants, just far enough to remove his knife from it. "Conner," Archie gasped. "Come closer. Here's my knife."

"What, Archie? I need to run back to the hangar and get you a doctor. You don't look too good. You are turning blue. I will be back."

"No, no! Conner, stay with me for a second. You need to go after that slimy fucker, Derek! But, before you do, I need to tell you something."

"Archie, don't try to talk. Lay there and stay still while I go back to get you some help. You are dying, Archie."

"I am already dead, Conner. I have been dead for a very long time, son. Don't you fucking leave me, you hear me? You don't fucking leave me!" Archie demanded of Conner. "I want you right here with me. I have to tell you something."

"What, Archie, what do you want to tell me?"

"Conner, I am your dad's brother. Ewald's brother. I am your uncle. I want to tell you that I am sorry for not being there for you over the years. Reasons I can't explain now. But, I have followed your every move and success. I don't have much time now, son. It's time for you to know."

Conner was stunned. He sat back in the mud next to Archie and said nothing for a moment. It suddenly all made sense to him.

"No shit. My uncle. You are that Archie? You're the brother that my dad talked about? I didn't even know my dad had a brother until this year when I talked with him."

"I know, son. Your dad and I walked different sides of the street and we just haven't stayed close over the years. It was for the best. I am sorry. It hurt me that I couldn't be near you, but I want you to know. I know all about you."

"You know Todd, don't you?" Conner said, realizing now why Todd seemed so comfortable around Archie.

"Yeah, he's a great friend of yours, Conner. I've known him for a lot of years. He made sure I knew what you needed so I could be there for you without you knowing it."

"Jesus, Archie. I am so sorry that I didn't know. Todd never told me."

"I made him promise me that he'd never tell you, son. He was helping me protect you. It was our secret. Don't blame him for my secrets, my mistakes."

"Archie, I need to get you some help. Stroebel can wait for me. Right now, I need to get you some medical help."

"No! I am fine. I will be able to get back inside the hangar on my own. I have some meds that will take care of me. You just be careful, but you go get that asshole."

"Are you sure, Archie?"

"Yeah. You need to go get him. He's calling you out. You are a Morley and we don't back off from anyone."

"Okay, Archie. I will make you proud."

"You already have made me proud, son. You already have. Just be careful. He's got a gun and he's tripping on something. Heroin, LSD or acid, is my guess. I have seen it before, Conner. He won't just go down and you will have to take him out."

"Yeah, Archie. He needs to be taken out and I am just the person to do it tonight."

"Go. Go and get him."

Conner took Archie's knife out of its holder and started his run to the clearing. He ran in a zigzag motion, being careful not to be exposed to an easy assault. The path was not very wide and he did not want to stray from it, since it was soft and wet from the rain. He could see the light from Derek's flashlight ahead of him. The intermittent lighting from the storm allowed him to find his way to the clearing. Conner did not have a good feeling about his position. He was at a disadvantage against Derek and he knew it. Stroebel had the flashlight so he could see where he was going and Conner kept thinking that Stroebel had something else in his possession but he did not know what it was. And the drugs. If Derek was truly spaced out, no telling what he would do if cornered. Conner understood a bar brawl, but this was no bar. He felt vulnerable in this situation.

Conner began to slow down. He realized that he was getting winded and he had to be ready to engage with the enemy at any second. He didn't want to be out of breath if he had to battle with Derek hand-to-hand. Derek had gotten out in front of Conner and he lost the light from the flashlight. He was hoping the storm would provide more lightning so he could get a glance at where Derek might be. Conner knew the clearing well and of all the places Derek could run, he felt best going to the clearing. If only the moonlight could be out he thought to counter the advantage Derek had with his flashlight. Conner did not like his position in the dark.

"Morley, you should have just sold me Blaney Park, you bastard! Then none of this would have happened."

Conner saw Derek leaning near a tree in front of him at the clearing's edge. Conner looked to his hands. Derek had nothing in them. Conner held the knife in his right hand.

"Why, Stroebel? What the hell was worth all of this? Money? Power? I don't get it. I don't understand why you are being such an ass."

Derek began to laugh.

"Why? Why? That is a good question, Morley. I have no fucking idea why. Why I have a dad that fucking hates me and never gives me a minute of his time unless money is to be made. Why do people need power, desire power over other people? I guess it's much like this wilderness here. It's survival of the fittest, Mr. Morley. And I plan on being fitter than either you or that cranky old man who has been funding you for all these years."

Conner looked shocked at Derek's comment. The rain had diminished greatly, which made the conversation easier but the lightning was steadfast around them. He could not see Derek as well as he would have liked, but then again, Derek could not see Conner, either. Only the intermittent flashes allowed each of them to see the other.

"Yup, that's right, little boy. That old fuck I left to die in the hangar has been funding you and you didn't even know it. How lucky are you? You get what you want without even trying. Hell, people are giving to you what I have to take for myself. It ain't fair. Life ain't fair, Conner."

"You are crazy, Stroebel. You aren't making any sense, man. I can get you some help. I can get you feeling better about yourself. So your dad is an ass, why do you put up with him?"

"Because he's all I have in this world. Nobody would like me for just me. Hell, my own dad doesn't even like me. I have to hide who I am, what I am, just to survive. You know what I am, Conner?"

"No, you tell me what you are."

"I am like that little northern Michigan deer tick that exists around here and everybody fears but can hardly see. It can bring down a huge buck by filling it with disease. That's me, Morley, just a little tick filled with disease and sickness, not caring who I hurt and why. I just need what I need and I am one of the sick ticks." Derek laughed at himself. "Sick tick. Hahaha, that fucking kind of rhymes, don't it, Conner? I just wanted to get inside my prey and bring them down. Like a tick, I just crawl along in life until I find my prey and I bore into them. I take just enough out of them that they are never the same after I have tasted their blood. Now I am going to take care of Emily and that old fuck. And, in the end, Conner, you will have wished that you never heard of Blaney Park and those activities that occur here. This place is sick, just like me, Conner. It needs to be cleared and rebuilt."

"I won't let you do that, Stroebel. It's not sick, you are sick."

"I figured you were going to say that."

As a flash of lightning lit up the woods and the nearby clearing, Conner went running after Derek. He had regained his oxygen and the lactic acid from his system was no longer burning at his lungs. He was refreshed and ready to do battle.

Conner was gaining on Derek as they ran into the clearing. He had no idea what Derek was doing. All he was sure of was that Derek, in his state of mind, could not be looked at logically. He knew he had to bring Stroebel down and, if necessary, he would kill him to do it.

The lightning was now being followed by the thunder, which meant another front was moving into Blaney Park. The rain began to fall in large drops. Conner could see ahead that Derek stopped just inside the clearing and he made his move. He was not going to talk anymore. He had the knife in his hands. A knife almost the size of a machete and he was going to cut Derek down at the legs so there would be no more chasing each other.

"Ugh!" Conner yelled out. The events that followed were in slow motion to him. He could feel pain from his ankle as it shattered in an instance. He was moving, falling forward when his momentum was halted by the pull of a chain that was attached to the trap that had just closed around his bone. He was downed like a tackle on the football field from behind and fell face first to the ground.

"Ah, Ah, Ah-haaa," Derek began laughing, hysterically. "Holy shit, was that fucking cool! Oh, my God. That was so fucking cool, Conner. That must fucking hurt!"

Conner began to groan. He instinctively reached down to his ankle and could feel the iron teeth of it deep inside his skin.

"Now that is one fucking tick, huh, Conner? Can you feel it boring into your skin and sucking out your blood? I am the tick and you are the deer. Now, who has the power, you spoiled mother fucker?"

Conner continued to struggle, trying to regain his composure. His mind was spinning from the intense pain going through his body. He had been hurt before, even stabbed a couple of times in street fights, but this pain was incomparable. As he was feeling for the trap to try and pull it open, he could feel the ankle twisted and hanging from the muscles and skin. The trap had snapped his anklebone and severed his skin. Blood was pouring out of the holes in the skin made by the trap.

"Conner, Conner. Mr. Morley, are you feeling okay? You look a little under the weather. Hahaha! A little under the weather, do you get it? Under the weather. The storm and you ... oh fuck it! You aren't smart enough to get it. You walked right into my trap. Hahaha... get it? You walked right into my trap. Oh, I slay me!" Derek continued to speak as he walked forward, becoming increasingly closer to Conner.

Conner realized that Derek was going to get into range of the knife. Derek never noticed, in his buzzed state of mind, that Conner had a weapon. The pain was intense but Conner never dropped the knife. He did place it next to him when he was feeling for his ankle. The adrenaline was keeping him going. While the pain was intense it began to diminish the closer Derek got to him. He reached down next to him and grasped the knife.

"So, do you want to kiss and make up, Conner? I have raped many women in my life, including your girlfriend, Emily, and her little niece. But, I have never had my way with a man before. Oh, would that make me a sick fuck. I have always wanted to experience new things and I'd say you are in no position to fight my advances. It's kind of like you are tied up for the moment. Hahaha, get it? Tied up for the moment. A moment you will never forget, Mr. Morley. I will make sure of that."

"Yeah," Conner winced against the pain in his ankle as it radiated up through the bones of his leg. "I know all about the rape of Emily. I also know that you tied her up when you did it. I guess you have a control problem, don't you, Stroebel?"

"No, I'd say you have the control problem, asshole. You don't have any. Do you know that when a person dies, they can't control their bowels any longer? I'd say in a few minutes, I will know what you ate for breakfast this morning." Derek continued to move forward towards Conner, laughing at his own comments.

"I don't think so!" Conner replied and with that, took the knife and swiped at Derek, striking him on his left arm and cutting it half off.

"Ouch! You mother fucker! That really hurt!" Derek yelled and fell backward from where Conner was now half sitting up. "I can't believe you did this to me! Why did you do this to me, Mr. Morley? Did I deserve this? No, I don't think so."

Conner hadn't been successful. He was looking to strike Derek in the neck, but when he swung the knife, the trap grabbed at him and pulled his swing down to Derek's tricep.

"Oh my God, look at my arm!" Derek was holding his nearly severed arm with his other hand, as blood poured from it. "You practically cut it off. Now what kind of lover are you to hurt me this way?"

Conner was shocked at Derek's composure, which only validated that he must have been drugged up to a high degree. For a person not to feel the intense pain of such a cut, they would have to be in an altered state. He knew he had to get up and do something, because to lie there was to die there. While Derek was looking at his wound, Conner scooted his body to where the chain attached to the trap was connected to a rod embedded in the ground. He pulled it out, and tried to get up to a standing position with the chain in his hand. He turned toward Derek, who had taken off his belt to tourniquet his arm with it. Conner was beginning to feel certain that he was going to die. The trap was too heavy and there was no way he could either run away from or battle Derek.

Derek pulled up his left pant leg and removed a pistol from an ankle holster. Conner watched, believing his time on earth was over, and looked to the stormy skies to pray during his last moments. A calm feeling came over him. He never really thought life was that wonderful, anyway, but meant to be lived. He never gave up at anything, but this situation didn't seem to offer anything more than to give in to the inevitable. He was making peace with his maker so he could go home without issue.

Derek raised his gun without comment. The rain continued falling and the increasing lightning flashes made it easier for Derek to get Conner in his cross hairs. Conner looked directly at him, holding the chain in one hand and the knife in the other. Conner raised the knife and made one final effort to save his own life. He threw the knife toward Derek. Derek never saw it coming in the darkness. Conner hoped a good throw would make a solid impact to Derek's chest. The knife flew high and to the right of Derek, missing him without him knowing how close he came to losing his life.

Lightning struck again, as Conner could see Derek taking aim. He did not close his eyes nor make any motion. He looked directly at the man who was going to end his life. His thoughts turned to his parents. How would they take his murder? And, his siblings. He never did make his relationship with his brother right. He'd never get another chance. And Emily, he let her down.

This man named Derek who violated her was the tick that did bore into her soul and sucked out her life little by little. He had let her down. He did not revenge her name or her existence. He wanted to rid her of the man who hurt her so badly many years ago. And, all that had happened to Conner. He felt it fitting that he die in such a violent way since his life had felt so unsettled. He could not even walk into a restaurant without sizing up those who might hurt him. He wanted to die like a hero. Now, he was going to die at the hands of a crazed person who wanted no more than to purchase a piece of land so he could destroy it to heal his own personal demons.

The gun was pointed directly at Conner when, to his left, he saw something jump toward Derek. The gun fired just as the object reached him. Pain again attacked Conner's body. This time it was his right hip that felt the heat of pain as a foreign object penetrated his skin. The bullet hit Conner in the right hip and he went down again hard to his back. The pain was just heat now, since the trap had activated all the endorphins in his brain. The organ that was trying to control all that was happening to his body. Conner pulled himself up to his elbows only to see Derek turn and point his revolver at the wolf that had jumped him. The wolf had its teeth in Derek's left forearm and would have been enough to deter him if not for the drugs and the injury already sustained by Conner's knife blow. Derek took the gun in his right hand and pressed it to the wolf's head and fired. The wolf yelped and fell lifelessly to the ground, only trembling once before dying.

"Shit!" Derek cried out. "This is bull shit, man! What the hell is going on? I can't even kill someone without trouble. Well, I am done fucking around with you, asshole. Now I am pissed!"

Derek walked up to Conner, who had no where to go and nothing to fight back with. He placed the gun to Conner's temple.

"Well, I guess this is goodbye. It was nice meeting you, Conner Morley. Tell grandma Stroebel hello when you get to hell."

Conner heard a shot ring out. He never closed his eyes. Again, it all was in slow motion. Derek was lifted up and thrown backward from the power of the shotgun pellets that just blew half his face off and populated his chest cavity. Conner was looking Derek in the eyes when he left his side from the power of the weapon that just took his life. He could feel heavier rain drops fall upon his exposed skin. Looking at his arms, he could see the rain washing away the blood that was spattered onto him from the shot. He could not move. He was losing too much blood and he was beginning to feel faint.

He kept his eyes skyward until the face of Elsie looked down at him. Elsie did not speak to Conner. She stepped over him, opened the chambers of her shotgun and reloaded. Conner did not witness what occurred but knew that Elsie emptied those chambers again into Stroebel for her. Not to kill the mind or soul of a man already heading to hell, but to put to rest her own anger for a man who she despised.

"You will never lay your hands on Emily, or anyone else, again, young man!"

Conner's hearing was accentuated by his state of pain and he heard her words as if she said them directly to him. It happens to the body when it is damaged greatly. The senses became more acute. He had no doubt that Elsie knew of Derek's violation against Emily, too. Conner laid his head down and felt the rain pound his face and the wounds that were exposed to it. He was working hard not to become unconscious. Even as he was lying there and he felt the pain from his wounds, he looked to the sky as the drops hit him on the face. He smiled and thanked God for allowing Elsie to rid Emily of the wound that was Derek Stroebel.

28

Gone With The Wind

Archie reached the hangar and went directly to his top desk drawer. He was wheezing from a rapid heart rate that was induced by both Derek's attack and his brief run to go after him with Conner. He pulled the drawer open and reached to the back of it for his heart medicine. The childproof cap gave him some trouble. He picked up a stapler and crushed the bottle, spilling the nitroglycerine tablets all over the top of his desk and onto the floor. He reached down and grabbed the first pill he could and placed it under his tongue to slow his heartbeat. He then went to the file cabinet, grabbed the scotch bottle from on top of it and took a swig from it. He took another, and then another. Stumbling back to his desk, he picked up the receiver, and dialed Todd's number.

"Sully, this is Archie," he said, with an irritated voice. "You need to come. Conner's in trouble. Cops will be crawling all around this place soon and I want him out of here. Too much has happened tonight. We need to protect him. We need to get him out of here, Todd. This shit has turned bad up here. Fuck!" Archie winced against both the pain in his knee and the tightness in his chest.

"The weather is like shit, Archie."

"I don't care if there is a tornado in the air! You get your ass up here, now!" Archie hung up the phone, not waiting for an answer. He knew Todd would come. Archie knew what happened to people when he placed them under a directive. Todd would first think about the risk to him and then say goodbye to his kids, in case something did happen to him during the flight. He would look into his kids' eyes and then question why he was going to take such a stupid risk by flying in such bad weather, no matter the reason. Then he would think about Archie and what he was capable of doing to anyone who didn't do as he said. Todd would be there within a few hours.

Archie could see the volunteer fire department trucks with their lights flashing arriving at Blaney Park. He did not call them nor alarm them. A Park guest must have seen the barn fire and made the call. Archie would have preferred it burn to the ground without incident. He met them in the drive leading to the barn.

"Archie, the barn, what do you want us to do?" asked the first volunteer fireman to reach him.

"Don't do anything. Just let it burn." Archie said coldly, as if it was the obvious thing to do. "It's too late now. Just turn around and go home to your families. The storm is getting worse and the rain will do much to put the fire out. There is nothing you can do for it now and you guys should be home riding out this hell of a storm."

"What happened to you?" the fireman asked, obviously concerned at Archie's condition. "You don't look too good. Do you need one of us to look after that cut on your forehead?"

"No, I am fine. The wind blew open a door and caught me. I'll be okay. Just go. I have to tie down some more stuff and I don't have time to fuck with you guys. I need you to get the hell out of here now."

"Well, okay, Arch, if you insist, but it seems like you'd at least want us to put out the barn fire since we are here."

"No, the barn is lost, so might as well just let it burn. Saves me from doing it later to clean up the mess."

"Do you know how it started?"

"Nope, not yet. Probably lightning."

"Then you know I will need to call the sheriff and have him file a report. You need to sign this sheet, here, indicating to us that you didn't want us to work on that fire. You know how lawsuits are. I trust you, Archie, but we can't have you telling a lawyer tomorrow we just stood here and did nothing."

"Sure, I'll sign it. I don't want anything to do with the law, period. Can you do me a favor?"

"What's that Archie?"

"Can you hold off calling the sheriff tonight? No sense getting him here when all will be the same tomorrow."

"Are you sure you are okay, Archie? What the hell is going on here?"

"Listen. This is private property and nothing is going on. I just don't have time for this shit, right now or later. The storm is causing havoc and now I need to make sure my paying guests aren't in a panic. I suppose lightning hit the barn and started the fire. I just ain't got time for you right now. So, please, go and leave me to my work and don't bring no sheriff here tonight. I have work to do, no time for his sorry ass."

"Whatever you want, Archie," said the fireman, shaking his head. All of the many firemen who responded were standing around Archie as he was telling them to leave and not act on the fire that was blazing inside the barn. Some of them called Archie an asshole as they turned to walk away, knowing that with the rain and their efforts, some of the barn could have been saved. They were displeased that they had drove the distance to respond and support the civil obligations of their duties, only to be told to turn around and leave it to burn. Yet, they knew not to, or just didn't want to, mess with Archie when he was in an ornery mood. A few had already made fire runs from the storms that day. They could use the rest and time to be with their family.

Archie signed the paper, as he was required. He watched as the trucks maneuvered to leave Blaney Park, hoping that none of them would take action on their own and call the sheriff.

As soon as the last truck exited the main driveway, Archie walked back to the hangar and climbed into the Park's old pick-up truck. He drove out across the grounds toward the clearing where he thought Conner and Derek would be located, based on the direction they were headed.

"Elsie! Oh, my God, what happened!" Emily screamed, as she ran up to them and found Elsie kneeling over Conner.

"Stay back Emily, don't come closer. It's not a pretty sight."

Emily did not obey Elsie's command. She just continued toward her.

"I thought I heard gunshots and then sirens. The barn is on fire! What is going on?"

"Here, help me get this trap off of Conner's foot."

Emily looked down with horror at his leg. Each of them grabbed a side of the iron trap that had dug its teeth into Conner's flesh. The grotesque ankle did little to bother Elsie, but Emily could hardly watch. She looked up to Conner's face. He was staring silently at her through the rain.

The lightning struck again. Emily caught a glimpse of two wolves just about 25 feet from them. One was motionless lying in the grass while the second was there as if it were standing guard over the other. The second, Emily recognized, was Wolfie.

"Oh my God, Elsie. It's the old black."

"You can't do anything for the old girl," Elsie responded. " She's gone. Derek killed her and was about to kill Conner when I blasted him. He won't be hurting anyone any longer." Emily raised to go to Wolfie when she stopped in her tracks at the sight of Derek. The lightning exposed his fatal injuries and Emily stood stunned at his appearance. She had so often wished he would be killed, taken from her world. But, a sense of sadness came over her, as she questioned why and how this all happened.

"Come on, Emily!" Elsie jerked Emily back to reality. "I need your help. What's done is done!"

The two women got Conner's ankle out of the trap.

"Conner, hang in there," Emily tried to sooth him. "Don't leave me, stay with me."

"I am not going anywhere," he managed. "I'm here with you... lost a lot of blood. Can't keep my eyes open. I am tired... too tired."

"Elsie, what are we going to do?"

Lightning struck again and Elsie looked to the other end of the clearing where more wolves were gathering. They weren't coming over to help, that was for sure. They were looking for a meal. Elsie knew the scavengers would be too much for Wolfie. She needed to get Conner away from the area and take Wolfie with them to prevent his pack from coming to fight with him.

With Conner's foot now free from the trap, Emily stepped away from him. She moved in the direction of Wolfie, who was still standing guard over his fallen aunt. Emily didn't think twice about approaching the young wolf she knew so well and had interacted with as if she were family to him. As she got closer, however, Wolfie's demeanor was not the same. He growled at her, not wanting anything to do with the kind of animal that had hurt one of his own.

"Leave him be," Elsie took Emily by the arm and her voice was stern. "We need to drag Conner out of here right now. Look to the other side of the clearing."

Emily waited for another flash of lightning to see that far. It came quickly and the site was very scary to her. The scavenger wolves had increased in numbers to at least two dozen. Everyone was in danger now.

Emily took one of Conner's arms and Elsie took the other. They began pulling him away from the clearing and into deeper woods for protection.

"Ugh, damn!" Conner moaned from the pain. "Keep pulling. No matter how loud I scream, or even if I ask you to stop. Don't listen to me. Just keep pulling me out of here. Fuck, it hurts!"

"Conner, help us!" Emily cried, as she continued to pull him.

Conner tried to assist with his one good foot and push his way to safety away from what all of them knew would happen if they were caught by the wolves looking for a feast. Derek was going to be dinner and the dead black was going to be dessert. It was not a thought anyone wanted to have, but it was the way of the wilderness. No kill was left to decompose. There would always be one species or another that saw value in dead flesh. And, wolves didn't mind taking injured flesh. Conner was injured and at risk of being part of the feast. Elsie knew this too well and Emily was getting the message, as Elsie was becoming fierce in her efforts to get Conner away from the clearing.

"Elsie, what about Wolfie?"

"Emily, just pull! Don't look back. We can't save them all. We have to save Conner first, and then we will worry about the animals. We can't interfere and your little one will follow."

Just at that moment, Archie came running over the hill. His worst fear was being played out in front of him. Of all places, Derek came here to the clearing to kill. The one place where Archie knew was no place to be when death was present and a wolf's meal provided. This was where he found them.

As the lightning confirmed what Archie suspected, he saw his pack of hungry wolves readying themselves for a feast they assumed was for them. The adrenaline was pushing Archie. Even at his advanced age, it was his first chance to assist Conner and he was going to save him. He had always been in the background, but now he was there for his nephew right out in front and he wasn't going to let him down.

"Stand him up on the good foot!" Archie yelled as he ran towards them. Archie picked Conner up over one shoulder as Emily gently placed her hands around Conner's broken ankle, trying to support it as they ran. Conner was over 185 pounds and Archie could feel every ounce on his old legs. He just closed his eyes and concentrated on moving one foot in front of the other. He could feel the sweat running down his brow even as the rain was washing it away. He opened his eyes just enough to stay on course and not run into any trees. He was worried about falling with Conner and causing him more pain.

Archie opened his eyes to see the truck. He began to grunt and yell forcing his body to continue when all his muscles were quitting on him. He had left the tailgate of the truck open. Feeling sick to his stomach from pushing his body beyond what it wanted to do, he continued to yell and scream to provide him the needed adrenaline to get his nephew onto tailgate.

Conner yelled and arched his back in pain as his legs flopped. Emily grabbed at his legs trying to secure them as she steadied his injured ankle. Archie went down on one knee and started to wheeze and cough.

He did it! He had carried his nephew to safety beyond what he thought he could do, but was now paying the price for his age and every muscle in his body was cramping up on him. His head was spinning and he was concerned that he'd not be able to drive nor even walk to the cab of the truck. Emily slid Conner by his armpits back into the bed of the truck. Conner was screaming in pain and didn't know which would be better for him, live or die.

After Elsie saw that Archie was taking Conner out of harms way, she looked back to Wolfie, still standing guard over his aunt. She clicked open the shotgun and loaded shells into each chamber. Lightning flashed and Elsie could see a couple of wolves had set out to take their meal. She ran a few more steps, stopped and began breathing out of her nose so she could control her emotions and shoot pure. She had come up to Wolfie who was now growling at her and posturing at her as if he was going to attack her. She ignored him and took aim out towards the bad wolves. Two of them she knew had become impatient and started their sprint to get first dibs on the meal that was provided by Derek and the black wolf.

"Come on, give me some light!" Elsie knew she must see them to shoot them. She had to take at least one of them down. A flash of lightning gave her what she needed and immediately when she caught their line of approach she fired one chamber of the gun. Not knowing what came from her shot she kept the gun against her cheek waiting for the next flash and the subsequent second chamber. Fortunately, it came soon and she emptied the second. Without waiting for a response, she reached into her jacket pocket and pulled out a 38-caliber pistol and shot multiple times in their direction. She then positioned herself in a crouch position waiting for the two wolves to appear not knowing if she had downed either one or both of them. She had to be ready for them if they came at her out of the dark. Another flash of lightning relieved Elsie of her worry. Two wolves could be seen down in the path. One was still moving while the other, the one that had gotten closer for the second shot, lay still.

Emily turned to speak to Elsie. She was not there. She looked to Archie who was still on one knee head down with his right arm resting on the gate of the truck, coughing and wheezing.

"Elsie!" Emily ran back to the woods, at the sound of more gunshots.

As more lightning flashed, could see Elsie standing near Wolfie with shotgun in hand and pointing towards the wolves. She heard another shot explode in the night, followed by the sound of Elsie's whistle. The wind was blowing in Emily's direction and the whistle seemed to be directed at her, even though Elsie's back was to her. Emily could see Elsie walking backwards, taking long steps but keeping her head focused on the bad wolves that could be approaching her. Elsie called out a second whistle. Wolfie hesitated, as his posture was not of anger now. Elsie whistled again, turned her back on Wolfie and began to run toward the truck. She could not risk her own life any longer. Elsie was scared beyond anything she had experienced before. She had confronted many types of wild animals, but the legend and stories about the viciousness of this pack of wild wolves was heard often around Blaney Park. While no one was known to die from them, the stories did persist and actually seeing them was frightening enough for Elsie. The thought of being eaten alive was too much for her to deal with. Elsie provided Wolfie the time he needed, and now it was time for her to save herself.

"Run, run, run!" yelled Elsie, upon seeing Emily standing away from the truck. "Don't stand there. Go!"

Emily turned, as Elsie was on her heels, and jumped into the back of the truck with Conner. Archie had regained some composure and had opened the passenger door for Elsie. Just before getting into the truck, she emptied the one remaining chamber into the air. She knew the gun needed to be unloaded before entering the cab of the truck.

"Go, go, Archie!"

Archie ground the manual transmission into second gear and popped the clutch, starting back toward the hangar.

Emily felt her body relax as the truck moved forward. She scooted up next to Conner and placed her hand on his chest as he was losing at his attempt to stay conscious. She thought it best that he be passed out for the ride back to the hangar. The ride through the woods was rough, causing Conner more intense pain from his ankle that was rotating without control with each bump.

Emily looked to the tailgate that was still open. At first, she was startled to see a wolf running behind the truck. Then, recognizing it was Wolfie, she began to whistle at him. Elsie had once tried, without success, to teach Emily the proper tone that Wolfie would respond to. Elsie tried to explain that the whistle was more appropriate than voice commands and that wild animals only would respond if they wanted to or felt the inclination. While Emily wanted to scream at Wolfie to come, she thought better of it and tried to whistle. His ears perked and his gate quickened. She reached up and banged on the truck's back window and Elsie looked behind them. She demanded Archie to slow down. Wolfie caught the truck and, to everyone's amazement, jumped into the bed of the truck and stood looking back towards the woods.

Archie reached the hangar. The door was already opened and he went to his bed in the back room and pulled back the covers. Elsie went straight to the medicine kit on the wall and pulled it off, taking it to the back room.

"Get two small boards, Archie. Something we can support the ankle with. I am going to try and stop the bleeding first."

"Okay, Elsie, I know what you are looking for and where to find them."

Archie went to the front of the room where there were two large, model airplanes. He pulled the props off one of the planes and then broke two of the three off the spindle. They were the perfect lengths and width to do what Elsie needed. Archie returned to her.

"Thanks, Arch," Elsie winked.

Archie returned her look the best he knew how and then ran back outside to the truck. Emily was pulling at Conner's good leg trying to slide him to the edge of the gate. Conner was just about unconscious. His low moans and groans let Emily know that he was still alive but also that she was hurting him in her attempt to move him. Archie jumped into the bed and went behind Conner.

"Grab both his legs and pull!" he yelled to her, lifting Conner by the armpits. "Don't worry about hurting him. We need to get him inside."

The rain again began to fall hard as Archie carried Conner inside. Elsie had the door closed and the heat turned up. She began working on Conner's ankle.

"Why, Archie?" Emily asked. "What happened tonight?"

"Girl, I wish I knew. I wish I knew." Archie patted her lightly on her arm. His mind flashed quickly through his life. "I wish I knew."

Emily moved to the bedside. Conner's eyes were barely open. She reached out to touch his hand and then began rubbing his forehead.

You may never wake up again, she thought to herself. She reached up and ran her fingers lightly through his hair. Don't you die on me, Conner Morley. Don't you die.

29

The Dream

Conner lay quietly upon the bed in Archie's room, as Elsie worked frantically on his hip and ankle. The fire was burning in the fireplace and he knew the room temperature should be toasty warm. The pain was no longer there for him, but a cold chill remained in his bones. Despite how his mind was spinning, Conner realized that the combined impact of the gunshot and the trap had caused a reaction and he was in serious need of help. He could barely hear Elsie's muffled voice and opened his eyes.

He could see only Emily, as what little strength he had left would only focus on her image. Her long, dark hair hung loosely around her beautiful face. Her complexion was tanned from the sun, but looked soft, not leathery. While Emily was no Bloomingdale's type, she knew how to keep herself looking nice. She was soft to the touch and it was the key to his passion. He reached out for her and felt both her one hand on his and the rubbing of her other across his fevered forehead. He was not afraid of death. He had only been afraid of two things in his life, failure and not touching the world in a way that provided proof that he indeed lived on this earth. All he ever wanted was to matter and inspire people, especially kids. His mind left the room and Conner began to dream.

"I'm here, Conner," Emily whispered. "I'm going to stay right here. I promise. You will be okay." She saw his eyes rolling, leaned over him and kissed his cheek. His eyelids lowered and Emily's heart was in her throat. She choked, as she could no longer see him through the tears that had filled her eyes and looked up at Archie.

"I need some hot water," Elsie said to anyone who wanted to assist.

"He'll be okay," Archie stated, flatly. "But no cops, you hear me? And, no questions. Just help Elsie get him well. Go get the hot water for her. You'll have to go to your cabin or the main house, I have no pans."

"Okay," Emily managed to whisper, intimidated at Archie's tone and the coldness he seemed to direct at her. She looked back at Conner. "Please stay with me..."

"Go, damn it!" Archie yelled.

Conner sees a woman. She is standing with her back to him. He enjoys her look, because she is tall and her blonde hair is full and beautiful. His eyes reach her shoulders and down to her back, to the strapless top she is wearing and then down to her rather short, tight skirt. It's the kind of look that turns him on. He tells himself that she is his for the taking and he walks forward.

When he gets to her, she turns and he realizes this is Samantha. Conner is shocked, since Samantha doesn't have blonde hair. She begins to criticize him.

'You want me to do what?' She laughs. 'You want me to touch you how? Where is this coming from? I am not going to kiss you like that. What do you think we are, teenagers or something?'

Conner turns to leave. As he does, he sees Jim Gordy standing in front of him. Jim doesn't look scared this time. Conner walks over to him and throws a punch. It goes right through Jim and he disappears.

The next moment, Conner looks back to where Samantha is standing. Jim is now next to her and he gives Samantha a kiss on the lips. To Conner's surprise, there is a bed behind them. Samantha smiles at Conner, as Jim takes her hand and leads her backward toward the bed.

"No!" Conner yells. He walks quickly towards them. Even as his walk turns to a run, he is not advancing on the couple. They approach the bed and engage, each taking off their clothing but never touching the other. Samantha is now completely naked and stretches her body fully on the mattress. Jim gets on top of Samantha and penetrates her with no emotion. She keeps her eyes open and begins to look at her nails, as Jim continues to thrust in and out of her. She then turns her head to Conner, giving him a smile. Jim groans with the intensity of his orgasm and then rolls off of her. She props herself up on her elbows and looks right at Conner.

"Do you see how it is, Conner? There is no kissing. There is no different ways of doing it. It's my way. What are you staring at? Oh, do I look like a slut to you, now? Come, Jim. Oh! I am so silly. You have already came, haven't you, Jim... in me!" She laughs at her own words and Jim's laughter joins her. Conner feels sick and he makes another attempt to run toward them.

Suddenly, Conner is in clearing along the river at Blaney Park. It's a beautiful, sunny day. He sees Emily along the opposite bank, running with the wolves. She is wearing simply a sundress and moccasins. Conner just watches and then he calls out to her. Emily sees him and, with her wonderful smile, she waves to him. She then kneels down and gives Wolfie a big hug. She stands back up and they run together alongside the river.

Conner follows them. The wolves have retreated back into the forest, leaving Emily alone to enjoy the coolness of the water. He catches up to her and finds her disrobing in front of a small waterfall. Dressed only in her bra and panties, she steps beneath the waterfall. It is a warm afternoon and the cold water coming off her body has caused her nipples to harden. She turns into the waterfall, her back now to him and Conner is aroused at the soaked material of her underwear, now transparent as it is clinging to the shape of her ass. She bends her knees and slowly lies down in the river on her back, beneath the waterfall, yet still wearing her undergarments.

Conner hears a wolf howl and is now in the bed of his cabin. The room is dark, except for a few, well-placed candles casting a soft glow around the room and the movement of their light is mixing with that of the roaring fire. Conner opens his eyes to see Emily, in her sundress, her arms outstretched to him. He gets up from the bed and stands bare-footed before her, wearing only his hiking shorts.

Emily and Conner are now standing face to face with one another. He steps closer to her, reaches up with both hands and softly pushes Emily's hair back away from her face with his fingertips. He looks her directly in the eyes and she returns his gaze for several moments, as the fire is reflecting the passion in her eyes. He gently cups her cheeks with both hands. He does not kiss her on the lips directly, but first kisses her softly on each cheek, as she stands motionless with her arms to her sides.

"Thank you for being with me and for being so nice to me," he whispers in her ear. Emily smiles at his words and kisses Conner on the cheek.

"Please kiss me," she asks softly. "Just kiss me once."

Conner moves his lips to her mouth. He first kisses Emily's lower *lip as it has opened for him to explore. Then he kisses her top lip. He slowly and gently reaches into her mouth with his tongue and begins a soft kiss fully upon her mouth. There is little movement in their bodies, as they stand in the fire's glow, looking into each other's eyes and kissing softly. Emily's breathing becomes deeper and Conner's craving grows in his loins. While there is much to do, he wants to complete her request as best he can. He kisses Emily's mouth for sufficient time and then moves his body behind her slowly, gently rubbing her shoulders. He then kisses Emily on the base of her neck and moves down her back, with light licks and kisses that make her entire body respond with goose bumps on her skin. She begins a soft moan and Conner continues his kisses and licks around her shoulders, slowly up her neck and down the backs and sides of her arms. He looks around at Emily's eyes and sees they are closed.*

Conner again provides Emily a soft, slow kiss, filling her mouth. As he kisses her, she gently sucks his tongue. Conner has to restrain the passion that is now burning hotter than ever before. He then stops and stands in front of her, seeing her reaction to him burning in her eyes. They still say nothing to one another. He then begins to tickle the front of her arms with his fingernails, moving slowly up and down each one, simultaneously. She rotates her arms so she can get full coverage on each. She now realizes he is not going to make love to her, he is going to become part of her.

He takes her hand and walks her to the bed. Before she sits, he reaches down to grasp the hem of her sundress and lifts it over her head. He glances briefly at the fullness of her now exposed breasts and then looks back up into her eyes. He unsnaps his shorts and lets them fall, his briefs straining against his erection. Emily lowers herself to sit in front of him, sliding her hands up his thighs and under his briefs over his buttocks. Her fingers lock around the waistband, and she pulls them down to his ankles, as Conner steps out of them.

She hesitates and tips her head back to look up at him, her eyes wide and moist. She stares into his eyes, as he caresses her hair with both of his hands. Emily slowly rolls her eyes closed again and her mouth opens. She tips her head back down and leans forward toward him, pressing her lips into his thigh and begins to kiss him softy, at the top of his thigh, slowly moving her lips across his skin towards the inside of his hip, next to his groin. She opens her mouth slightly and gently licks the skin of his leg with the tip of her tongue.

Conner begins to feel drugged. Never before has he felt so comfortable. He is sure that what she is doing, she loves and what he is doing, he loves. He is truly making love for the first time and it will be an experience that he will compete with for the rest of his life.

Emily rises and twines her fingers within Conner's hands. She guides him back to sit on the edge of the bed. She then moves her hands upward along his arms as she gently pushes him back. Conner pulls himself backward with his elbows to the head of the bed and Emily crawls upon him, positioning herself between his opened thighs. Conner reaches behind his head and pulls a pillow down. He then sits up and places it between her legs.

Emily drops her back slightly, raising her ass and allows Conner to position the pillow. She then pulls her knees together and arches her back, pushing her crotch against the pillow between her thighs. Her breasts are resting against the top of his legs, on either side of his erection and, as she moves her body slowly up and down to enjoy the sensation of the pillow, her hardened nibbles rub lightly across the insides of his thighs. Emily groans and lowers her body, stretching her arms upward. She drops her head and begins to lick and suck the full length of his erection. Her arms remain outstretched above her head and she gently curls her fingers so that her nails float lightly along the outside of his body and across his chest and stomach. She continues to moan softly, moving against the pillow in perfect rhythm with her lips. Her mouth is upon him, yet her entire body is sucking him, feeling him, reacting to him.

Emily hears Conner moan each time she squeezes her ass against the pillow and she tastes him against her tongue each time she tightens her lips around him. Conner is anticipating and finally getting what he is hoping for. Emily's mouth engulfs the head of his erection over and over, and she moans with enjoyment as she does it. Conner relaxes, for he never wants this moment to end.

"Please don't stop, never stop," he asks her. "I want this evening to last forever." Emily continues to move her mouth against Conner and her thighs against the pillow. Conner feels he is about to explode with excitement for her. He sits up, takes her face again in his hands *and kisses her passionately, placing his tongue firmly in her mouth. He moves his lips away for a brief moment between kisses, each time telling her how wonderful and beautiful she is. He leans forward on the bed around her, and kisses her ass, rubbing it with his hands. He massages her for a few moments, his hands caressing beneath her underwear, being careful not to touch her sex. He lies back down in front of Emily.*

She rises up on her knees and looks Conner in the eyes. He lifts his hands and again tickles Emily's arms. Emily allows him to continue for a few moments and then leans forward pressing her flat stomach against his erection. She stretches up to him and gives him another slow, passionate kiss. Conner slides out from beneath her and stands, pulling Emily to her feet in front of him, but with her back still to him. He begins to softly massage Emily's shoulders and back. Emily turns her head to him with an almost hypnotic look and opens her mouth indicating to Conner that she wants to kiss him.

She then walks around to the opposite side of the bed and crawls upon it, facing him, and lays flat on her stomach. Conner allows her to kiss his stomach for a moment, but then moves away and around behind her. He takes a path onto the bed and over it so he is at her feet. He gives her a pillow to lay her head upon as he reaches down beside the bed into his toiletry bag and pulls out a bottle of scented mineral oil. He pours some on Emily's legs and begins to massage the oil into her skin. He moves right up to her ass and close to her fiery crotch. Emily is dizzy. Her body is arching and squirming slowly, sensually, in a way she has never before felt. She is captivated by her desire to mate with Conner, mate with him completely, not just with her body but with her soul. Never has she felt drawn to someone like she is drawn to him at this moment.

His hands continue to be firm, but gentle. Emily reaches up and takes her hair in her hand, moving it to the side so Conner has full access to her back. Conner occasionally kisses and licks Emily, each time, getting closer and closer to her sex. He is both teasing and inviting her. He wants her to share the encounter and understand that her soul is one with his if they just give of each other. When love is for all the right reasons, there is no wrong in its execution and Conner wanted Emily to know that she was he and he was she. He is hard and ready to explode as the chance to regain his composure is welcomed. She is lying on her stomach and, with her head turned to the side, is looking at Conner wondering what was next. It is clear she is enjoying the fact that he is taking control. She trusts him, feels good about his techniques and the way he makes her feel like a lady while allowing her to be free to express her womanhood.

Conner suddenly stretches out beside her, grabs either side of her hips with his strong hands and rolls her on top of him, he on his back, both facing the ceiling. Emily feels free with him, excited and encouraged by their body contact.

He slowly reaches down between her legs for his erection and rubs her vagina with it. Electricity goes through Emily. She begins to tense up, realizing her first orgasm has begun. She begins to groan aloud, as her orgasm is both unpredicted and very powerful. As it subsides, she does not, however, lose the excitement and the feeling she has.

Conner, in his wisdom, leaves that place and begins to kiss and feel Emily's breasts that are above him. Gently, at first, and then he begins to tease the nipples. He also turns his head up and kisses Emily on the mouth and around her neck. She stays there, recovering from her orgasm but realizes she does not have enough of him on this night. She wants more.

He makes her feel like a woman, without the guilt or restraints that men cause with women. He continues to touch her and his hands move down to the moistness between her legs. She is still sensitive from her orgasm, but Conner is gentle and soft, as he soon stimulates her again. He knows just when the time is right, and quickly places his erection into her, pumping in and out of her with a rhythmic motion. Emily is receiving him fully and begins to move in alternating directions to allow herself the maximum sensations. He knows just what to do and, after some time of making love, his skillful fingers return to her clitoris. Emily has never felt the sensation of a man's soft touch. He is as skillful as she is at playing the border between pain and sexual sensation.

'Touch your breasts,' he softly asks her, knowing that if she does it will be the ultimate compliment, watching her respond to her pleasure as if he isn't there, but appreciating that he is. The passion

never decreases, as Emily again comes to another wonderful orgasm.
He does not leave her, but allows her to remain on top of him until she
is completely finished.

She slides her body off of Conner and reaches for him. As she
pulls him close, Conner mounts her. He kissed her with passion as once
again he slowly enters her as their eyes are fixed on each other. The
fire is causing Emily to glow like the sun and Conner is feeling the heat
from continuing satisfaction. Conner maintains eye contact the whole
time his member is stroking the inside of Emily. Softly, rhythmically,
he continues as they look in each other's eyes. It is Conner's turn to
enjoy and he knows it. He also knows that he does not want to ruin
the wonderful feeling that is within her. They are one on this night.
Conner cannot hold his restraint any longer. He opens his mouth as
his orgasm bursts through him and into her. Knowing he is over the
edge, she begins to kiss his chest and then grabs his head to bury her
tongue into his mouth, so they can be one. Each inside the other.

Emily stumbled to her feet at Archie's commands and ran from the hangar. She was sobbing and could not gain solid footing along the familiar path. She had walked this path a thousand times in the dark, yet tonight it felt strange to her.

She reached her cabin and searched frantically for her cell phone. Her hands were shaking as she tabbed down to 'Sky Guy' in her directory.

"Please, be home," she prayed, as the phone rang.

"Hello," she heard Austin's voice.

"Austin..." she managed, then choked.

"Em? Emily, is that you?"

"Yes.... Austin, you have to come."

"Emily," Austin laid his newspaper aside. "What's wrong? Are you okay?"

"Yes, yes.... I'm fine. Oh, my God... it's Conner, Austin.. He's ... well, he's hurt. You have to come...please, he needs help. Please."

"Jesus, Emily, its ten o'clock at night. It'll take me a good three hours to get there. Can't Archie just call 911?"

"Austin! Please! I can't do that. I can't explain—there's no time. You must come now!"

"I can't, Babe. The weather won't allow me."

Emily didn't wait for another word, but instead angrily threw the cell phone onto her cot. She grabbed a pan and filled it with hot water and stepped back out into the light drizzling rain.

The damp, Michigan air pierced her skin as she hurried back to the hangar. Once reaching it, she leaned against the door, gasping for air. Her heart was pounding and she slowly entered. Once inside, she looked at Conner. He was lying still on the couch. Archie had dimmed the lights and Conner's face was expressionless. Archie was staring at her, also without expression. Emily felt her lungs tighten and the excitement of the evening began to take over, clouding her common sense and heightening her fears. She looked at Archie as her heart pounded wildly, tears beginning to fall.

"He's okay?" she asked, weakly. "Just tell me he's okay." Archie dropped his gaze to the floor. Emily was afraid to move. "Archie, tell me he will be okay. Please."

"Why?" he snapped, as he looked back up at her. His eye sockets had deepened and his jaw was clenched. "What the hell difference would it make to you? What are you to him, anyway? You're not his family."

"Archie, please," Elsie scolded.

Emily lowered her head, her mind was spinning and she felt weak. She slowly walked over to the couch and knelt beside Conner. Her hand was shaking as she reached up to caress his cheek with the back of her fingertips.

"Just some damn broad from the city, you are," Archie growled. "Some spoiled brat who doesn't want to deal with her own family or her own responsibilities. He don't need what you got, lady."

Emily was hurt by his words, but knew there was nothing she could say. Should she tell him of her separation from Austin? Would it make a difference? He was right, she was not family. Who was she, where did she belong? Who had she become to Conner, to herself and her life? Or, was she truly just some wolf woman in the woods.

Emily was relieved at the slight warmth she sensed in Conner's face. You are still here, she reassured herself. I'm still here, and I will not ever leave you. I am with you and you are with me. Always, Conner, always and forever. She did not respond to Archie, but rather laid her head on Conner's shoulder, closing her eyes.

Archie watched them for a moment, as he allowed his own face to soften. He liked her, and knew how she felt, yet hated her circumstances because he felt it would only mean more pain for Conner. His loyalty to protect his family remained the same. He lowered into a chair at his small kitchen table. As the cold, October rain fell like sand on the hangar, they said nothing. They prayed, and they waited. Archie listened for the distant sounds of Todd's plane to approach.

30
Take Off

Archie walked to the radio in the front room and lowered the volume. "Charlie Frank Sam 444, do you read me?"

"Charlie Frank Sam 444, do you read me?" Archie repeated.

"This is Charlie Frank Sam 444. I read you, go ahead."

"Todd, its Archie."

"Hey there, old man!" Todd laughed. "I'd call you what you really are, but Minneapolis dispatch would get an earful. No more fowl language fines needed here BPR165."

"No laughing matter here, boy. I have some sensitive cargo I need you to pick up, Todd."

"What the hell happened, Archie?"

"Don't want to talk over the radio. What's your ETA?"

"Oh, I am in some heavy shit up here, Archie. Weather is bad and getting worse. I had a hell of a time filing a flight plan, but I altered it mid flight so I could stay high and dry for as long as possible. I am planning on dropping in on a severe downward landing pattern, so make sure those cows and deer are no where to be seen on the runway, okay?"

"Roger, I read you."

"I will be there in 20 minutes."

"20 minutes? Jesus, that's too long. Did you leave right away, Sully?"

"Listen, Arch, don't give me none. I had to leave my family and not tell them why and where I was going because you wanted to keep this hush, hush. Come on, you have to cut me some slack here, baby. I did my best. And you didn't even bother to tell me the details as to why I had to come, so I did what I had to do."

"Alright, alright. Fine. Just get here ASAP. BPR165, out."

"Okay, boss man. CFS444, out."

Archie walked back into the hangar to check on Conner. Emily was sitting next to him at the head of the bed. Elsie was picking up the medical items she used and was putting them in their proper places.

"Is he going to make it, Elsie?"

"I don't know. He lost lots of blood and not knowing what internal injuries are posing issues for him makes it tough to know what degree of risk he's at. Actually, the gunshot wound is less severe then the broken ankle. That trap was not clean and its impact severed the bone completely apart. An infection is a possibility. I am doing my best to stop the bleeding and keep him going. I do know this, it will be a while, if ever, before he walks on that leg again. He's going to be in some great pain."

"Okay. Thanks for all that you have done for him. Do you want a drink?"

"Sure, Arch," Elsie smiled at him. "My usual."

"All I have is your usual," Archie replied with a grin and a wink.

"I know," she said, as she watched Archie walk to the file cabinet and pour a couple ounces of Jack Daniel's into a small water glass. "What about calling the sheriff and an ambulance? If he lives, he'd have a better chance of walking on that foot if he had medical attention now, rather than later."

"Absolutely not! I won't have a sheriff here. No cops, period."

Elsie did not even try to respond to Archie's answer. It was what she expected. Elsie was one of the few people on this earth who had the courage to ask such a question. She did not, however, agree with Archie's attitude. His nephew needed medical attention now and Archie was still trying to protect himself from his ghosts.

"I have to step out for a second, Elsie. Keep an eye on them, will you?"

"Where you going? Don't you think you should stay here with your nephew?"

"Jesus, woman, don't be questioning my intentions. I have good reasons to be leaving and I will be back soon."

Archie left and jumped into his truck. He wanted to drive the airstrip and make sure it was clear of deer, or any other animal that may cause a problem for a plane. He was also worried about tree limbs the way the wind was blowing. Todd was going to drop in with a hot landing and he would need as much of the runway as possible to stop.

Archie made his run up and down the airstrip three times and then pulled off to the side, comfortable that all was well. He opened his glove box and removed the flask. He drank three gulps in a row and placed it back in the glove box. He then reached to his visor and pulled a cigarette out of the pack held in place there and went to his pocket for matches. They were soaked from rainwater.

Looking down at his rain-soaked pocket, Archie noticed, for the first time, all the blood that had covered his clothes. From his shirt down the front of his pants to his shoes he was covered with blood. The blood of the child he never got to be with during good times and now he was wearing that child's blood from a tragic event. An event he knew he could have prevented a long time ago.

He opened the truck door window and threw out the damaged matches. He pushed in the lighter inside the truck's ashtray. He waited for it to pop back out and then pressed the red glow of the lighter against the cigarette he was going to enjoy. He inhaled deeply, not having had a cancer stick for a couple of hours. He sighed with relief of the nicotine fix he was receiving. The alcohol buzz was approaching and even though Conner was in the hangar dying, these vices were mentally and emotionally necessary to Archie. He wondered if he shouldn't go back to the hangar and be near the radio. With the inclement weather, he was thinking there was a chance that Todd may not make it to the Park and might be calling for help at that moment.

He decided not to leave. He sat just off the runway waiting for Todd's airplane to show itself from the stormy clouds above, thinking about the night's activities and reliving all that had happened. The guilt he was feeling from the fact that he had witnessed the rape in the barn that evening so many years ago. The fact that his sick mind was such, he enjoyed the sexual entertainment more than he had concern for the girl who had emptied his trap that night. So much so, that he allowed Derek to rape Emily that evening because he didn't want to stop it. Now, after all these years, he was being punished again and again for his lack of action and preventing the rape from happening.

Archie reached for the flask again. His high was beating in his head. He was experiencing residual effects from the earlier blow to his head. His legs were aching already from the work they had to do to get Conner back to the hangar. He chained smoked a few more cigarettes when a plane appeared out of nowhere on the runway. Todd had landed and Archie never saw the approach. He must have truly dropped straight down out of the clouds to land.

Archie started his truck and drove back to the A-hangar that housed Conner. He jumped from his truck and got the tie downs out of the storage bin attached to the hangar. As an afterthought, he went to the B-hangar, the only hangar that could house a plane at Blaney, and slid open the door. He then grabbed the orange light sticks used to guide planes to their parking spots, turned them both on as he saw Todd coming his way, and motioned them up and down, indicating to Todd where to park the plane. He then waved them to his right where Todd knew he would go to the B-hangar to park the plane. Todd approached the hangar and made a 180-degree turn so the tail was facing the opening of the hangar. He shut down the engines and did his post-flight routine.

Post flight checklist is not necessary tonight, Sully, Archie thought to himself. He waited impatiently for Todd to open the plane door, deplane and get Conner out of Blaney Park before the sheriff showed up.

Todd opened the door and with a smile greeted Archie.

"Hey, old fuck! Nice color red you are wearing tonight. Had a good hunt today, huh? What's that called, blood light? You should model in a hunting magazine."

"Not tonight, Todd." Archie jumped into the tractor and drove it to the nose of the plane. Don attached the metal bar to the front wheel and secured the bar there. Archie then rolled the plane back into the hangar and Todd released the bar.

"Come on," Archie yelled, as he jumped off the tractor and headed to the hangar where Conner lay. "I need you in here." Todd followed and his smile turned to a scowl.

What the hell is going on? Todd asked himself. He ran just behind Archie to the A-hangar, and they both entered the back room. Todd gave a few quizzical looks around as the room was trashed with paper and debris spread around it.

"What the hell happened here tonight?" Todd exclaimed when he saw Conner on the couch, realizing he was unconscious. "Conner, Conner! You alright? What the fuck happened? Who did this to him? I will kill the fucker who did this to my brother!"

"Too late. She already shut his faucet off," Archie nodded to Elsie.

"Thanks, ma'am," Todd tipped his hat to Elsie. "Fuck, Archie! He looks bad. He's white like a ghost. Why didn't you guys take him to the nearest hospital?"

"To protect him," Archie replied.

"Protect him? What good is protecting him if he dies from this shit? We need to get him to a hospital now."

"No! He ain't going to no hospital around here. I have everything worked out, Todd. I've made the appropriate phone calls and you know where he needs to go!"

"Archie, man, your paranoia is fine most of the time. But there is no reason Conner doesn't go to a hospital, man. You are fucking up this time."

"Shut up, Sully. Don't say another word."

"I agree with him," Emily spoke out.

"Oh, so you agree with him, too, huh? Okay, then I change my mind." Archie stated with severe sarcasm. "I don't give a shit less if you do, or do not, agree with me. He's my blood and I will tell all of you what we are and what we are not going to do with him. You hear me?"

"Go to hell, Archie," Emily said, angrily. "You don't care about him. All you care about is protecting yourself. You don't want cops here because of you, not because of him. And, you will allow him to lie here and die before you'll risk yourself. It's all wrong, Archie. What you did was to you. Don't let Conner pay for your mistakes."

"Okay, I have heard enough," Archie replied to Emily's outburst. "Let's get him out of here and onto the plane."

"No!" Emily stood up in front of Conner. "Nobody takes this man out until a sheriff and the EMS are here, first."

"Todd, get her out. Elsie, you go with him and keep her out of my face while I get this done. He's hurt bad and he needs medical attention. We have no time to argue about this. We do what I say, period."

Todd approached Emily. "Now this can be nice or it can be rough. It's your choice. I know he means a lot to you, so leave the hangar on your own and I don't have to touch you. He wouldn't appreciate me putting my hands on you. But the way I see it, you have two choices, nice or rough. Nice means he gets help quicker."

"Todd, don't do this," Emily pleaded. "You know he needs help, right now. Help me help him. Don't do this, Todd. I want to stay with him, be with him and help him recover."

"He will get help," Todd said, reassuringly. "He'll get the appropriate help. Archie is right. We don't want just anyone working on him. We need to take him where good people know his medical history."

"I am sorry, Conner," she whispered, as she sank onto her knees next to Conner and kissed his forehead. She realized she wasn't getting any help from anyone in that room. "Please know that I love you."

Elsie walked over to Emily, gently took her arm and guided her to her feet and they walked toward the door. Elsie looked up at Archie with a stern look on her face. Her loving posture that had been there earlier in the night was gone. It was obvious that Elsie agreed with Emily and wanted Conner to get attention from local resources. Emily looked back one last time as she reached the door, then turned and walked out.

Archie pulled a stretcher out from underneath the couch in the front room. He carried it to Conner and laid it on the floor next to the bed. Todd took Conner by his armpits and Archie grabbed his legs at the knees, being as careful as possible not to place pressure on the injured ankle. Conner was deep into his unconsciousness and never reacted. Archie was fighting the thought of just getting him to the closest hospital facility available. They lifted Conner on to the stretcher and as soon as they had him secured in the plane, Todd began his pre-flight check.

"Jesus, Todd, can't you just take off? Why must you do everything by the book every time? Time is of the essence here."

"Listen, you old fuck! I have done everything you wanted over the years. I have been doing my job to the best of my ability and never did you ever give me even a thank you. Now my best friend is hurt bad and I know where you want me to take him. So leave my ass alone and let me get him there in one piece! If I don't do this, I don't know for sure that this plane will even get to where I want it to go. I do things right. I do it by the book, no shortcuts. So, shut the fuck up and get the hell off my plane!"

Archie never said another word. He descended down the ladder to the pavement below. Todd interrupted his pre-flight checklist and followed, closing the door immediately after Archie cleared the ladder. Half because he had to close the door, eventually, and half because he was unsure how Archie would react to his scolding. Men had died for lesser actions. Todd had never gone there before with Archie and, while he needed to say what he said, he was afraid of the repercussions of his words.

Todd didn't feel good about flying on that night. He would never have flown on a night like that, if it were his choice. Todd was frightened of Archie and wanted to isolate himself from him. He was pissed at Archie for making him fly.

Smart move, you asshole, Archie thought, as he climbed into the tractor and saw Todd shut the plane door. He had thoughts of going back up and slapping Todd around for his comments. Instead, he hooked the plane up, rolled it out from underneath the hangar, and then did what was necessary to detach and put the tractor away again. Archie plugged the electricity into the plane, so Todd had power to start the engines and get the heater started. Conner needed to stay warm.

Todd tried to stay focused on the task at hand and did his whole pre-flight check wondering if Archie was going to hurt him at some point during the process. He intermittently looked out to the front of the plane, worried that Archie might be down there with a gun aimed at him. He started first one engine, then the other, and then looked for Archie so he didn't run him over. Once Archie unhooked the plane from the generator, Todd tried to wave as he was walking away, in order to make amends, but either Archie didn't see him or wasn't in a waving mood. Todd suspected the latter was true.

Archie didn't stay and watch the take off of the plane. He went to his office, where he picked up the radio microphone.

"Alpha Beta Charlie 555 do you read me?"

"I say again. Alpha Beta Charlie 555 do you read me?"

"This is Alpha Beta Charlie 555 I read you, go ahead."

"Yea, this is BPR165. What's your ETA, over?"

"Two minutes. Two minutes. Over."

"Roger, that is affirmative. Dime4 is taking off now. Feather is ruffled, repeat, feather is ruffled. Will need full veterinarian support, over."

"Roger 165, all is well. Pet will be fixed."

"Roger 555. That is a go and good luck. Thanks again ABC555."

"Roger and out."

"Out." Archie walked to the front window of the hangar and looked outside to see if Todd plane could be seen. The rain was hitting hard against the windows. At that moment, the wind blew open the front door that had been damaged and was not latching correctly. Archie ignored it and walked to the back room looking for a smoke and drink now that everyone had gone from his space. He felt the peace of loneliness again and wanted his vices to keep him company.

"Minneapolis Dispatch, this is CFS444 requesting permission to depart Blaney Park airport, runway 13 heading east."

"Yeah, Minneapolis Dispatch here. CFS444 do you realize there is a weather warning in your air space? Advise to abort flight, sir. I say again, advise to abort flight."

"Minneapolis Dispatch, This is CFS444. Negative, say again, negative to abort. I have emergency clearance for the flight. Your warning is so recorded on flight records. Say again, Minneapolis Dispatch, this is Charlie Frank Sam 444 requesting permission to depart Blaney Park airport, runway 1-3 heading east."

"Roger, CFS444, so noted is the warning accepted and rejected, and the negative on the abort. Good luck. You are free to dispatch Blaney Park airport, runway 1-3 heading east. Not a plane in the sky within 400 miles of you, sir. All other buses have heeded warning."

"Roger, Minneapolis Dispatch. This is CFS444, out."

Todd could not see the end of the runway in front of him. The rain was coming down so hard that he could hardly see 20 yards. He got the plane rolling and looked at his instrument panel. He didn't worry about anything else; he put this flight in the hands of God. He was gaining speed down the runway, yet never looked to it, perpetually focused on the instruments in front of him. When the plane reached a speed for a solid take off, Todd pulled up on the wheel. He could feel the lift of the plane and he stayed on the instruments knowing he could not see out the window, anyway. Once the plane was airborne, he did as he always did. He raised the wheels and softened the rudders.

Todd had all the training. He practiced all he could. He would place pilot blindfolds over his eyes to try and emulate instrument-only flight. The blindfolds were specially made so a pilot could see his instruments but could not see out the cockpit window. They were used to simulate this exact situation. The truth is, he never truly flew only on instruments and he was scared to do so. He always heeded weather warnings. It was too risky. Conner often would be pissed at Todd for grounding his plans by grounding the plane due to weather issues. Now, he was forced to fly.

He shivered with fear as the plane went skyward. At 800 feet, Todd knew he had at least made the takeoff and was not in danger of trees or power lines bringing him down. Until he reached that altitude, though, he was waiting to crash into an object that he could not see. He felt his take off was low. The lightning was both awesome and dangerous. A plane could take a bolt of electricity most times but if the instrument panel were to go out due to it, Todd and Conner would be in extreme danger. Todd's fear went from the trees and power lines knocking his plane down to the lightning above the plane while airborne. He was in danger of losing his instruments to a bolt of lightning and he knew it.

"BPR165, this is CFS444. Do you read me?"

"Say again, BPR165, this is CFS444. Do you read me? Come on, Archie. What the fuck, are you pouting? Say again, BPR165 this is CFS444. Do you read me? BPR165 this is CFS444. Do you read me?"

Emily walked to her cabin with Elsie next to her, neither saying a word. Emily opened the door and walked in. Elsie grabbed a log from the pile out front before entering and placed it on the fire that was nearly out.

"Should we call the police, Elsie?"

"No, Emily. I learned a long time ago. Don't cross Archie. It's not worth it. In the end, he gets his way and that is the way it is around here."

"God, Elsie, you are so independent most of the time. Why do you let that man make choices for you?"

"That's not fair, Emily. He's there when I need him. I can't tell you how often he was there for me over the years, never expecting anything back in return. And to be honest, most of the time, he was right."

"He's not right this time, Elsie. I have a bad feeling about this. I will blame Archie if anything happens to Conner." They both stared at the fire. "What about Derek's body? Don't we need to call the police for that?"

"There isn't any Derek body, Emily. The wolves have eaten what they wanted of him and scattered the rest across miles of the Park. Oh, I guess if someone really wanted to find something of him, they might. My guess is his family will be interested in justice until all the rape charges start coming out against their evil son and then they'll just say it was a horrible accident and let it go. They'll give him a hero's funeral and tell everyone what a great son he was, when he was nothing but evil. We can only wait to see what happens when he is reported missing. And he will be reported missing, eventually. How do we know he told anyone he was coming here?"

At that moment, both Elsie and Emily heard a plane fly above the cabin. It was low and frightened both of them. The winds silenced the prop noise within seconds. Emily felt a shiver go through her body and she waited for the noise of a plane crash.

"Wow, that plane was low," Elsie stated.

"God, I wish Austin was flying the plane," Emily said, with a soft tone. "I trust him so much more in bad weather. I don't know what kind of pilot Todd is, but I know Austin is good."

"I know, Emily. Todd was put into a bad position. I know he'd have not flown if it weren't for Archie and the pressure he put on him. You now have to put your trust in God."

"Elsie, I have lost him," Emily began to cry. "I feel it to my core."

"I know, sweetheart. I know," Elsie put her hand on Emily's arm. "I am going to leave you for a while, okay? I will lock the cabin behind me, you cuddle up in bed and I will be back soon. There is no one left here at Blaney Park who can hurt you, my dear. You are safe here. The only intruder is the moon and tonight you will welcome him."

Emily smiled at Elsie's statement. After all that had happened, that was one of the first things she heard when she came back to Blaney Park.

"I am so tired. I will stay here and rest. I don't feel in danger now that Derek is gone."

"Good, now you rest. I will be back to check on you soon."

Elsie left the cabin and locked it behind her. As she left, she saw Wolfie standing a few feet away, looking at her, as if he was trying to get her attention. He took a few steps away from her, stopped, and then looked back at her. He repeated this over and over. Finally, Elsie whistled in acknowledgment and followed him.

Elsie got an eerie feeling in her gut. She pulled the 38 out of her jacket again and followed Wolfie. Were there more of Derek's friends hanging around? Fear fell upon her just when she had started to relax. She wasn't sure where he was going, but it seemed Wolfie was taking her back to the A-hangar. She cautiously looked inside the front door. Nothing seemed unusual from the scene earlier that evening. Just then, Wolfie appeared from the back room. Elsie was startled since, to her knowledge, Wolfie had never entered the hangar before. Elsie entered the back room, only to find Archie lying on the ground motionless, face down.

"Archie!" Elsie yelled and went to him. She rolled him over onto his back. A nitroglycerine pill was stuck to his cheek and she swept it off. She took his pulse by his neck and there was no beat. She held it there for a few more seconds and then realized Archie was dead.

Elsie stared down at him for a few moments. She began to cry, softly at first, and then began to sob when her heart started to break from what her brain was telling it. She reached down, raised his torso to hers and hugged him. She hugged him tighter and tighter, rocking him in her arms as if he was a sleeping baby, stopping occasionally to look into his face. His eyes were open. She thought how attractive his eyes were and always had been. His eyes were his best features and that was all she could focus on at that moment. She just lost the best friend she ever had. They were partners. She would no longer have him to help run Blaney Park. Who would control the rowdy fisherman? Who would ease the fears of the children who always worried about being eaten by some wild animal in the woods, until they met Archie, who would tell them no animal would dare hurt them while he was around?

So many memories were flooding her mind. Memories were all that she would have left. She didn't want Archie to be dead. So many people disliked him and feared him. Because he was there for her, protecting her, she loved him and feared nothing.

She reached around her neck and removed a chain with a wedding ring dangling from it. It was his mom's wedding ring. A very long time ago, during one of their drink and talk sessions, Archie presented the ring to Elsie. He told her that while he knew she'd never love him enough to marry him, nor feel at ease enough with him to make love to him, he wanted her to know he loved her. Before even a drink reached their lips that night, Archie got down on his knee and gave the ring to her on a gold chain. He had showered, shaved and even put on his best suit and tie, as well as placed a few dabs of cologne on his neck and proposed lasting love and devoted friendship for Elsie.

Elsie reflected on that moment and on the words he had spoke to her.

"I am used to nobody loving me, Elsie, I don't blame you for that. But I am not used to loving someone as much as I love you. Please accept this token of my love. It was my mom's. She gave it to me just before she died. I don't expect to love anyone as much as I love you in my lifetime, Elsie. I know you don't love me back and that you wouldn't want anyone to know how I feel for you. No one needs to know but you and me. I'd write it on every mountain on earth that I love you, but I know that would embarrass you, Miss Elsie. So we'll just keep it our secret. That is good enough for me."

She had allowed him only one sensual kiss all those years on the night he gave her the ring. Now, looking into his lifeless body, she felt guilt come over her. She never went anywhere without his ring. She cherished it. Yet, she never let anyone see it. It was her secret and she was not comfortable wearing it on the outside, in fear someone would ask her who gave it to her. She wanted no scandal or gossip over it or anyone to question what was going on behind closed doors at Blaney Park between the Harrison singles. She had always hoped her Robin Hood would someday enter Blaney Park and sweep her off her feet, onto his horse and ride away with her.

Maybe Archie was my Robin Hood and I never gave him credit for being there when I needed him? she thought. That realization broke her heart. She took the ring off the chain and placed it on her ring finger. It fit perfectly.

"I do love you, Archie," Elsie said, with sensitivity and passion. "I am so sorry I didn't tell you before this, my dear. I love you, Archie. I love you. Please wake up, Arch. I want you to know. I don't want you to die without knowing it. I love you, dear. I love you. I am so sorry. God forgive me!"

Elsie stayed with Archie for two hours, holding him and caressing his forehead. Perpetually admiring her ring, she thought back to all they had shared together. Wolfie lay quietly beside them. They had both lost loved ones that day. Wolfie's aunt died to save someone and so did Archie. His heart must not have been able to take all the stress that happened to him that day. He died with a broken and lonely heart and Elsie knew it. Now Wolfie and Elsie were left alone to carry on and take care of each other.

31
May Day

"Open frequency, Open frequency. Mayday, mayday. This is Charlie Frank Sam 444 announcing mayday. Someone copy?"

"Open frequency, Open frequency. Mayday, mayday. This is Charlie Frank Sam 444 announcing mayday. Please someone copy."

"Open frequency, Open frequency. Mayday, mayday. This is Charlie Frank Sam 444 announcing mayday. Please someone copy."

"Minneapolis Dispatch Copy. What coordinates are you, Charlie Frank Sam 444? You came off scope. Say again, what coordinates are you, Charlie Frank Sam 444? You came off scope."

"Did you block us? Did you block us?"

"Charlie Frank Sam 444, do you read me? Mayday registered but no radar of you indicating. Charlie Frank Sam 444, do your read me?"

"Charlie Frank Sam 444, do your read me?"

"Say again, Charlie Frank Sam 444, do your read me?"

"Minneapolis dispatch announcing to open frequency, Charlie Frank Sam 444 now missing. Date and time registered."

"Say again, Minneapolis dispatch announcing to open frequency, Charlie Frank Sam 444 now missing."

Emily awoke the next day without the aid of her alarm clock. She didn't even know what time it was. She hadn't heard from Elsie since the night before. Elsie never did return. Emily was a touch concerned yet she didn't have the energy to go looking for her. She trusted that her old friend had done what she had to do.

Her cell phone rang. It was Austin.

"Hey there. How are you?"

She only heard silence on the other end of the phone.

"Austin? Are you there..."

"Em... listen."

"What Austin? What's the matter? Are the girls okay?"

"Yes, babe, we're all okay."

"What's wrong? Why are you so quiet?"

"I called the airport to get a flight plan to come get you today."

"Great. What time will you be here?"

"Em, listen to me. Conner's plane had a mayday last night. They lost it somewhere over Lake Michigan. Its official, registered as missing. That's not good."

It was Austin who heard silence on the line now, as Emily held the phone against her stomach while choked back her tears. She didn't want Austin to hear her and she struggled to regain control of her emotions.

"Em, are you there?"

"I knew it," she whispered calmly into the phone. "I knew it when they flew over the cabin last night. I had the emptiest feeling, Austin. I knew something bad was going to happen."

"What kind of fly by night pilot goes out in that weather?"

"It wasn't the pilot, Austin. It was Archie. He made Todd fly. I will never forgive him for that."

"Made him fly?"

"It's a long story, Austin. I'm tired. It's been a crazy couple of days. I can't believe all that has happened. Please Austin, I have to go. Just please come get me, now. I want to come home." Emily was working to stay composed, but she was losing it. She closed her phone, curled into the fetal position on her bed and cried herself back to sleep. She was numb and too tired to deal with life. She wanted to sleep and dream of better times that were good and pure at Blaney Park.

Hours earlier, Todd was sweating bullets. He had to get Conner on the ground for much needed medical assistance. He also had to get the plane on the ground in one piece or none of it mattered. He was flying to a remote island in the middle of Lake Michigan, in the middle of nowhere. Todd knew many pilots flew over the island, but no one knew who owned it, and its airstrip was well camouflaged. As usual, Archie made sure of that and did it well. Only the Michigan Department of Natural Resources was pushy about walking the island. Archie boasted a long time ago that he bought off some decision-maker at the DNR who was made comfortable to provide assurance that there would be no issues with his island. A pilot could fly directly over it and see the strip, but would not risk trying to land in such a remote place with such a narrow landing.

Todd was fighting the crosswinds. The airstrip was a challenge on a good day with the normal high winds out on the lake. With an east to west runway, and a southern wind reaching 60 mph, the plane was difficult to steady. Todd knew he had to trigger the runway lights by flying 1000 feet over the airstrip, a task he really didn't want to have to do with the current weather conditions. The sensors would detect the heat from the engines and the runway lights would turn on automatically. Archie had them installed for night flights into the island so he could control the lights without someone on the ground needing to manage them. He wanted as few people as possible to know about the island and what it was used for. Todd had only flown in there at night. He appreciated the automatic lights then, but not now.

He was comfortable knowing what he had to do, but it was the execution in the weather conditions that concerned him. Just as he was descending to do his fly-by over the airstrip, the lights came on to his pleasant surprise. That's when he saw the other planes that had preempted his landing onto the field.

Leave it to Archie to have all the bases covered, Todd thought, relieved that his only task now was to land his plane. He dropped it right in the middle and started breathing again, having held his breath most of the landing and almost hyperventilating from the fear of it all. It was a landing he never wanted to make again under those conditions. As he turned off the number two engine, he taxied to the others, still trying to compose himself before he reached them. Two planes had already landed on that strip and Todd's pride was much like Conner's. He was going to get in there on the first attempt or crash trying. It was a "kiss my ass" landing, as pilots called them. Todd had never made that type landing before, but he had heard other pilots talk about them. A "kiss my ass" landing meant no aborting, no pulling up, land or crash. It was named that because, if the landing was a crash, the pilot's ass would be sticking up for all to kiss, and he was sure to be called an ass for trying to land, whatever his reasons might be.

He taxied to the others, shut down the plane and, for the first time since getting into flying, there was no post flight checklist executed. Todd's first and only concern was to get the plane's door open for the EMS people on site to get to Conner.

He looked down at Conner as he stepped to the door, realizing that his friend may already be dead from his injuries. He dropped the ladder and just stood back as four men entered the plane and worked on Conner for about twenty minutes inside the plane before they carried him off and into one of the two planes waiting. They flew him out immediately to a destination not even known to Todd. But, he knew he was going somewhere that would provide him the best medical help available and save his life, if it could be saved. Once Conner was away from the plane, Todd went to re-enter his plane.

"Where you going, man?' One of the men grabbed him at the elbow.

"I am going to get on my plane and fly it home."

"Ah, no you're not."

"No? What the hell you mean, no?"

"We are going to take this plane apart and you are going to help us. Then we are going to use the same torch that we break it apart with and burn the skin just right making it look like there was a little fire going on here. You know, so the authorities think it crashed and burned. And, then we are flying you home so you can pack you and your family up to chill out for a year or two out of the country."

"What? Take me and my family where?" Todd demanded.

"Hey, man, I don't make the rules, I just enforce them."

With that, the man and a few others pulled out pistols and pointed them at Todd.

"You've got to be fucking with me! No way this is happening. This fucking isn't happening. Tell me it ain't fucking happening!"

"Afraid so, man. We have orders. Come on, Todd, don't make this shit stink. You are going to be a cool, right? "

"Fuck!" Todd yelled.

"What's the big deal man? You will live the best life you have ever lived while being gone for a year or two. We just have to let this bullshit play and chill for a year. After that, no one is going to care who you are or whether you are still alive."

"I know, man, I know. I am looking forward to doing Jack for a year to let this all fade away. Living high on the hog in the Caribbean is for me, but trying to get the wife to do it may be worse than you just shooting me in the head right here."

The boys all started laughing at Todd's humor and downed their weapons.

"By the way, great landing, Sully. Our pilots all took three or four tries getting on this slab. I thought for sure we were going to die tonight."

"Thanks." I am an asshole, Todd thought to himself.

"Let's break her down, boys," said the man with the gun, who was now putting his weapon in its holster.

"We don't need to treat her like a lady tonight. Let's get it done ASAP."

They went to the other plane parked nearby and removed the equipment that was needed. Todd got the feeling of melancholy as the boys started to break down his plane. The plane he loved so much.

"What are you going to do with it?" Todd asked.

"We'll store most of it away here on the island until we can remove it. Some of the more common parts that float during a crash we'll drop into the lake far from here. We will make it look like there was a crash and you all perished. I did this type of shit for years working for the government. It's not that hard making a plane disappear."

"Well, I ain't helping you tear her down. I ain't going to do it."

"I figured you'd say that, Sully. I know this will be tough on you. There's coffee and grub in the cabin over there. Why don't you go eat and get some shut eye? We'll be at least three hours breaking her down. We'll do our thing and pick you up for the flight back. It's all set up for you. Oh, and don't use your cell phone or the phone in the cabin. You are a dead man for two years. How does it feel to be dead?"

"Thanks," Todd replied. He really didn't want to thank them at all. He wanted to take one of their guns and blow them all away so he could rescue his girl. They weren't going to be easy on her. They were going to be rough. Todd felt strange about it. His thoughts turned to the program he and Conner use to watch as kids, The Twilight Zone.

As the first air tool started up, Todd turned and walked away. When he got to the porch of the cabin, he walked to the railing and looked back to the boys tearing down his plane. He stood there for a while, not too long, and said his good-bye. He was thinking how sick he must have been to fall in love with a girl of sheet metal and rivets. How well he took care of her and she did him. But there was nothing he could do. He had to walk away and he knew it. He turned and entered the cabin.

He went to the coffee machine and started to pour a cup of Java. He looked to the kitchen table where there was a bottle for the taking.

Coffee or whisky? he thought. Stay awake or pass out? He didn't finish pouring a cup of coffee. He picked the liquor bottle up off the table, went to the stereo in the front room and turned the volume way up. He went to the cot up against the wall, sat down and swallowed the whiskey that was going to help him get through the death of his most prized possession.

The girl had been with him from the start. She was the first and only. He'd take a drink.

He picked her out of the catalog and managed her custom build. He'd take a drink.

He took his family on vacations with her. The pride they felt for her. He'd take a drink.

He'd fly sick kids to places they needed to go, so they'd get well. He'd take a drink.

He thought about how good he felt that he had such a beautiful lady. He got drunk.

32

Chimes At The Door

Six years later.

It was not the daylight that woke her, but rather the sudden gusts of wind and sounds of a million water pellets against her bedroom window which told Emily it was another typical rainy October morning in Southern Michigan. In past days, these sounds would have only prolonged her dreaming and mesmerized her return to a deep, early morning slumber that carried her back, back to Blaney Park. It was days like today, when she awakened peacefully from her dreams and was welcomed by the place her soul called home. It was days like today when she would lie in bed with her eyes closed, listening to the flurry of nature's elements outside the protective walls of her cabin. She would imagine what it all looked like... the wind, the rain, the bows of the evergreens against her windows, and even the sun as it tried to burn its way through the thick cloud mass that hovered beneath it.

If she opened her eyes now, would she find herself back there, in the solitude and peace of her cabin? Would she listen more closely and hear the soft hissing of the fireplace coals telling her they had been neglected during the night and would soon die out completely, taking with it the warmth that had been emitting into her domain? Or, would she rise to see her home in the city, in the place where she had found a life, yet where she had always felt misplaced. Emily had started a marriage here, raised a family here. Yet, this was not truly the place she called home. There was only one place that held her heart and soul, and that place was Blaney Park.

Emily's mind drifted to her friend, her companion, as it did every morning when she awakened. He never left her thoughts. Where would he be now, she wondered? Was he now leading his own pack? Had he become the alpha? She missed Wolfie, his playfulness and how, even when he was a young and inexperienced wolf cub, he made her feel safe when they were together. She sometimes thought of him when she was doing the most removed activities, like grocery shopping or paying bills. He would suddenly flood her mind and it seemed that she could feel his presence within her soul and she could sense that he missed her, too. He had sensed something was wrong, something was changing the last day she was there. He had sat quietly on the rug in front of the fireplace while she cleaned, packed and secured the cabin. Usually, Wolfie would pace back and forth to the front door, impatiently waiting for her to take him outside with her and they would spend their days playing around the Park and the river.

That particular day, he was very quiet. Reluctantly, he had risen when she opened the door with her travel bags in hand. She had cried when he simply sat down on the doorstep outside her cabin and refused to accompany her to the airstrip, as he had always done. He knew she was leaving and chose to say his good-bye's to her at the cabin, not the plane. And then, as the plane lifted from the airstrip, she had looked down to see him running through the field, circling as if he didn't know which direction to run. Emily longed to go back to the Park, to the riverbank, just to see him again.

It had been very difficult for Emily during the past nine years to be away from Wolfie and from Blaney. So much had happened there. The memories and the wounds were still very fresh in her heart. Except for a few brief visits, she had not been back for an extended period of time, as she had during that one, very powerful year of her life. Now, however, she had a clear plan. Emily was anxious to get back to the one place she felt was truly home.

The gusts increased, showering the rain pellets against her window. Emily drew herself tighter into a ball beneath the covers, trying to escape not only the cold October morning, but also the memories of a time and place that was her own personal heaven on earth. The harder she tried to resume her sleep, the more awake she became. Damn the rain, she thought. The rain always awakened Emily. It was a welcomed morning friend in the quiet of Blaney Park, as it meant cleansing and renewal and almost always burned off beneath the warmth of the afternoon sun.

Today, however, it was the misplaced and untimely sound of soft, distant door chimes coming from outside her bedroom telling her that someone was at the front door which kept her from drifting back to her dreams.

I'm not moving, Emily told herself. They will go away and then, I can go back. The door chimes were intermittent and irritating to her, as she had no guarantee the person at the door would still be there if she chose to investigate. Emily still did not move, but instead contemplated whether to rise from beneath the warmth of her down comforter and answer it, or simply allow herself to be persuaded by the hypnotic rhythm of the soft rain outside and go back to sleep.

The chimes called to her again. Emily tried to think of who it could possibly be. Anyone important? Should she answer the door? Perhaps it was Austin. No, Austin had already been there. He arrived early to make breakfast for the girls. They were pretty much grown up now and spent most of their time at the college. It was such an easy routine for her to see them on weekends and continue the role of their mother as they were growing up, as Austin always brought them along when he flew up to Blaney. They had simply learned to accept the fact that mom was gone during the week. Now, however, they were older and much more aware of the dynamics that accompanied life's choices and relationships. They watched her more closely now, and were very attentive to her when she was home.

Emily had intended to sleep in and enjoy the solitude of her house as much as possible before she prepared for the evening's activities. That's why no one was answering the door. They were gone. She had awakened a little earlier, when Austin came in to give her a kiss and wish her a good day, and she heard the girls call their good-byes to her from the kitchen. There was no one else she expected to see today, nor anyone she wanted to see. Austin and the girls had been so excited about this day and they wanted to give her some quiet time this morning. After all, tonight was the biggest night of her life. Her book, her work with the wolves of Blaney Park, was being honored tonight. This would most definitely lead to grants and more work for her at Blaney. She needed this award. She needed to return to the Park. There was still much work to do there, and not just on the book. She had so much unfinished business to attend to. Promises that would be kept, promises she had made to a very dear friend.

Emily Renae Stewart was less than twelve hours away from receiving the most significant public recognition of her life. She had written a first-hand, soul touching account of why we should cherish and respect the natural wildlife of our earth and, more specifically in this case, those creatures we call wolves. Emily had spent far more time with a pack of Northern Michigan wolves than even she had anticipated. Past and present events of her life kept her there, and bonded her to the wolves as part of their pack, at a time when it seemed her own world was falling apart. She had found peace and purpose with them, and within the beauty of Blaney Park. Her soul bonded with the Park and with its natural citizens so deeply that when she returned to her own life, her own domain, there was a great emptiness in her heart. She knew that some day, regardless of her success and achievements within the world of man, she would return to that place, to her pack, and when she did, would vow to never leave it again.

Why today, damn it. No more reporters, no more questions. Just leave me alone.

It was probably Becky, coming to raid the kitchen before going to work. Emily was glad that her niece had decided to attend college close by years earlier, and was even more pleased when Becky graduated and decided to stay permanently. Becky's world had been shattered during her second year of college, and Emily had felt responsible. She protected Becky after that, and kept a close connection to her, but the frequency with which Becky now dropped in on Emily was beginning to get old. Emily was more used to her privacy, now with Austin living full time in their condo and her own girls almost out of college and on their own. She worried about her niece, who had always insisted she was fine. Emily knew first hand how the wounds upon one's soul were the hardest to heal and left the deepest of scars. She had remained close to Becky and tried to stay conscious of any changes within her, in order to anticipate the resurfacing of those wounds which Becky, like her aunt, had buried deeply under the rug.

Reluctantly, Emily rose and reached down for the white cotton robe that lay in a heap on the cold, hardwood floor beside her bed. She rose and slowly pulled it on, still hoping that it was all just a dream and she would soon find herself back in the warmth and solitude of her bed and blankets. She looped the sash around her waist and fought with her slumber while shuffling toward the chimes.

"Alright, alright! I'm coming," Emily called hoarsely, not hearing the chimes again, but responding anyway as long as she was standing and now making an effort to approach the door.

Emily sighed and reached for the doorknob. When she turned it and opened the door, she found no one.

"Great," she said aloud. "No niece, no stranger. I got up for nothing." Confused, she stepped out onto the porch in order to get a clear view as she glanced up and down the sidewalk in front of her house. After waiting a few moments, she shivered and decided the warmth of her bed was more important. She stepped backward into the house, and her attention was caught by the hem of her robe which did not follow with her body.

She looked down at her feet. There, lying in front of her on the welcome mat with its thorns pulling slightly at the bottom of her robe, lay a large, long-stemmed red rose, glistening with moisture from the cold, autumn rain. Emily stared at it for a moment. She knelt and carefully wrapped her fingers around its stem, avoiding the sharp points of the thorns. Small, icy raindrops fell lightly upon the top of her hand and wrist. The droplets created tiny rivers cascading down the curves of her fingers and wrapping beneath her palm into one stream flowing along the bottom of her wrist and forearm, soaking into the cloth touching her skin at the elbow.

As she took the flower in her hand, her eyes were drawn to something gleaming at the base of the rose. Lifting the flower slowly, Emily's eyes were caught by a delicate gold chain as it fell in the air, suspended from the stem of the rose. Dangling from the chain was a sort of medallion. She cradled the medallion in her other palm and gasped lightly upon recognizing its shape - a beautiful golden triangle. A strong, sunken feeling grew rapidly above Emily's stomach, as she cradled the triangle-shaped gold piece in her free palm and looked for the symbols she knew would be pressed within each corner of its shape. Her eyes snapped shut when she focused on the cross at the top, preventing her from recognizing the other symbols and she clutched the medallion tightly within her fist.

Her hands now trembling, Emily suddenly felt icy cold standing in the doorway. Her legs were weak as she rose from her crouched position and her attention was then drawn to the faint sounds of a small group of Canadian geese, the first she had seen this season, as they flew bravely overhead on their journey south for the winter. Fall must finally be over, she thought, lifting her gaze toward their calls in a failing effort to ignore the item she cradled in her palm, a symbol she had tried to forget. Emily stood shivering in the doorway, and watched the large flock as they flew directly over her house. The tears began to well in her eyes and she longed to rise from the doorstep and join them in a journey southward.

As they disappeared behind her over the roof of the house, their calls diminished. She wiped the tears from her eyes, as her emotions settled back down and she slowly lowered her head. Before turning to re-enter the house, she opened her eyes and noticed in front of her, within her path of vision, was an unfamiliar, black sedan parked at the curbside across the street, clearly out of place in her quiet, uneventful neighborhood. The rear passenger window was slowing rising to a close and she was unable to see inside.

Damn reporters, she thought, as her eyes fell once again to the familiar symbol that she held safely in the palm of her hand. Was this somebody's idea of a sick joke? For an instance, her imagination thought of all possibilities. Her heart sank almost as quickly as it had risen and she refused to consider she would ever see him again.

Her legs began to weaken and she felt as if she would sink back down onto the doorstep where she had retrieved the rose. Her heart was pounding and her mind was ignorant of the rain soaking through her robe to her skin. Her eyes stared at the beautiful red rose and the medallion. An old, familiar image flashed through her mind and Emily felt barely able to breathe from the lump that had formed in her throat.

It can't be, her mind told her. He's gone... they told me, I have the death certificate, the deed... I have clear proof.

The emptiness within her grew as she thought about that place and about Conner. How she missed him. Emily could return to Blaney Park and to Wolfie, but could never return to Conner, or he to her. The delivery of paperwork two months earlier had confirmed what she had feared for so many years. Conner had been killed that night, the night of the plane crash, as everyone assumed. The delivery of Conner's death certificate had seemed strange to her, at first. After all, she had read about his death in almost every newspaper published within the state of Michigan for almost a month. However, her copy was notarized and included the same triangle icon that matched the medallion in her hand. It had been accompanied by the property deed for Blaney Park. Conner had left its legacy to her for protection. Wolfie and his family were now under her care in every way. It was for all of these reasons that she knew it was inevitable that she return to Blaney, to assume responsibility for the preservation of that beautiful place, and also to say good-bye to her friend.

She shuddered as a gust of wind reached her and the tiny droplets suddenly seemed to sting like needles against her face. Realizing that the rain was quickly reaching through to her skin, she stepped backward into the house, closing the door. Still clutching the rose and the medallion in one hand, her other trembled as she slid the door's deadbolt into place.

No locks here, ma'am. Your only intruder is the moon. Her memory fought with her, teased her, and it flooded her mind. She paused briefly behind the security of the door, asking herself if she should reopen it and look to see if the dark car remained. As another shiver overtook her, she quickly dismissed her thoughts and ran lightly back down the hall to her bedroom. Dropping the rose and the medallion onto her bedside table, she crawled back into the warmth of her bed, without removing her rain-soaked robe, and her body was shaking with cold and emotion.

Perhaps I am just dreaming, she tried to convince herself. Please, God, if I can only go back to sleep.

The telephone rang and startled her. Her hand searched the bedside table for the receiver. She picked it up, but said nothing.

"Emily?" Austin's voice was broken, as he was obviously calling her on his cell phone.

"Hi," she answered faintly, trying to sound awake.

"Why didn't you answer? Are you still in bed, you lazy thing?"

"Uh.... Oh, I'm sorry. Ya. I'm awake. I was just deep in thought. Dreaming, I guess..."

"Ya, I'll bet. Dreaming about all that attention you'll get tonight, huh?" His voice revealed his smile, as he teased her.

"That's it. All that attention. I admit it."

"Okay, okay. Sorry I woke you. I'm on my way back to the office and just called to see how you were doing. I should be leaving early tonight, so I can pick up the girls on my way over, and we should be there around five o'clock. I'll bring some take-out, or something. I doubt you'll be thinking about dinner. We'll have to hurry to get to the theatre by seven. I've put my tux and stuff in the car, so I can change at the house. Is that okay?"

"That's fine, Austin. However you want to do it. Thanks for thinking through everything for me."

"You're welcome." He paused, sensing something in her voice. "You okay?"

"Fine... fine. I think I'm just tired. I didn't sleep very well last night. You know, last-minute stage fright and remembering everyone I have to thank."

"Em, you need to just relax. I'm so proud of you, and so are the girls. You've earned this, y'know? It's been a long and emotionally exhaustive journey for you, for all of us. But just look what you've got to show for it. You're being honored, for Christ's sake. Remember, me and the girls will be there, as always... your own private fan club. Just relax, and you'll be fine! You always are. Always will be."

Emily smiled lightly at his never-ending optimism, as her eyes closed and her mind began to drift again with his words. You always are... she thought. Always... Always and forever.

"Em?" Austin's voice interrupted her thoughts. "You still there?"

"Ya, I'm here. I'm sorry. I'm just... you're really breaking up, and I need a shower. I better get up. If I don't, it'll be five o'clock and I'll still be in bed. Will you call me this afternoon?"

"Don't I always? Go back to sleep. You've got an hour or so yet."

"Okay. Listen, can I ask you a question?"

"Sure, Em. What is it?"

"Do you think I'm making a mistake? Y'know, the plans up north... moving."

"No, Em. You're not making a mistake. We've been over this thing a million times. If you don't do it, you'll always have regrets. Just give it some time, like you have planned. I'll be here and you can come back when your ready, when its time. You'll just have to put up with us all pestering you on the weekends." He laughed and Emily smiled at his optimism.

"Thanks, Austin. Thanks for everything. I'll see you later." Emily replaced the phone receiver onto its cradle and looked at the medallion, lying on her nightstand next to the rose. Her eyes filled with tears, as she gently lifted it from the table. She felt weak as she pulled her arms back under the covers, clutching the delicate gold piece in her hand. Emily drifted back to sleep, as the tears steadily fell down her face and disappeared into her pillow.

Do you journal?

33

The Delivery

"Aren't you ready yet, Todd?" Conner Morley was losing his patience. "Jesus, man, it seems like I have been waiting for you all my life. Get the fucking lead out! I need to get there when they are not home. Did you get the cane from the shop, and did you check to make sure the handle was done in 17-karat gold, not 14? Did they get the symbol right this time?"

"Con Man, relax! Of course, I have it right. Have I ever let you down before?"

"I won't answer that."

"I brought the smaller sedan, so we won't look so obvious."

"Great." Conner stared out the window. "Wow. I wish I could just get one look at her, Todd. It's been a while since I've seen her. I'm almost afraid to see her. I know I look like hell, but she...? She was as beautiful as the moon on a clear October night at Blaney Park. Her eyes were like the stars and her face, the moon."

"Jesus, Con Man," Todd laughed and shook his head. "Get over it! She's been happily living with her own family now for six more years, and you have one leg in the fucking grave!"

Conner coughed, as his cancer-filled lungs tried to extract the phlegm inside them. He limped over to the table for the medicine that was supposed to relieve what ailed him. He only smoked an occasional cigar and most often only while on the golf course. Once in a great while, he would smoke a cigarette in social situations. It was unbelievable news to him that his lungs were filled with emphysema.

The disease was not kind to Conner or his family. His grandpa, his dad and now he, too, had lost life to cancer. Many new treatments had been predicted and publicized. Some medications that even the doctors thought would work, but the FDA wouldn't allow, as they were untested for human consumption. He was always a man of principal. He had the money to make a difference. He could bribe or pay off a doctor to provide him the drugs or treatments not available to all persons, if he so decided. But, somehow, he felt it was wrong and immoral that the common man, who was captured by this disease, was punished with death and no special treatments would be provided. He knew he could travel the world and possibly even get some of those new discoveries that would prolong his life, even cure him. Yet, he had been alone, without spouse or child, ever since Samantha. After such heartache, there didn't seem much point to allowing his heart and soul the risk of a relationship with another woman. The crushing blow that came from her betrayal was devastating to him. He never trusted a woman again.

Or did he? Perhaps he did find the necessary trust for one deep relationship. His soul never really let go of Emily, or the wolves that helped him survive both the breakup of his marriage and the death of his father. He trusted Emily, yet she was never an option for him. She was married to Austin and Conner was too value-conscious to take their relationship beyond that of an intense friendship. And now, Emily believed he had died, lost to the waters of Lake Michigan.

Conner was a dead man limping, and he knew it. He just wanted to get his accounts in order and say goodbye to Emily before his life was over.

"Did you get the red rose?" Conner asked, as he finished dressing in suit and tie.

"Yes, I got the rose."

"Well, how do I look?" Conner stood in front of the dressing mirror. He had selected his most expensive silk suit and the best accessories money could buy.

"How do you feel?" Todd would never offer his opinion to Conner, as Conner would always bite back to the contrary.

"Like shit."

"Yyyyaaaa, well... that's how you look," Todd said with a grin. "Sorry, Con Man, you were the one who told me to tell you the truth at all times. Only the truth, you've always said that I can handle the truth, you said."

"Fuck that, Todd. I change my mind. Lie to me from now on." Conner was half kidding with his friend.

"You are so damned handsome and you walk as if you were the queen queer, boss."

Conner broke out into deep laughter, followed by his familiar cough. "Don't make me laugh, Todd," he choked.

Todd put on his chauffeur's cap, shook his head and walked out. A few moments later, he pulled the car around to the front of the hotel. He got out and walked inside to the lobby to see that Conner had sat down to catch his breath. There were better days than these and Conner just hoped for a few more so he could be near Emily when she received the award she had worked so hard for during the past several years.

Todd was bringing Conner two canes. One was the one that rarely left Conner's hand, and the other was to be given to Emily at the awards ceremony. Todd helped Conner up from the lobby couch and they walked slowly out to the car. Without speaking, Todd opened his own door and Conner winced with discomfort as he climbed inside. As they drove off, Conner looked out the window at a typical, dreary Detroit October day.

How appropriate, he thought to himself.

His life was ending and he knew he would not see Emily again until they both were in heaven. He so wanted to get one last glimpse of her, perhaps even speak with her. Perhaps allow just one kiss before he passed away. He smiled, not knowing what heaven would be like, but thinking maybe, for a short time, he would be in purgatory and able to see her. All of her. Naked, like he had that night so very long ago in the moonlight by the river.

He thought back to the dream. It was the only time he had experienced love with Emily and it still brought warm feelings to his loins. With all that had happened, perhaps he should have simply gone from that dream straight to heaven, never returning to his consciousness and state of mind of being alive on this earth. For him, the dream was heaven. Maybe it would have been best to remain that way.

The dream was certainly better than the real thing ever would have been.

His thoughts were interrupted by his cough. He coughed so hard and so often. He leaned over in the seat, trying to release the pressure from his lungs. It was painful to die such a slow death, yet he knew God has His reasons and Conner would not ever ask, 'why me?' So many had asked that question for him. He looked forward to the peace he would know being in a perfect world, a world so different from the one he would leave.

The drive was long. There was a purpose for that. He did not want there to be any chance Emily, Austin or the girls would encounter him. He knew that Emily never really knew what had happened to him after he left Blaney Park. She knew the wounds that had been inflicted upon him were serious and she most certainly assumed the worst with the staged plane crash.

Emily had wanted to stay with him, wanted to be with him. Conner knew he, and his life, was not an option for her and to prolong the temptation was only self-serving to him, not to Emily. He sensed that Austin was also anxious to have him leave their lives alone. The overwhelming feeling of being rejected by so many, in such a short period of time, was just too much for Conner. He went into exile, with only Todd at his side. The money and connections were there in which to disappear. What person, who could, wouldn't? That was Conner's rationalization. After all that had happened, he saw no reason to ever expose himself, nor his soul, to that kind of pain again. He could not face the public any longer. After just a few years of seclusion and no public appearances, life went on without him. He had imprisoned himself within his own exile. To allow an appearance would most assuredly raise more questions than would be solved. People died at Blaney Park and some authorities believed Conner needed to be questioned. While he had relieved himself of that burden, he realized he might have lost all his own answers in life by running away.

Oh, there were a few women in his life after he disappeared. But, they were not the types you marry. Those women were there for a specific reason and, like most of those who serviced Conner, they were well paid. He felt no disgrace for his satisfaction, only the broken heart for one woman who had spoiled his soul by betraying family and a longing for another who would not betray hers.

This morning's trip was a pre-emption to the trip they would take later that evening to the awards ceremony. Conner had too much unfinished business with Emily. First, he had the rose and the medallion, both which must be provided to her. They symbolized who she was to him and what he had done with his life since she touched him. Later, at the awards ceremony, Conner would bid her his last goodbye while sneaking a peak of her on stage. As with everything else, he had made arrangements for this to happen. All who needed to be paid in order for Conner to take care of business had received their compensation well in advance.

And, finally, the cane he would leave for her. This was the one symbolic item that Conner believed would express all appreciation to the woman who saved his life and whose memory he leaned on while building memories in the hearts of others through his Kids at Risk foundation. This was a place where he included Emily's spirit, but not her physical being.

Death. Conner knew it so well in his life. As they continued to drive along the freeway, he turned toward each passing car and tried to look into the eyes of those inside, attempting to pull something from their souls. He had always been a soulful person and, while he knew it, never admitted it, until Emily. He judged people so harshly throughout his life because he felt burdened with his knowledge of the soul and what it meant, how it exposed the truth of a person. He knew it meant everything. He knew that those who had no connection with their own soul were not truly living life, seeing life for all its joys and fulfillment. Samantha was one of those who could not see the soulful meaning of life. He learned that the soul, and one's ability to recognize it, was a gift of life. While his life would be cut short long before normal statistics would predict, he knew that he had lived a far more productive and intuitive life than many who would live many years beyond him. He often told those who would listen, 'Some people just breathe through life. A soulful person creates a scenic picture for life.'

Todd turned the car into a suburban neighborhood and they pulled in behind a car waiting at the curb across the street from Emily's house. A man got out of the car and walked back towards them, as Todd lowered his window. Conner turned on the speaker in the back, in order to hear the conversation in the front. He wanted to hear, but did not want the man to see him. Everyone, including the police, believed Conner to be dead and never cared about Todd. The media had a field day predicting the causes. It was a strange existence, being dead to the public while actually being very much alive and working. He would, at times, venture out and risk the moment. He loved life too much and would feel too caged to even move around to his different domains. He often thought of himself much like the creature he loved so much, the wild wolf that must always have the barn door left open just enough to slip through and run freely to the moon.

"Husband and two girls left about thirty minutes ago. I have a scout car tracking and they are at least forty minutes out even if they turn directly around and come back. She is all alone in the house."

"Okay, thanks," Todd replied as the man walked away. His window rose back up to join the others. They were clear to see out, but once they were closed, no one could see inside the dark car.

Conner lowered the divider window separating the front seat from the back.

"All set, Con Man?" Todd asked, looking in his rear view mirror. "You are the man. It's your game now. Are you sure you don't want me to walk up there with you, or drop the stuff off to her later? I'm sure she won't remember me after all these years. She never really saw me, Con Man."

"I'm sure. I am ill, but I am not dead. I need to do this.... My last act!"

"And, don't start coughing, for God's sake!"

"Todd, fuck you."

Todd smiled, knowing his comments would get the blood running in Conner. He seemed to be the only one in Conner's life who still had meaning, other than the kids who came to the foundation for his help. It would never change. He was Conner's soul brother and knew that he could do anything, except steal or cheat with Conner's wife, and pretty much be exonerated from his actions. Since Todd had no reason to steal, he had everything he could want and more. Conner never remarried, so Todd was smooth. Just as Todd was to Conner's dad, he was free to be himself.

Conner took his inhaler from his pocket. It was the one device that would suppress his cough for up to fifteen minutes. While he always hated the way Todd communicated, he knew that Todd was telling him to use his inhaler. Instead of just saying 'Take a whiff of your inhaler", Todd would make some wise crack like 'Don't start coughing, for God's sake!" He also knew that Todd wanted him to break down and see Emily privately before the cancer beat him. Todd had tried many times to convince him to invite Emily to his remote estate in St. Martin and allow her to know where he was and that he was doing fine. Conner refused. To him, Emily was married and family was everything. He would not attempt to contact her, for fear that by doing so, he would tempt her to remain with him. With his current condition, he was pleased that he had kept to his values. What kind of man would he be to her now? A dead man.

He inhaled the beam of spray and coughed. He hated the inhaler and seldom used it. He hated devices and doctors. He hated admitting that, had he responded more quickly to his condition, he may have defeated the cancer. Yet, he would not take the time while in his seclusion to even walk to a doctor in the same building as his office, just to see if anything of contempt was invading his body. He ignored it, took aspirin and waited for it to cure itself. Cancer doesn't go away like the common old and now had infiltrated his lungs and was divorcing him from his life. He often joked that the cancer was like Jim Gordy. Jim had taken the life out of Conner when he stole Conner's wife and the cancer was doing the same thing to him now by stealing his lungs.

Conner climbed out of the car, with the rose and medallion in hand. He took a deep breath of air, knowing the medication from the inhaler would allow it. It felt great. He had left his cane in the car and began his walk to Emily's front door. Walking felt good, and he picked up his pace, reaching the house in what seemed like no time at all.

He stood at the door. He so wanted to see her. Was Todd right? Would she be pleased? Or, would she faint at seeing him, thinking he had come back from the dead? He so wanted to see her just one last time. He half wished she would just open the door, as he stood there, and surprise him. Then, he could be with her, tell her how wonderful she was, how much she meant to him. How she had motivated him to quit working in big business and help hundreds of kids feel better about themselves, to get the medical care they needed and begin preparing for college. He wanted to tell Emily that her story of saving the wolf and caring about the environment touched him to such an extent that he consciously changed his life to become more like her and do for others who were in need, like the wolves of Blaney Park.

He stood at the door. His hand rose and he rang the doorbell once. Conner then bent his knees and placed the rose on the mat in front of the door with the medallion dangling from its stem.

Conner knew he was supposed to turn and walk away. He did not. The weather was cold and damp, and a slight breeze began to pick up. He felt it, but did nothing to protect himself from it. He stood there waiting, watching the door handle, and expecting it to turn. I look like shit, he thought to himself, knowing he would not impress the woman he had dreamt about for so long, but his courage and desire to see her was steadfast. He rang the bell again.

A car turned down the street and came towards the sedan. He feared it was Austin, even though he knew it could not be based on the comments of the investigator who had spoke with Todd when they drove up. Yet, ever since his divorce, Conner never believed what anyone told him. He had lost trust and faith in people, betrayed enough that he always made decisions based on his own gut instincts.

The car continued past the house, but had startled him. He reactively reached for the doorbell and rang it a third time. This time, he heard movements within, a woman's voice, and he lost his nerve. Conner turned around abruptly and walked as best he could, as quickly as he could, back to the car. As he approached, he half expected the door to open behind him and began having an anxiety attack. He would occasionally get these. His self-induced incarceration caused this, at times, for him. He would worry who was walking up to him, fearing they recognized him. Of all the people in the world, he worried most he would run into Emily one day.

Now, here he was at her doorstep, first hoping to see her and now praying that he would reach his car before she saw him. His mind went back to the times when he was walking home from school in the hood thinking that, at any moment, someone was going to pound on him from behind. Conner would run or cross the street to rid himself of the uncomfortable feeling. He wanted to climb quickly into the back seat of the car and be free of the emotional distress he was experiencing.

On rare occasions, Todd would get out of the car and open the door for him. However, he was street smart. While he, personally, wanted Conner to be seen by Emily, his devotion and loyalty remained to Conner. He knew that it was quicker to stay in his place and let Conner manage the door himself. Too many times in their life did they have to sprint to a vehicle together because someone was chasing. They both had extensive experience in this type of situation.

Todd was laughing at Conner. He knew Conner couldn't see him. Conner had the look of a man carrying a football, trying to reach the goal line, with only a few seconds left in the game and the whole defensive unit chasing him. To Todd, it was both somewhat humorous and sad to watch Conner. Conner had been such a good athlete in school and his body always so perfect and in shape. To see him deteriorate like this was sad, but also caused Todd to find some humor due to how he knew Conner would have treated him if the situation was reversed. Todd was sure he would be trash-talked to no end about being a big pussy and letting cancer get the best of him.

Conner reached the car door, opened it and fell into the back seat, pulling the door closed behind him. He was winded and began coughing as the inhaler was already losing its effectiveness and his lungs were beginning to tighten within his chest. Coughing and hacking, he reached up and opened the dividing window. Todd was laughing out loud now and threw Conner his towel. Todd called it Conner's drool towel.

"Fuck you, Todd," he choked between bouts of coughing.

Todd was still laughing, as he looked toward Emily's house.

"It's open, Conner. The door is open. There she is."

Conner pushed up from his bent over position and saw that his window was lowered slightly. His paranoia got the best of him and he closed it completely.

"She couldn't see it through that little bit, Con Man."

"Look! Look, Todd... there she is. Oooooo, she is even more beautiful six years later, isn't she?"

Todd did not answer. He left the divider window open so he could share this moment with his life long friend. He had to hold his emotions. He looked to his dying friend and saw the smile on his face. It crushed him. Here was a man who loved so many. He cared about everyone, kids he knew and kids he didn't know, loving them as if they were his own. Here was a man who gave his heart and soul to people. Yet, he never experienced the true feelings of love and sharing himself with a special woman.

Todd wanted to close the window and provide Conner this moment, but he could not. He just sat there, watching the great big grin that seemed to reflect having seen Jesus himself. He looked back at the door, praying to himself that she would see the car and walk over to them or, at least, just stand in the doorway for eternity so his best friend could cherish this moment until he was done with it. They watched silently as she bent down and examined what had been left for her. She looked toward the sky, and rose to her feet. For an instance, she glanced in their direction and Conner gasped to himself. Then, as it was with all his experiences with the women he had loved, her eyes pulled away from them and she turned to re-enter the house.

As the door closed, Todd looked in the rear-view mirror and saw the smile turn to pain. He was not the compassionate, sensitive person that his friend was. In fact, many times he felt Conner wasted his time with his concerns and feelings for people who just turned around and kicked him in the teeth. Todd never wasted much time on tears, privately or publicly. Even his wife asked periodically throughout their marriage if he even had a heart. But this time, Todd had to close the divider window separating him from his cherished friend, not for Conner's privacy, but for his own.

As he shifted into gear and began to pull away from the curbside, Todd felt the tears begin to well up in his eyes. He just couldn't hold it back. His stomach began to pump with his unexpected and unfamiliar act of crying, not just a couple of tears like those which occurred when his football team lost and cost him big dollars. This was a heartfelt cry.

For Todd felt, for the very first time, that his friend, his brother, his boss and mentor...this man who had been so much to him, was to die soon, very soon. And Todd knew that his friend would die alone.

34
Awards Night

A man dressed in a long, dark overcoat shuffled inside the back door of the theatre and winked at the doorman sitting on the metal folding chair just inside. He raised his finger to pursed lips, indicating to the doorman that he wanted his presence to be a silent one. The doorman was not concerned, as he looked up and down at the obvious wealth and great class that this man possessed which was evident in the way he presented himself. The doorman had been compensated in advance and was expecting the gentleman, who was limping and leaning on a gold-handled cane held tightly in his right hand. The doorman looked more closely at the cane, and noticed it was gold-tipped with a triangle-shaped handle - a very unique and unusual design for a walking cane.

"That author lady been up yet?" the gentleman asked.

"No, just next, though. You'd better take a seat if you want to watch. You need help into the auditorium?"

The man just shook his head. "Can't stay," he replied. "Here, take this." He handed the doorman the cane. "I am leaving this cane for her. You make sure she gets it, okay?" The doorman never had met Conner before. He prided himself in knowing the players in town. He didn't know this man, but there was something about the style and the class of this man that made him compliant. The doorman stared at the cane again.

What an unusual cane, he thought.

He could not stop staring, but knew it was not his business and he didn't want to risk the bulge in his pants from the roll of bills Conner gave him to be let in. No matter, if this guy could afford to pay himself into the back door of this event, he was not to be messed with.

"Sure, sure thing."

"Good night," the gentleman replied, as he turned and shuffled back out through the doorway into the dark, damp Detroit evening. The doorman rose and stood in the doorway. He watched as the man walked with a more distinct limp because there was no longer a cane to keep him balanced. He watched him get into a black limousine and continued to watch as the car drove away. He took notice they were driving towards the river down the street.

The doorman's attention was then distracted by loud applause inside the auditorium, followed by Emily's exit from the stage towards him.

"Uh, ma'am?" he called out.

"Yes?" Emily was smiling and breathing heavily from her excitement. She glanced over her shoulder towards the audience, obviously waiting for someone to meet her backstage. She was holding a large plaque tightly in her hands against her chest.

"What is it?" Emily asked, with some impatience.

"A gentleman just left this. Said to be sure you got it." He held out the cane and noticed a medallion shaped the same as the triangle tip of the cane hanging from a chain around her neck.

Emily's eyes dropped to the handle of the cane and her smile vanished. She recognized the triangle, the same triangle as the medallion she found dangling from the rose earlier that morning, that she now wore. His triangle. His Triangle Of Life.

"Oh, my God!" she gasped, looking up at the doorman and not noticing that Austin had walked up behind her. "Where... When? Where is he... where did you see him? Please! Tell me!"

"Out there," the doorman pointed towards the theatre exit door. "He left just before you took the stage."

Emily dropped the plaque onto the metal chair as it was now insignificant and, still clutching the cane, ran outside. She stopped and stared down the foggy street. She turned back to the doorman, her eyes filling with tears. Austin approached her and placed his suit jacket around her shoulders.

"Where did he go? Was his name Conner? Did you see him? Did he have a driver with him? Did you see them drive off?"

"Well, yes... yes, I did. They went towards the river, but it's a good five blocks from here..."

He stopped short, as Emily was already running toward the river.

Conner walked to the top of the street. It was a cold wet night. A night he would rather be home sitting in front of the fire with a stiff drink than out carousing along the streets of Detroit. The inhaler was working better tonight and Conner thanked God for that. Tonight was different. A smile spread over his face, one that wasn't like his own, but more like a child's smile. Tonight was special. He walked up to the jet-black limousine.

"Let's go to the river, my friend," he told Todd. He then pulled out two fine Cuban cigars and cut their ends off. He gave Todd one. He then proceeded to tongue his cigar to give it the proper moisture for smoking. Todd got to the pier and then proceeded to light both cigars. Smoke filled the car, and the cigars were appreciated for both their taste and aroma.

Nothing was said between the two men. Even though they had become very close over the years, Todd still realized when and when not to interrupt. Interrupt tonight, he would not.

The smile was unusually long and broad this evening for Conner. Todd smiled, too. He had not seen such a look on him since those days at Blaney Park. Conner opened the door. He must do it himself.

"I'll be looking out over the river for a while, Todd," he said, as he pulled himself up out of the car. "I expect to have a car pull up behind you. Do not interfere or interrupt with what takes place. All is well on this night."

"Whatever you say, boss."

Conner stood by the wooden guardrail and continued to peer out at the water, smoking his $100 cigar. He was not moving much except side to side to disperse the pain that was constantly riddling his lungs. The cigar and the beverage of choice assisted Conner in dealing with a pain few in this world could endure. The cigar tonight would be his last in life and God had suppressed his cough for at least that moment.

Todd, as was told to him, saw a car approaching in his rear view mirror. He also saw the image of a nicely shaped woman in front of it, running awkwardly towards them in a pair of high heel shoes. The woman slowed and then took the shoes off to better her gate towards the limousine.

The car stopped and turned off its lights and engine. Todd was confused. Conner seldom went out in public and even less rarely interacted with street folk. He was concerned, but did as he was told.

Maybe it's Emily, he thought.

She approached Conner slowly the last several yards. He remained still, with his back to her, and gave no indication that he would acknowledge her. She waited patiently... seemingly longing to find the appropriate words. She had a suit coat hanging from her shoulders, but it did not impede the view of the low cut gown and her full breasts heaving as she attempted to catch her breath from her unexpected run.

The sounds of foghorns from ore and coal ships as they passed through on the Detroit River were heard in the distance. Conner continued to smoke the cigar with grace and class. Still, he did not acknowledge the beautiful woman standing behind him. In her hand, Todd saw Conner's cane. It was his Sunday cane, his prized cane, not the one Todd had expected Conner to leave at the theater. He looked back at the car in his rear-view mirror and began to feel uncomfortable. Conner gave his cane to Emily, but he did not know the party in the other vehicle. His distrust could not be settled for those in the vehicle behind him. Police was his biggest fear.

The cane was a present to him from the kids of all the youth centers he opened across the nation, while they never knew they gave it to him. Conner had it made for himself. He would do that, on occasion, to make himself feel good for all that he was doing for society's children. He missed the reward of getting back for all he gave. Never expecting anything, he genuinely felt great when someone would return his kind heart. He mentioned often that the cane meant more to him than all his riches combined. It defined and represented who he was.

Conner straightened out and stood on his own, no longer leaning on the rail. Still, never looking back. He continued to take more drags off of the cigar and the woman began to compose herself. She then realized she had just run five blocks to a man she thought she knew. Was it him? Was it Conner? Of course, it was.

She was obviously dressed for a special event. A tear began to fall from her face. She looked back towards the vehicle that had parked behind the limousine, as a tall man dressed in a suit and cowboy boots began to walk towards her. She looked towards Conner and then back to the tall man. She seemed confused and anxious, as if time was running out on her. She continued to look, as if she was going to speak, as if she had something to say... she did not.

The tall man approached and it was obvious the coat she was wearing belonged to him. He took hold of her arm and gently pulled her, as if he wanted her to go with him. She resisted and pulled away. Holding the cane with both hands, she walked up behind the man with the limp. She reached out with her hand and he complied with his own. She placed the triangle shaped handle of the cane in his hand. While still holding his hand, she raised it to her lips and gently kissed it.

She walked from Conner and buried her head into the tall man's shoulder. They both walked back to the car and got in. The car started and turned around without turning on its lights. Once it had backed away from the peer, the lights turned on and the car disappeared over the hill.

Gone. Gone was Emily, forever, from his life.

Conner Kenert Morley was steadfast for several moments. He stood looking out to the water.

Todd saw him wipe a tear or two away from his eyes and from his cheek. Conner was trying to compose himself before returning to the car. Todd was looking at Conner as the light from the street provided a silhouette of him. It made him look solid again, the man he had known all his life. He then, at that moment, realized that this would be the very last night he would share with his best friend.

The emotions were getting the best of him, too. Never had he cried in front of Conner. So much had happened in Todd's life and made him harden to feelings and emotions. Conner's way, too, was never to show his emotions. Not since the murder of his brother, Ken, on the train tracks of Flint had Todd allowed release of his emotions. At that moment, Todd's mind went back to Ken and how he was killed way before his time in an inhumane and senseless way. Conner was there for Todd during those difficult times. He was at the funeral and by Todd's side during it all. He was there when he heard the news, not from his parents, but over the local radio broadcasts that Todd's older brother was gone. Conner was there and had been there for him ever since. He had paid for some of the relatives who could not afford the trip. They were brothers, too.

Todd had bottled it all up inside himself, not wanting to let it out. And now, he realized he was going to lose another brother. Again too soon, and before his time in an inhumane way, to cancer. He could feel the emotions begin to take his skin and tighten it as if the sun had beaten down on him and burned it. His eyes were swelling up with tears. He worked hard to suppress them. He was sad, not for Conner, but for himself. Conner would be going to heaven, the perfect world. But for the first time since the seventh grade, he would have to live life without his very best friend in the whole world. Conner had been his family and he to him.

Conner used his cane to walk back to the car. He walked to the driver side window. Todd rolled down the window, hoping for any kind of explanation for what just happened.

"My friend," Conner said, taking another drag of his half-smoked cigar. "That woman sees life from the big picture! It's time to go fly and die, my friend."

Todd opened his door and stepped out. He placed his cigar in his left-hand fingers. He then extended his right hand out to Conner. A tear was unable to stay in place. It rolled down Todd's cheek. Conner looked into Todd's eyes for a short moment, surprised at this outwardly expression of emotion, and realized he was not able to contain his tears from shedding. He knew it was appropriate now. It was okay. It was going to be their last evening together. Todd had never shed a tear in front of him. Conner was not about to lose the chance to let Todd know his feelings for his friend. How much he loved his brother and how badly he would miss him when he was gone.

He looked at Todd's hand and then reached out to reciprocate the offer and the two long-time, school boy friends shook hands. As they did, Conner pulled Todd closely to hug him. They had never embraced that way before. Never, except during that street fight so many years before in a fit of violence.

"I am going to miss you, bro," Todd whispered into Conner's ears.

Conner squeezed his eyes closed on Todd's shoulder trying to keep his emotions in check. "Be careful, my friend. I pray to God we will meet again in heaven."

"I know you are going to be there and I will be working to get there with you."

"Deal."

"Oh yeah, and one other thing."

"What?" Conner said, as his emotions were returning to him.

"I'll be there."

"Where?"

"I'll be there at your funeral. Right there, by your side. I won't leave you until the dirt has covered you and your soul is skyward... until you are with the Coach."

Conner grabbed Todd and hugged him tighter, disregarding his emotions or perceptions. He hugged Todd and they both spent a short while sobbing in each other's arms, not caring or even considering who was watching or what it may have looked like even to each other. Their toughness from all those years released to a caring and kindness they both always wanted for each other, and needed from each other, but never shared.

Todd released Conner and opened the back vehicle door to the limousine. And, for the first time since Todd had the job, for the first time since he'd been Conner's driver, he played it by the book.

"Sir," He motioned for Conner to enter the car, while wiping the tears from his eyes, which were now flowing freely.

A grin came to Conner's face. It broke the extreme emotional tension that had been created by the sad moment.

"It's about God damn time," he responded. "Finally, you give me a fucking reason to give you a raise!" He would be going to a private hospital the next day for the balance of his life. He asked to receive the pain relievers needed to allow him to die with dignity. He knew, too, this would be the last moment that he and his best friend in the world would share any quality time together and they made good use of it.

Conner entered the back seat and pulled two glasses from the limousine bar. He removed his most expensive bottle of cognac from the rack and poured it into each glass. He then picked up the phone from its hook and made a call.

"Edward, its Con Man. Use the tracking device and find my vehicle. I need you to send me another driver. Todd has just announced he has retired. Take your time. There is no hurry."

With that, Todd stepped out of the driver's seat just after entering it, expecting to take his friend anywhere he wanted to go on his last night. He climbed into the back seat next to Conner. Conner waited until Todd was settled into his seat and then handed him his drink.

"Well?" Conner asked.

"Well what?"

"How does it feel to be me?"

"Makes me want to cough," Todd replied, and then started to laugh. They both began to laugh.

"Con Man?"

"What?"

"Which end of the human body is heavier when it's dead, the front or the back?"

"Shit, I don't know. Why?"

"Because if I am carrying your ass out of the funeral home, I am sure as hell taking the light end of the box."

They both laughed again. Conner wheezed a bit from the phlegm that was building in his lungs. He stopped laughing, took another puff of his cigar and looked up through the sunroof in the limousine.

"Remember when we were kids and I beat your ass in the school yard?"

"Bull shit, you didn't whip my ass!"

"Those were the good old days, huh?"

Conner and Todd sat in that limousine for hours and tried to exhaust all the alcohol stocked in it. They talked about old times... good times... and, before the evening was over, Conner thought about Emily and smiled.

Conner looked up through the limousine's sunroof at the clearing sky. The stars and the moon were bright, as they often were at Blaney Park. He took one last drink and emptied it. He picked out one star in the sky and finished his night by praying to God.

"Emily, please take a moment of your life and let it be mine. Goodbye, my soulful love. Goodbye."

35
Conclusion

Journal entry—October 16, 2001

Dear Conner:

I drove to the Park tonight, on the familiar, smoothly paved highway and I noticed the sun was hidden away behind deep blue clouds that were the remnants of a recent autumn storm. They were tall clouds, secured to each other and covering the sky. Only a glimpse of the evening's golden sun peaked out from the clouds as they rested on the earth's horizon and it reached upward beneath the rim of the deep blue sea above. I drove, mesmerized by the continuous deepening of the sky's color as if the lowering sun were bowing to the massive clouds.

I turned north, and it was as if the seasons had turned with me. The sun suddenly cascaded down from its evening retreat and set fire to the landscape. On one side of the road, its gaze rolled lazily upward with the faded green earth, still wet and freshened from the late afternoon rains. A small group of cattle grazed at the beaded grasses around the rotted wooden benches and arbors that were once enjoyed by golfers on a lazy afternoon, and swished their tails at imaginary flies. The other side was a smooth carpet of shining gold, as the sun reflected from the wheat like a million bronzed candles, and a gentle breeze made the flames seem alive and flickering. This golden carpet was once smooth as the pavement beneath me and lined with man-made stars to guide pilots for a safe landing, bringing guests back to their favorite retreat.

Beyond the hidden airstrip bordered a deep, green forest of pine, dotted with the fall hardwood colors. The sun accentuated the shades of green and made each stand out as if it were like none other. The eastern sky had darkened to a soft, rich purple, as if to subdue its own beauty in order to give equal respect to all of nature's brief exhibitions.

Just beyond the wheat field, and set a bit closer to the green forest, a slightly different shade of gold caught my eye... then two, three, four, and I focused on a group of deer feeding at the edge of the field. The largest one lifted its head to look at me, and it seemed as if we recognized one another.

Then I felt content. I realized that they, too, were witnesses to this display of nature's own fireworks. I was glad that they were there to watch it, as you could not be. I had been thinking how you would have appreciated it, how we had watched the sun set dance on the earth so many evenings together. But the deer did see and grasp all that was around them. Then, they looked at me (I had stopped by the roadside), as if to let me know that they shared it. They saw it, too.

They looked... and it was if they understood me.

As Emily's car neared the driveway in front of the Harrison, the sun was completing its evening retreat, slipping down through the tops of the trees that bordered the airstrip at the top of the hill. Bright rays landed on the grounds of the little village, shining for a moment on the clearing by the river. As the soft, evening glow of amber light stretched out over the riverbank, it scattered the shadows of the trees over the rippling waters.

One shadow, however, had a different shape from that of the pines and even from that of a beaver walking lazily along its bank a few yards away. It was cast from the twin markers honoring Blaney's most beloved caretaker and his nephew, both which had been placed beneath the protection of the large pine tree in the middle of the clearing.

Not far away, the arrival of the new owner was announced to all by the dogs of the Park, circling her car as she stopped in front of the House. Elsie sat in the front porch swing, anxiously awaiting her dear friend to live out her last few years with.

At the moment of Emily's arrival, a beam of bright sunlight slipped through the trees at the edge of the clearing, and came to rest on the handle of the walking cane which was secured in the face of the smaller black marble headstone. The sun's reflection exploded from the golden triangle, shining brightly like a beacon for the souls of the two men who would lie there forever, reunited for eternity.

It was the end of another day. The morning would bring the sunrise and, with it, new possibilities to those who would come here, whose souls would find a home within this seemingly untouched beauty and Michigan wilderness called Blaney Park.